FAME'S
PERIL

FAME'S PERIL

Martha Smilgis

POCKET BOOKS

New York   London   Toronto   Sydney   Tokyo   Singapore

This book is a work of fiction. Names, characters, places and incidents are either the product of my [the author's] imagination or are used fictitiously. Although there are references to real people contained in this work, the story is not based on the real activities of those people or on any real events involving them.

POCKET BOOKS, a division of Simon & Schuster Inc.
1230 Avenue of the Americas, New York, NY 10020

Copyright © 1992 by Martha Smilgis

All rights reserved, including the right to reproduce
this book or portions thereof in any form whatsoever.
For information address Pocket Books, 1230 Avenue
of the Americas, New York, NY 10020

Smilgis, Martha.
    Fame's peril / Martha Smilgis.
        p.   cm.
    ISBN: 0-671-72818-0 : $19.00
    I. Title.
    PS3569.M42F36   1992
    813'.54—dc20   91-28421
                                                        CIP

First Pocket Books hardcover printing May 1992

10 9 8 7 6 5 4 3 2 1

POCKET and colophon are registered trademarks of
Simon & Schuster Inc.

Printed in the U.S.A.

For P.J.C.
and Marion

I want a hero, an uncommon want,
When every year and month sends forth a new one,
Till after cloying the gazettes with cant,
The age discovers he is not the true one.

—Lord Byron, *Don Juan*

PART
I

1

East Hampton, New York

The late September sun cast a pale, translucent glow over the white sand of the public beach. A few remaining stragglers, there to catch the nearly spent rays, packed up to depart. A cool sea breeze chilled the afternoon air as they busily snapped sand from their towels and folded aluminum beach chairs.

No one noticed the slender fiberglass motorboat that cruised eastward along the shoreline. There were two people in the small boat. About a quarter-mile past the public beach, they abruptly cut the engine. Mindful of the treacherous whitecaps that lashed and sucked at the long slope of sand, they cautiously maneuvered the boat toward shore. Their goal was a decayed pier that extended from a rocky escarpment pockmarked with water-filled craters and clusters of sharp barnacles.

As the boat bumped against the rotted pilings, a tall, dark-haired man wearing a black wetsuit looped a rope over a wobbly stump of wood. He leaped from the boat, then turned to help a petite woman, also in a rubberized suit, climb onto the pier. The man bent to retrieve a collapsed duffel bag from the boat.

Once on shore, the couple walked to a neighboring crescent of beach-front property. On the hill behind them, a new mansion was near completion. Ribbed dunes of sand marked the path of a bright orange Caterpillar tractor, at rest now that the crew had gone home.

They continued on and, slipping behind a conspicuous NO TRESPASSING sign, hiked up a narrow, winding trail. At the top of the ridge a giant four-story house rose before them. It resembled a huge church with domes of gleaming Plexiglas encircled by thin steeples of tubular blue steel.

The man smiled at the sight of the lavish futuristic mansion, an architectural testiment to great wealth and power. But unlike the grand summer cottages up the coast in Newport, Rhode Island, built in the late 1800s by America's manufacturing families, this monument was the product of show-business money.

The man squinted into the receding sunlight as he lifted the bag from his shoulder and gave it to the woman. He yanked the rubber hood of his wetsuit up over his hair, then checked the time on his nautical watch. It was 4 P.M.

One mile from the mansion, a navy blue Mercedes 560SEL sedan with bulletproof windows careened down Route 114 toward the Montauk highway. The chauffeur, a lanky West Indian man named Saar, drove the heavy car at breakneck speed, as was his style. In the backseat sat Doni Shay, a honey-haired boy with corn-flower blue eyes, apple cheeks, and a mischievous smile presently directed at his nanny, Sarah Silverman. Beside him, a silky cocker spaniel industriously licked the boy's baby-soft arm.

"Sticky hands?" asked Sarah, a faint reprimand in her voice. She was pretty in a plain, wholesome way, with a moon face and a quick, easy smile.

"I only ate one. A big red one," said Doni. He stretched the corners of his mouth with his fingers to make a werewolf face.

"Did Millie give it to you?" Sarah prodded.

The boy dropped his head sheepishly.

She studied his dark lashes as he lowered his gaze. His head bobbed an imperceptible yes as he reached to scratch the dog's underbelly. It wagged its tail and pawed at Doni's shoulder.

"Your dad's calling at seven tonight," said Sarah. "Don't tell him you ate candy before supper or he'll squeal to your mom. Then you and I'll be in the doghouse with Snickers."

While Sarah gazed out at a stretch of farmland Doni quietly uncinched his seat belt and slid across to the other window. He stood up, oblivious to the mud prints left on the creamy leather seat by his cowboy boots.

"Doni, sit down!" Sarah shouted. "It's dangerous to stand in a moving car." She swiftly yanked at the tail of his checkered shirt. He turned and lunged at her. As she caught him, his small arms hugged her neck and he deposited a splatter kiss on her cheek, then sat down properly for a moment.

Sarah's eyes strayed back to the forest of scrub trees along the Montauk highway. Traffic was light. They sped past the Quiet Clam and the twenty-four-hour deli, catering now to the après-summer crowd. Soon they turned on to Lily Pond Lane. On either side of the street, manicured hedges framed forty-room white-shingled cottages with vast emerald green lawns.

"How's Foxy?" Sarah asked, bending down to get closer to Doni's face.

His eyes gleamed at the mention of his pony. "Fast," he said. He spoke excitedly, swallowing tiny gulps of air. "He's like lightning."

"Lightning?"

"Uh-huh."

"Who said that?"

"Millie," Doni answered.

"Do you know what lightning is?" Sarah asked, an amused twinkle in her amber eyes.

Doni thought for a moment. He played with the cowlick at his temple as he concentrated, then wiped his arm across his cheek. His small shoulders rose and fell in a shrug of defeat. "Dunno," he replied.

"It's a streak of light that shoots through the sky during a storm."

Doni scrunched his nose up like a rabbit as he listened to Sarah's words. His hand found hers.

"How old is Snickers?" he chirped. It was a familiar question, one he loved to repeat.

Sarah nudged him gently. "You know. Snickers is two years older than you are."

Doni eagerly shot all five fingers in front of her face.

"Right," she said.

Doni tilted his head. "But I want dog years not my years," he said very distinctly.

Sarah looked at him lovingly. "Oh my, dog years, eh?" She pursed her lips in exaggerated thought. "Let's see. There are seven dog years to one human year, so Snickers is thirty-five years old."

Doni concentrated on this information. He knew his mommy was thirty-five years old. This meant that Mommy and Snickers were somehow the same.

Saar brought the Mercedes to a full stop at the metal voice box beside the electronic gates of the thick granite wall. He buzzed down the window and repeated the proper code numbers. The steel bars opened slowly and he drove through to the gate house where Doni's bodyguard, Spike Pappas, waved them on. The regular guard was off duty.

A stretch of polished brick road heralded the approach to the mansion. Saar picked up speed and swung the car past the front of the house to the row of concealed garages at the back. Doni and Snickers tumbled from the car. The spaniel trotted to the kitchen door, anticipating rightly that Maria, the Shays' cook, had filled his bowl with dinner kibble.

"Can I go play? Pleeeease," Doni whined at Sarah as she reached back into the car to fetch his cowboy hat. He tugged at her blouse as he tried with all his might to pull her away from the car and toward the ocean. "Pleeeease. Daddy would let me."

Sarah stood upright, the hat in her hand, and laughed. "Daddy would let you jump off the Empire State Building if you wanted." She looked down at him. His disarming eyes begged and coaxed, tears imminent.

She glanced at the Cartier tank watch Emily Shay had given her for her birthday. It was 4:15. Shadows extended out from the house, but in the distance the steel ladders of the playground still sparkled in the tangerine sunlight.

"Okay, buster," she said. "But only for ten minutes. I've got to pee. I'll get your jacket and be right there."

Doni bolted toward the playground, his arms outstretched like an airplane.

Sarah looked at Saar. "Watch that monkey, would ya, so he doesn't break his neck."

Saar nodded as he buzzed open the garage door. The Land Rover was parked in the space reserved for his Mercedes. He swore under his breath as he got out of the car. Once again Maria had thoughtlessly left the Rover there, and, as usual, she had forgotten to leave the keys. Saar slammed the car door angrily and followed Sarah into the house.

At the beach Doni scampered over to the dragon slide and hurled himself headfirst down the slippery metal tongue, slithering along the curves to finally belly-flop in the cold sand. Ignoring the seesaw, he tackled the pint-size jungle gym next. His fingers curled around the steel rungs as his small feet kicked wildly. With an effort he hoisted up his rear end and locked his knees over the bars. Then he let go with his hands, giggling and shrieking gleefully at the upside-down sensation.

Inverted, he saw them: two black figures deathly still against the vivid blue sky and sea.

Doni dropped with a somersault onto the sand.

Perplexed, he studied the man and woman quizzically for a moment, then shot to his feet and cried, "Seals!"

Proud of his identification, he sprinted over to them fearlessly. There was a benevolent smile on the woman's face. As Doni reached up to touch her shiny, slick skin the man leaned over and flipped the small body under his muscular arm. The woman quickly slapped a piece of white adhesive tape over his mouth. Doni wriggled violently, but the man lowered him onto the grass and held him firmly while the woman wrapped more tape around his arms and legs. The man lifted him into the open duffel bag and zipped it shut swiftly. He hoisted the bag over his shoulder like a carry-on satchel and in seconds they were gone, back down the cliff.

2

Los Angeles, California

"You're some dish," said Frankie Fontana as he leaned back in his chair. "Why ain't you in movies?"

Ceci McCann wasn't about to be sexually intimidated by this weasely, wall-eyed detective. In fact, it was laughable that the self-serving whimp had the gall to come on to her. "I'm already on television," she said firmly.

"I watch Tommy Train. I've never seen ya. There's that sexy brunette, Lisa somethin' . . ."

"Proudfit." Ceci supplied the name. "Yes, she's on the show. But I've also reported several important segments—"

"Train's king of that show," Fontana interrupted. "Guy's got an ego the size of Everest, he'll never share the spotlight. If you're smart, you'd move over to entertainment, where the big money is. I got a friend, great guy, great agent. Made Charlene Tilton's career."

Ceci was dumbfounded. She couldn't believe this smarmy runt was telling her how to manage her life.

"Thanks, my job's fine," she said abruptly. "I prefer being a journalist."

"Yeah, yeah. It's a boom business. Take that Mary Hart. Now, there's a cute piece of ass."

Ceci deliberately changed the subject. "Mr. Fontana, I hope you're aware that you must reveal the outcome of your case on camera. Did the clandestine affair you so expertly documented result in divorce? What became of the adulterous spouse? The marriage?"

Fontana rose. "Don't ya worry your pretty li'l head. You'll hear a great story from me. And get some juicy snapshots to sweeten the act. Just lemme know when to show up at the studio."

At the door Fontana unexpectedly grasped her arm. Ceci felt the sweat from his clammy fingers through the sleeve of her silk crepe jacket. "Remember, babycakes," he whispered. "I got an agent for you."

Ceci recoiled. "Sure, thanks," she mumbled as her free hand found the doorknob.

"Here, let me," he said, reaching around her. To avoid further contact, she swiftly backed into the blazing sunshine. The sweltering heat of the San Fernando Valley had never felt so refreshing.

Safely locked in her Saab Turbo, Ceci disconnected the car alarm. She popped the sun roof, then checked for messages on the cellular phone. In seconds, she was racing down Lankershiem toward Ventura Boulevard.

She couldn't escape Frankie Fontana fast enough, but the trip to his Van Nuys office had been worthwhile. At least he'd provide show-and-tell material. Whether the photographs and stories were accurate was another matter. Ceci felt uneasy with the deal, but the pressure was on. Mitch Creed had generously saved her ass by sharing the adultery segment with her. She couldn't let him down.

She made a left turn onto Beverly Glen, the mountain pass that connected Sherman Oaks to Beverly Hills. The frisky Saab hugged the steep curves nicely, holding steady at a decent speed.

She quickly ejected Madonna from the tape deck and flicked on the radio. KJOY blasted "Bye, Bye, Miss American Pie." Ceci punched up the volume and hummed along until the words of the song suddenly unsettled her. Right there, in her hip new car, she had the awful, sinking feeling that the tune might be her swan song at the ripe age of twenty-four.

From the time she was a little girl in Kansas City she had dreamed of a career in television. More than anything in her life she wanted to become an anchor star. She had a rich, husky voice and telegenic good looks. With a confident smile, she recalled the words of her journalism professor at Northwestern: "Miss McCann, you have an innate gift. Your ability to read from the teleprompter is perfect. Your delivery is smooth as a player piano."

After an unrewarding two-year stint as a local weather girl in St. Louis, Ceci had sent her résumé and videotapes to thirty established news shows. Within the month, Shorty Smith, the executive producer of *The Tommy Train Show*, had called and offered her a job. She had been ecstatic. It was her big break, a chance for national exposure.

But something had gone dreadfully wrong. Even this midget

detective had noticed that she hardly ever appeared on camera. Moreover, her last segment, on pet hotels, ran barely fifty seconds. For some reason, she wasn't clicking.

She knew she had to wise up and correct her current course. She was a fighter after all. And a little problem like a slow start wasn't going to cause her to roll over and disappear. She simply had to work harder and pay attention to every detail.

Ceci cut a sharp right off Olympic Boulevard into NTN's headquarters, a complex of modern buildings located south of Century City in West Los Angeles. The uniformed guard winked at her as he inspected her windshield stickers and waved her past.

She parked in her assigned space in the back lot. As she rushed past executive row she noted Train's Silver Shadow tucked into his shaded slot. She planned to be parking up there soon.

Quickly cleared by lobby security, Ceci ran down the drab, windowless corridor to her office. From an accordion file on her desk she collected a folder fat with fresh story ideas. Shorty Smith's mandate for a "commercial edge" replayed in her mind as she slipped through the back door of Tommy Train's spacious office.

As usual, Train presided over the story meeting. He was shirtless, a terry towel draped over his tan shoulders, a can of Bud Light in his hand.

Ceci grabbed an empty chair next to the window. There were ten people in the room, a poor turnout. Over half of the show's producers were on the road.

Tommy's razor-sharp eyes acknowledged her, then traveled back to Nelson Grinker. The young producer was hyping a story in the current issue of *Newsmakers* magazine, something about an exposé of Ivana Trump's childhood in Czechoslovakia.

"Sensational story for us," boomed Grinker. "Rags to riches— and back to rags."

"Come off it," said Train. "Pussy pablum for ladies who lunch." He lifted his feet onto his desk, his muscular thighs evident under his worn denim jeans. "The cow's got the franchise on that market."

The cow was Oprah Winfrey.

Tommy's hooded eyes wandered covertly down Lisa Proudfit's legs. She sat directly in front of him, a short spandex skirt revealing slim, bronze thighs. Ceci noticed that the red steeple-high heels were new.

But Train didn't focus on anyone for more than a few seconds. Like a shark, he continuously hunted for prey. If anything could hold his attention it was his own image; every few minutes he lifted a mirror from his desk to check his reflection.

"I need a gimmick to get in the tabs," he said as he tilted his head back and examined his jawline. "Oprah prattles about her weight. Carson battles his ex-wives. Even Geraldo broke his nose." Train pinched his cheek flesh back with his fingertips. "How 'bout some on-air nips and tucks . . ."

"Better hire an irate fan to shoot Tommy Train," volunteered Lisa.

Tommy flashed her a get-real look.

"Donate your kidney to a sick kid in Ethiopia," declared Shorty. "We'll visit your organ in an Addis Ababa slum."

"Speaking of organs," said Lisa, "how 'bout a penile implant?"

Train laughed. "Real cute, Hot Lips. Almost as clever as your vasectomy suggestion."

His trigger smile revealed the whitest, most perfect row of teeth Ceci had ever seen. Tommy caught Ceci's glance. She looked away quickly.

He rose to his feet. His sculpted pecs and washboard stomach were in a league with Sly Stallone's. "C'mon, folks, let's roll," he prodded. "Flip the switch. Where are the new ideas? We've got vast stretches of airtime to fill."

Mitch Creed looked up from the L.A. Weekly on his lap.

Tommy's eyes met his. "Any fresh goodies for Ted Bundy fans?"

"Two boys are on line in Florida," Mitch said. He was a handsome black who spoke with a velvet-soft southern drawl. "They're set to be electrocuted next month."

"Crybabies?" Tommy asked.

Mitch shrugged.

Tommy paced back and forth in front of a bulletin board stapled with news clips. Finally he halted and stared directly at Mitch. "Voices of the Damned," he said flatly. "There's decent promo here." He was wired, anxious. "We're desperate for a blockbuster for the November sweeps," he shouted at them. "The National Television Network isn't payin' us six million for nothin'. We gotta save their ass."

"Payin' you," Ceci heard Grinker whisper under his breath.

"We've gotta galvanize these moronic couch potatoes," Tommy bellowed. "Any news on Elvis? Crazed fans exhume the king?"

"Stage a resurrection," muttered Shorty.

"What's wrong with teen drunks?" Lisa asked. "We've got Drew Barrymore."

Train plopped down in his chair. "Too moo-cow, too Donahue. C'mon, guys, up tempo, we're hands-on journalists. Guts and gristle."

Unpredictably, his face flushed. "And no more saccharine celeb profiles. We're not shills for those press fuckers. Whatever the flacks offer is junk. If they want us, we don't want them."

Ceci focused on her notes. This outburst scotched her suggestion on Farrah Fawcett: working mom.

"How 'bout a cult in Malibu that practices animal sacrifices," offered Grinker. Ceci cast a sidelong glance at him. He appeared so corporate in his tasseled loafers and tortoiseshell specs. "A painted and feathered preacher is hacking apart live cats and chickens," he announced.

Train frowned as he poked the blinking light on his telephone console. It was Tanya, his wife, calling from the detox unit at the Betty Ford Clinic.

Annoyed, Lisa suddenly came alive. Second billing wasn't her style. She sprang from her chair and, ignoring Tommy, addressed the group, her agile tongue wetting her glossy peach lips with the frequency of a windshield wiper.

"Before you give me any back talk, hear this full out," she said. "It needs to be done in series with the panel treatment. Shrinks, sexologists—"

Tommy slammed down the phone. "Hot Lips, hold on a minute." He pointed at Grinker. "Animal sacrifices will rally the animal-rights gang. Picket lines bring fat headlines. Let's shoot this cult before the competition wakes up." He looked back at Lisa. "Back to you, toots."

Lisa was visibly perturbed. Ceci observed that their affection for one another was built on a series of little power plays.

"Masturbation," Lisa said deliberately.

Mitch whispered to Shorty: "That's somethin' she doesn't know much about."

Ceci stifled a grin.

Lisa ignored the sniggers. She continued calmly in a detached, clinical tone. "Human beings develop masturbation fantasies before puberty. The basic theme of those fantasies is replayed throughout adult life. Surveys indicate that married people masturbate as much as the unmarried. Frequency has nothing to do with the amount of sex people actually have."

"Where'd you get this?" Train asked.

"My shrink."

"Will he come on the show?"

"She . . . but let me finish, there's more. We can debate familiar taboos, explore historical references. Even analyze how-to techniques."

"I sense a landmark show in interactive television," deadpanned Grinker.

The room erupted with laughter.

Train circled again, stopping beside a midnight blue tux hanging on his closet door. He flicked a piece of lint from the lapel. "Okay, slate masturbation for next week," he said to Shorty. "It'll pump the adrenaline of our teenage Tarzans."

Tommy's eyes landed on Ceci. "Snow White, not a peep from you?"

Ceci swallowed hard. "That valley detective Fontana came through."

"X-rated snaps?"

"He says he'll deliver them."

"Get blowups made." Train turned to Mitch. "This means we've got three guys ready to sing, right? Schedule 'em for Monday. Call the segment 'Peeping Dicks.' "

Train looked at Ceci again. "You got more? What else?"

"Ah, well, I've noticed that singles bars are increasingly passé . . ."

Tommy's face brightened. Sex always revved his engines.

Ceci continued, her voice stronger. "The hot new pickup spots are fresh-brewed coffeeshops—"

"Too yuppie," he interrupted. "It's the BMW buyer. We're not playing to the *New Republic* crowd. Downmarket, honey, think downmarket."

Ceci felt a river of perspiration drip down her back under her silk blouse. "There's an environmental conference sponsored by the New Age people next month," she blurted. "Top scientists meet to discuss the greenhouse effect."

Tommy stood stone still. He took a deep breath.

"Get with it, McCann," he suddenly yelled. "Eject this cosmic

13

save-the-world crap. We live in a world of caged store fronts. Flipper and fluorocarbons aren't sexy unless you grab the public by the balls."

Tommy stopped cold. "But the mini-mall bomber is." He swung around to Mitch. "What happened to that crackpot anyway? We got mail ten to one in favor of the guy."

"The last explosion was in a San Diego mall," he replied. "Since then, *nada*."

Tommy's needle gaze returned to Ceci.

She looked down nervously at the sheet of paper clipped to the folder on her lap. "Well, along those lines," she said weakly, "the pesticide scare has ruined fruit sales—"

"Christ, Ceci, this isn't Betty Crocker does Ralph Nader," Train barked.

Ceci sank down in her chair. There was a victim at every meeting and she sensed she was today's sacrifice.

Tommy again lifted the hand mirror from his desk. After preening like a girl preparing for her first date, he said wearily, "Ace reporters, please keep in mind civic spirit spells ratings death." He leaped to his feet abruptly. "I want bad-assed cowboys!" he shouted as he scanned their faces. "JC multiplied loaves and fishes for the masses. We've got to stage a magic show."

The intercom buzzed. Stan Lutz, the president of the NTN network, was waiting for Train in the lobby.

From his closet Tommy grabbed a chamois shirt with two-inch fringe. Ceci saw a flash of his orange briefs as he tucked the shirt into his jeans.

"The cupboards are near empty and Papa Bear's hungry," he called back at them as he left the room.

Ceci ambled back to her office. On the way, she observed Lisa in the glass recording booth practicing voiceovers for her "Castrated Rapists" segment. A carton of tissues and several boxes of cough drops were scattered on the counter.

Tommy's secretary pushed past Ceci with Train's limo driver in tow. In a shrill, bossy tone she instructed him to fetch Tommy at 7 P.M. for the Cancer Foundation dinner at the Beverly Hills Hotel. Ceci speculated who Tommy's date might be. Probably Lisa. Tanya was conveniently locked up for a month.

The studio bustled with activity, but Ceci felt totally left out, irrelevant. And although she appreciated Mitch's kindness in shar-

ing the detective series, she couldn't help but feel she'd been un-
officially relegated to the job of gopher. *The Tommy Train Show* was
her big break and she was blowing it.

Wheezing heavily, Shorty Smith caught up with her. His Rock-
ports made a thwopping sound as he trotted along the linoleum
floor. He looked tired. The skin around his eyes was as wrinkled
as his powder blue seersucker suit. "Don't take it too hard," he
said. "Tommy's jealous of you. That's what that's all about."

She peered at him incredulously. "Jealous of me?"

"You've got twenty-five years on the guy." His lugubrious eyes
reflected a protective warmth. "He's envious of anyone who doesn't
need a face-lift."

She smiled faintly. "But he's not jealous of Lisa."

"He's bangin' Lisa," said Shorty humorlessly. "Anyway, it's no
contest. She's held together with toothpicks. Every time the sutures
come out another implant goes in."

Ceci gave him a grateful peck on the cheek. He was a kind,
dear man, always trying to cheer her up.

Ceci sat in her Saab, hopelessly stalled in traffic. Every evening
the exodus of cars from the parking garages under Century City's
skyscrapers created gridlock around the broadcasting complex.

She clicked off the relentless chatter of radio news to reflect on
the story meeting. Though she disapproved of Train's boorish behavior she had to admire his seat-of-the-pants smarts. The man was
a genius who knew exactly what he was doing. Granted, it was
"shock journalism," but these days the competition for ratings was
savage. Train had deftly maneuvered his show through a mine field.
All his producers were pros. Ceci knew she had a lot to learn. There
was more to journalism than the lessons her genteel professors at
Northwestern had taught her.

When she first arrived on the show she had been horrified by
Lisa's overt sexual come-on. Ceci still thought it was tacky but she
had to acknowledge the results. As crass and vulgar as Lisa's ideas
sounded they always reaped airtime. If Ceci planned to survive, she
had to learn to think more like her.

Lisa didn't limit herself to Tommy; she dated other powerful
men—actors, sports stars, movie directors. Ceci once overheard her
tell a friend, "The only reason to date is to get your name in the
columns. Otherwise, settle for a fast fuck." That's where Ceci knew
she had to draw the line. She could never adopt Lisa's values when

it came to sex. Long term, Ceci wanted marriage and children. She had hoped to have two babies by the time she hit thirty.

The chirp-chirp of the car phone interrupted her thoughts.

"Where are you?" Shorty's voice was high-pitched, anxious.

"A block from my apartment."

"Great. Get upstairs, pack your bags. You're on the ten P.M. American flight to New York." He paused. "You got paper?"

Ceci's stomach fluttered as she steered to the curb. She pressed the emergency lights with trembling fingers.

"Ready," she said, yanking a notebook from her purse.

"Robert Shay's baby was kidnapped from his mansion in East Hampton . . ."

Ceci's mind raced. Shay was the richest movie mogul in the world. His company, Starlight Studios, was valued at over a billion dollars.

". . . The AP reports that Shay's in Thailand. His wife Emily's the lead in a Broadway revival of *A Streetcar Named Desire*. The baby was en route from nursery school—some type of holdin' pen for rich kids. Tomorrow's early edition of *The New York Times* can confirm this for you."

Shorty shouted at somebody in the background, then promptly returned to the phone. "There's more. Tommy asked Lisa to cover the story but she's tap dancing." A split-second pause. "This is your break, kid. A chance to shine, get a chunk of airtime, show us what you can do."

Ceci gulped nervously. "Yes, yes."

"We'll need chatty stand-ups in front of the mansion, the school, the police station, the courthouse, any landmarks in town. We expect good cutaway filler for tomorrow night's show. In the studio we'll round up law-enforcement types, kidnap experts. We're digging up photographs from the Lindbergh case."

He paused. "Here's the crunch. The satellite feed must be in-house by two P.M., that's five P.M. East Coast time."

Ceci's hand shook violently as she jotted down the time.

"You only have two, maybe three hours to get the first batch of tape up on the bird."

A blast of static broke their connection.

"Shorty? Shorty?" Ceci shouted into the phone. Sweat poured down her face.

"Yeah, I'm here." His voice was clear again. "NTN already has a team out there to feed their nightly news show," he said. "Jim

Armstrong's been assigned to you. He and his boys'll meet you at JFK. You're bedded at the East Hampton Motel." He paused. "Any questions?"

"Why did Tommy choose me?"

"He didn't, I did," Shorty replied. "And Ceci . . ."

"Yes?"

"Have you ever been to the Hamptons?"

"No," she said weakly. She'd never even visited New York.

"Ceci?"

"Yes?"

"Have fun."

"Right, right," she stuttered. "I'll try . . . try to do my best."

3

Chiang Kham Province, Thailand

"Shit, cut, hold it."

Robert Shay shook his head angrily. He removed his baseball cap and wiped his sweaty brow against the sleeve of his T-shirt. The steamy night air of the jungle made every breath difficult. He exhaled with exasperation, then stepped between James Whitney and Lee Mack. He moved in close to the blond actress, his lips nearly pressed against her ear.

"Cut the white-glove routine and slap the hell outta him," he said. "Wallop the bastard." Then, in a whisper, "You showed me what you can do with those scissor thighs, now slam him."

The actress smiled bashfully. She closed her eyes, mustering concentration. Once again the klieg lights ignited.

Shay retreated a few steps. "Ready?"

Mack's eyes popped open. "I can do it."

On cue, Whitney disappeared behind the chipped plaster wall of the abandoned infirmary. The crew fell dead silent. Only the chorus of crickets continued their staccato chirping.

With a practiced twist, Shay secured the baseball cap over his dark blond hair.

"Action!"

The lone clack of the clapboard's black-and-white jaws echoed through the vacant building. Almost immediately, Whitney, dressed in a stained and tattered surgical gown, lunged around the corner. His dazed eyes registered surprise when he spotted Mack. She jump-started backward and then in one fluid motion lifted her arm and slapped him hard, open palm, across the face. Whitney reacted instantly. "Darling, such a brutal welcome for your hero."

"You're no healer," snarled Mack. "You're a tortured soul who came here to die. But dying wasn't enough, you had to inflict your misery on others. Then greed took over, didn't it?" Mack's pale skin reddened, her fists balled. "Didn't it?" she screamed wildly.

18

With deft professionalism Whitney transformed himself from the assured seducer into a whimpering coward, a pathetic doper breaking down. "No, my beauty, my altruistic innocent. Greed's too simple an explanation. Rather, boredom."

Her face a mask of disgust, Mack turned to walk away.

"Cut!" Shay yelled. "Take eight's a wrap."

At ease, the two actors hugged one another warmly. Lee Mack flashed a sly look of relief at Shay. Sweating profusely, Whitney lifted the stethoscope from his neck and grunted a curt phrase of thanks to the Almighty. A seasoned actor, he knew instinctively when he hit the sweet spot.

Shay was pleased, too. Whitney's performance in this stifling rain-forest drama scored right up there with Michael Caine's in *Educating Rita*. And *China White*'s late summer release date positioned it perfectly for the Academy's review schedule.

A swarm of costume and make-up people emerged from behind the cameras to fuss over the actors. Shay watched as Mack shook her hair free from the soiled nurse's bandanna and combed through her tangled curls with splayed fingers. She flinched self-consciously when she realized he was watching her.

Robert looked away, down the empty corridors of the bombed-out hospital. Tufts of mossy vegetation had sprouted from every crevice—the jungle's inexorable claim on the sprawling cinder-block building. He gazed out beyond the overgrowth to the expanse of rice paddies. The misty drizzle had subsided. From the east, the suggestion of dawn came in a deep scarlet line narrow as a needle.

He was thankful the scene had finally clicked. The sky was too light for another take, and an extra night of shooting was out of the question. The film was already four million over budget due to the ridiculous cost of generators necessary to power this swamp.

As if reading Shay's thoughts, Harry Pine, his executive producer, bumped his shoulder triumphantly. "Three takes on the narc raid and it's liberation from Sing Sing."

"The chase is all yours," said Robert. "I'm flying to Bangkok this afternoon to run the dailies at Bakstree."

He could have simulated the entire mission compound on the sound stages of Bakstree Studios for less money, but he had purposely moved the set to this remote location to escape the prefab interiors. The gamble had paid off. The choking heat, buzzing flies, and nagging beggars lent a gritty reality to the film. After a week in this hellhole any reasonable person would understand why an embittered doctor might decide to smuggle a ton of heroin into the New York City hospital system. Shay's gut told him he had a winner with *China White*. Rarely, if ever, did he call a movie wrong.

Tired and satisfied, he left the infirmary and walked across a dirt road to the Gulf Reef Officer's Club, a Eurostyle colonial structure of latticed wood and tin roofs built in the 1920s. The fancy name was some sodden Brit's idea of a joke since the compound was tucked up near the Laotian border hundreds of miles from saltwater of any kind. Taken over and then abandoned by Anglican missionaries, the decrepit building had been temporarily salvaged as the production headquarters for Starlight Studios.

Shay ambled down the wide, airy hallway to his office, originally the dining room. The space was decorated with mismatched rugs of frayed yellow straw and random pieces of cheap Danish modern furniture. He spied the movie's shooting schedule tacked to a cork bulletin board. October 13th shone like a beacon. D-day. On that glorious morning the ruins would be returned to the rats and lizards.

On the far side of the water cooler, Chicki Zenker, Shay's personal secretary, viciously pounded the keys of an antique Olivetti, transcribing production notes for *Red Planet*, Starlight's next film. On the sawhorse table next to her sat four defunct computers, the victims of power outtages.

Robert was aware that Chicki had been testy of late, her usual can-do attitude soured by the difficult working conditions. He noticed her housedress of lightweight cotton was damp with sweat; she had traded her ever-present Gucci loafers for cheap rubber flip-flops, a concession to the tropics. With a free hand she irritably waved a pile of orange message slips at him like a flag. "Seventy —URGENT, UNRETURNED—messages from yesterday."

She ripped a sheet from the typewriter. "The phone line's on the blink again." Surreptitiously, she shot a sidelong look at Robert to check if he heard her. "You're not listening."

"I am." Shay riffled through a batch of new slides of Mars sent from NASA.

"Sketches of the Martians are underneath," she said.

Robert liked what he saw. The Milan design firm had created a spectacular array of intelligent-looking frog-eyed creatures.

Chicki chattered behind him. "A half-message came through the fax before the phone went down. Sarah's tried to reach you at the Hilton. And Robert"—her voice resounded with a naggy whine he prepared to ignore—"please, I beg you, get Harry to take these ghastly creatures out of here. I don't care who steals them."

Robert stared down at three miniature pythons asleep in the closed glass aquarium. Neatly coiled Slinkies, the slippery babies only thrashed about when they were hungry. He didn't see Chicki's problem. He tucked a marked copy of the *Red Planet* script under his arm and strode out to the veranda for breakfast.

The hot sun climbed higher in the cloudless blue sky. Despite the night shooting, he walked briskly, charged with energy. A band of emaciated cats scattered at the slap of his sandaled foot against the warped floorboards. The building was infested with the ferret-eyed creatures, prowling stealthily in their endless hunt for rat meat.

Kicking a fan-back rattan chair beyond the shade of the awning, he noticed that his pilot had parked the twin-engine Cyclone alongside the amphibious cargo airplane on the tarmac runway. Farther out, beside a wooden shed, two beggars squatted in the mud.

Before Shay could stretch out his legs on the wobbly footstool, a waiter appeared from the kitchen bearing a silver tea service for eight with a basket of brioche and toast and a platter of fruit.

As the waiter poured him a cup of tea, Robert noted his stiff, gray linen jacket. Where the man found the electricity to iron was one of the mysteries of the Orient.

Shay tossed a few cardamom seeds into his tea and draped an Irish linen napkin, also freshly ironed, over his crumpled Bermuda shorts. Perversely, at that moment, what he most craved was a Winchell's glazed doughnut polished with sugar so thick that it cracked into dime-sized flakes. Much as he loved sushi, a second-generation California Jew from a Fresno suburb wasn't meant to subsist on rice cakes and octopus.

After a few sips of the strong, dun-colored tea, he tilted back in the chair and closed his eyes. The tropical sun had toasted his face light brown and streaked his hair with golden highlights. In spite of the fact that he hadn't had a decent night's sleep since the week before, in his air-conditioned suite at the Bangkok Hilton, he felt damn good. Terrific, really. The monotonous diet had trimmed his muscular frame to 170, and his mind boiled with creative ideas. He also knew that Lee Mack had more than a little to do with his newfound burst of happiness.

The soft memory of her strong Germanic beauty and the cute, four-beat flutter fuck under the clanking propeller fan in his room made him smile. Even the smell of insect repellent on her skin was a turn-on. And those nipples—extraordinary: big, fat, pale, and round as pancakes. Old-fashioned, pink, translucent LPs floated past his eyes, whirring slowly around in his brain . . .

"El Snoro, it's rise and shine time." A familiar female voice blasted behind Robert. "Problems multiply."

Startled from his soothing slumber, he squinted at Libby Babcock, his financial manager. Robert closed his eyes again, listening attentively as she shuffled the papers on her lap.

"Y'know the incandescent-light effect in the first scene," she began. "It translates as a grainy halo. Seven hundred thousand to reshoot. Or seventy thousand if the lab plays with it."

"The lab."

"Oh, yes, here's somethin' nice. Universal slated six sneaks of *Blue Lightning.*"

"Six?"

"The boys are talkin' mega roll-out, a thousand theaters."

"Did we get a marketing budget for *China White?*"

"Twenty million."

Robert twisted his head to look at her. "I must be doing somethin' right."

"Sorry," Libby said with a speedy smile. Puncturing his ego was her favorite pastime. "Uni wants first dibs on *Red Planet.* They got plans for humungous merchandising. Dog bowls. Sports equipment. That Berkeley whiz kid has devised three computer games."

"Remember to try 'em on Doni."

She furiously scribbled a note. Shay watched her fondly. Libby was his organizational alter ego, shouldering all the details, giving him the freedom he needed to create new film projects.

Robert adjusted the silk pillows in his chair and slouched down again. The hot sun warmed his eyelids. A passing cat brushed against his bare shin.

"ILM accepted *Planet.* Four thousand special effects for ten million bucks. Thus, we're desperate, repeat *desperate,* Robert, for final storyboards."

Shay shifted toward the table and squirted a quartered lime on a slice of papaya. "Too much storyboarding stifles creativity."

Libby's dark eyebrows shot up like chevrons. "An epic techie feature can't have too many storyboards and you know it."

"What about the scoring?" The question was sure to get her off the guilt button.

"Good news. John Williams said yes and Michael's sniffin' for a piece of the action."

Behind them came the suck-drop of encroaching flip-flops. "Ah, I forgot," interrupted Chicki. "A fax of your controversial quote in *Premier* magazine came through last night."

Robert and Libby tilted their heads expectantly.

Chicki slipped a pencil above her ear and assumed a mock oration posture: "Making a film is like losing your virginity. Once you do it, you know. The touches come later."

Robert's brow crinkled. "I can't believe that caused a ruckus?"

"You're supposed to be Walt Disney," said Libby. "Family movies, environmental concerns. Anything risqué brings complaints."

"That's risqué?" He thought for a moment. "Isn't our new PR man being paid to prevent this sort of thing? Damage control."

"Short of taping your mouth shut, what can he do?" came Chicki's parting shot as she headed back to the office.

Robert closed his eyes again. He folded his hands on his chest in casketlike calm while Libby blasted forth.

"We've got a potential catastrophe on the home front. Duke thinks Whitney's gettin' loaded."

Duke was Shay's bodyguard, now an extra in the film.

"Smoking our samples?"

"No, we switched to baking soda after the opener," said Libby. "It's more serious. Duke suspects a dealer among the extras. He thinks Whit's Fed-Exing dope to his old lady in L.A."

"That jerk," Robert muttered. From the start he had disliked the jittery Brit's public-school posturing. "Tell Duke to search every package Whitney touches. We get ourselves a *Heaven's Gate* rep and *Premier* will have something to write about."

Shay poured himself more tea. "Why wasn't I told about this sooner?"

"Coach, you've been occupied." Her snide crack referred to his liaison with Lee Mack.

Shay gazed at Libby as she industriously tallied figures on her calculator. At thirty-six, her dark looks were handsome and sleek rather than pretty. Her face was too long, her ankles too thick, and although she was trim, her big-boned frame made her seem squarishly unfeminine. The shingled haircut, madras shirt, baggy khaki shorts, and neat little black watch on her wrist added to her PTA Mom look. And, despite the fact that she earned well over three million a year, she drove a four-year-old Volvo station wagon. Though Robert would never fully understand her, he'd taken to her from the day she walked into his office to apply for a secretarial job. Fifteen years later he'd come to love, respect, and trust her like his own mother. They'd survive her self-righteous fit over his little affair.

"Do me a favor," he said. "Tell Harry the final cut for *China White* is Jan one. We're going to Cannes in May."

"You think you got a mini *Zhivago?*"

"I do. Lee Mack's a nineties' version of Julie Christie."

Libby flashed a quirky smile. "A chubby Vanna White's more like it."

He laughed hard. He loved to bait her.

"Wise up, dork," said Libby. "Mack's after the lead in *Planet.*"

"Well, she's a possibility."

"Impaired judgment on your part. Whitney saved Mack's ass. He's making *China White* work."

Robert pulled a pair of sunglasses from his shorts pocket. "Exactly what do you have against this woman?"

Libby emitted a gurgly chuckle. "Turquoise eye shadow for starters. And she doesn't know squat about acting. Even worse, she's in that 'Learning to Love Yourself Is the Greatest Love of All' stage of life. Face it, Roberto, she's another A.S.S."

"What's that supposed to mean?"

"Ask Harry." She nodded toward the tall, lanky man coming toward them across the porch, moving swiftly as if mindful of the thousands of dollars every minute in the steamy jungle was costing them. "We're short six magnesium flares," he said as he grabbed a piece of crustless toast from the bread basket. "Gawd, this tastes like cardboard."

"What's an A.S.S?" Shay asked casually.

Harry winked at Libby. The tropical sun had enhanced the drizzle of freckles over his nose. He leaned over Robert, shedding breadcrumbs as he said, "Another sychophant starlet."

Libby pulled on his arm. "Sit."

"Can't," he responded. Behind him Lee Mack drifted on to the veranda and took a chair on the other side of Shay. The ends of her wet hair dripped down her white muslin shirt. Its oversized pockets barely concealed her loose breasts.

"Great scene, baby," said Robert. "Great."

She returned the compliment with a dreamy, sustained smile. Shay felt a sexual charge. He slipped his hand into hers. Long, tapered fingers teased his palm.

"We blocked the narc raid," said Harry. "It's a clean demolition of three thatch huts."

Lee Mack leaned forward. Plastic ivory bracelets clacked together as she reached for a cup. Harry, still standing, poured her tea. "Any chance for a trip to the Hilton for a real bath?" she asked.

"Not yet," said Harry. "There're two more shots of you whipping through the hospital. Plus retakes."

The actress pouted dramatically and hooked a shapely waxed leg over the footstool. In front of them a troop of green chameleons emerged from a hole in the floor.

"Robert, look!" Childish wonder elevated Mack's voice.

Libby glanced at the lizards and groaned. Thousands of chameleons crawled about the building. Even the cats didn't bother with them.

Robert felt sorry for Lee. Her forced exuberance was a clumsy attempt to be chummy, but they were too tight-knit a group. It was impossible for a newcomer to achieve their degree of intimacy.

"Robert!" hollered Chicki.

Shay rose from the chair and affectionately patted Mack's head. In the office Chicki held the cheap French phone out to him. From ten thousand miles away came Sarah's voice through a blast of cracking static. He caught just a few of her words. ". . . Doni's disappeared, vanished . . ."

Panic seized him. "What? What, Sarah? Louder. Speak louder." He clamped his hand over his other ear. His face tightened with concentration and the muscles in his back tensed. Through the drone he heard her say, ". . . we returned from the stable. Then he ran away."

Robert took a quick breath of air and began to yell. "Sarah, Sarah. Doni wouldn't run away . . ."

The line cleared for a moment. "No, I don't think so," she cried hysterically. "We're looking for him. Maria's on the beach. Saar's over at the Tuckers'."

A fist of fear punched Robert in the gut. He lost his breath. With desperation he fought back an overwhelming feeling of impending doom. Feverishly, he calculated the distance to the Tuckers' estate. A quarter-mile. It was walled. Inaccessible.

Facts, for Chrissake, he needed the facts.

"Listen to me, Sarah. Get your wits about you," he said with steely control. "Has Doni been kidnapped? Has my son been kidnapped?"

No response.

Suddenly frightened, he shouted, "Where's Emily?"

Libby stood beside Robert now, repeating numbers into a portable phone. Lee Mack, uncertain what to do, reached to stroke his shoulder. He slapped her hand away roughly.

The deafening static ceased and Spike Pappas came on the line. "Cap'n, we can't figure it." He spoke in a clear, hard voice. "It happened very fast. I was at the gate house. There's still a good chance he's wandering around in the marsh grass. Even down some hole. It's a bloody black night. Pitch. But those little legs of his can't carry him too far."

"Where's Snickers?"

Spike hesitated. "In the kitchen."

"Doni wouldn't leave him," Robert shouted, his voice filled with despair.

"We know that. The police have twenty men searchin' . . ."

"The police? Who called *them*?"

"Emily."

"Where is she?"

"In a limo, on her way out."

Shay blinked hard. His sweaty fingers tightened around the receiver. "Spike, listen, don't call anyone else." He slammed the phone into the cradle, then seized the walkie-talkie from Chicki. Duke was on the line. "Call Bangkok," he ordered. "Get the Peugeot to the airport. And the Gulfstream fueled." He turned to Chicki. "See if there's a Concorde connect in Paris."

As he shouted orders to his staff the sinister word—*kidnapped*—reverberated louder and louder in his brain. A vein pounded brutally in his temple. Nausea clawed at his gut. With trembling fingers he grabbed the edge of the bamboo table, hunched over, and threw up.

He rubbed his dry lips with the back of his hand. A grip, he must get a grip on himself. His gaze fixed on the cats. Posed, their long tails switching, they waited patiently. Greedy, molten eyes stared into his. Predators were everywhere.

4

Desert Hot Springs, California

Jack Werts thrust himself into Sherry Cox's lithe body with accelerating force. He stared down at her fluttering, iridescent eyelids and moist, full mouth. Long strands of her silky copper hair were tangled around his hand, pressed flat against the crisp hotel sheets.

Gradually Sherry began to pitch and twist under his body. Jack's weary eyes fastened on the gold-lettered charm around her neck. SPOIL ME, it read. His concentration began to wane. It was fortunate that his reliable cock performed independently of his leaden, jet-lagged brain.

A pint of Jack Daniels sat on the Victorian nightstand next to the bed. With one hand Jack reached for the bottle and, swallowing a gulp of warm whiskey, picked up the tempo again.

Sherry was clamped to his tanned muscular torso, her legs locked around his back, her firm breasts pressed to his chest. "Pleeeease give it to me, daddy," she begged. "Harder, harder. Do it, daddy. Do it."

Jack rammed into her. He dropped his face down to hers. His probing lips found her ear.

"I've missed you," he whispered. He breathed hard. "God, I've missed you."

Sherry wriggled wildly. She nipped at his chin with her teeth. Her aggressive tongue slithered along his lips as she emitted a soft moan.

"I'm coming now. Now, Jack."

He slammed into her again, this time to explode in her simmering dampness.

"You swine," she sputtered. Jack felt her sharp nails dig into his taut buttocks. "You promised me three to one."

"Promises, promises." Jack laughed as he gently slapped her hands away and rolled away from her body.

But Sherry wasn't about to quit. Her greedy mouth scuttled down his chest to his groin.

"Hey, Fifi, take it easy," cautioned Jack. "I'm an old man, remember."

"The horniest old man I know," she said as her soft mouth closed over him.

To get a better view Jack propped himself up against the mahogany headboard and lit a cigarette. Sherry had a truly magnificent spine. The flawless skin on her back was all mocha and apricot with a spray of tiny freckles across her delicate shoulders. She had a cheerleader-cute face and well-proportioned limbs. Not an ounce of fat anywhere. There was just one problem: low brainpower.

He inhaled the smoke deep into his lungs and then exhaled slowly through his nose. Leave it to her to find this funky hideaway. "Authentic desert deluxe," she had called it.

Decorated with ersatz Tiffany lamps, frayed Persian rugs and chintz love seats, the bedroom reminded Jack of a Vegas brothel. Though he was impressed with the Deco bathroom, he contemplated the adobe ceiling of unreinforced concrete with skepticism. He remembered reading somewhere that these desert towns north of Palm Springs were situated on a major fault line. This wasn't the place to be during an earthquake.

Rather miraculously, Jack felt an awakening sensation in his cock just as Sherry chose to abandon her enterprise. She crawled to the top of the bed and reached over him for the tall plastic bottle of Evian water on the table. After a long swig, she plopped down like a little anchor, creating a wave in the mattress.

Jack closed his bloodshot eyes.

At last he felt totally relaxed. His flight from Geneva to Palm Springs had taken thirty-two frustrating hours.

Sherry rose to her knees and nudged him to flip over onto his stomach. With experienced fingers she began to knead his pinched neck muscles. "Sweetie, the reason you're knotted is because you're stuck in alpha state," she said solemnly. "To achieve mental symmetry you've gotta float in delta twice a day."

Jack caught Sherry's wrist and pulled her down alongside him. "Listen, my little guru, you might notice I relax fine inside of you.

You forget I've been to London, Prague, and Geneva in one week. I ran my friggin' tail off."

"The story's a big hit, though, everybody in the office grabbed to read it."

He breathed a sigh of relief when she rattled on about her boss, Morgan Camp. The last thing Jack wanted from Sherry was a cross-examination on Ivana Trump.

"He insists that you're the best reporter in the business," she cooed.

"A frightening assessment."

"You can't accept a compliment," said Sherry, biting at the cuticle around her lacquered thumbnail.

"I'm considering the source." Jack looked at her thoughtfully. "And what if I wasn't a hotshot reporter? What if I was a laidback guy who ran a used-book store?"

"Stop it," said Sherry. Her hazel eyes softened. She gazed at him with the adoring innocence of a six-week-old puppy. "Why do you say such things? You're too talented for that kind of job."

He reached for more whiskey. "I'm hardly Seymour Hersh."

"Who's Seymour Hersh?"

Jack sighed. He was tired of playing teacher. "C'mon, get dressed," he said. "Let's go see if these mineral pools are worth three hundred bucks a night."

According to the slick brochure, Two Bunch Palms had once been Al Capone's desert hideout. After viewing the grounds, Jack thought it possible. The village of crude stone cottages could well have been built in the 1930s. The original site, however, had been enlarged by a series of developers to include an artificial lake and tennis courts. Despite these additions, the resort managed to retain a listless desert atmosphere. Vultures circled overhead. Pencil-thin lizards darted across the sandy pathways.

The dry evening air was warm but not unbearably so. Sherry soaked quietly alongside him in the larger of the two mineral pools. After a while she draped her arm around his sweaty neck, kissed him warmly with parted lips, and mumbled something in his ear about an herbal wrap—an eighty-five-dollar-an-hour beauty session he was paying for.

Jack's eyes followed her compact ass, abundantly displayed in a canary-yellow bikini, as she climbed the steep ladder out of the pool. Grateful she was gone, he floated alone in the palm-enshrined grotto. Eventually he paddled over to the edge, where he stretched out on an underwater shelf, his head resting on a pillow of ferns.

Jack briefly contemplated why he always seemed to end up in bed with women he had no desire to talk to. Most likely because he was a sucker for beauty. He smiled as he recalled his diverse conquests. An equal-opportunity seducer, his sweethearts ranged from Miss Israel to a Dallas Cowboy cheerleader.

Rationally he knew these pursuits were depressingly puerile, but he had always been a creature of impulse and instinct, too much like an animal when it came to sex. The truth was, he followed any direction his dick pointed. Later, of course, came remorse. Remorse from the blowtorch invectives inflicted by his steady lady.

Ironically, the same gut instinct that got him into trouble with the ladies served him admirably in journalism. He had an inborn sixth sense when it came to uncovering stories, nailing con artists, or just defining the real agenda at hand. Unfortunately, this rare talent had been misspent by chronicling the lives of movie stars or, more accurately, gaseous balls of hot air inflated with fame and ego. For him show-biz journalism was a personal tragedy. He could have been a contender: a David Halberstam, Bob Woodward, Joe Mc-Ginnis. Instead he had wasted his precious gifts on show-biz dreck.

Sure, he was competent. He had delivered landmark stories: Princess Grace's death, John Belushi's overdose, Rock Hudson's gay life-style. He had reported the significant weddings: Charles and Diana, Sean and Madonna, Burt and Loni.

But he didn't give a shit.

The hype didn't matter anymore. He was bone-tired of trans-continental flights and nouvelle cuisine. The celeb news business had escalated to a battlefield crowded with officious, self-important twerps: agents, lawyers, publicists, and accountants. Even more disturbing were the hordes of newly graduated journalism students—earnest, ambitious children fighting for stories.

Unfortunately, Tom Harrington, the editor of *Newsmakers*, sensed his disillusionment. The more dispirited Jack became over his work, the more money Harrington offered him. Already his expense account was lavish. But Jack had no illusions. He was just another parasite who fed off the celebrity gravy train. The perks had made the prostitution worth it.

He closed his eyes. Relaxed by the steamy hot mineral water he greedily anticipated his upcoming vacation, a quiet month to go fishing, play a few hands of poker, and get the brakes fixed on the Wrangler. He was burnt out, running on empty.

After a late dinner in the Casino, a rotunda where Capone once gambled the night away, Jack and Sherry hiked back to their cottage. Hundreds of stars twinkled in the black sky. A lone coyote howled in the distance.

"Morgan made a pass at me," she confided.

"It's about time."

Jack caught a glimpse of her sultry smile. He wasn't in the least jealous. Their relationship had endured because he had been out of town for the last two months.

"I plan to ask for a promotion," she said tentatively.

"Mmmm. Sounds fair."

"Morgan'll beef about it," she fretted. "He'll say I'm not qualified to be an associate publicist."

Jack vaguely recalled that she'd been a hair stylist at Blow Gun, a beauty salon in Santa Monica. "Ask for another position," he suggested. "Does he need a secretary?"

As Camp's secretary, Sherry's value to him doubled. But no sooner had he uttered the statement than he tried to dismiss his opportunistic thoughts. He hoped to extract himself from the relationship, not become indebted to her.

Back in their room Jack stretched out on the bed and lit a Marlboro. Halfheartedly, he perused Thursday's *L.A. Times.*

Sherry slipped off her red halter and Navaho-patterned skirt. She wore no underwear. She paraded back and forth before her reflection in the mirror on the bathroom door, then she pirouetted and complained: "You look more like Tommy Lee Jones than I look like Victoria Principal."

Jack ignored her. He turned the front page of the paper and kept on reading. Only when she began vigorously stroking an oily cream on the underside of her breasts, chin, and buttocks did she snare his attention. He figured the localized massaging had something to do with gravity but dared not ask. To his surprise, the swelling in his groin returned.

"C'mere. I've got something for you," he coaxed.

Sherry obediently strutted to the edge of the bed. She stood over him, arms akimbo.

"Bravo! What a surprise," she taunted. She brushed the newspaper from his chest and scratched playfully at the zipper on his chinos. Her voice decelerated to a purr. "But remember, this time, no deposit, no return."

Right then, he knew he'd miss *Nightline* with Ted Koppel.

Shortly after 3 A.M., the antique phone on the night table next to the bed rang with a vengeance. Jack reached for the complicated receiver and lost his grip.

"Werts? Werts? Is that you?" squeaked a voice from the dangling earpiece. Jack groped for the cord.

Sherry hissed at the racket and rolled to the far side of the bed.

"Yeah," Jack grunted.

"Where are you? What's this place?" It was Mara Stykes, the L.A. bureau chief for *Newsmakers* magazine.

"The desert," he groaned.

"Near Palm Springs?"

"Yeah, near Palm Springs."

"Have you heard the news?"

Jack's groggy brain began to function. "News" always meant his getting on another airplane.

"No."

"Well, listen to this. Robert Shay's kid has been abducted. Harrington wants an on-the-scene story from you."

Jack's head throbbed. Too much red wine at dinner.

"Where'd this happen?" he asked.

"East Hampton."

"Shit."

Mara adopted her schoolmarmish tone. "Because you didn't leave your whereabouts with the bureau, it's taken six hours to locate you. You've missed the red-eye."

"Whadda shame."

"We got you on a seven A.M. flight out of Palm Springs." She sounded intolerably cheerful. "Sammy Voight will meet you tomorrow night at Bobby Van's. Y'know where it is?"

Jack remained silent.

"Jack?" Mara persisted. "Jack, don't be difficult."

"Yeah, I know."

"The story's Monday's cover," she chirped. "Copy must be filed to Harrington by Saturday night. Forty-eight hours from now. Dig it."

Jack slowly digested the information.

"I didn't know you and Sherry Cox were an item," Mara added. Jack visualized the smirk on her face.

"It's fortuitous," she continued. "Very fortuitous. Because Shay signed with Morgan Camp Associates last month."

With a click the line went dead.

Jack poked for the operator button, requested a 5:30 wake-up call, then scooted over to Sherry. His tired arms hugged her warm body as the memory of Mara's words disintegrated into blotchy fragments.

5

Robert Shay's Gulfstream III jet flew east over the Swiss Alps. The steady thrum from the powerful engines produced gentle vibrations in the luxurious sleeping compartment at the rear of the aircraft. The narrow cabin was dark; ecru silk shades were pulled taut over the porthole windows. On the satinwood side table a cone of light from a tiny halogen lamp illuminated a cluster of graphite-framed photographs. In one, Robert hoisted his first Oscar aloft. In another, Emily Shay beamed brightly under the marquee of *Lila,* the film for which she won an Oscar for best actress. The other photographs were of their son, Doni, clowning with an inflated Mickey Mouse.

For over an hour, Robert had lain perfectly still on the double bed. His strong, angular features were ravaged by grief, and deep grooves sliced the corners of his mouth. His flat, blank stare was directed at the ceiling.

Without warning, the pain came again, the raw, excruciating stab in his intestines. This time, he twisted on to his side and yanked his knees up to his chin to relieve the pressure. But there was no release. The pain stuck in his gut. He cried out to ease the ache, a loud, detached wail. Then, another. Finally, he curled into an embryo position to block the agony. Never before had he known such horror, such grief, such numbing, incapacitating pain.

Robert Shay's worst nightmare had come true. From the moment his son was born he had feared that someday the baby might be kidnapped. Because of that fear, he had done everything to ensure his son's safety.

But he had failed.

In the last twelve hours, trapped like a caged animal in this fiberglass prison, Robert had made every pact with God he could think of. Although he never prayed or attended temple, when he saw the first televised news reports of his son's abduction he fell to his knees and promised Almighty God the works—his fortune to bring world peace. He'd buy the goddamn West Bank and force the goddamn Arabs and Jews who lived there to love each other. He'd buy each one of them off if he had to. He'd confiscate their weapons and personally brainwash them into burying their hatred.

Years ago, Shay had given up a successful acting career to become a director because he wanted control. As a director, and now producer, he had won that control. Now he'd give up everything, he'd do anything God asked if only Doni was back in his arms.

The boy meant everything in the world to him, more than his own life. Now every memory echoed with the tinkle of Doni's small voice: "Daddy, read to me. Daddy, play with me. Daddy, find the stars." Every time he closed his eyes he saw his son's rosy, loving face, his buttery little hands, those precious baby fingers they had spent hours counting one by one. The memory of Doni's giddy, innocent smile ignited the pain again. Shay doubled up and gagged with dry heaves.

The hotel doctor had given him medication but the chalky liquid had no effect. The gut-wrenching spasms continued every hour. Rationally he knew he must drink to avoid dehydration, but he could barely keep water down. He breathed heavily. He knew he must rest but he was afraid to close his eyes. His skull held an inferno of grisly images.

In desperation, he sat upright and placed his feet on the floor. With a jittery movement, he ran his hand through his sticky hair. He was wearing the same T-shirt and crumpled shorts he had had on in Thailand when word came. He stared at his open closet. Dozens of silk shirts hung beside a rack of leather jackets and cashmere overcoats. An adjoining compartment held three Christian Dior tuxedos and a Russian beaver coat.

In the cramped, bronze-plated bathroom a pile of plush monogrammed towels had been stacked beside a tray of bath oils, colognes, and aftershave lotions. A graduated collection of boar-bristle brushes were neatly arranged alongside an oblong, velvet-lined jade case that held ten pairs of reading glasses and six gold watches.

Robert reached over and unlatched a brass-fitted cabinet under the desk. A half-bottle of Absolut stood beside a cache of pills: Halcion, Flurazepam, Valium, Seconal. He unscrewed the Valium bottle and gulped down a batch of tiny white tablets, then poured an inch of vodka into a crystal tumbler. The warm liquor burned his parched throat.

There was a gentle rap at the door and Duke Thompson entered the compartment, ducking down as he did. He was a hefty black man with the oversized shoulders of a prize fighter and the clever mind of a jewel thief. "We land at Orly in twenty minutes," Duke said softly. "I figure twenty minutes to refuel."

Robert nodded.

Duke sat down lightly on the edge of the bed, his concerned eyes scrutinizing Shay's face. "I got this East Hampton cop, Drake, on the line," he said. "Six escort cars are meetin' us at the airport."

Robert felt the drop-kick of the booze and tranquilizers. "That's the entire force," he said sharply. "Why aren't they searching for my son? Doni's lost, not me."

Duke let it pass.

"Still no news from Emily," he went on. "Libby's burnin' the wires talkin' to her shrink, the new guy, Dr. Reiss." He paused. "Chicki left word she's on a commercial flight."

Robert gave Duke a startled look. "I need her," he said. "I need you all."

Duke hunched forward and his strong muscular arm encircled Robert. "Things are never as bad as you imagine. Small fry's goin' to be okay." His massive jaw twitched slightly. "He's okay," he repeated. "We'll find him and break those cocksuckers' necks."

Robert's lips trembled. He choked back tears. For too many hours he had obsessively considered all the horrible possibilities, vividly gruesome scenarios that replayed mercilessly. He gestured toward the closet. "Should I load the thirty-eight?"

Duke shook his head. "Only if you plan to ice a few photographers." Powerful muscles visible under his black shirt, he rose from the bed, and left the compartment.

Robert covered his face with his hands. Why hadn't Duke stayed in the Hamptons with Doni? He kicked himself for his naive, misguided fear that Thailand was dangerous. Jesus H. Christ! He had bought his own stupid movie fantasies. The menace wasn't there in the jungle, it was at home in his backyard. And who did he leave to protect his son? Spike Pappas and a hired lackey. The B team. The fucking B team had been guarding Doni. He had failed all down the line. A 2.8-ton armor-plated 560SEL for what? A half-million-dollar security system for what? There was direct access to the mansion from the beach because the goddamn construction crew was a week behind schedule.

With his seething anger barely held in check, he made his way down the narrow corridor to the executive parlor at the front of the plane. Libby rested in a leather club chair, her feet propped up. Robert hurled himself into the chair opposite hers. "Why the fuck did Emily call the police?" he bleated at her.

Libby jerked forward. She lifted her feet from the table and reached out to him. "Relax, relax. Please try to get some rest."

"Who the fuck can rest?" he shouted. "My son's been kidnapped. Doni's . . ." Tears blinded him.

Libby put her hand on his. "You look like hell," she whispered gently. "Go take a shower, clean up. You've got to pull yourself together." Her voice shifted from a tone of concern to one of encouragement. "Doni's alive. I know he's alive," she said. She paused for a long, deep breath, then spoke in a calm, clear-thinking voice. "For once, Reiss made some sense. Emily's hysterical. She lost her grip on reality, flipped. He says it's a nervous breakdown. Apparently Nina called him immediately. He went to the apartment, sedated her, and drove her out to the house."

Robert stared at Libby, a strange light in his eyes. "Fine, great. So now she's got Thorazine up her ass. She can't talk because she's a medicated zombie. The question remains: *Where was she? Where the fuck was she when Doni was taken?*"

Libby shrugged. It was pointless to argue with him.

"She doesn't leave for the theater till six-thirty," he raved. "Reiss didn't say where she was, did he? You and I both know if she wasn't simpering on his couch then she was bouncing up and down on Reno Ventura's dick. In that hotel. What's it called? The Chelsea? That downtown joint with her phony downtown friends."

He lowered his head and linked his hands in back of his neck. He could barely contain his anger. He wanted to kill. It was because of Emily that Doni had postponed his karate lessons. It was her protective bullshit that prevented him from learning any form of self-defense or achieving any level of street smarts. Robert flashed on the urchins in Bangkok, the ghetto kids in Manhattan. Instinctively, these little tykes knew the game of survival. Doni was brilliant and brave but what did he know? Nintendo, telescopes, music. He was trusting, terribly trusting. The traits he desperately needed for his survival had been denied him.

Red landing lights flashed overhead. Absent-mindedly, Robert buckled his seat belt and gazed out the window at the pointillistic grid of Paris at night. To him it was a postcard cliché. They couldn't take off fast enough.

"Why did she accept this two-bit, retro Broadway production anyway?" he asked irritably. "And when she did, why didn't she force him to stay in the city with her?"

The jet's descent was smooth as cream. Unfolding landing gear thumped under their feet. Libby's eyes remained dull and still.

"Doni stayed in the Hamptons because of Foxy," she said softly.

"So why didn't she think to truck the horse to the stable near Central Park? Why in God's name did she buy that stupid pony for him in the first place?"

Libby glared at him. "You bought Foxy, remember?"

Robert turned to the window. As the jet's tires clicked over the runway reflectors he flashed on Doni's birth at Cedars Sinai in West Los Angeles. The twelve-hour labor had been torturous agony for Emily but she never complained. When Doni was an infant, she kept him with her at all times. He had been raised in trailers on movie sets. It was only now that he was older that she insisted he needed a home, a place to run and play and make friends. He recalled her words vividly: "Doni's not a football to be tossed between us."

Of course, Doni had homes—their Beverly Hills mansion; houses in Malibu, Aspen, St. Bart's, and Santa Fe. But for reasons neither of them fully comprehended the child had taken to the half-finished space-age estate in East Hampton. He developed an immediate attachment to the potato fields, the ducks, and the cold, pounding Atlantic. He watched for hours as the giant bulldozers ploughed up the soil. He had pretended to hammer along with the big workmen in their dusty jeans and shiny yellow hardhats. These men were his heroes.

The plane rolled to a jerky stop. From the window Robert watched two fuel trucks drive onto the tarmac. Behind them in the mechanics' hangar a burst of white lights flashed. Two photographers broke loose and ran toward the plane. French security guards stopped them and wrestled the men to the ground.

Robert quickly returned to his sleeping compartment. He lay down and closed his eyes. Something that Libby had said shone like a prism of light. He sifted through her words. Yes. She had said, "Doni is alive." Of course. His son's value to the kidnappers hinged on keeping him alive.

A message would come. A ransom note in some form. A demand for big money. He must reply properly. Cautiously. Emotion must be held in check. Every detail must be analyzed and reanalyzed. No mistakes could be made by bumbling half-witted bureaucrats. Every detail must be handled by him. His son's life was at stake.

6

Doni Shay sat on a red blanket on a big floor. There were no toys. He stood up and walked to the wall. It was tall, taller than his daddy. He went over to where the floor changed to cold. Hard, white, cold. There was a potty. A tub. They were the kind Mommy used. The floor was cool. He sat against the tub.

At the top of the wall he saw sunlight. He knew about the sun. Daddy had told him the hot center was far, far away. But the beams came all the way down to Earth. He couldn't see the sun. But he could see the tops of many trees.

Doni put his hand in his pocket. The Pez machine was still there. That was good.

He looked back at the red blanket. Maria put a blanket on the floor for Snickers. But where was Snickers? At home with Maria and Sarah.

He started to cry. He missed Snickers so much that it hurt inside. He cried louder. No one came.

After a while he stopped. He knew that Snickers was okay. He remembered that Snickers had gone into the house to get his food. He loved his food. This made Doni feel good. Snickers was always so happy eating his food.

But where was Sarah? And Maria?

They were at home too. He was somewhere else. He was with the seal people. He hated them. He thought they wanted to play a surprise game. Daddy always played surprise games with him. But Daddy's games never hurt. This game hurt his head and his arm. He looked at his arm and started to cry again.

The tears made his shirt wet. He remembered the boat. It had rocked like his cradle. That's what hurt his arm. And later, the car stopped too fast. Sarah said people should never stop fast because it hurt the tires. When he was wrapped up in the dark he heard many hurt tires.

The seal people were like Dr. Bee. Mommy always said Dr. Bee was good for him. But Doni hated him. The seal people stung him like Dr. Bee. But when he went to see Dr. Bee he sat on Mommy's lap. She sang him a song. He felt very sad. He wanted his Mommy. She always kissed him.

Doni returned to the blanket. He remembered that Daddy was going to call. He was coming home with presents. He always brought presents. He must talk to Daddy to tell him to take care of Snickers.

Something was wrong. He started to cry again. Snickers never went away. Sometimes Sarah went away to see her mommy and daddy. But Snickers always stayed at home with Doni. Even when Doni went to see Grandma, Snickers came with him.

Snickers was with Sarah and Maria. That was right. But somehow he was in the wrong place. He was a lost baby. Maria told him about little lost babies in big stores.

He put his head down on the blanket and thought about the devils that lived in the dark under his bed. They had something to do with this. At night they tried to grab his legs. They played bad games in the dark. Now the devils had caught him and taken him far away.

Sarah showed him a devil in a picture book. It was red with horns. But the book was wrong. Devils were tall and short and flat and round. They could fill any space if they wanted to. They knew how to sneak up on you when you didn't expect them. One night they chased him into Mommy's room. She told him that if the devils were under the bed then Snickers would eat them. The devils were afraid of Snickers. But Snickers was gone. Who could protect him from the devils?

The door opened.

Doni sat up.

The seal woman came into the room. She was no longer black and shiny. She had bare feet. Mommy didn't let him wear bare feet.

The woman sat down next to him. From a bag she took a white box. It was a toy. He started to turn it over but she made him put the box on the floor. Then she opened the top. There was a hamburger inside. She took a cup from the bag and pushed a straw through its hat. Then she put the straw into his mouth.

The liquid was sweet. It was Coke. Mommy and Sarah didn't let him drink Coke because it was bad for his teeth. But when he and Daddy drove in the car, Daddy stopped and they drank Coke together. It was their special secret.

"Good?" she asked.

He nodded.

The woman stood. "C'mere," she said.

Her brown hand pulled his. It was browner than Sarah's. But not as brown as Maria's.

They walked into the bathroom.

"Stay there," she said.

Doni stood by the potty.

She came back with a square black box. She put the box in front of the potty and lifted him onto it.

41

"Unzip your pants," she said.

Doni knew how to do potty by himself. Sarah taught him. He knew how to tie his shoe laces too. He wore tear snaps but he knew how to tie a bow by himself.

The woman waited.

He pulled his pants down. Tinkle came. It felt good.

Seal woman pulled his pants up. After she lifted him down from the box, she patted it. She was happy that she put the box there.

Back in the room, she left him on the blanket beside the hamburger. The big door closed. He heard her steps go away.

Doni walked over to the door. He reached his arm as high as he could but it was all flat.

He returned to the blanket. He picked up the hamburger and took a bite. It was good. He took another bite and then drank the Coke.

The empty white box made a good fort. He took the top off and turned the bottom down on the floor. From the straw, he made two soldiers. Then he tore a tiny piece of straw from the taller soldier. He placed it inside the fort. A baby soldier, like himself.

Again he felt very sad. He put his head down on the blanket.

By the time Jack Werts landed at Kennedy Airport packs of foreign journalists were roaming about the TWA terminal. In the baggage-claim area a crew of swarthy Australian cameramen shouted and laughed as they collected crates of video equipment. Nearby a group of Japanese photographers had turned the car-rental counter into a war zone, refusing to accept the beleaguered agents' announcements that every available car had been rented.

Mara's secretary had yanked some fancy strings to find Jack a secondhand Chevette on loan from a Brooklyn car lot. The flimsy little compact started up okay but an unidentifiable ping began to tick in the dashboard the moment he accelerated. He cracked the window to release the odor of stale french fries.

The Long Island Expressway was choked with traffic. In the slow lane a line of TV vans rumbled along like a caravan. Their wobbly satellite dishes swayed in the wind. Just three years ago, Jack would have killed for the opportunity to participate in this media superbowl. He would have been flying high from the intense rush and frenzied competition to get fresh news to his editors in New York. But this afternoon he was tired and annoyed by the whole affair. Even Buddy Holly, crooning from the cheap radio crudely tacked under the dashboard, couldn't dispel his grouchy mood. The battered and weatherbeaten New York automobiles disgusted him. During the last five years he had been happily spoiled by the gleaming cleanliness of L.A. autos as well as by their law-abiding drivers.

Of course East Hampton, at the tip of Long Island, was another story. It was a fairy-tale Gatsbyland of immense summer cottages built by wealthy New Yorkers who came there to escape the suffocating heat of the city. Theirs was a life of golf tournaments, polo matches, and sailing regattas held at local beach clubs. Over the years, the natural beauty of the dunes had attracted less affluent artists and writers as well, boosting the populations of adjacent communities like Bridgehampton and Sag Harbor.

In recent visits Jack had seen the tranquility of the exclusive resort increasingly disturbed by an influx of yuppies. Flexing economic muscle gained from Wall Street jobs in the skyrocketing stock market of the 1980s, these urban professionals invested heavily in Hampton real estate, remodeling decayed farmhouses and converting barns into high-tech residences. With this prosperous environment came the accompaniments necessary for the survival of their species: fine wines, gourmet restaurants, well-stocked bookstores, and designer boutiques.

Celebrities had also migrated to the Hamptons. Dustin Hoffman, Yoko Ono, Alan Alda, Chevy Chase, Faye Dunaway, Carrie Fisher, Billy Joel, and Ralph Lauren were among the rich and famous seen shopping along village streets. Media stars were also well represented. Clay Felker, Tom Brokaw, Carl Bernstein, Diane Sawyer, Mort Zuckerman, Ben Bradlee, and Sally Quinn had settled in long ago.

Back when Jack worked in the magazine's New York headquarters he had frequented Bobby Van's, a cozy piano bar in Bridgehampton. For hours he listened to sauced, cynical writers berate lame-brain Californians obsessed by screenplay money and real-estate prices. Overnight, the old-timers woke to discover that Perrier had become the local drink and Jags were parked in the garages next door. Movie deals were the hot topic of conversation.

As usual, Werts was late. He forced his way through an army of TV technicians to get in the door. Inside, the bar was jammed with every size, shape, and persuasion of media voyeur. Two dozen sweaty bodies queued up for the public phone. By sheer chance Jack spied Sammy Voight perched on a bar stool.

He deftly weaved toward her. A dishy TV reporter shoved past him in the direction of the exit. At the same time a tweedy Brit elbowed him while a frenzied waitress screamed drink orders in his ear. The place was a zoo.

"Get yourself outta the line of fire," called Sammy. He dodged a revolving tray of drinks and with a bear hug scooped her petite body into his arms. She was his favorite photographer.

Voight's bright green eyes took him in, examining him like a doctor searching for telltale signs of decay. "It's about time," she said after he set her down. "Five hours late."

"Time's relative," he said. "If Harrington wanted punctuality he should have sent one of his New York wiz kids."

"God forbid."

Jack slid his body into the narrow standing space next to her and surveyed the crowd. Everywhere were faces he recognized: two old buddies from *Newsweek*, the *Post*'s entertainment editor, the ace feature writer from *Vanity Fair*. In the restaurant section Geraldo Rivera yakked to a well-known black news anchor. At a front table under a blanket of blue cigarette smoke the junk press congregated, an entire gang of *National Enquirer* graduates. The crowded room crackled with energy. Jack had to admit the event had produced a smash turnout—the full media spectrum: stars, scum, and serious journalists.

"Nothin' like a little competition to whet the appetite," Sammy said, her eyes on him. Jack noticed that she had cut her flame hair even shorter, tomboy style.

"How 'bout a progress report?" he asked.

"I took the requisite snaps of Doni's school—Lycée whatever-the-fuck-it's-called. The headmistress is a certified she-bitch. If you want spittle in your face, try her for a quote."

Sammy swirled her drink. It looked like Scotch.

"Did you eat?" he asked.

That instant she was bumped by a Japanese photographer with three telephoto lenses around his neck.

"Fuckin' Nips are everywhere," she said under her breath. Like all crack press photogs, Sammy was a killer competitor. A bull raged in Tinkerbell's body.

"It's a battlefield out there," she snapped. "The whole town is the floor of the Democratic convention."

She pushed her empty glass to the far side of the bar. The

bartender's arms were moving like a windmill. It was obvious they would have to wait.

"Forget food. It's too late," she said. "The restaurant owners are paralyzed." It had been a rough day for her. Jack was grateful he had missed it.

"Just wait till you check into the Motel from Hell," she said. "It's the Kuwait Hilton under siege. The phones are totally fucked. The water's puke green and the power shorts. BBC has six guys bunkin' in the room next to me."

"Any chance of my gettin' laundry done?"

"You jest." Sammy pulled a tiny black transmitter from her camera bag. "Your beeper."

Jack tucked it into the pocket of his safari jacket.

"Shay's chauffeured Bentley has been parked at the East Hampton airport since sundown," she said. "I'm cruisin' over there for a blurred shot of him steppin' off his plane—along with four hundred other mad hatters."

Sammy stood on the rungs of the bar stool. She leaned over and aggressively grabbed at the bartender's arm. He shook her off as she ordered Glenlivet for herself, a Dos Equis for Jack.

"Nice goin'," he said, casting an eye on her tight, round tush. If Sammy weren't a lesbian he would have slept with her long ago. Though she did everything to camouflage her femininity, Jack knew she'd be dynamite in the sack.

"I shot in the toy store for two hours," she said.

"The toy store?"

"Doni Shay got new toys to the tune of eight hundred dollars a week." Suddenly Sammy gave Jack her medical examiner's look. "Don't you want to write this stuff down? Some reporting to go with my pictures, maybe?"

Jack laughed. "Don't worry. I got it."

"Well, whatever you decide to write, it'll fly off the stands," she said. "Harrington said they unearthed a tear-jerk picture of the kid for the cover. Big saucer eyes guaranteed to rip your heart out."

Jack had never seen any pictures of Doni Shay in print. "Where'd he find it?"

"Bought it off somebody. Probably a relative. Maybe a professional photographer who shot a portrait, then quietly pocketed the negatives. Some lucky slob is counting half a million greenbacks."

"Wheeeee," exclaimed Jack.

The drinks came. The fatigued bartender brought him a Miller Lite.

"Did the afternoon papers have any news on the kidnappers?" Jack asked.

"Idle speculation," Sammy replied. "Money's got to be the reason. Doni Shay isn't exactly your average ghetto kid." She rubbed her eyes with her knuckles. "I hear that tomorrow's *Daily Mail* has Charles Lindbergh on the front page."

"Lindbergh's baby was found dead in a ditch," he said matter-of-factly.

"That's a bad omen," said Sammy. "What happened to the 'napper?"

"Bruno Hauptmann fried."

"Serves the bastard right."

"Who knows?" said Jack. "His ninety-year-old wife claims her husband was innocent." His eyes strayed about the room. Lou Rauscher, the tireless press reporter for *The New York Times*, gave him the high sign.

"Did you get any dirt from Morgan Camp's office?" Sammy asked.

"My, my, gossip travels swiftly."

"Sherry Cox?" Skeptical eyes searched his. "A receptionist? If you fucked higher up the ladder we might at least get some exclusive info."

Jack moved to punch her. She ducked.

"Your standards are slippin'," she teased. "Before I forget, Harrington's got three reporters fixed on the Beresford—Shay's twenty-room Central Park West duplex. They're after Emily's extra-curricular activities."

"Her too?"

"Yeah, but I don't know who. His latest is Lee Mack. Her flack's been leaking items to the columns for the last two months."

Lou Rauscher came by and slapped Jack on the shoulder. "I'm impressed. If *Newsmakers* flew you in from the Coast then you're not over the hill like the rest of us."

Rauscher, in his late fifties, was nattily dressed in a summer-weight Brooks Brothers suit and striped power tie. Jack became acutely aware of his crumpled khakis.

Sammy gave Rauscher a wary look as she rose and hoisted her canvas camera bag over her shoulder. *"Au revoir,* love," she said to

Jack. "I've reserved a chopper for some aerial shots of the Shay estate. You wanna come?"

"What time?"

"Six A.M."

He frowned.

Sammy smiled at him. "Keep in touch," she said. He watched her bright carroty head vanish into the crowd.

"Fun and games, eh?" said Lou, sidling up.

Jack always recognized the "pump" in any guise. "I just joined the party."

"Why so late?"

Jack liked Rauscher. He wrote hard, lucid prose and his press stories were always on target. "What exactly are the ground rules?" Jack asked with a wry smile.

Lou came clean. "Tomorrow's *Times* runs my paean to idyllic life in the Hamptons. The lengthy poem—rather artful if I do say —was written to assuage my editor's fear that the Southampton shack he bought was exorbitantly overpriced."

Two draft beers magically appeared on the bar. Lou paid. He glanced at Jack. "For my next act, I'm taking in the media circus. From you, I want to know what *Newsmakers'* cover angle will be?"

Jack laughed. "Who knows? I haven't written the story yet."

"Then give me a perceptive quote about the magazine. Ace reporter predicts the biggest cover sales in history . . ."

"Better you call Tom Harrington," said Jack. He pulled out a small address book and recited the editor's home number. "He'll blab your ear off. Harrington loves to read his words in *The Times*."

"Don't they all."

Years ago, Jack learned that when pressed against a deadline, fellow scribes made quick, relatively accurate sources. He turned the tables. "So who's here?" he asked.

"*Le Monde, Stern,* the *Economist.* The *Journal's* doin' a piece on the global reach of Starlight Studios. Their theory: massive publicity from the kidnapping will boost cassette sales of Shay's films."

"Undoubtedly accurate," Jack acknowledged.

"There's another item. A tip, actually." Rauscher hesitated.

"Well, what is it?"

"Okay, okay, but do me a favor and don't pass it around. The *New York Tattler* is on first base."

Jack cocked his eyebrow. "Malcolm Bates? You're kidding."

Behind him the *Tattler's* star correspondent was getting shit-faced with the table of tabloid reporters. His paper was a daily rag dedicated to celebrity mischief. Sports scores passed for hard news.

"It's impossible to figure how or why," said Rauscher. "But he's got a pipeline to Joe Krugger."

"Krugger?"

Rauscher was taken back. "Where'd they parachute you in from? Khartoum?"

"Two Bunch Palms."

Confusion registered in Rauscher's eyes.

"Forget it," said Jack. "But if you mention my being airlifted in, I prefer Bali. Harrington will shit neon marbles when he reads it."

Rauscher smiled agreeably. "Let me give you the basics, my boy. Krugger heads the FBI investigation team . . ." Just then, his roving eye zeroed in on Liz Smith. Rauscher tapped Jack gently on the arm and trotted away after the gossip columnist.

Jack finished his beer and approached the noisy table of mud-slingers.

"Christ, it's Black Jack," Bates yelped through a haze of smoke. "Where was it last? Paris? The insane press conference where Rock Hudson admitted he had AIDS? Was that the last time I saw the likes of you?" Scruffy red whiskers sprouted from the reporter's fleshy cheeks. Three empty shot glasses were lined up on the table in front of him.

"Join us, mate," said a skinny fellow in a Hawaiian shirt. A pair of Porsche sunglasses were shoved over his forehead.

"Jimmy Leggitt!" said Jack with genuine shock. His eyes fixed on the reporter's lean, deeply tanned face. "I'd expected by now you had married money and retired to Monte Carlo."

"We sleuths never sleep," chirped Bates in his drunken, sing-song Welsh accent. A manic light played in his watery eyes. With a clumsy, graceless gesture he waved for the waitress, his bulk almost overturning the chair under him. "Service in this establishment stinks," he hissed loudly.

Leggitt's shifty eyes glowed with whiskey. Red capillaries fanned out across his nose. "You been doin' some nice work," he said to Jack. "They must be payin' you well."

As always, money was Leggitt's number-one concern.

Jack deflected the question. "Who you workin' for?"

"Friggin' *Express*." He turned from Jack to greet an approaching waitress. Meanwhile, the neighboring table of Australians rose to leave. Jack grabbed an empty chair.

Bates hunched over the table. Despite his loss of bodily control, there was single-minded intent in his eyes. "When's your deadline?" he whispered hoarsely to Jack.

"Tomorrow night."

Leggitt interrupted, "The public expects a love story. Not cops and robbers."

"That's all mush-mush," said Bates, poking Leggitt's arm. "I'm three-quarters to the finish line. I've landed the crown jewels. America will read the story in this Sunday's *Tattler*."

Leggitt glared at Bates. He lowered his voice. "For Godsakes!"

"Black Jack's not gonna jabber," said Bates. His face resembled a badly peeled potato.

"He might tip the *Post* or *Daily News*."

"Why?" asked Jack. He knew the game they played.

"Repay somebody a favor," said Leggitt. "We all owe favors."

Bates dipped a red cloth napkin into the water glass and wiped his sweaty face with it. "Jack's a good boy," he said softly. "He's done me some nice turns. I owe him."

Bates was drunker than Jack had estimated. Sober, he wouldn't have been so generous.

"Here's the dope," said Bates confidentially. "The FBI's targeted the nanny. They're sure it's an inside job. Estate's a fortress, you seen it?"

"Not yet."

"It's impossible to crack."

Leggitt leaned forward, a merry twinkle in his eye. "Before dawn, super-sleuth Bates here got loaded and dressed up like a sand dune. He pinned twigs to his back and crawled along the beach."

The story brought a round of hoots.

Bates ignored their banter. He flashed a cunning smile. "The FBI thinks the nanny and the chauffeur transferred the kid to a third party. Arranged the snatch." There was a smug, self-satisfied expression on his face. "Tuesday's *Tattler* will have her life story on the front page."

Rauscher was right. Bates had a snitch.

"What's with the police?" asked Jack.

"Dimwits notified the media before they erected roadblocks," said Leggitt. "Y'know how uniforms think."

"Where's the wife?"

"That's my secret. The bitch is given to tantrums. She can't function without a shrink 'n' hairdresser strokin' her hand."

Bates beamed at Jack. "Legs here has dirty details on both of 'em. But the lad's a mite tight-lipped with the grime."

A sneaky smile lightened Leggitt's face. He relished the attention. Once a shrewd reporter, he, like many, had been reduced by his indulgences. Tonight, however, he appeared in control. But before he could respond to Bates, there was a loud commotion at the entrance to the restaurant. A blast of hot white light ignited the corner behind their table. Jack twisted around to take a look.

In the center of the bright glow stood a stunningly beautiful young woman. Her body was draped in a silky peach suit, her slender, shapely legs shimmered in peach-tinted stockings. With great concentration she was speaking into the eye of a minicam held by a burly technician in a gray jogging suit. Behind her the smoke-filled barroom exploded with noise.

Jack was mesmerized by the girl. She had pearly white skin, a generous, inviting mouth. Her hypnotic blue eyes were surrounded by a cloud of flaxen hair. She looked like a mirage standing there serenely in the midst of the inebriated herd of boisterous reporters. But she was no dream. A ripe voluptuousness assaulted Jack's senses. Her intense sexuality was barely concealed by the elegant, expensive suit.

Jack's skin felt damp and prickly.

"A sparkling bit of cracklin'," said Leggitt with a wink. He fully enjoyed Jack's evident appreciation.

Jack turned to him. "Who is she?" He attempted to contain his enthusiasm.

"Ceci McCann. Some variety of field producer for *The Tommy Train Show.*"

"That trashmeister?"

"I grant you, it's weird, but Train specializes in beauty queens. Female producers are hired for their looks—that's it." He leaned closer to Jack. "I think it's a harem arrangement myself."

Bates waved his stubby hand at them. "That lass is green as clover, not at all friendly. Our boys tried to chat her up. She wouldn't give them the time of day."

"Update me. What's the show's format?" Jack asked. These days, he rarely watched anything but CNN.

"It's standard teleporn," scoffed Bates. "Slo-mo stabbings, Satanic prophets. Uplifting fare."

"Train's smarter," Leggitt defended. "His studio's state of the art. Pure *Star Trek*."

As Jack turned around to get another look at Ceci McCann, the camera lights went down. She and her crew quickly vanished into the crushing crowd at the exit.

Jack felt a pang of despair. He smashed the butt of his cigarette into the glass ashtray on the table. The fact was, he was grounded in the Hamptons for several days. Ceci McCann was too. Why not sleep with her and bring a little happiness into his life—and hers? For no apparent reason, the cover line BILLIONAIRE BABY 'NAPPED resounded in his head. He was bleeding angles. A passion for work suddenly returned.

Blip-blip-blip erupted from under the table. Bates fetched a portable phone from his rucksack. After a mumbled exchange his weary eyes fired with fresh news. "Shay just touched down," he informed them. "The lads are gettin' decent snaps of him."

A sense of relief permeated the group. The more pictures and information they had to feed their respective editors, the better. Jack often thought of himself as a zookeeper paid to throw sirloin strips into cages. If the meat wasn't rare enough, the beasts banged the bars mercilessly.

Shay's arrival meant good things for Sammy. Harrington might use an airport shot for the cover. That meant big international residuals. A change-up had advantages for Jack as well. With Robert Shay the focus of the cover, he was off the hook. The bulk of reporting would come from L.A.—details of the filmmaker's charmed life before this sinister twist of fate.

Jack leaned back against his chair. He liked this new scenario. He'd unwind, kick back, go to the beach. Track down Miss McCann's luscious loins.

Nostalgically, he looked back to where she had stood. He knew one thing for certain about the blond minx. She had been in the wrong place at the wrong time. She totally missed Robert Shay's arrival at the East Hampton airport.

A cold, drizzly rain had begun to fall. Libby Babcock stepped onto the aluminum stairway, followed by Robert. Showered and shaved, he had changed to cord trousers, a blue crewneck sweater and loosely tied gabardine trench coat. His eyes were hidden by dark glasses. Duke Thompson hovered protectively at his side.

Almost immediately to their right came a frenzied roar from the photographers. A huge lake of flashing white strobes was dammed up behind a double line of squad cars.

Spike Pappas stood at the foot of the ramp. He quickly introduced them to Police Chief Drake, a heavyset man with passive eyes and a flaccid handshake. Drake escorted them around the aircraft to a navy blue Bentley.

Libby slid into the car first, Shay next. Just as his leg touched the leather seat a pudgy man broke from the ranks of airport security. He wedged himself into the car after Robert. Flashbulbs pierced Shay's eyes like pieces of shrapnel. Almost instantly, Duke laid a hammering karate chop across the back of the man's thick neck, forcing the camera to tumble from his hands. As the man attempted to stand, Duke bent down—his buckled jacket revealing the white strap of his shoulder holster—and jabbed his clenched fist into the pit of the man's soft belly. Quickly he kneed him in the groin and then hoisted his limp body by the collar of his shirt and jammed the man's head against the laminated walnut molding on the inside of the car door. A bubble of blood gushed from the photographer's open mouth.

"Cool it, Duke," Shay mumbled. "That's enough."

Thompson lifted the body delicately, as if handling a baby, and dropped it unceremoniously on the pavement at the feet of Police Chief Drake. He slipped into the car and slammed the door shut.

Twenty sirens wailed as the Bentley inched forward. The sedan was buried in a procession of police cars bedecked with pulsating blue and white lights.

"This is ridiculous," said Libby, her nose pressed to the smoky window as she watched a mounted policeman with a hand-held megaphone fight back photographers at the fenced entrance. "We're media fugitives."

"How many of 'em at the house?" asked Duke.

Spike turned around toward them. His nut-brown skin was slick with sweat, his dark eyes tormented. "Four thousand."

Libby gasped audibly. "You're kidding!"

"I wish I were. They've been planted there since before dawn."

Robert felt a surge of anger. He forced himself to slouch down in the plush leather seat as the sedan sped through the foggy night.

After six weeks in Bangkok, everything appeared immense: the streetlights, sidewalks, roadside signs.

Libby scooted forward and got Spike to repeat the details of the abduction. Robert listened, acutely aware of the self-reproach in Spike's voice. The guard's guilt was palpable.

And WHAT THE FUCK DO I PAY YOU 100,000 DOLLARS A YEAR FOR, Robert screamed into the void.

"Maria and Saar never got along," he overheard Duke saying as a piercing roar descended from above. He cranked around to look through the back window. A low-flying helicopter hovered over the car. "Police?" he asked.

"More press," replied Spike. "Aerial battalions are cruisin' night and day."

The parade of TV vans began on Lily Pond Lane. Satellite receivers lined the road like an honor guard.

"At least the police are keepin' the lane clear," said Spike just as the Bentley was besieged by a ground swell of humanity. Between the flashing strobes, Robert could see makeshift campgrounds— tents, picnic tables, luncheon wagons. "A Roman circus and we're the Christians," Duke muttered under his breath.

As they approached the gate, the dreamlike scene turned ugly. Harsh spotlights strafed the granite walls. As the steel gates opened, legions of fiercely determined media soldiers launched a blitzkrieg. Like a sea of antennaed insects they swarmed around the car. A line of volunteers from the sheriff's department fought them back with billy clubs. Loud clacks beat against the tinted windows.

Finally liberated from the crush, the big car sped down the private drive in silent darkness. In the distance came the crisscrossed glare of flashlights. "Twenty cops are on the inside," Spike explained. "Gotta have 'em to keep the buggers off the grounds. One joker parachuted into the pool."

Robert nodded. "Do anything to keep them away from the house."

"We have, boss. We're usin' Mace and rubber bullets."

Within minutes, the mansion came into sight. It glowed like a molten radiator through the soupy fog. The iron-railed parapets, cylindrical elevators, and geometric stairwells were perfectly clear against the solar walls of glass and steel.

Saar, dressed in his chauffeur's uniform, waited stiffly beside the reflecting pool at the front entrance. Maria stood in the open doorway, a wan Sarah at her side.

Robert jumped from the car. He caught a whiff of garlic as Maria pressed her face to his. Before he could speak, her soft brown eyes flooded uncontrollably and a grieving moan came from her. His arms circled her round body. "Shhh, steady," he whispered while she sobbed into his shoulder. As she began speaking in a garble of Spanish and English, Sarah stepped forward, quaking with fear and guilt. Her pleading, dark eyes were filled with terror. She pulled compulsively at a strand of hair with nervous fingers.

"I . . . I'm so sorry I failed you . . . I, I . . ." she stuttered. The expression on her face reflected shame and self-condemnation. "For only a minute I went into the house . . . for this."

From behind her back, she produced the little purple-and-gold baseball jacket. Tears running from her eyes, she offered it to him, the pathetic evidence of her contrition.

"It wasn't Sarah's fault," Saar spoke up. "I said I'd watch him—" Robert stopped his confession with a gesture.

A chopper swooped low, its blades beating overhead. "Get inside, they're dropping down for a picture," Duke cautioned.

Inside the glass atrium, a thin man with sharp eyes gave Robert a fast handshake. "Joe Krugger, FBI." Before he could go on, a bespectacled, black-haired man in a double-breasted suit hurried down the circular steel staircase: Emily's therapist, Dr. Reiss.

Shay approached him. "Where's my wife?"

The psychiatrist's eyes darted nervously behind his thick glasses. "Sedated."

Robert pushed roughly past him. "Fuck it," he said as he charged up the stairs.

7

Robert opened the door to his wife's suite without knocking. The oval bedroom was dark and humid. Emily slept propped up in a hospital bed, a clear IV tube dripping solution into her arm. Behind her bed tiers of satin curtains were draped over the floor-to-ceiling windows. A nurse in a white uniform sat quietly under the glow of a night-light.

Robert snapped on the overhead lights, bringing to life the colors of the Impressionist paintings that hung on the pale walls. "Get out," he commanded.

The nurse scurried for the door.

Emily's eyelids fluttered open. Her blue-violet eyes blinked at him as she fought her way through a fog of drugs. "I'm fine," she whispered.

Rage seethed in Robert. He didn't care what she was. He walked up to the head of the bed, his body a few inches from her face. Her vacant stare followed his movements.

"Where the fuck were you Thursday afternoon?" he spat out. "Just where the fuck were you?"

Fear tinged with hate filled her swollen eyes. "I didn't know you cared." Sarcasm made her voice grow stronger.

"You were in the sack fuckin' that two-bit country musician, weren't you?" he said hotly. "What kind of mother are you, anyway?"

Provoked by his insult, Emily tossed her head arrogantly. The mane of tangled ebony hair bounced along her half-naked shoulders. "Who says I was fucking anybody?" she cried. "Since when are *you* Mr. Morality?" Her voice was thick with contempt. "You chase every piece of jailbait you can lay your paws on. How many little film students did *you* nail?" Her tormented eyes glinted, sizing him up like a gunfighter in a duel. She emitted a bitter chuckle, then taunted: *"I'm a great lay, Mr. Shay. I'm a great lay, Mr. Shay. I'm a great—"*

Robert reached over, threatening to slap her.

Her eyes froze. She laughed, her voice curdled with mockery. "Wasn't that the chant of that cunning baby bitch? That runt who had the nerve to call you at home?" She smiled coyly. "Hubby dear, I long ago figured out the psychological subtext here and it's ugly. Fidelity never made this marriage work."

Robert looked away, unwilling to listen.

"It was you, my dear, who gave your son permission to stay here during the week." She was on the attack. "Weekends weren't enough, remember? I suggested we get him a pony in Sherman Oaks, near home. As usual you ignored me. Then you fucked that French model after the polo match and impulsively bought a horse to show off your macho wealth. Well, that little horse is the reason Doni wouldn't leave this . . . mausoleum."

"Your mausoleum," Robert exploded. "I built this house for you and your 'intellectual' East Coast friends."

"*My* East Coast friends," Emily screamed. "You bastard! You came here to play Mr. Mogul with the Sammy Glick movie crowd. You were the one who designed this towering monstrosity—to show the eastern establishment you knew more than station wagons and backyard barbecues."

"Save your performance for the camera," he said with a sadistic smile. As he stepped back, his heart pounding violently, he noticed the huge bouquet of flowers. With trembling fingers he separated the fireworks of orchids and curly willow branches to extract a small white card: *I'm sorry I cannot be with you in your hour of need.*

He turned back to her. His voice had an eerie calm. "So it *was* Reno? Reno Ventura over your own son?"

"Stop right there," Emily cried. She jumped up from the bed. The IV needle snapped from her arm, leaving the tube to leak onto the blue satin comforter. "Reno's a kind, sweet, sensitive man," she said, pressing her fingertips to the spot in her arm where the needle had been. "The man has time for me, he cares for me and for my career. He supported me when I was ill."

"Ill?" Shay laughed patronizingly. "Was that your excuse this time? Were you too sick to play with your son—or was his presence just too disruptive? Did Sarah and Maria interfere with your afternoon trysts? Perhaps you grew tired of explaining to your son why Mommy was never in bed with Daddy."

"Shut up. Just stop it," she lashed back, fire in her eyes. "Don't point the finger at me. Where were *you*—Father of the Year?" Her words came like bullets. Years of accumulated pain and resentment scorched her voice. "Halfway round the world on another asinine action-adventure film. You call that love for your son? You've always put your movies before him. And before me."

Shay absorbed the sting of her words. His eyes skimmed over her long ballerina legs exposed by the lacy satin negligee. "You look very beautiful," he said with forced calm. "That's a very sexy outfit. For Dr. Reiss? Did he enjoy it? Is he your new conquest?"

Emily clicked her tongue. "Robert, for godsakes, the man is a professional, a psychiatrist. Has your dense shitkicker's brain heard of professional ethics?"

Before he could answer, she went on. "Sure, I spend my afternoons with him. Y'know why? I'm trying to understand why I married a self-centered megalo—"

"He's a goddamn mind-fuck."

"A height you'll never reach," she shot back.

"You married me to conceive Doni, that's why," he said. "We both wanted a baby, remember?"

Emily began to tremble violently. Pain distorted her exquisite beauty. "Our baby fell between the cracks," she wept. "Between the cracks in our marriage." Tears streamed down her face as she sobbed. "We lost him," she moaned. "We . . . lost him . . ."

At that moment an icy chill went through Robert. He sensed Doni's presence in Emily's frail delicacy. He must stop. This was useless.

Reiss hurried into the room with Maria behind him. "That's quite enough, Mr. Shay," the psychiatrist said primly as Maria helped Emily climb back into bed.

Robert shoved by him rudely. He felt no better for having released his anger. Anger wouldn't bring Doni home.

Ceci McCann felt beaten, defeated, rejected, as well as physically exhausted. She peeled away her crepe suit jacket and hung it over the back of the plastic chair in the motel room. She kicked off her high-heeled pumps and removed her stockings. Finally, her skirt, blouse, and silk camisole. With shaking fingers, she unclasped her Bulgari bracelet watch and laid the delicate crystal face up on the Formica night table. It was 2 A.M. She hadn't slept in forty-two hours.

She staggered into the tiny bathroom. With sloppy strokes she removed the thick coat of television make-up. The reflection from the avocado walls gave her face the greenish cast of illness. Suddenly she was dizzy. Her knees buckled and she sank down on the rim of the tub and began to cry. The pressure was too much. Her flight from L.A. had been delayed. The airline had lost her suitcase with her on-camera blouses and jackets. She'd worn the same suit for two days. Tommy would surely question why—in every shot—she was wearing this rumpled peach outfit. She felt ridiculously over-dressed. Why hadn't she worn her sporty linen suit on the plane? What in God's name made her change her mind?

But Ceci knew her clothes were the least of her problems.

This had been the worst day of her life. Every moment of the never-ending drama had been a nightmare. It had been impossible to get any information. By the time she arrived in East Hampton, the few newspaper boxes in town were empty. The deli newsstand was sold out. She desperately needed help: a researcher, a producer. Instead she faced alone the hordes of uncivilized, pushy reporters. The most primitive laws of the jungle applied. The blatant rudeness of her media colleagues astounded her. These so-called journalists were pirates, barbarians, savage idiots who ignored all aspects of human decency. One malicious jerk actually walked in front of her as she taped cutaways.

But what was it she was taping? Nothing of merit. Not a minute of her tapes was used on the show, and to add to her problems, Jim Armstrong didn't like her because she was young and didn't know the ropes. In point of fact, he was a lazy SOB who expected her to do his job for him. He had tried to sabotage her psycholog-ically. Again and again, he told her she didn't know what she was doing. To make matters worse, he was out of favor with the other NTN crews. If they had any inside info or shortcuts to share, they weren't about to tell Armstrong.

She put her hands on the edge of the rust-stained sink and pulled herself up. She wet the threadbare washcloth with cold water and pressed it to her bloodshot eyes. Ceci studied her face in the mirror. All she had ever wanted to do for a living was look pretty and read news copy written by someone else. She had the telegenic features, the diction, the charisma. Why didn't God allow her to do what she was designed to do best?

Another wave of tears washed down her cheeks. She'd be fired after this fiasco. She knew it. This was her last chance to show them that she could perform. There'd be no breaks of this magnitude again. She reached for a tissue, but the tarnished wall box was empty.

Back in the bedroom she unwrapped the cellophane from a tuna-fish sandwich that had been lying on the seat of Armstrong's van since noon. Cautiously, she parted the soggy slices of white bread. A gray-green foam covered the lumps of canned tuna. Although her stomach growled with hunger, Ceci dropped her dinner into the cardboard wastebasket.

From under the hem of the mustard-colored drapes a cockroach scurried toward the basket. Ceci shuddered.

Her glance came to rest on the ashtray on the fake teak bureau. Glittery flecks in the glass spelled out Golden Nugget Hotel, Las Vegas, Nevada.

Just as she was about to succumb to another burst of self-pity the phone on the night table rang. It was Shorty. He sounded flustered, impatient.

"Is this Ceci McCann's room?"

"Shorty, it's me," Ceci whispered as she crawled under the skimpy motel blanket. She wiped the back of her hand against her runny nose, the receiver cradled to her ear.

"That joint has the screwiest switchboard," he railed. "The bozo who answers the phone refuses to take messages. Then he disconnects the call."

Ceci managed a warped smile. "The switchboard is the most luxurious feature of the place." She rolled over on her side. A cigarette hole at the corner of the overwashed pillowcase confronted her. She closed her eyes.

"How's it going?" he asked.

Ceci fought back her tears. "Between us, honestly, it's a disaster."

"Relax, honey, you're doing fine," he lied.

"No, I'm not," she said. "But it's impossible. Camera crews are everywhere."

"Calm down," said Shorty. "Your beautiful face will grace every scene."

Shorty was always so supportive. It was as if his arms reached through the phone to hug her. But tonight the fact that he was such a doll, so nice to her in spite of everything, made her want to cry all the more.

Three quick breaths helped her regain her composure. She

cleared her throat. "The French teacher at Doni's school barricaded herself in her château," she said. "Armstrong taped the play yard, but so did everybody else."

"How's Armstrong behaving?"

"Okay, I think." She tried to sound diplomatic. "But he stands around like a lump on a log and expects my direction. I don't know which way is north."

"Yeah, Armstrong has a bad rep. He's on suspension."

Oh terrific, thought Ceci, that's just terrific.

"His stuff is quality though. Tommy saw some tape of the town dump he liked."

"Mmm . . . the garbage collectors. But Shorty, they were fakes, local clowns who tried to horn in on the publicity. When I asked the contractor about the security system, he clammed up. He said the police instructed him not to talk to the press."

"Is that on tape, his answer?"

"Somewhere in the interview."

"Good, we can salvage that. It demonstrates a blackout."

"I did cutaways of the library, the Episcopal church, the fish market. But this is a very snooty village. The owner of the toy store chased us from the premises. She was livid because the press portrayed Doni Shay as an indulged spoiled brat."

"Did you get her sayin' that on camera?"

"Are you kidding? The woman kicked me—literally, her heel in my shin."

"Tell Armstrong to tape that—the shove-off." Shorty was emphatic. "It translates well. Good drama. You, the sincere, hardworking reporter, harassed by irate townsfolk."

At this point, any angle sounded reasonable to Ceci.

"Did you tape Shay's arrival?" Shorty asked. "The network newsbreak had clips of a scuffle."

"Damn it." Ceci hit her fist into the pillow. "We waited three hours. I got impatient and made Armstrong scout some new locations."

"It's okay, we got pickups from NTN." Ceci heard the ring of disappointment in his voice. "Listen, baby," he said softly, "Tommy says shoot through the weekend. To paraphrase our master: 'Suck this tit as long as it gives milk.' " He paused. "Ring me if you stumble onto anything we can use on Monday's show."

* * *

Jack Werts found the East Hampton Motel easily enough, a mile past town on the north side of the highway. The office was a neon-lit glass enclosure that evenly divided two rectangular barracks. A rusted bronze sunburst hung over the entryway.

He tapped the silver desk bell.

"Be with you in a minute," called a crusty voice. An elderly bald man in an athletic jacket appeared and fetched a hoop of keys from a desk drawer. Before Jack could decipher the bowling-team insignia scripted on the back, the old gent swung around and peered at him suspiciously.

"Brazilian radio technicians are asleep on my new pool chairs," he said. "Very shabby. We can't have it." Without further explanation he disappeared out the back door. Jack heard loud groans from the yard.

Behind the desk, tiny red lights blinked randomly on an antique switchboard. A guest ledger lay open on the wooden counter, hand-written names on each line.

Like all good reporters, Jack was expert at reading upside down. He spotted his name near the top of the page. Room 8 had been assigned to him. *Newsmakers* was scratched in the margin in blue ink.

He read slowly down the page. Sammy Voight—room 34. Two names from the bottom his eyes skidded to a halt.

Ceci McCann—room 18.

Jack grinned triumphantly. He lifted the ballpoint pen tied to the book and hastily jotted a number 1 before the number 8 after his name. His room number now read 18. He replaced the pen and ambled over to admire a 1946 Rotary Club plaque.

The clerk returned and deposited the keys in a drawer in the desk. The untended switchboard continued to buzz incessantly. "Can I help you?" he said. There was no apology for the delay.

Jack came forward with an eager smile. "Jack Werts. I believe a reservation was made by *Newsmakers* magazine."

The clerk pushed his glasses to his nose as he hunched over to examine the ledger. His calloused forefinger traced down the names until he came to *Werts*. "Indeed, here you are. A three-night prepaid deposit."

The fellow turned to unlatch a wall box. One key hung from the nail marked 18. "Doughnuts and Mr. Coffee in the lobby," he said, handing the key to Jack. "Ice machines at the end of the building."

Jack picked up his bag and headed through the glass door and down the cinder path. The cheap plywood doors had toy locks. Safety chains would be too costly. At room 18, he stopped. With a pious smile on his face he turned the key in the lock. He pushed the knob and the door opened with a loud thwack. Jack stepped in, purposely banging his suitcase against the walls of the narrow hallway as he flipped on the light.

Awakened by the racket, Ceci McCann jolted upright. She swung around to blink at the tall, dark stranger standing in the garish yellow glare. "Who are you?" she shrieked in fear.

"Sorry, sorry." Jack's voice was laden with embarrassed apology. "Obviously, there's been a mixup." He scanned her lustrous hair, her long, porcelain arms. The thin sheet had slipped to expose the steep slope of her ample breast.

"Obviously," said Ceci indignantly. She promptly yanked the skimpy sheet up to her neck. Without makeup she was even more beautiful than Jack remembered.

"Ah . . . it seems that the clerk has accidently given you my room," he said. He took a step forward. Ceci flinched. Jack quickly held his key up to show her the number 18. At the same time, with his other hand, he subtly lifted his bag onto the double bed across from her.

She dismissed his key. "What do you mean, your room? Sir, this is my room. I checked in this morning."

Jack disagreed firmly. "Listen, madam, if you'll excuse me, I'll call the manager." Before Ceci could protest he picked up the telephone on the night table between the double beds.

She burrowed down under the cheap bedspread. She noticed he had left the door wide open. That was good. She could scream if she had to.

As he waited for the clerk to answer he took in her expensive clothes, the leather Gucci suitcase in the closet, the open purse on the bureau. His eyes returned to her face. "We could share the room," he said in a playful, mischievous tone.

Ceci glared at him with hostility. "Get the clerk," she said. Still, she noticed his broad shoulders, tapered waist, and coal-black hair flecked with gray at the temples. Handsome, but old. At least forty.

"Who are you?" she asked stiffly.

His eyes sparked as he extended his hand. "Jack Werts. *Newsmakers* magazine."

Ceci didn't budge. "A journalist?"

"Aren't we all."

At last the clerk answered. "Yes, Jack Werts, room 18. It seems you have given my room to a lady, Miss . . ."

"Ms. Ceci McCann," she said distinctly.

"McCann," repeated Jack.

The rattled clerk found Jack's reservation and repeated his room number. "Perhaps it's best you talk with Miz McCann," Jack said, handing over the phone.

Ceci listened a moment and then exploded. "That's ridiculous! Well, if it wasn't my room, it is now. You find Mr. Werts here another home. My bags are unpacked and I refuse to move." She slammed down the receiver.

The young beauty had a temper. Jack was relieved to see her gunsights were directed at the hapless clerk. Best not push his luck. This introduction was memorable enough.

He lifted his bag, then turned back to her. With an ingenuous expression on his face, he said, "Ceci McCann? Haven't I seen you on television? That show from Los Angeles . . . what's the name of it?"

Ceci's lips broadened into a warm, responsive smile. *"The Tommy Train Show.* You must have seen one of my segments."

"Yes, yes. I remember it being quite informative," he said respectfully. "I hope to see more of your work."

The door closed.

Ceci instantly felt much better, almost cheerful. The public recognized her. So did other journalists, print journalists like this man from *Newsmakers.* She must not toss in the towel. She must work harder. Eventually, she'd rise to the top with her idols: Connie Chung, Katie Couric, Diane Sawyer.

The phone jangled in Ceci's ear. With reluctance she forced open her eyes. The motel room was still dark. She lifted the receiver.

"Jack? Hello. Hello. I must get in touch with Jack Werts. Is this his room?"

For a split second Ceci had no idea what the shrill female voice was talking about. Gradually, from her tired, jumbled mind came a recollection of the handsome reporter.

"Is this Jack's room?" the girl asked again.

"No, not exactly," Ceci mumbled.

"The motel operator told me to leave my message with you." Desperation filled her squeaky, high-pitched voice. "I have an extremely urgent message. Will you please make sure he gets it?"

Ceci knew that he was somewhere in the motel. "Yes, I'll take it."

"Thank goodness," said the girl appreciatively. She had already been disconnected several times by the motel clerk.

"First, tell him 'Raspberry' called."

"Raspberry?" repeated Ceci. Certainly she had misheard the girl.

"It's a code name. He'll understand."

Ceci smiled. The girl sounded tanked.

"Tell Jack that Raspberry said that Doni Shay wasn't at school on Thursday. He was at the Devon Riding Academy. His riding instructor is Millie Farnsworth. There's a good chance she'll talk to him."

Ceci swallowed hard. She spoke evenly. "I'll see he gets the message." She hung up the phone with a burst of excitement. If true, this was a dynamite scoop. Maybe he wouldn't mind if she tagged along with her camera crew.

Then, at once, the reality of the situation hit her. God, was she nuts? This was exactly her problem. Miss Goody Two Shoes. Always too much of a good sport. Lisa Proudfit wouldn't hand this scoop over to Werts. She'd polish her face and hustle straight over to the Devon Riding Academy. For weeks Ceci had been telling herself she had to learn to think like Lisa if she was going to survive. Here was her chance for a hot exclusive. This was war.

8

From the window in his bedroom Shay watched dawn brighten the sky over the steely blue Atlantic. Beside him a white enamel telescope with a barrel the size of a cannon was pointed at a yacht anchored a half-mile from the house. The boat had been chartered by a team of Japanese cameramen. They huddled together on the deck like a flock of cold sea gulls, their telephoto lenses fixed on the house.

Shay stared down at the long, gray swells that battered the shore with their spitting whitecaps. Down the beach the police had erected metal barricades trimmed with spirals of razor wire. Robert observed two officers with M-16 rifles stationed beside a dune buggy elevated on balloon tires and racked with roof lights.

From the bedroom window the sprawling grounds of his property resembled an unfinished resort complex. Near the east wall two bulldozers sat on a ribbon of road that webbed over a valley of tilled soil. Every day dump trucks hauled in mountains of rich, black dirt from Riverhead to create fertile acreage capable of supporting a future vineyard. On the far side, on a section of landfill, a small recycling plant was under construction. Beyond the cinderblock building, the natural marshlands had been carefully preserved. An endless sweep of sand dunes sprouting spindly reeds and scrub pine stretched out untouched.

Near the towering house was a village of solar-heated guest cottages alongside six north-south tennis courts. Directly below, a huge trapezoidal pool glistened in the morning sunlight; its mosaic bottom copied the square patterns of Josef Albers's boxes. A circle of triangular cabanas framed the pool like a silver crown.

Suddenly a thunderous buzz came from overhead. Robert's eyes narrowed to follow a twin-engine Squirrel as it jittered about like a mosquito. The chopper abruptly tilted to descend on the Tuckers' beachfront property. Dispassionately, he noticed this chopper was lighter than those that circled at dawn. A low-rent operation.

The prying vultures were everywhere. During the dark morning hours, Robert had devised a plan to hire a band of murderous mercenaries, plus a few F-15s, to launch a counterattack. For a small bonus they would strafe the armies of vipers that had established their nests at the front gates.

Robert didn't fully comprehend this brutal invasion by the media. He had always treated the press fairly. He had given long, detailed interviews before the release of his new films and supplied more than enough background material to satisfy their greedy appetites. True, he didn't choose to share his personal life with the public. It wasn't his style to bring family matters into the limelight. But since when was that a crime? Essentially he thought of himself as a hardworking filmmaker. He had no illegitimate kids, no closeted gay life. He had always tried to keep smut out of his films. Focus on environmental issues. Employ women, blacks, and Hispanics. Except for a few private bank accounts in Lichtenstein, he had supported the American tax structure wholesale. Why should he now be punished for his gift for entertaining big audiences and making money?

He went into the study that adjoined the bedroom and sank down into a cherry red leather reading chair. He closed his eyes. Again, Doni came into focus, as if he stood next to him. Doni's little hand clutched the broken arm of Robo Cop; blue and gold wires hung from the toy in a snarl. He wore his frayed pajamas with the tiny fishes. How Doni loved those old pajamas. So did Snickers. Whenever the boy came within reach, the dog gnawed at the cuffs. At night, when Snickers curled up next to Doni—his furry body and Doni's breathing in tandem—he would chew and chew until wispy threads hung down over Doni's little feet and hands.

Everyone bought Doni new pajamas. Shay's mother brought home the boys' wear department from Neiman Marcus. But Doni ignored the expensive designer sleepware. The fishes were special to him. Maria had purchased them at K Mart in East Los Angeles and for months, Robert and Emily had sent maids to search through K mart stores for more "fishies."

A tear rolled down Robert's cheek as he recalled Doni telling him that he was "Big Tuna." He explained that Mommy was "The Butterfly," Spike "Gupper," and Sarah "Flipper." Snickers was "Mr. Fisherman," which gave them all reason to ponder their fates.

Recalling their happy games brought a stab of pain, the increasingly familiar depth charge. Robert gazed despondently at the colossal black onyx mantelpiece imported from Italy, the Rodin sculptures, the Giacometti figures that danced about the giant crystal obelisk on the terrace, the bronze sculpture that hung like a frozen waterfall from the ceiling, catching glints of the early sunlight.

The house was beautiful.

And he hated it. He hated every fucking inch of the forty-million-dollar mausoleum with a venom he hadn't known was in him. Every stick of furniture, every piece of sculpture, every painting, every carved door, were like tombstones now.

If anything happened to his son, he'd destroy this architectural monstrosity by hand. He'd bash in every block of marble, burn each panel of wood, rip out every electronic gadget, demolish the crypt to its foundations. He'd steamroller the grounds. The plowed sand dunes would be all that remained. For eternity.

At this moment he hated equally the career that had brought him such enormous wealth, made him a billionaire before he was forty. He would trade every fucking cent, every accolade, every Oscar, for his son. Emily was wrong. It meant nothing to him. Years ago, his success, his fame, had become an immense prison. And now, the unheard-of wealth it brought was solely responsible for Doni's abduction.

The Devon Riding Academy was a ten-acre spread of glistening green lawns and white-fenced paddocks. In the oblong training ring near the main ranch house, a silver-haired gentleman in a jockey cap and black velvet jacket put a high-stepping bay gelding through his paces. Two perfectly matched Dalmatians trotted a measured distance behind the horse and rider.

Ceci found Millie Farnsworth in the tack room, a blue-shuttered shed behind the ranch house. Farnsworth was a patrician-looking woman with a broad forehead, high cheekbones, and calm hazel eyes. She wore a white cotton blouse, tan jodhpurs, and cavalry-style boots of polished leather.

Initially aloof, the elegant lady was reluctant to discuss Doni Shay. Ceci gradually conquered her resistance by explaining that Tommy Train hoped to help the Shays find their son. If Millie could describe the boy on camera, give a detailed account of his afternoons at the stable, describe his mannerisms, well, then, it might make the public personally aware of him. After all, someone knew the kidnappers. Suspicious neighbors might recognize the child or report unusual behavior to the police. Ceci suggested that Mrs. Farnsworth mention only those traits of Doni's she felt comfortable revealing.

Finally, after an hour of persuasion, Millie agreed to be interviewed. Ceci sat her down in the club room on a hardwood bench amid saddles and horse blankets for a two shot.

Mrs. Farnsworth told Ceci that Robert Shay had paid $4,000 for Foxy, a rare miniature Palomino less than five hands high. This summer, the boy had come by the stable daily. He was a clever, fun-loving child who always brought his pony a bag of carrots. His nanny usually sat in a white wicker chair on the porch; his bodyguard stayed in the chauffeured Mercedes and read the newspaper.

Because of Doni's youth, Millie used a lead rope on Foxy. But the boy rode well and had a feel for animals. He was destined to become a great equestrian.

After the interview, Millie instructed the stable boy to bring the pony around for the camera crew. At Millie's command, the boy unharnessed the tiny apricot mare. Her sensitive ears twitched to attention. Wet honey-brown eyes focused on the open corral. With a sudden start, she galloped away from the stable hand. Then, on delicately tapered, white-stockinged legs she pranced back to where he stood. Her arched wheat-white tail rippled in the warm breeze —a balletic performance for the camera.

Millie Farnsworth watched the pony with great pride. "Whenever Emily was at home, she brought Doni for his lesson . . ." She abruptly stopped speaking as she spied a silver Chevette barreling down the roadway from the gate.

Ceci peered at the car. She recognized Jack Werts behind the wheel. The car screeched to a halt in a cloud of red dust and Werts jumped out, slamming the door.

A red-headed woman also got out and studied Armstrong's men in the corral. Two hefty cameras were strapped around her neck. Werts stood beside her, his square jaw clenched. He said something to her and then came toward Ceci.

McCann fidgeted nervously with her tape recorder. Fortunately, he ignored her and introduced himself to Mrs. Farnsworth. When he mentioned *Newsmakers*, she nodded approvingly. "My daughter-in-law reads every issue."

Jack asked if he might question her about Doni Shay.

Faint lines knit her broad forehead and she spoke in a martyred voice. "Mr. Werts, I'm tired now. I've talked for hours with this lovely young lady . . ."

Jack scowled at Ceci.

". . . the FBI was here most of yesterday. I have a jumping lesson to give." Millie Farnsworth tilted her head toward Ceci. "Perhaps Miss McCann will share her interview with you?"

"I'm sure she will," said Jack.

Ceci discreetly lowered her tape recorder into a leather briefcase.

"But our stories are quite different," he went on. "My deadline is tonight. May I call you sometime later this afternoon?"

His polite professionalism won Millie over. "All right," she sighed. "About four."

Ceci smiled at Mrs. Farnsworth, shook her hand, and thanked her effusively.

"My dear, it was painless," she responded. "You're a lovely person."

Jack followed Ceci from the porch. His strong hand caught her roughly by the arm. "Thanks for the message," he said with bitter irritation.

"Let go of me." Ceci wriggled her arm away.

"I'm not finished with you yet."

He followed her as she rushed toward the television van. Her high heels sank into the soggy carpet of sawdust; the hot, dusty air stung her eyes. Ceci noticed enviously that Werts was appropriately dressed in a safari jacket and light khaki pants.

"You owe me," he said abruptly, blocking her way. His eyes were fastened on her leather bag.

"If you think I'm handing this tape over to you, forget it." She blew a strand of loose hair from her sweaty brow. Nonchalantly she tried to step around him. "Excuse me, I have an appointment."

"Hold on there, young lady," Jack said, somewhat surprised by her gutsy belligerence. "The very least you can do is spill the Farnsworth interview"—he paused and winked at her—"over dinner tonight."

Ceci was stunned by the invitation. She considered it. In a few hours her Farnsworth tape would be safely in Los Angeles. She knew Jack Werts had excellent sources. Lisa would go to dinner— even to bed with this man—to extract every bit of relevant information he possessed. Ceci tossed her head gamely. "All right. I do owe you a favor."

"An understatement," he said flatly. But Jack liked her spunky attitude. And the sensuous symmetry of her body. "I'll pick you up at your room at nine." He broke away to meet his photographer.

"I'm set," Sammy called to him. As they got in the car, she said, "It was lucky that Sherry left a message for me. Goldilocks wasn't about to share the wealth."

"Oh, she will. We're having dinner tonight."

Sammy gave him a bemused grin. "What good's that after your deadline?"

"None."

Sammy glanced back at Ceci standing idly by the NTN van as the crew packed to leave. She looked like a frazzled starlet in her smudged peach suit, puffy hair, and high heels. Her pancake make-up was melting in the hot sun.

"Why's she always in that Easter Sunday outfit?" Sammy asked. "She may be gorgeous but she doesn't look too bright."

A devilish light burned in Jack's dark blue eyes. "I know. I like 'em that way."

"This really worries me about you."

The steel doors of the cylindrical elevator opened into the hall of the solarium, where Libby Babcock stood arguing with Joe Krugger. Robert's arrival ended their frosty exchange. "Mr. Shay, I must talk to you in private," said the agent, edging Libby out.

Her dark eyes flashed at Robert. "I told the staff to convene in the den in ten minutes." She looked at Krugger, her thin lips twisted with disdain. "Robert might wish to meet with his staff first."

Shay studied Krugger. From his thatch of thick brown hair and boyish face Robert figured him to be six years his junior, thirty-five or so. This morning the agent wore a sober navy suit, red suspenders, and expensive Ralph Lauren loafers. He looked more like a junk-bond trader than a man who ran one of the most powerful departments in the Federal Bureau of Investigation.

"Relax, Libby," said Robert softly. "They can hold up a bit." No sooner had Shay nodded for Krugger to precede him into the bright room than Babcock hooked him by the arm. "Be careful," she whispered. "You're dealing with a high-tech maniac—a pin-the-wings-back type of guy."

As he descended the slick marble stairs into the splendid solarium, Shay was once again amazed by the beauty of the vast room. Sunlight streamed through the ceiling of solar panels, casting an opalescent shimmer on the quartz walls and the aquamarine marble reflecting pool. Life-size marble statues were tucked into neatly spaced recesses about the room. The overall effect was one of ethereal spirituality, a glacial cathedral of ice blocks awakened by the sun.

Robert walked to the narrow deck overlooking a small meadow of autumnal wildflowers in bloom. He contemplated the half-row of Japanese maples nearby. Each tree had cost fifty thousand dollars. On the ground six more waited to be planted, their roots wrapped in damp burlap. Robert's face suddenly paled. Why in hell had he allowed Doni to live in this house before it was completed? Gardeners and builders came and went like midtown buses. His son was safer walking alone down Fifth Avenue. What in hell had gone wrong with his brain . . .

"Mr. Shay."

Krugger called from the midst of the makeshift office his team of FBI agents had established in one corner of the room. Behind a planter of leafy palms, a radio man wearing headphones pressed the buttons of a high-frequency multiband receiver. Next to him, two heavy-duty computer terminals bleeped messages from Washington.

Three men and a woman rose as Robert approached them. Introductions were quick. The team wore government-issue suits and cold smiles. Their leader, the boy wonder, perched on an overstuffed silk chair. His attention was focused on a map spread over the large Lucite table.

Robert's eyes skimmed the squiggly lines. "That's seven hundred yards of ocean frontage," he said. His forefinger landed on a boxed figure: "It's twenty-five, not twenty-three, acres total."

"The architects are bringing the blueprints this afternoon," said the female agent. Robert had already forgotten her name.

"Give Chicki, my secretary, a list of what you need," he told them. "Anything. It's yours."

Krugger spoke up quickly. "Most of our tracking equipment stays in Washington. Another team of forensic guys will be here tomorrow."

Robert took in the turquoise-and-silver ring Krugger wore on his left hand and immediately suspected his electric blue eyes were tinted contacts. Either this guy dressed against type or FBI agents were straight-laced pencil pushers only in the movies, his movies.

Captain Drake lumbered into the room and extended his hand to Robert. "Good morning, sir." The police chief was stuffed into a flappy checked sport coat and too tight gray slacks that emphasized his walrus belly. His thick fingers ran nervously up and down his red cotton tie as if checking for lumps. It was a sad sight. One of the thousands of America's gridiron guys gone to fat.

Krugger stared at Drake in silence. Robert sensed a tense competitiveness between the hapless resort cop and the yuppie technocrat.

"I know how you love your kid," Drake began. "I got three boys myself . . ." He rambled on about his sons.

Shay's attention shifted. He didn't have the patience for sympathy. Both of the men made him skittish. He only clicked back when Drake said, "Since yesterday morning, early, I've had my men pickin' through every handful of soil. Your workers done a good job because we found nuthin'—no sand traps, ditches, mud holes, abandoned wells, septic tanks—nuthin'." He rubbed his thick hands together. "We got a body watch down the coast. If he washes, it'll be two miles east, somewhere on the Amagansett beach."

He stared at Robert with serene complacency. His words were slow and ponderous. "Mr. Shay, I gotta tell you straight. Unless your boy's body is pinned under a hunk of coral out at sea, he's gone. And given the circumstances . . ." Drake's droopy eyes scanned the opulent room. "Given this—and your position, well, the police department's officially concluding——"

Krugger cut him off. "It's a kidnap."

Shay dropped into a chair. The cold reality of Krugger's words filled him with bleak hopelessness. The agent went on in his clipped style: "Yesterday, we alerted every travel terminal on the eastern seaboard . . ."

Trying to control the unexpected surge of rage and terror, Robert lifted a Steuben vase from the table. His hot, sweaty fingers curled around the cold crystal. A rashlike chill began to creep along his arm.

". . . We are backgrounding every child between the ages of two and six who was officially in transit from Thursday night on. We've dusted the playground for prints and"—Krugger glanced over at Drake with contempt—"sifted the beach sand for footprints, marks, anything. We've also begun surveillance checks on the immediate staff."

Krugger's bloodless smile focused on the female agent. "The polygraph department sets up shop tomorrow morning." His full attention returned to Robert. "I ask you to insist that the entire household take the tests."

"Lie detectors?" said Shay faintly.

"Yes. Libby Babcock and Duke Thompson as well."

"They've been with me ten years. They love Doni like I do."

Krugger looked him straight in the eye. "For big money people take big risks."

Shay felt as if a fist had landed in his gut. He sprang up and walked to the window. He had to think this one through. Certainly, many times during the course of his career he'd been cheated by people he trusted. In fact, it was an operative rule of his that if only money was involved, a screw job was likely to follow. For that reason he tried to deal with artists, those who cared about the quality of their work first, money second. But he was also a realist—he operated in a financially slippery business that included swindlers and less than reputable studio czars. Early on, he had carefully handpicked an inner circle of associates who passed the test of time. The same was true of his domestic staff. They were a cohesive family, one that migrated with him to whichever residence he inhabited. It was difficult for Shay to accept Krugger's suspicions. Money was a poor motivator. Robert had been generous. Everyone on his staff was a millionaire. There was, however, a revolving cluster of maids, valets and waiters.

That ugly thought prompted a burst of uneasiness, a burning desire to take charge and find out what the hell was going on. He beckoned for Krugger to follow him. The agent obeyed, though visibly annoyed by Robert's short attention span and reluctance to listen.

Shay pushed through the swinging cherry doors into the kitchen. Almost immediately, a yapping bundle of curly blond hair bounded toward him. "Hey, scout." Robert bent down to hug Snickers. The dog's wet nose burrowed into his neck in a frenzy of affection. "Calm down," said Robert. "We're gonna find your little master. You and me."

Maria came toward them in a torrent of Spanish. She beamed as she took Robert's drawn face affectionately between her hands. For the first time since Thursday morning Shay felt warmth, loving warmth. In that moment he understood why Doni had spent so much time in the kitchen with Maria. He remembered his own childhood, the lazy hours he spent watching his mother preparing family meals. Perhaps this explained why there were so many kitchen scenes in his films, so many happy suburban homes.

"*Un momento*," Maria muttered. Her fingers tugged the collar of his shirt to free it from his sweater. He kissed her cheek. "Let's go," he said to Krugger.

Outside the sun on the kitchen deck was hot. The cool, salty air refreshed his tired brain as they went down a black ramp with steel-cord banisters to the wide circular drive and walked past the pool. Robert froze when his eye caught the silver gleam of the dragon slide, and his composure cracked. A flood of tears washed down his face. He swallowed hard as huge sobs burst from his chest.

Krugger's hand pressed on his shoulder. The man's presence meant nothing. Two policemen approached them from the pool house. Krugger waved them back.

Robert exhaled. Get with it, he told himself angrily. These wild fluctuations in mood were becoming increasingly uncontrollable. He was on an emotional high wire, either delicately balanced or crashing to the ground.

With forced calm, he walked over to the edge of the cliff where the strong breeze from the ocean cooled his hot cheeks. The Japanese yacht had been chased away by two coast guard boats patrolling the waters offshore. Directly overhead, a huge helicopter buzzed annoyingly.

"Ours," said Krugger.

Robert's kidskin loafers sank down into the sandy soil. He inspected the loosely shoveled footpath that twisted its way down through clumps of wild grass to the boulders of the breakwater. An orange Caterpillar rested silently on the wide beach below.

Krugger pulled a notebook from his pocket. His fingers skipped gracefully over the pages, barely touching them. "Each man from Crawford Builders knew your son. The foreman shared his lunch with him—and Sarah. Picnics."

Shay grimaced. He spoke quickly. "Doni loved those guys and their trucks and tractors."

Krugger seemed disinterested. "Twenty people in their office knew the Caterpillar was busted. The job was a week behind schedule." He gestured to the west. "Somehow the 'nappers transported your son along the beach. There's a dead-end road a mile down that's seen plenty of fresh tire tracks."

Much as Shay disliked Krugger he had to admit the agent made sense.

"Are you aware that your cook, Maria Benez, has a brother with a record? Sergio Benez transports illegals across the Rio Grande."

Shay shielded his eyes from the sun. "Even if that's true, she's honest. She'd stake her life for Doni."

"Have her relatives ever visited?"

Robert thought hard. "Only at the L.A. house. Doni played with her nephews. That's how he learned Spanish."

"He speaks Spanish?"

"Yeah, like a three-year-old Mexican kid."

Krugger jotted down another note. "I need a release for personal records from Starlight Studios."

"Done."

"The bodyguards you hire for special occasions . . ."

"Chicki handles that."

Krugger snorted. "Well, she's employed some tricky characters . . ."

Shay faced him. "I've tried to be cautious. We all use P.O. boxes. The cars, plane, everything for that matter, is registered in the studio's name. Our credit cards are in my account's name. Our fan mail is screened by Easton Services. They alert Duke to the nut cases." Robert paused, bent his head down, and nervously ran his hands through his hair. He looked up at the agent. "I'm not fightin' you, I'm just exhausted."

Krugger spoke tonelessly. "Because the operation was expertly executed—with no resistance or witnesses, we're assuming it's an inside job." He went on. "From you I need a complete list of friends and business associates. People who have visited the house or know your son's schedule."

Because of the ongoing construction only a handful of Shay's close friends had visited. There were, however, bankers, lawyers, scriptwriters, and "last summer some girls came out with me," Robert said. "I had to check on the contractors. A film student, a model. Chicki has their names."

Krugger didn't miss a beat. "Was Doni here?"

"God, no. He was home in L.A."

Krugger returned the notebook to his pocket. "We need your phone records for the last two years." He turned to Robert, his eyes like granite. "It's important we tap the phone lines going into the house. We'll leave your private line free—and your wife's—unless you feel we should—"

"Tap it."

"That brings up another problem. This doctor. Reiss. He won't allow me to talk with her."

Robert stared up at Emily's window with venom in his eyes. "Oh yes, he will."

Doni woke to hear voices outside the room. He sat up and pulled the blanket over his head. Steps came from the other side of the door. Big steps. Little steps. More big steps. The door opened.

"The kid's freezin' to death," said a big voice.

Doni peeked through the window in his blanket. It was the seal man. He was dressed in regular clothes.

"It's hot as an oven in here," the woman said. She tried to pull the blanket away from Doni. "You're just playing. Aren't you?"

"Clean him up so he looks normal," the man ordered.

Doni saw the camera in his hand. His daddy had many cameras. Much bigger. Doni had one too, but his was smaller.

"We need more light," said the man. "Get that gooseneck lamp from the living room. And find a brush for his hair. He looks deranged with his hair like that."

The man spun around. He walked into the bathroom and found the black box. "Sit here," he said to Doni.

The woman returned with a light at the end of a crooked pole. She stood it behind Doni. She had jeans like Mommy and Sarah. She took out a brush. When he lifted his face to her he saw her black eyes. Mommy had see-through eyes.

"There. You're as good as new." Her eyes moved to his arm. "The bandage shows."

"It'll give 'em somethin' to worry about," said the man. "Move over." He spanked the woman's bottom in a friendly way. Doni wondered if the man and woman were a daddy and mommy.

The man came close to Doni. He didn't look like anyone Doni had ever seen before.

"Okay, kid, I'm going to shoot a home movie. You're the star. We're going to send the movie to your father, so I want you to tell him how happy you are, how much fun you're having with us. Do you understand?"

Doni stared at the floor. He was afraid. He wanted his mommy. He started to cry.

"You've frightened him." The woman's hands touched Doni's cheeks with a tissue. "How was the hamburger?" she asked. "You want some more?"

He nodded.

She lifted the bun to his mouth. He took a small bite.

"He liked the Coke better," she said to the man.

"How long do we have to humor him?"

"He's almost ready."

The man started the camera. "Stay outta the way," he told her.

She didn't move. "Wait, I got an idea." She came close. "When's your father's birthday?"

Doni didn't know but he said, "May fourth." That was his birthday, the only birthday he knew.

"What do you do for your father on his birthday?"

Mommy and Daddy and Snickers sang "Happy Birthday" on his birthday. He sang with Mommy for Daddy's birthday.

"I sing."

The woman smiled at the man. "Wonderful, Doni," she said. "Why don't you sing 'Happy Birthday' to your father. He would love to hear you sing for him."

Doni wasn't sure about singing just now. But Mommy and Daddy liked him to sing. He knew that. They always kissed him after.

"Why don't you say 'Hello, Daddy' and then sing 'Happy Birthday.' "

Doni blinked at the woman.

"C'mon," she said. "I'll help you." She swung her head and clapped her hands.

Doni tried to sing, but his voice cracked. The woman sang along with him. His voice grew bigger.

"Now, you shut up," the man said to the woman.

All alone in a strained voice, Doni sang:

> "Happy Birthday to you,
> Happy Birthday to you,
> Happy Birthday, dear Daddy,
> Happy Birthday to you."

The woman wiggled her hand at him. "Wave to Daddy."

Doni lifted his hand. He moved his fingers. He did want Daddy to see him. He missed Daddy so much he started to cry.

Click. The man stopped the camera. "That was effing unbelievable."

The woman put her hand on Doni's head. "Stop crying. Everythin's okay.

We're goin' to have a lot of fun, you and me. We're goin' to take a nice trip together."

But Doni continued to cry. He took lots of trips. He didn't care about trips. He wanted his mommy and daddy.

The man came over.

Doni cried harder.

"I've no patience with screaming kids," he said to the woman.

"You think I do?"

He lifted the camera again.

"Maybe we can wait a day for this," said the woman.

"You know we can't. I'm busy," the man said. "Now make him say something for Emily."

The woman came close to Doni again. He cried louder. She slapped his cheek. Doni stopped crying. No one had ever hit him like that.

"We're in a hurry. We're giving you one chance to talk to your mother. What do you want to say to her?"

Doni looked at the woman. He didn't want to say anything. He wanted to run away.

"He's a stubborn brat," the man said. "Like you."

The woman tried to kick the man but she wasn't really angry. "I have another idea," she said, looking back at Doni. "I'm going to say something. You repeat it after me. Okay?"

Doni stared at the floor.

"God Almighty," the man exclaimed.

The woman stepped back. "Hi, Mommy," she said. Then, to Doni: "Say 'Hi, Mommy.'"

Doni didn't respond. He didn't want to play with them anymore.

"The kid needs a few swats," the man said. He put the camera down and left the room.

The woman sat down. "Listen, kid, say hello to your mom. Otherwise my boyfriend here'll explode. We'll both be in trouble."

Doni knew the word *trouble.* Sarah and Maria were not happy when he made trouble. He looked at the woman.

"C'mon," she said. "The movie's fun. Tell your mommy you love her and you'll see her soon. If you do that, you *will* see her soon."

What the woman said made Doni feel good.

"How 'bout Snickers?" he asked.

"The dog?" The woman laughed. "Sure, you'll see the dog too. Maybe you want to say hello to him?"

The man returned with a glass in his hand.

"I think we're getting somewhere," the woman told him. "Let's go. I think he's ready."

The man put the glass on the floor. He lifted the camera to his shoulder and turned it on.

"Doni," said the woman, "tell your mommy how much you love her. How much you miss her."

Doni looked at the man and the camera. "Where are you, Mommy?" he said softly. "I miss you so so much. This big." He reached his small arms out and made a circle. "I miss Snickers. I put his bone under my truck. Don't forget to give it to him. He misses his bone."

He started to cry.

The woman stood up. The man whispered, "Wait."

Doni didn't mean to cry. He wiped the tears from his cheeks with his hand. He looked at the camera.

"When will I see you, Mommy? Please come and take me home. If I can come home I'll never be trouble again. I'll be a good boy. Forever 'n' ever."

Tears came again.

Click.

"We got it," the man said. He was happy now. He touched the woman and gave her a kiss. After he left the room the woman came over to Doni and pulled him up by his arm. Then with her other hand she took the box back into the potty room.

At the big door, she turned around.

"Go pee."

The lights went out.

Doni sat back down. After a while he went into the room with the cold floor. It was getting dark. But he was okay. He knew that the devils weren't there just now.

9

The 1770 House is an authentic colonial dwelling located on Main Street, in the heart of East Hampton. Over the years the small shingled cottage had been enlarged by a series of entrepreneurs to capitalize on its charm. In the 1990s, complete with white picket fence and smart black shutters, it was the perfect setting for a cozy restaurant.

Its rustic parlor was crammed with a wealth of antiques. Every inch was taken up with grandfather clocks, ornate mirrors, duck decoys, bowsprits, pewter kettles, and ceramic figurines poised on lace doilies. In the corner a ginger cat perched on a tartan wing chair.

"Pretty kitty," Ceci cooed as she lazily ran her hand along its arched back.

Jack hovered as close to Ceci as possible. Her presence was unnerving. From the moment she opened the door of the motel room he wanted to devour her. Standing there now, inhaling her perfume created the sweetest ache in his groin. As they headed into the bar he admired her beauty in the soft lemony light from the hurricane lamp overhead.

"Terrific outfit," he remarked casually. She was resplendent in a black silk tunic and red lizard sandals. The bodice of the slinky garment draped artfully along the slope of her breasts.

"Thanks, my luggage finally arrived."

A divine smile lightened her face. The hostility of the afternoon had vanished. The change was infinitely agreeable and Jack was grateful.

"How'd your story go?" Her eyes met his with warm interest.

"Sent in an hour after my deadline." He extracted a pack of Marlboros from his pocket and lit a cigarette with the matches on the bar.

Ceci frowned. "I don't know anyone who smokes anymore."

"Then you know the wrong crowd."

Jack regretted the mini confrontation but it was necessary to establish smoking rules early on. Otherwise, there'd be endless carping. Especially with these yuppie types. Jack signaled the bartender and ordered a Glenlivet on the rocks. He looked at Ceci.

"Diet Coke," she said.

Jack peered at her. A diet Coke at the onset of a date was a bad omen. He expected substantial rewards after the three intense hours he had spent hunched over his laptop in the dreary motel room. Passionate sex with stacked blondes always topped his list of treats. A porterhouse steak accompanied by a decent Bordeaux scored second. Tonight, he'd anticipated the possibility of a double whammy. The diet Coke, however, worried him.

The bartender delivered their drinks.

While Ceci sipped her Coke she discreetly took in the outline of Jack's shoulders under his soft suede jacket. There was a raw sensuality about the man; he must have been devastating in his youth, before the onset of his adult personality. "Charming restaurant," she said politely. Friendly, seductive allure was the way to play this game, she decided. Already the two hours she spent on her hair and makeup had had the proper effect on him.

"This dollhouse is s'posed to serve the best food in town."

She leaned toward him, her voluptuous body moving at odds with the silk dress. "I'm impressed you were able to get a reservation."

Jack savored a long swallow of the fine scotch. He wasn't about to tell her he had bribed the owner.

Ceci moved even closer to him and lightly touched his arm with her hand as her magnetic blue eyes sought his. "Did you discover anything new this afternoon?"

Jack smothered a smile. This glorious creature was attempting to seduce him for information. She couldn't have found a more willing candidate. "In fact, I did," he said softly. He tilted his head toward hers. He pressed the flat of his hand firmly against the small of her back. "The FBI sent a polygraph team to the mansion."

"My God," she choked.

Jack loved the way her breasts trembled when she became excited. He removed his hand. Best to take her slowly.

"The ongoing theory is that the kidnappers climbed over the breakwater," he said.

Ceci looked puzzled. "How did they escape? By boat?"

Jack watched the tendons in her slender neck constrict. She became serious when she talked about work. He found this trait in her lovable. Even more endearing was her clumsy sexual come-on. So endearing in fact that he wanted her right there on the floor of the bar.

Instead, he rattled the ice in his empty glass. "They don't know," he said distractedly. He ordered another round of drinks from the bartender. "Still diet Coke?" he checked.

"I shouldn't drink. Puffy eyes show on camera," Ceci said fretfully. "But, well, okay. A glass of white wine."

This was a promising sign.

"The kidnappers might have carried the kid down the beach— concealed in a canoe possibly—to a getaway point," Jack continued. "Certainly they had plenty of time to escape."

Ceci had read none of this in the Saturday newspapers. Werts was a terrific reporter. "By now, Doni Shay might be in Chicago," she speculated.

"Peru's more like it."

A plump woman in a polka-dot dress waved to Jack. Their table was ready.

The quaint New England atmosphere prevailed in the low-ceilinged dining room. A tiny oak table was set with boldly patterned country plates, lead-crystal goblets, and white cotton napkins embroidered with tiny black sheep. Ceci appreciated the homey touches after the cavernous cold stucco of Los Angeles restaurants.

With the care of a connoisseur, Jack chose a bottle of Jordan cabernet from the wine list. Ceci agreed to sample a glass. She rarely drank, but the glass of white wine had pleasantly soothed her after the travail of the last two days. Moreover, it was appropriate she celebrate the Farnsworth interview with Mr. Werts.

Over steamed clams they chatted about Los Angeles—the traffic, earthquakes, auto insurance rates, and finally, the Dodgers. Jack was surprised to learn she had been living in southern California for only six months. This explained her virginal charm, an innocence he found increasingly irresistible.

During the meal Ceci talked shop. She told him that Tommy Train planned a piece on the Charles Lindbergh case. "The story's stalled," he said. "Everybody's tryin' to generate new angles. I suggested the magazine do a filler act on the survivors of kidnapping—average people who had been 'napped and then lived to tell about it. Our crackerjack researchers unearthed twenty of 'em. My lunatic editor killed it. He's after the razor's edge, the ransom note."

Ceci considered his words. "The Survivors of Kidnapping" would make a decent segment for Tommy Train. She admired the way Werts thought—one step ahead. Her mind was always two steps behind. She must learn to develop his talent for projection. Already she had gained so much from the man. Ever since he barged into her motel room wonderful things had happened. Her faith in herself as a journalist had been renewed. At last, she felt happy and exhilarated. She finished her glass of wine and signaled the waiter to pour her another. The life of a roving correspondent wasn't so terrible after all.

Even Shay's fagged brain registered that they weren't making any progress. The two men who sat with him at the marble table in the library obviously hated each other.

Joe Krugger remained stone-faced while Morgan Camp pleaded his case. "Listen to me, just listen to me." The publicist addressed first Robert and then Libby, who had impatiently left her chair to watch the sunset. Behind her, the leather-bound tomes that lined the mahogany shelves added to the room's somber tone.

"We got the world wired with this tragedy," Camp exulted. His pouchy round cheeks wiggled and sniffed like a gerbil's. "Doni knocked Gorbachev off the front page of *The New York Times*." His pudgy torso bundled in a white tennis sweater was in constant motion, but his bulging eyes never strayed from Robert. "You're the prince of Hollywood," he rasped. "The prince of Hollywood can't bury himself in"—a meaty arm vaguely paddled the air—"in drifting sand dunes. If you can't fight 'em, use 'em. A press conference'll help us find Doni. Look . . ."

He reached down and produced a recent close-up of Shay's son mounted on a piece of cardboard. "Take this picture—or one like it—and print MISSING or KIDNAPPED underneath." With clumsy fingers he blocked a space where the letters might be printed.

Libby came over to look at the photograph and noted with distaste the coat of clear nailpolish that covered Camp's manicured nails. That instant, she realized Camp's dyed black strands were woven into a toupee, a scalp doily.

"Run off ten thousand," Camp explained. "Add some details

like height, weight. Simple stuff." He smiled broadly. "Put television to work for you. By Monday morning the entire world will be hunting for Doni."

Robert tried to analyze the publicist's pitch. He studied Krugger for some sign of his reaction. The young FBI agent barely blinked. Robert wasn't able to get an accurate reading on the guy. He was impassive, impenetrable. Morgan Camp, on the other hand, was vintage L.A.—one of many polo lounge lizards dressed by Fred Haymen.

Krugger addressed Robert in his low-key mechanical tone. "You already have my opinion. I stated my reasons. Do I have to repeat them every time this moron does his jig?" His hard eyes were coldly objective. "Our plan is to safeguard the channels of communication open to the kidnappers. Already hundreds of crank calls have jammed local police precincts. Every mother's uncle thinks he's seen Doni. Thousands of letters are pouring in. This so-called press conference will just generate more interference. It serves no purpose."

Morgan Camp slid forward, his chubby face turned to Robert. There was a defensive surliness in his voice. "We've printed a list of celebrities who have sent flowers, notes, condolences. Since yesterday, two thousand bouquets have been delivered to the post office."

Libby lowered herself into her chair. There were dark circles under her eyes. Exhaustion had drained her face; she looked ten years older. Her words came slowly. "We've rerouted truckloads of the stuff to a senior citizens' home in Southampton."

Camp bounced up energetically. "*My* idea," he bragged. "I arranged that. It looks good. Real good. Chicki suggested the children's hospital but that's too ironic, given the circumstances . . ."

Libby scowled at him and he clammed up immediately. He knew enough to treat her with the same respect his employer accorded her.

Robert's head ached. Little knife pains stabbed behind his eyes. He looked at Babcock. "What do you think?"

Before Libby spoke her eyes passed icily over Krugger's face. "It's plausible," she said. "A press conference might relieve the media pressure. It can't hurt."

Krugger folded his hands together on the table, his attention directed on Shay. "The kidnappers may not have counted on the magnitude of the press response. If they are frightened they may change their course of action. Unless, of course, we're dealing with international terrorists . . ."

Robert paled. "International terrorists? My God!"

A shrewd chess player, Krugger manipulated Robert's fears. "Ransom demands are usually made in the first two weeks. This is the most critical period."

Camp churned about again, his fat hands waving in the air. A gold Rolex flashed from under silk cuffs. "Joe, listen, you're the star here, the country's foremost expert on kidnapping." He decided to try a new tack. "I wouldn't have the audacity to challenge your expertise," he said with patronizing flattery. "Believe me, I wouldn't dare. But I know the press side of this. This ain't some estranged angry parent stealing back a baby. What we got is the crime of the decade, the world press at our fingertips . . ." Camp's rodent eyes glowed red with the thought of it. "The public loves Doni, they'll help us," he said. "Blow the whistle on the bastards. The photos circulating are dated . . ." Again Camp lifted the glossy photograph of Doni. "Nothin' of this quality."

Shay crossed his arms and dropped his head down on the table. Until now, his son had been hidden, guarded, never in the public eye. He felt a wave of anger overtake him.

Camp's ingratiating words rolled on. "Practically speaking, we've got to remove tent city. We can't allow the press to stampede around like a herd of scavengers, poking in everywhere." His gaze focused on Krugger. "Even you've complained that they monitor police radio calls." Back to Shay. "We give 'em scraps, crumbs. That's what press releases are about. Give 'em a photo op. It works to our advantage the way it works for the White House." He looked at Krugger with false affection. "At least they get the spelling of everybody's name right. How many people you got in Washington on this?"

"None of your damn business."

Unfazed, Camp rocked forward. He yanked a silk handkerchief from his back pocket to blow his nose.

Krugger stifled his rage. "They'll nail you for details on the investigation," he said to Robert.

"He doesn't answer them," said Camp. He folded his hankie without acknowledging the agent.

"An eight hundred number is as far as I go. That siphons off the crank calls. My advice is to lie low."

"Sooner we do this the better," said Camp. "Drake'll provide security. We invite the networks, prime overseas press. Let 'em know we care about 'em."

Robert looked at Libby imploringly. She stretched her arms out on the table, an empty coffee mug clenched in her large hands. She nodded ever so slowly. "Okay."

Krugger rose and walked soundlessly from the room.

"I gotta scramble to organize this event," Camp said.

Libby spoke quickly. "Make it short and painless."

He flashed a triumphant smile. "Believe me, I will."

While Jack and Ceci were finishing their chocolate soufflé the plump hostess appeared at their table to tell Jack he had an emergency call. He excused himself politely and found the telephone buried in a British-style red booth behind the restaurant. He hunched over uncomfortably to keep from banging his head on the low ceiling.

"Hi, buns," chirped Sherry. "Sorry to disturb chow time but I got a hot tip."

"What's up?"

"Morgan just called the office in a tizzy. Shay's scheduled a press conference for tomorrow morning. Half the staff is on the red-eye to East Hampton."

"Where?"

"High school auditorium. Noon."

"Who's goin' to perform?"

"Morgan, natch," said Sherry. "Shay too, I think." She took a breath. "Morgan says Shay's unhinged. His wife's totally outta commission. A house of zombies."

Jack heard a male voice in the background ask Sherry to make a hotel reservation. She returned, flustered. "Okay, toots, I gotta jet." A second later, she whispered, "Jack?"

"Sweets?"

"You behaving yourself?"

"What makes you think I'm not?"

"The female who answered the phone in your room at three A.M."

"Honey, that's the crazy motel. A room mix-up."

"Good."

"Raspberry?"

"Yes?"

"I appreciate what you're doin'," said Jack. "I'll have a reward for you when I get back to L.A."

"How 'bout an engagement ring?"

He emitted a thorny chuckle.

"A key to your house then," she said coyly.

"You're a persistent devil."

"Be a good boy."

Back at the table the dessert plates had already been cleared. Ceci twirled a spoon in a cup of milky white tea.

"Guess you might as well hear this from me," he said. "Shay's scheduled a press conference."

Ceci hunched forward, keenly interested. "Why?"

"Who knows?" Jack sighed. "But whatever the reason we'll find out herded and tethered."

Ceci could hardly believe what a valuable source he was. She'd tape the press conference. That was worth yet another segment.

After dinner they settled on a tufted leather sofa in the intimate bar. Jack ordered Ceci another glass of wine, a double scotch for himself.

It had been Jack's experience that tipsy women become amorous. He put his arm around Ceci's waist and took her hand. More than anything he wanted to peel the expensive dress off her ripe young body. But inexplicably she squirmed away and began to yammer about her journey from the wilds of Missouri to the smoggy streets of L.A. He listened patiently until she expounded on journalism school.

Jack called for another scotch.

What was with females these days? All of 'em were on a mission. Stella, his old girlfriend, had been consumed by the sisterhood rap. After their relationship ended, she became a "hypenate" who slept with a revolver under her pillow. Sherry's gospel was the world according to Shirley MacLaine: chakkras, alpha waves, and wheat-grass juice. With Miss McCann, the prayer chant was the power and glory of the media.

"Journalists perform a positive service for humanity," she said earnestly. "We serve the world by illuminating complex issues of life. Information makes people better human beings."

Jack felt a wave of depression. He aimed for a flirty fuck with this delectable creature, not a pompous lecture. She was too pretty to ruin the evening's spell with such drivel. He wished she would give her luscious lips a rest.

But Ceci was determined to talk. "From the time I was six I knew I'd be a television journalist——"

Jack interrupted rudely. "Listen, honey, if you think that *The Tommy Train Show* is contributing to humanity then America's in serious trouble. Train's a video barbarian. He panders to perverts. It's crap—waste product to force a visceral rush. The crud is jamming America's air waves. His show, and the others like it, reduce the viewer to a jackass. The guy's a threat to democracy."

"Ridiculous," Ceci objected indignantly. The expression in her crystal blue eyes sharpened. "You print people are jealous because he makes so much money. Because TV people make more than . . . than you hacks! What do you think you are? Your magazine runs the same stories."

"Me? What do I think I am?" Jack slurred. He wiggled his empty glass under her nose. "I'm a sane man in an insane world. I'm a vestige of what once was a journalist. And this kidnapping is just another hyperinflated celebrity orgy."

"If you dislike your job so much, why do you do it?" she challenged.

He smiled sourly. "Because you learn how to adapt to the phony environment. The sterile smiles, the insincere friendships, the vacant minds obsessed with their press coverage. Celebrities live to see their nipped and tucked faces stretched across magazine covers. For them, being interviewed by Barbara Walters is the supreme orgasm."

His bitterness frightened her. "You're drunk," she accused.

"Uninhibited perhaps, but not officially drunk," he said coolly. "My beautiful child, you'll soon learn that in this business, like most others, calculated gain motivates all of us."

They drove back to the motel in silence. The streets of the village were empty. The night had turned cold. Ceci rested her head against the seat, overcome by an unbalanced whirling sensation, a distant drumming in her ears. She closed her eyes. The scalding tone of his words echoed in her brain. He was such a cynical, sarcastic man. Life was too short for such negativity. Downbeat people never got anywhere. Ceci had always made an effort to steer clear of negative thinkers.

She opened her eyes and looked over at him. His attention was concentrated on the road. Squares of light from the street lamps cast a blue sheen on his black hair. It was a shame he was negative because she found him terribly suave and experienced. Even though she knew he didn't have fame enough to get her mentioned in the gossip columns, she still liked him. Trusted him. "You married?" she asked.

A faint grin lightened his face. "Once, in my early twenties."

"Do you have children?"

"No kids, thank God."

They turned into the motel parking lot. Jack removed his jacket and draped it over her shoulders as they walked to her room. Ceci gazed up at the sky. Clouds sailed past the bright full moon like battleships.

He waited quietly behind her as she unlocked the door. When she turned to say good night he backed her into the darkened room. "I hate public displays of affection," he said as his arms circled her waist. His lips found hers.

Then, in what seemed like just seconds to Ceci, Jack had her pinned under him on the double bed nearest the door.

"Whoa!" she said, regaining her senses. She wriggled out from under his strong body. "Hold on. This isn't exactly fair."

"Fair's no fun." He nuzzled the nape of her neck. Ceci switched on the lamp and Jack squinted with irritation. "Fluorescent light isn't for lovers." The top button of his shirt was opened. A moist sheen covered his tanned skin.

Ceci jumped to her feet and modestly straightened her dress. "Look, you're very nice," she said, flustered. "But I never sleep with men on the first date."

Jack had a bemused grin on his face. "Who says I wanna sleep with you?"

"Well, whatever this is then, I just don't do it." She hurried around to the end of the bed. "Thanks for dinner. Now please, go."

She was adorable. Once he got her back in his arms, he hoped he could muster enough control to make love to her properly. He hadn't desired a woman like this for a long time. He immediately bunched the pillows behind his head, settling in. "You forget that this is my room," he said. "Tell you what, you come over and give me one more kiss and then I'll split."

Ceci knew that line. She'd fought men off since she was sixteen. There wasn't a come-on she hadn't heard. Part of her desired him but a tumble in the sack with some drunken journalist she met on assignment wasn't worth it. It was dangerous, given the times. "If you don't leave immediately, I'm calling the police." Making good on the threat, she lifted the receiver.

Jack frowned at her. "Surely you're kidding."

"When I say good night, I mean good night."

Jack blinked at her incredulously. It had been years since any woman kicked him out of bed, either before or after sex. This little hellcat was a throwback to the fifties.

"Okay," he said, rising from the bed. With a surprise lurch he captured her again. "Someday soon you'll beg for it," his lips whispered in her ear.

Ceci squelched a smile. "You wish."

He let her go abruptly and, fetching his jacket from the floor, walked to the door. "How about lunch after the press conference? My reward for being a gentleman."

"Maybe," she said teasingly.

As soon as Jack left the room Ceci called Shorty.

"I left two messages for you," he said when he heard her voice. "Did you get them?"

"No. Forget messages. I'll call whenever I'm free."

"I've got great news. Your exclusive with Farnsworth is Monday's show. The entire half-hour. Your ass is golden, baby."

"Shorty, there's more. Shay's holding a press conference tomorrow."

"Dynamite," Shorty trilled. "Make sure birdbrain Armstrong gets tape of you asking him a question. Also, you takin' notes, quizzing the police. The networks will bombard the public with head-on footage. We'll have an oblique angle. The old 'you are there' with Ceci McCann."

"Shorty?"

"Yes, honey."

"I've an idea that I think is real strong. But Mitch must help me."

"Sure."

"How about a show on 'The Survivors of Kidnapping'? We find ten people who were kidnapped as children. It's unlikely they were kidnapped for money but they can give graphic descriptions of being held captive."

"Fantastic idea," Shorty boomed. "Sort of before and after, then and now. You're right. Most of 'em were 'napped by perverts. But that adds excitement. If Tommy says go, Mitch is your partner." He hesitated, then added, "Ceci, I knew you'd come through."

Right after she dropped the receiver in the cradle the phone jangled again.

"Is Jack Werts there?"

It sounded like Raspberry.

"I'll see him soon," Ceci said. "Can I take a message for him?"

There was a heavy silence.

Finally, the woman spoke. "Yes, you can. Please let Mr. Werts know his fiancée is trying to reach him."

The line went dead.

Mr. Werts? His fiancée?

"That shit," Ceci fumed aloud. "That two-timing lying weasel." Thank the Lord she had kicked him out of her bed. What did he think? She was the preview attraction for his bachelor party? Jack Werts better think again.

10

Shortly before noon Robert Shay peered from behind the brown velvet curtains at the front of the auditorium. Cumbersome studio cameras rolled down the wide aisles like battalions of Sherman tanks. On the hardwood floor, fat black television cables tangled with discarded strips of red, white, and blue crepe paper. Throughout the jittery crowd, isolated sound booms sprouted like spindly trees.

Familiar network reporters were stationed in the front rows, mouthing lead-ins to whirring cameras. At that moment Shay had nothing but contempt for these "fighter pilots" of TV broadcasting. He prayed Camp's theory was correct, that the public sacrifice would get the bloodsuckers off his back for a few days.

Numbly resigned to this slaughter he crossed back to the cubbyhole where Camp's assistant had unfolded a chair. He sat down and impatiently smoothed his hands over his fashionably slicked-back blond hair. He had dressed for the occasion in a simple Italian sweater, twill slacks, and handmade English loafers.

A few feet away Krugger stood with Police Chief Drake. This morning the agent was dressed in a khaki suit and running shoes. A leather knapsack was casually slung over his shoulder. "Where'd Camp go?" Shay called to him.

Krugger came over and squatted down, eye level. "He's countin' heads." Like a banker he snapped open a gold pocket watch. The spidery hands showed 11:50. "You can bet he'll be back before the music starts."

Libby emerged from the backstage shadows. She carried an open bottle of Perrier. Shay lifted the bottle from her hand and took a long swallow. "Good luck," she said softly, ignoring Krugger. "I'll be in the wings." She trotted away on low stacked heels.

Krugger spoke with maddening precision. "We've got a lead with some credibility." Robert stared into his improbably blue eyes.

The agent's masklike face reflected nothing. "Two teenagers flying kites on the beach saw a motor launch with two surfers near the house. The girl thought it was weird because a few hours earlier her brother had told her the waves were too choppy to surf." Krugger shifted his position to ease his knees. "A week before, a similar boat—again with two surfers—was spotted by the Tuckers' gardener."

Boiling with excitement, Morgan Camp came slashing through the heavy curtains, the glint of victory in his eyes. He looked like a carnival barker in his scarlet blazer, white ducks, and white tasseled loafers.

"Restless natives, restless natives," he repeated to himself with an air of absentmindedness. Spying the two men, he came over and settled his hand on Robert's shoulder. "Ya feel good?" His avid eyes were riveted on Robert's face.

Two maintenance men dragged a podium from the apron of the stage. The sharp metal corners scraped the wood floor. "Trixie," yelled Camp. From nowhere his short, buxom assistant galloped forward, her mountainous chest in motion. Like a heat-seeking missile, Camp hurled himself at her and saluted the rafters. "Is the right mike on stage?" Trixie ducked and curtsied, then ran around the curtains to find out.

Robert had accepted the commotion like a dumb prize fighter who had taken too many blows to the head, but when the publicist reached to hug him again, he slapped his arm away. "Get this charade over with."

Camp recoiled and smiled obsequiously. "Aye, aye, skipper." He mumbled a spate of mumbo jumbo to himself and then dissolved between the curtains. From the other side came screaming bedlam—a storm of boos, hisses, grunts, belly laughs. Krugger flashed a tight-lipped smile at Robert. "The audience has good taste."

There was another eruption and Robert heard the faint rumbling of a chant: "Go home, Morgan. Go home, Morgan." Camp's amplified voice blared through the high-pitched yells like a fog horn. "For two long days Robert Shay and I debated—in good conscience—whether or not to hold this press conference." The crowd quieted. "Thanks to the wise counsel of FBI Chief Joe Krugger we decided it necessary to include you here today. From the bottom of his heart, Robert Shay thanks you for your coverage and your concern for his son."

"That toad," hissed Krugger as Robert rose to his feet and slipped through the curtain. His appearance released an artillery fire of scorching white light. Blinded by a sheet of glaring heat, Robert felt Camp awkwardly embrace him in a misplaced gesture of camaraderie. The moment Camp stepped back there came another torrent of scalding white light. Shay blinked, aware of the great mass of humanity that confronted him like a raging surf. The entire auditorium seemed to swell in his direction.

He could make out a row of silhouettes at the base of the stage apron. A human fence of police officers had lined up to protect him. Duke stood in the wings, a .38 strapped to his chest.

After a few minutes a second wave began. Like a field of crickets the rapid clicks of the flashing cameras blended into a continuous thrum. Finally, Robert lifted his hands.

"Emily and I are devastated . . ." he began. A metallic screech from the microphone pierced his eardrum and he jumped. To steady himself, he clutched the podium, a catatonic glaze in his eyes. "Questions are best—"

Tumultuous shouts interrupted his words. Again, hot lights. Black silhouetted bodies leaped up. Quickly, he pointed down into the front rows.

A twangy professional voice shouted, "What's the name of the movie in Thailand?"

Robert's lips grazed the microphone. *"China White."*

"What's it about?"

Shay ached to awaken from this suffocating nightmare. The sobering thought of his son prevented him from turning on his heel. He spoke in a detached tone. "A missionary doctor lends his hospital to a gang of heroin smugglers."

"Where's Emily?" a female reporter shouted. "Why isn't she here?"

Shay's fingernails dug into the oak podium. "Emily's under enormous strain. She's ill . . ."

"What's wrong with her?" the woman persisted. "Describe her symptoms."

"Next question?" He pointed back into the crowd.

"Is there a ransom note?" a man with a heavy Spanish accent called out.

"No, no ransom note."

A familiar anchorman's voice came from the front. "Does the FBI have any leads?"

Krugger stepped forward. "We have no leads at this time."

"Back here . . . back here," came a heckler's yell. "Are you offering a reward?"

Robert looked puzzled. "No, I am not offering any reward."

A chorus of anonymous voices shouted through the silvery haze. "Why not?"

Jack awoke at half past noon. He had an aching hard-on prompted by sweet dreams of Ceci McCann's legs knotted about his sweaty neck. He bashed the pillow and pulled the sheet over his head. God, he wanted to fuck this woman—if ever he managed to get his hands on her. The thought of her naked, unattended body sleeping twenty rooms away brought another surge of horniness.

He kicked away the sheet and yawned till his eyes watered. The twinking digits on the cheap electronic clock were frozen at 4 A.M. Broken, like everything else in the dump. Only his cock seemed in supremely good shape. He smiled as he stretched, savoring his intense desire for the snappy young blonde.

Attempting to ignore his hard-on, he padded to the window. Rain clouds gathered in the sky. He was in no rush to join the lemmings. Never in his life had he learned anything from a press conference.

After a long hot shower he dressed in a white shirt and chinos—the last of his clean clothes—and grabbed his battered Burberry.

Already late, he stopped by the Buttery, a chic muffin shop on Main Street. He forswore the blueberry popovers for a large carton of freshly brewed coffee and claimed the last copy of the Sunday *New York Times*. He flirted with the cute cashier, a local kid with a remarkably snug uniform.

By the time he arrived at the red brick high school a ring of blue-and-white squad cars were successfully keeping a boisterous throng of curious tourists at bay. News choppers buzzed overhead. Twenty moon-faced satellite dishes vibrated softly; their passive white surfaces soundlessly uplinked footage to tiny transponders hurtling around the globe.

Jack backed up and drove past the congestion. He made a right at the corner and parked the Chevette on a sleepy residential street across from the football field.

Carrying his papers and coffee he ambled under the goalpost. As he approached the rear of the high school two plainclothes cops emerged from the fire exit. Precariously balancing the coffee, Jack fished around in his pocket for his press ID, but the tall guy simply held the heavy metal door open for him. "Delivery? Go right ahead, pal."

He'd better get himself a new raincoat, he thought, as he circled aimlessly about the basement corridors. At last he discovered a staircase to the front entrance of the auditorium where Camp's army had established its beachhead. Like lacquered geishas, obedient female publicists papered every reporter who passed by. Jack ignored their handouts, focusing on the fireman who patrolled the aisles. When an AP photographer abandoned his seat to get a shot from up front, Jack dashed for his empty chair.

At the podium Robert Shay appeared ghostly white, hardly a matinee idol. Jack diligently scanned the ranks of the television gladiators. McCann was in the fifth row, waving her arm frantically. She was strictly dress-for-success in a tailored jacket with a pointed white collar. Miraculously, Shay acknowledged her. Although her voice was strong it was impossible to hear her question. Shay responded with what sounded like "Snickers." A candy bar?

Finished with his coffee, Jack slouched down in the hard-backed theater seat. He was pissed at himself for being such a curmudgeon last night. Who was he to lecture this sweet kid about the darker side of journalism? Why spoil her enthusiasm? She was a gold-star gal—first in line, bright, eager, full of confidence, a real trouper. He knew better than anyone that in journalism, showing up ahead of the pack was 90 percent of the job. Hell, he'd rather have McCann as an opponent than those geeky dames he usually had to confront. He'd apologize to her over lunch.

Across the aisle Jack spotted an empty seat next to Bill Leggitt. Jack hustled over. The tabloid reporter looked like a candidate for membership into the Palm Beach Hunt Club. He wore a double-breasted linen suit, oxblood silk tie, creamy suede loafers. As Leggitt leaned over, Jack got a whiff of his fragrance: Bombay Gin.

"Did you see this?" He floated a sheet of paper Jack's way. Morgan Camp Associates was elaborately scripted above a long list of celebrities who had sent condolences to the Shay family.

Jack frowned. "All of his clients are on this list."

"A smart sponge," Leggitt croaked.

Jack put his elbows on the armrests and knitted his fingers together. He looked around the auditorium. "Where's Bates?"

"The guy lives hand-to-mouth," said Leggitt. "Last night he lost seven hundred bucks to the FBI. The agents love him."

"Where's the game?"

"American Hotel in Sag Harbor."

"He shacked up there?"

"Naw," said Leggitt. "Bridgehampton. The *Tattler* rented a proper pad. Pool, tennis courts. I wasn't invited."

Jack directed his attention to Camp down on stage. The publicist's piranha smile was at war with his maudlin spiel.

"How much is Shay bankrolling Camp?" Leggitt asked.

"Rough estimate? An easy twenty grand a month."

"Shiiit."

Jack knew he'd see that figure quoted in next week's *Midnight Express*.

While Camp blathered on about the poster campaign, Shay abruptly disappeared behind the curtains. The audience immediately erupted with activity: camera caps snapped, briefcases flapped and buckled, cables retracted. Jack watched Ceci pack her notes away. He took in her long, shapely legs below the narrow miniskirt as she marched up the aisle.

Jack rose. Surely she'd see him standing there. But she continued right past, eyes straight ahead. He immediately edged his way through the crowd after her. "Hiya, beautiful." Then, very cheery and merry, "Ready for lunch?"

Ceci halted. She spun around. Pinpoints of hate sharpened her eyes. "No, thanks."

Technicians and reporters rudely banged into them, annoyed that they had blocked the flow of traffic.

Jack was baffled by her anger. "Any particular reason?"

"Yes." Her voice had the thrust of a dagger. "You're a phony two-timer. A breed of men I avoid."

Before she could turn away from him he clutched her arm. "Hey, wait a minute. What'd I do?" he said with the start of an impish grin. She looked so cute when she got mad it was hard to take her seriously.

Ceci slapped his hand from her arm. "Your fiancée called my room searching for you." The word *fiancée* chimed like a bell. Her accusation hung there in the air between them.

"Is that what she said?"

"Yes."

Jack frowned. "Well, she's not."

"Funny, she certainly thinks so. Something you said must have given her that idea."

"The lady's a friend from L.A."

Ceci glared at him. "I hate liars. Get lost."

She turned and, using her elbows like swords, sliced through the crowd in hot pursuit of her crew.

"Has Casanova lost his magic touch?" Leggitt asked from behind him.

Jack's eyes followed Ceci through the exit. "In this case, I never got the chance to demonstrate it."

The woman brought Doni more hamburgers. He now had many white boxes, many forts. But he missed his Ninja turtles. And the smile-face cookies. And the bow-tie cookies. Maria chased Daddy when he put the bow-tie cookies under his neck. Snickers loved Maria's cookies too. But Mommy got mad if he gave Snickers the cookies.

Doni turned one of the forts upside down. It was now a boat. He put some straws into the boat. These were pirates. He moved the boat over the ocean but there were big walls around the ocean.

He abandoned the boat to tear apart an empty cup. Now it had wings. It was a big airplane. It could carry many soldiers. To get ready for their trip, the soldiers borrowed the pirates' boat and went fishing in the ocean. Doni tore tiny pieces of paper from the white bags the woman brought the boxes in. They were fish. He tore off more pieces of paper. They were blankets. The soldiers needed food and blankets for their trip.

Doni put the fish, the blankets, and the soldiers in the plane. It was ready. The plane took off from the floor and lifted slowly. It circled higher and higher around the room. The soldiers were happy they were going to the sun and the trees. Then something went wrong. The soldiers pushed the button that made the plane go higher but the plane was stuck. It was going as high as it could go, making giant circles in the room.

Doni started to cry as he ran faster and faster around the room. His arm was straight up, the cup in his hand. Unexpectedly, he tripped and fell. The plane crashed to earth. The soldiers were dead on the floor.

Doni cried very loud. He hurt inside. The men were dead. Then he felt something small in his hand. He stopped crying and looked at the little soldier. Doni felt much better. The littlest soldier was alive. He was the smartest soldier too. He knew he must build a rocket to take him to the sun. The other soldiers had thought an airplane was enough.

The big door opened.

"What's with all the racket?" asked the woman. She looked at the boxes, torn cups, and pieces of straw strewn across the floor. "This place is a pigsty. If you expect a fancy maid to clean up this mess, forget it, sonny boy. I ain't no housekeeper."

She brushed his forts, boats, and soldiers into a brown bag. She held the airplane in her hand. "What's this? You chewin' on Dixie cups now?" She was angry. She tossed the cup in the bag and disappeared through the big door.

Doni took the littlest soldier from his hand and hid him under the red blanket.

The woman returned. This time, there were clothes in her arms. "C'mon," she said.

Doni followed her into the potty room. She reached for his arm and yanked him to her. In her hand, she had a buzz machine. When she put the buzz machine against his head his hair dropped everywhere. It was on his jeans, his cowboy shirt, and all over the floor. The buzz machine hurt his head.

"Sit still. I'll be done in a minute."

The buzz machine cut his ear.

"Stop squirmin'," she said. With her hand, she snapped his head back. The buzz machine circled his head again and again. Pieces of hair went into his nose. He started to cry.

"For Chrissake, stop the bawling."

Doni tried not to cry but the buzz hurt. Then suddenly it was gone. "There." She laughed. "You're a bowling ball."

She started water for the tub. She unzipped his pants and took his cowboy boots and put them into her bag. "You stink," she said as she lifted him into the water. "Don't you know how to wipe yourself?"

Doni didn't know what that word meant. He shook his head.

"That's pathetic." She was jumpy and heated up again. "A billion dollars and they can't teach you how to shit."

She left the room.

Doni stood up in the tub. From there he saw more of the trees. There were no houses nearby.

"Get down and start washin'," she said as she came through the door with a bundle of clothes in her arms. "Move it, Dumbo. I'm not your nanny. You wash. There's the soap."

Mommy had taught him to soap his hands. But Sarah washed him in the bathtub. He tried to do like Sarah. The woman didn't bother him anymore. After a while, she lifted him from the tub and gave him a small towel. "Here, dry yourself."

But before he finished, she put something wet and soft all over his face. Sarah put this soft, cool feeling on his face before he went to the beach.

She waited a few minutes, then said, "Thank God, it works." Then she pulled a pair of black pants over his legs. They were not like the pants he had at home. Then, a long shirt. Funny red shoes went on his feet. She took some black hair from a bag and put it on his head like a hat. It felt hot. With his hands, he tried to push it away.

A sharp slap stung his face. "Don't you dare touch that wig," she yelled at him. Her face was red, her eyes small and black. Doni quickly put his hands down.

"If you ever touch your head, I'll beat the livin' hell outta you. Ya hear?"

She took a real hat from the bag and put it on his head over the hair. Under his chin, she tied a bow.

"Perfect," she said. "What a pretty baby girl. Now go sit on your blanket while I pack. Remember, if you mess yourself I'll kill your goddamn dog."

Before she left she turned and said, "Oh, yeah. Your name's Tina, Tina Sanchez. I'm Rita, your mother."

When the door closed, Doni took the little soldier from under the blanket and put him in the pocket of the dress. He sat down, still as a rock. He didn't want anything to happen to Snickers.

11

By the time Shay returned to the mansion turbulent black thunder-clouds had laid claim to the sky. Chilled from the cold, salty air, he immediately went upstairs and took a hot shower and sauna. The water recharged his batteries. He toweled down briskly, then pulled on a pair of cashmere sweats. He slapped some aftershave on his face and combed his hair in the mirror. Camp had been right about the press conference. The media vultures had vanished from the gate. They were busily occupied, digesting the scraps of information Camp had prepared for them.

Before heading downstairs, he crossed into the glass hallway that connected with Doni's bedroom. He padded noiselessly down the marble floor to the walnut door carved with the faces of Ninja turtles.

The moment he opened the door a bolt of lightning electrified the sky. A ray of white light ricocheted around the steel door frame. Robert remembered the mezuzah his mother had sent from California. It was stashed in a box in the basement of the mansion. Emily had refused to allow the carpenters to attach it, even to the back-door jamb. At the time he had agreed. How could an old Jewish superstition bring protection?

Robert was distracted from this thought by a gust of heavy rain that splattered against the giant windows. The storm sent blue shadows undulating over the lunar maps that papered the walls. Large and small moon craters, like inverted saucers, pockmarked the stucco ceiling. In the corner sat Doni's spaceship bed. The heat shield canopy, control panel headboard, and aluminum space blanket came alive with every bolt of lightning. On the floor an empty astronaut suit with quilted gloves, a bubble helmet, and disconnected air hoses rested like a dead body.

Robert's foot came down on a small toy. He bent to pick it up—a pink '56 T-bird. He tossed it onto the bed and walked into the playroom, where dozens of stuffed animals were herded in a barnyard corral behind painted foam-rubber fences. Shaggy gorillas, tawny goats, black-faced sheep, seals with glass eyes, pink rabbits, and striped skunks huddled absurdly together. A spineless orange carrot was folded over the pliable railing; its feathery green top mopped the hardwood floor.

The architectural firm that designed the house had created a miniature stone castle with a working drawbridge for Doni. Dwarf knights and horses made from laminated plastic littered the artificial turf that surrounded the castle. Robert swung around to face a row of steamer trunks that had been sent from Beverly Hills. They held Doni's favorite collections of soldiers, representatives from every major war in history. Next to the brass trunks were inflated replicas of *The Queen Mary* and *The Spruce Goose*, gifts from the city of Long Beach.

Last summer dinosaurs had commanded his son's attention. Mounted models of pterodactyls, saber-toothed tigers, and mastodons patrolled the room. The models were so accurate they rivaled their cousins at the Museum of Natural History in New York. Robert smiled at the memory of Doni insisting his wooly mammoth spend the night with them at the Ritz hotel in Paris.

How extravagant the rooms were. Having grown up in a middle-class suburban home, Robert knew this better than anyone, but he had found it impossible to deny his son anything. Happily, Doni seemed to be unfazed by the wealth. He always shared his toys with his friends. And kept his eye on important things. His son already had his feet on the ground. Then Robert remembered the ducks.

Last July he and Doni had discovered a brackish backwater pond nicknamed the Oil Spill by local fishermen. A mangy flock of brown ducks inhabited the swampy area. Every time Robert returned to East Hampton, Doni insisted they go feed the ugly duckies with the rat eyes. His son had no interest in the iridescent ring-necked pheasants in Hook Pond at the Maidstone Club. He had explained then that the pretty duckies had plenty of food but the ugly guys needed the bread. His little kid was a fucking genius. A genius with a heart. Robert couldn't have invented or designed a better child than Doni.

Another streak of lightning flashed through the room. Shay walked over to a blob drawn on a white tablet tilted against a small easel. He studied the forbidding shape. It was unlike his son's other watercolors. Then he noticed a drippy square of prongs in the corner. A blurred, disconnected pitchfork. The painting looked like an image of the devil. He retreated quickly.

Back on the second-floor landing, he heard the sound of the television in the den. The heat-sensitized door opened automatically. Emily was watching a videotape of the press conference on a screen embedded in the stone wall.

"You handled yourself well," she said, her back to him.

He came around and faced her. She looked better. Her face had been scrubbed, her thick ebony curls secured with a rawhide cord. Except for the signs of stress around her eyes she was beautiful. As beautiful as she had been fifteen years ago when he first saw her playing Portia in a back-alley production of *The Merchant of Venice*.

She stretched forward to set down a steaming mug of coffee. "To them, we're freaks."

"Had enough?" he asked.

She nodded and he punched off the set. She rose quickly. A billowing silk shirt dropped down to cover her black leggings.

Robert spoke softly. "It's time we talked. Like adults."

She sank back down willingly, but before he could formulate his thoughts he was distracted by a framed montage of Doni's baby pictures on the desk next to a bank of computer terminals. He walked over to the amber-lit stock quotations scrolling noiselessly across the smallest screen.

His eyes filled with tears. "Six fucking satellite dishes. Forty international data banks. This crap gives me the weather in Zanzibar, the density of Neptune. But it can't tell me where they've taken . . ."

Emily watched him like a sphinx, the only animation in her pale blue-violet eyes. Specks of Antarctica.

Challenged by her calm, Robert dried his eyes on his sleeve and sat down beside her.

"Associational transference," she said deliberately.

He smelled the familiar dusty-rose scent of her body. "What are you talking about?"

"Those lie-detector tests are a witch-hunt."

"What else can I do?"

She didn't respond. He pressed the service button at the base of the quartz table.

"*Sí, señor?*" came Maria's voice.

"Send up food. A salad. Whatever you've got."

Quietly distancing herself, Emily retracted into a corner of the deep leather divan, her legs folded gracefully under her. Shay recalled her critical comments about the big rooms. Airplane hangars she had called them. She had insisted that this den be small.

"I know a good parapsychologist in Santa Monica. She'll fly out tomorrow."

Robert ignored her, his voice stony. "Krugger's correct about one thing. It's a waiting game for the ransom note. Did you give him the names?"

She nodded.

Robert fought the urge to add "of all the men you've been with." He was glad he didn't. He had to let go of the jealousy. He gently laid his hand on her leg. Her thigh muscle tensed.

Her eyes drilled into his. "This woman in Santa Monica connects the unconscious. Doni's thoughts with our thoughts," she persisted.

"I don't buy that," he told her. "Any more than I buy Reiss."

"Thanks to his shots I slept," she replied, her voice edged with anger. "You're a mess. The pills don't work. You need help. Let him knock you out."

"Krugger's wired our computer system into FBI terminals throughout the world," he said, changing the subject. "Camp got us digital readouts from the AP wires."

"Robert, listen to me," she hissed. "Pay attention to what's going on under your nose. The staff is loyal. Krugger and Camp are opposite sides of the same coin. They aim to profit from this freak show."

She turned to him, her body taut with excitement. "Snickers won't leave the kitchen door," she said. "He waits there for Doni. At night, he howls. Awful, plaintive howls . . . Maybe, just maybe, if we take him to town he can track Doni's scent . . ."

"This isn't a movie," said Robert. "After three days it's unlikely that Doni's anywhere in the vicinity."

Maria arrived with a platterful of sandwiches. A red-cabbage-and-mushroom salad filled a huge ceramic bowl. She blanketed Robert and Emily with linen napkins.

"Señor Camp expects I bring his people food by the pool." She was smiling but her eyes were dead.

Robert nodded. "Yeah, they're movin' into the guest villas."

"The man's a yahoo, a fool," Emily protested.

"He got the press off my back."

"For ten lousy minutes."

Robert took a bite of a sandwich. "Give 'em some of these," he said to Maria.

Maria wiped her hands deliberately on her stained white apron. "Not so easy. The police, they stop our delivery. People from the market try to take pictures."

Robert lifted a fluted glass of iced tea. "Duke'll straighten it out."

He visualized the Amagansett market and thought about the kidnappers. They had to eat. They bought supplies. Food. Rope to tie up Doni.

The rapid clack of Libby's stout heels sounded on the marble floor. She ran in, breathless. "Pick up line six," she stammered. "It's the president."

A soft twilight rain pelted the windshield of the Chevette as Jack drove toward Southampton. There was nothing as depressing as a summer resort off season. All along the Montauk highway sad, rain-streaked signs advertised corn and fresh strawberries. A misty fog hung over the potato fields—boutique farmlands protected by local preservation committees.

Jack was pissed at Sherry for the fiancée nonsense. Now he had to prove to Ceci that he was single and unattached. Unfortunately, until the kidnapping story was resolved, Sherry served as his pipeline into the Shay household. She had already saved him hundreds of dreary phone calls chasing dead leads.

He turned left on to a quiet street of old brick buildings. He parked in front of the library and walked down to the Driver's Seat, a local hangout.

In the windows of white-shingled shops the emblems of wealth were blatantly displayed. There were enough duck decoys and hunting-dog placemats to stock ten English manor houses. Yet despite the abundance of pretentious Anglo artifacts, the neighborhood had changed. The town of old WASP money—hard-drinking Episcopalians in chauffeured station wagons—had been transformed into an East Coast Beverly Hills. Rolls Royces with curvaceous blondes now filled every other parking space.

Before the florist closed, Jack ordered a dozen red roses sent to Ceci's motel room. From there he ambled across the street to the restaurant where he found Sammy at a back table hunched over a steaming bowl of mussels. He caught a whiff of garlic broth as he sat down. "Where's everybody tonight?"

"Movin' in to private rentals," said Sammy. "They're rootin' in for a long stay."

The waitress appeared. Jack ordered a Heineken, mussels, and a hamburger.

"I took a shitload of pictures at the press conference." She nodded at the TV sets posted at the end of the bar. "God knows why. The public's saturated."

Jack watched her dissect another mussel.

"Want one?" she offered.

He declined. "Thanks to your cover shot Harrington upped the press run to five million copies."

"For fifteen minutes I'm a pig in shit." Sammy wiped her mouth with a napkin. "What are they doin' for an encore?"

"We, my dear," said Jack. "We."

"You." She winked at him. "I'm booked on United for LAX *mañana*."

"You're kiddin'."

"Nothin's happening," she said. "Let a New York bozo baby-sit the story. I've got cats to feed. And there's my gallery show on Main Street, remember?"

Jack had missed the Rice Gallery opening. The *L.A. Times* art critic gave her exhibition four stars.

"The owner expects me to make nice with the buyers," she said. "They expect to shake hands with the sensitive artiste who lensed the masterpiece."

Jack's food arrived. Each tureen of mussels came with a separate bowl for the empty shells. The table was gridlocked with plates. He yanked a hunk of bread from the warm loaf.

"By the way, the tabs have fresh dirt on Shay."

"Which one?"

"*Midnight Express*, I think."

Wormball Leggitt had failed to mention it.

Sammy tipped one of the shells to her mouth and noisily slurped the broth. "Why so quiet? You down?" she asked.

Jack focused on his food. He wasn't about to explain that Ceci McCann had her hooks in his soul.

"You plan on hangin' in?"

"Somethin' might pop."

"In that case I've heard about a nice house on Lumber Lane. Take a room. You'll get a working phone."

"No, no."

Sammy stared at him. "You wanna stay in Motel from Hell? Are you crackers?"

"It's best to stay put," he said absently. "Plenty of background work to be done."

Sammy smiled. Werts was conning her. He never activated his brain until three hours before his deadline.

When he saw the cellophane-wrapped roses on the counter in the motel office Jack froze. "Those are for Ceci McCann," he fumed at the clerk.

"That's a problem. Miss McCann checked out two hours ago."

"Where'd she go?"

The clerk exhaled dramatically. "You think I'm Houdini?"

As Jack turned away, he said, "She mentioned a flight to Los Angeles." Jack gave him a dirty look and pushed through the door.

"Mr. Werts, wait. Your flowers."

"Eat 'em," Jack called over his shoulder.

Back in his room he phoned Mara Stykes. She answered on the first ring. "You did a super job on the cover," she said. "Since when do you have FBI—"

He interrupted. "This place is BOR-ing. Release me."

"Have you flipped? You're writing history."

"I'm supposed to be on vacation," he complained. "Harrington's got a squadron of snoops cryin' to play ball."

Mara sighed audibly. "Werts, you're psycho. What do I tell Hairface?"

"Make up a rumor," said Jack. "Robert Shay's headin' for the Coast."

Late that same night in the flats of Beverly Hills Tommy Train sat naked on a cushioned pool chair. Under the glow of garden spotlights he rolled two joints, tight and hard. Factory-made, said his wife Tanya of his technique. An expert's opinion.

Before him on the patio table was a bottle of San Pellegrino mineral water. With the edge of his hand, he swept the spill of leftover grass onto a crumpled sheet of aluminum foil.

A rustle of leaves came from the bamboo forest that camouflaged the bedroom wing of the house. Lisa Proudfit emerged from the semi-darkness. The garden lights gave her whippet-thin body a ghostly whiteness. She appeared transparent except for the black patch between her long legs. Behind her, the oval pool glistened like an aquamarine jewel.

Tommy sucked in his guts as he took a long drag from the joint. His head lolled back over the metal rim of the chair. He stared into the hot, smoggy night. Two stars blinked back at him through the soupy air. "You wanna hit?" he called, not bothering to look at her.

She tossed a plush bath towel over the armrest. "Does the sun . . ."

He felt her soft fingers gently pry the joint from his.

"Fine dope, eh?"

He squinted at her through one eye. "It's decent, but you shoulda tried the shit Tanya brought home . . ."

Lisa kicked him in the shin with her bare foot. "Ingrate."

Tommy closed his eyes and listened to her inhale. She forced the joint back between his fingers. Her high-heeled sandals clacked against the flagstones as she walked to the pool. He finally looked over at her, a receding figure of frizzy black hair atop two symmetrical half-moons of flesh.

He studied the curliqued *T. T.* embossed on the border of the towel. Tomorrow he must call the contractors. He planned to have his initials embedded in gold tiles on the bottom of the pool.

Tommy's eyes focused on the gingerbread gazebo perched on the artificial hill at the far end of the property. Biggest fuckin' gazebo he had ever seen, big as a band shell at Disneyland. He bought the house because Tanya promised to throw grand Hollywood parties in the gazebo. He made the decision to spend three million bucks on those goddamn parties.

Lisa dove into the pool with a thin, clean splash. Tommy's eyes wandered to her naked body undulating through the translucent water. He took another hit, then quickly another.

The sky transformed into a reddish brown helmet. The shadowy palm fronds became flat black spiders that clung to the stucco walls of the house. He took another hit. It came. At last. The mood he craved. He was light years away. He savored the separation. Full and quiet.

"Suck dick," Lisa yelled from the pool. She laughed hard like a hooker. He remembered how he felt when he opened the front door and saw her in the skintight biker pants and zipper jacket.

Tommy staggered over to the ledge of the pool and dangled his legs in the water. Lisa's head emerged. Her hand slashed across the blue surface to splash his body with a fan of droplets. Wet fingers crawled along his arm searching for the remainder of the joint. "There's a roach clip in my purse," she said.

The water that sloshed against Tommy's ankles was too warm. Like the night. Like Lisa.

She placed his toes on her breasts. She slid her hands along the inner side of his thighs. He pulled away.

"Later," he said. He swallowed the tiny piece of leftover ash, then went to find the other joint.

"For Godsake, get your body in the Jacuzzi," she prodded.

The fresh drag gave him the jolt he sought. He wanted the charge again and again, rapid-fire like a cap pistol.

Lisa stood in the Jacuzzi and splashed like a windmill. "Tommy's a sissy," she yodeled.

Grudgingly he came over and slipped down into the bubbly pool. He held the joint high, away from the spitting surface. Lisa splashed at his side. She grabbed the joint from him and sucked it hard. Once, twice, three times.

"Hey."

She handed it back. "Next time, I'll bring my kilo," she said. "There's coke in my jacket, if you want."

He shook his head and settled on the concrete bench under the water. The jets forced his spine forward. When a headband of sweat formed on his brow he hoisted himself onto the ledge.

"You're such a putz."

Usually, Tommy liked the abusive lip she gave him. It served as verbal foreplay. But tonight he didn't have the energy to shut her up. He leaned back against a terra-cotta planter filled with tulips. His eyes flickered over her. She was off in a dreamy trance.

An itch began between his brain and cock. Yet he was unable to imagine how he wanted her. Greased? Spread-eagled? No, he was tired. Something simple and uncomplicated.

Lisa came up the steps and arched over him. Tears of water dripped from the shaved strip of wiry hair between her legs. "Gimme, selfish," she demanded. With her ass thrust out she leaned forward to take the dwindling joint.

As she inhaled, Tommy lunged at her with bared teeth. His mouth clamped down on her. Lisa immediately pressed the palms of her hands against the back of his head. She smashed his face deeper. "Can't we finish this in the bed?" she moaned.

Reclining in the canopied poster bed, Lisa surveyed the bedroom. She adored Tanya's taste in furniture. It was classic kink: red velvet settees, gold-embroidered armchairs, mahogany-framed mirrors. It reminded Lisa of East European porn films—low-budget versions of the Marquis de Sade where horny young men mounted passive, big-breasted women.

Even kinkier than the furniture was Tanya's collection of exotic vibrators. She had an ebony wand inlaid with ivory, from Africa. Lucite sticks with chrome heads, from West Germany. Chinese friction balls. A veritable hardware store.

And Tommy hardly noticed any of it.

Lisa smiled to herself. She predicted a divorce by Christmas.

Tommy emerged from his mirrored bathroom in a silk Dior robe with *T. T.* stitched in satin piping on the breast pocket. He always showered immediately after sex. Then came the forty push-ups. This evening, however, he fidgeted before the smoky mirrored panel against the wall. He stretched the skin above his eyelid. "How 'bout another tuck? This new doctor didn't snip enough. In a year, it'll hood like a reptile."

Lisa gave him a critical look. "Do it. I prefer taut. The 'natural look' is meaningless."

Before he joined her in bed, he pressed a lever on the floor. A painting of a female nude retracted to reveal a six-foot screen. The late news replayed Shay's press conference.

Lisa's stomach knotted with envy. She was livid at herself for passing up the assignment. Everyone in America was obsessed with Doni Shay. Even her delinquent son called from his reformatory for inside info.

"There's Snow White," said Tommy.

McCann rose to ask Shay a question.

Lisa scooted forward. "Shut up, I wanna hear."

"A nothin' question about the kid's dog, but nice promo for Sweet Lips."

Lisa couldn't take it. She swung her naked body around to block Tommy's view of the screen. She arched her back, the hard plum nipples of her small breasts aimed at him.

"Send me to East Hampton."

With his leg he pushed her aside. "You had your chance. Those who snooze, lose."

She crawled up to him. "C'mon. If prim-and-proper Pollyanna managed to squeeze this equestrian lady, I'd have found the kid by now."

His eyes skimmed over her crotch. "I prefer you stay where the action is."

"What action?"

"I'm the action."

Lisa's nostrils flared. "And suck my dick till Tanya comes home. Is that it?"

Tommy's eyes remained fixed on the tube. Three male reporters whistled and waved to get Shay's attention. The director stonewalled.

Lisa began to scratch the black belly hair above his cock. "Listen," she said. "I'm askin' straight, no bullshit, send me to East Hampton."

Tommy sighed. "What's to cover?"

"This Krugger guy," she said nodding at the screen. "I'll pull down the pants of the FBI."

"You'd screw that guy?" Tommy was vicariously interested.

Lisa ran her long nails over Tommy's ear and down his cheek to his mouth. "I'll sleep with anyone to get a story—or an assignment."

Lisa's m.o. bugged him. He wanted her off his back. "We need footage of Shay's office at Starlight."

Lisa's tongue fiddled in his ear. "I'll get it, doncha worry."

PART

II

12

It had been seventeen days since the kidnapping of Robert Shay's son, and Ceci McCann was on top of the world. Lying in her own bed at home in West Los Angeles in the early morning light, she finally felt proud of herself as a journalist. While the rest of the media rehashed tired information and reran old video clips, she had hit gold with her "Survivors of Kidnapping" series. True, the pace had been grueling—ten victims in seven different cities—but the results on tape were spectacular and she knew it.

Ceci gently pushed away the polished-cotton comforter and padded across the thick white carpet to the windows. She yanked the cord of the miniblinds, revealing a panoramic view of the Santa Monica mountains. She swiftly unbolted the sliding glass door and slipped out onto the terrace.

It was a smogless, cloudless October day. From the twenty-second floor she gazed down on the residential neighborhoods of Westwood and Bel Air. The hilly terrain was sprinkled with terracotta tiled roofs and turquoise swimming pools. Vivid splashes of fuchsia bougainvillea blossomed over walls and chain-link fences.

Ceci craned her neck to check the penthouse balcony of the high rise next door. It had become a morning ritual ever since Nelson Grinker told her that Johnny Carson lived there. Once a sultry blonde in a thong bikini and straw hat had emerged from the apartment. Possibly his wife, Alexis Mass.

This morning the balcony was deserted. Ceci stepped back a few feet and, holding the rail, did ten pliés, then a series of leg lifts. She raised her arms and twisted back and forth to loosen her stiff spine. The bones and muscles in her back popped like plastic packing bubbles. Plane flights were ruination.

After taking a long, soothing shower she rubbed her skin vigorously. The erratic schedule had caused her to lose weight. Her waist, now wasp thin, made her breasts appear even larger. She twirled around, observing herself in the mirror. If she changed her style of dress, turned up the volume a bit, she could wipe Lisa Proudfit off the map. But why change her style? Beverly Hills didn't need another frizzy-haired mermaid in lycra stretch pants.

She sighed unhappily. Her physical beauty was wasted unless she found a man to share it with. She thought about Jack Werts. The memory of his strong kisses sent a warm tingle over her flesh. But, like the actors she had dated, these male journalists were arrested adolescents, infants who refused to be adults and accept the responsibility of family life.

Even more unsettling was the fact that he turned out to be a con man, a liar who tried to get his last licks in before he settled into marriage. Pity that poor woman who planned to marry him. But then who knew? Maybe they were perfectly suited. She sounded like a nitwit.

Ceci brewed a pot of Jamaican coffee and watched the morning sun stream into the living room over the white marble fireplace, white leather sofas, and Lucite coffee table. One thing was certain: she wanted this luxury for the rest of her life.

She lifted a pile of mail from the counter—a fat American Express bill, notices from the gym, catalogs, and invitations to movie screenings. She had always kept her domestic life in order. For her, organization was the key to a happy life. This crazy week of travel had upset her methodical routines.

For this morning's videotaping she planned to wear her Calvin Klein box-shouldered jacket softened by a double helix of seed pearls. She'd shine, she knew it. This was her strength.

Lucky. Lucky. She kissed the back of her hand before she took a sip of the rich brown coffee. Finally, God had let her into the big league.

Charlene slathered a thick glob of yellow grease over Ceci's bare face. "Pore protector," she explained. With a handful of tissues she blotted away the excess.

A plastic bib was tucked into the neck of Ceci's blouse. She closed her eyes. Supervision was unnecessary. Charlene was the best. She knew when to stop.

Charlene unclipped her pearl earrings. They clattered against the Formica makeup table. "Pearls suit you. Very Grace Kelly."

Ceci sputtered through the corner of her mouth, "Faux pearls, very Barbara Bush." Two cool pads stung her eyelids. She melted into the soft leather of the barber chair.

"Jez moved her crew into an apartment across the street from Starlight Studios," said Charlene as she combed Ceci's hair back from her forehead. Jez was short for Jezebel, Lisa Proudfit's nickname among the support staff.

Ceci jerked forward.

"Don't move," Charlene barked.

Ceci felt the wet line of a fine brush traced along her eyelid. "When was this?"

"Yesterday. Same day Tommy took Julie Cordero home after work. You can bet those two didn't make cookies."

Cordero was the new secretary on the show. Her style was strictly North Beach leather.

"Why?"

Charlene nicked at Ceci's eyebrows with short, hard strokes. "The man requires sex like the rest of us breathe air." She rattled a bottle next to Ceci's ear as she talked. "Tommy's an exhibitionist. He gets his rocks off by fuckin' the help. It ensures a captive audience."

"Lisa'll be furious when she hears."

"You kiddin'? Jezebel loves soap operas. There's another sexual work of art."

"Well then, I guess I feel sorry for Cordero."

"Don't bother. She's the office pump. Even Shorty's been serviced."

"Really?" Shorty was so kind and fair to all the women on the show. Ceci never considered him to be particularly sexual.

"When the boys itch, Cordero provides a comfort station."

"What's in it for her?"

Charlene didn't answer. "The masterpiece is complete," she said. "Open sesame."

Ceci looked in the mirror. A pair of shadowed eyes stared back at her.

"Frosty platinum powder works nicely for you," said Charlene. She screwed on a few lids, then forged through a basket of bottles. Her harness of puka beads shimmied as she shook a jar of skin base. Using an organic sponge, she stroked the makeup over Ceci's skin.

"Any news on the kidnapping?" Ceci asked.

Charlene raised a stick of coral lipstick up before the row of makeup lights like a syringe. "You're a superstar," she said. "The ratings skyrocketed. Tommy slated 'Survivors' for another week. He nixed Wright's interview with Kim Basinger."

Shorty bounced in, a clipboard under his arm, and pitched a freshly mimeographed script to Ceci. He spoke rapidly. The closer to air time the more impatient he became with the English language. "The intro launches the second half of the show. Veil's on twelve minutes. Tommy closes." He paused. "Tomorrow, you and Mitch will open the phones." The revised schedule meant that Ceci was on air all week.

Before exiting, Shorty flashed Charlene a hangdog smile. He nudged her affectionately with his elbow. "Make her beautiful. The kid here, she's good."

Ceci sat erect at the anchor desk. Three banks of studio lights ignited in a burst of white. In front of her, giant black letters began to roll silently down the teleprompter. When the first sentence hit the arrow cue Ceci began to read in a loud, honey-smooth voice.

Her eyes remained frozen as she followed the script. She never analyzed the content or imagined an audience of viewers beyond the letters. What she saw was the faintly reflected silhouette of her own face transporting the sounds expertly defined by her mouth.

The script moved at a comfortable pace, neither too fast nor too slow. After a few seconds, she hit her stride. The whole process became effortless, as natural as walking over evenly spaced lines in the sidewalk.

When Ceci had first learned to read from the teleprompter she had been troubled by an involuntary tic in her right eye. To cure the annoying defect, she forced herself to stare wide-eyed into three 100-watt bulbs for an hour each day. The exercise had enabled her to regulate the rate of her blinks under the searing camera lights.

Ceci lowered her voice as the arrow cue flagged the end of the script. She cut the final phrase dramatically, her eyes drilled straight ahead until the red light in the camera blinked off.

"*Wunderbar!*" boomed Shorty's voice from the control booth.

Ceci unclasped the button mike from her lapel and crossed into the fishbowl, a glass-partitioned rec room adjacent to the studio.

This large space always seemed to have been visited by a tornado. Chairs faced every direction. Coffee cups and food wrappers littered the tables. She opened the communal fridge and claimed the last diet Coke. Behind her, Nelson Grinker balanced precariously in a chair tilted back against the wall. Between bites of sandwich he glanced up at the monitor suspended from the ceiling where Ceci's taped interview with Madeline Veil, a fifty-eight-year-old kidnapping victim from Des Moines, replayed continuously.

"You win the brass ring for this," he called out to her. Ceci turned around and looked at the screen. Madeline sat next to a ceramic donkey-cart vase filled with philadendrons. She clutched a tissue to her nose as she retold the sordid details of her abduction fifty years ago.

The camera effectively highlighted Veil's tremors. The sack of fat under her chin jiggled, and choked breaths interrupted the woman's ragged voice. ". . . I cried for months. I wished I was dead. I had been raised as a Catholic. I truly believed that if I died I'd meet my parents in heaven so one night I tried to kill myself with a shard of glass I found in the yard . . ."

A close-up caught the tears brimming in Madeline's sad eyes. Then the camera pulled back to include McCann in the shot. Ceci examined herself critically. The red suit looked crisp and fresh. Her hair, however, was dry as straw. She needed a cut-and-oil treatment.

From across the room, Grinker hummed Joe Cocker's "You Are So Beautiful." Ceci dismissed him with a smirk. The office clown. A likable smartass.

"We'd save mega bucks if we stocked a few tear tracks," he said with a broad grin. He hurled a folded newspaper at her. "Did you see this?"

Ceci caught the paper and opened it. Robert Shay's picture was on the front page, his arm around a slim woman with straight black hair parted in the middle. SON KIDNAPPED WHILE ACTOR FROLICS WITH TOP MODEL, the headline screamed.

Ceci stumbled over to the nearest chair and sat down to scrutinize the photo. Shay's windblown hair was unfashionably long, and a two-day stubble grew on his face. He only vaguely resembled the man she had seen at the press conference. The caption below the photo read: BOBBIE'S A MANIAC IN BED SAYS MADISON COLE. Ceci turned the page. Shay and Cole walked arm in arm down a country road: VERY MUCH IN LOVE LAST SUMMER IN EAST HAMPTON.

There were two more photos of Madison Cole. In one she wore a sequined couture jacket. The other was a nude shot cropped strategically above her nipples. EX-*PENTHOUSE* PET SAYS SHAY TOLD HER NUDE SCENES RUINED HER FILM CAREER.

The final photograph was blurred. It was a foggy picture of an unidentifiable man and woman entangled on a hotel balcony: SHAY AND COLE RENDEZVOUS AT JET-SET RESORT IN MARBELLA.

"Quality trash, eh?" Grinker said with a laugh.

"You don't buy it, do you?" Ceci replied. "Anyway, who cares about this nonsense? It makes Shay into a depraved man. An uncaring father."

Grinker shot Ceci a skeptical look. "*We* care. 'Invasion of privacy' is our motto."

Grinker's wisecracks irritated her. The relentless one-liners precluded serious conversation.

"By next week 'Survivors' will be sucked dry," he said, focusing on the monitor. "We'll be desperate for fresh blood. Every booker in TV land has already called Madison Cole. The tramp can name her price."

Ceci glanced back at Madeline on screen displaying her scrapbook for the camera. Yellowed newspaper clips showed a chubby, myopic girl in the arms of her smiling parents. Ceci had seen the edited tape three times already. Shorty had done an excellent job. She considered what Grinker said about Madison Cole. She'd be pissed if this pseudo-model knocked any of her survivors off the air.

She began to read the tabloid. Buried under the gush of "they were very much in love" was a chronological account of Shay's affair. Several of Cole's girlfriends were quoted. Their predictions ran in favor of Shay ditching his wife for the model.

Grinker watched Ceci devour the gossip rag. "Hey, I'm sure Shorty's lookin' for volunteers to investigate Miss Cole."

Ceci gave him a disgusted look. "Forget it."

Joe Krugger had moved his FBI command post from the solarium to a thirty-thousand-foot chamber in the basement of the Shays' East Hampton mansion. Night and day a dozen agents scanned computer screens linked up with FBI and CIA data banks throughout the world. A special team of forensic experts had been flown in from Washington to analyze minuscule fragments of auto paint, wood, and cotton extracted with tweezers from the sandy lanes that dead-ended near the house. Another team spent four days excavating fresh tire prints in an attempt to identify the getaway vehicle.

Massive FBI computers were hooked into the data banks of local real-estate offices. Agents painstakingly scanned thousands of listings, searching for residential properties leased or rented within the last year. The credit and tax status of each new resident was carefully checked. The slightest irregularity was immediately coded and sent to Washington. In the last three days Krugger's agents had inadvertently uncovered the secret hideout of a Colombian drug czar as well as an elaborate money-laundering operation supported by offshore banks in the Cayman Islands.

Every phone call to the Shay mansion was recorded and each caller was taped and his location determined. A team of experts listened for particular speech patterns, local accents, or any other vital information that might distinguish the authentic kidnappers from the bluffers. Meanwhile, a team of handwriting analysts pored over volumes of letters that had come to the house.

During the last week Robert had spent all his waking hours in the basement command post. In the past he had often concentrated on learning about a subject to ensure the accuracy of his films. Now he took on the FBI's research-and-statistics division in much the same way except that in this case his diligence could possibly mean life or death for his son.

This morning he found Krugger and a radio technician hunched over a bank of radar screens. The agent swung around immediately and guided Robert to a dark corridor lined with rows of crisscrossed walnut wine holders. From the back of the basement Robert could hear the faint strains of *Don Giovanni*.

"Two teams in the field have been activated," said Krugger with a wintry smile. "Yesterday we had credible 'sightings' in Nantucket and East Lansing. Both reports were of towheaded youngsters matching Donald's description. Neighbors say the first child is being hidden in a barn by a deranged female. The second child was identified by the owner of a trailer park. Apparently the baby boy appeared just hours after Donald's abduction. The suspicious couple vanished the next day."

Robert smiled dubiously. He knew better than to get excited. So far, all of Krugger's 'credible sightings' had fizzled on follow-up investigation.

"I don't get it. Why don't they speak out? Why don't they make contact?" Robert asked.

Krugger looked pensive. "Their operation may have backfired." He fidgeted. "We can find the bastards without their making contact. We're getting closer every day."

A panicky expression shadowed Robert's face. He felt ill. Had he foolishly given Krugger too much control? Had he stupidly interpreted his ambition and slick jargon for intelligence?

Morgan and Trixie were at lunch poolside, under the shade of an oversize pink canvas umbrella. "Certainly, I'll tell him to do the interview," Camp purred into a remote phone. His eyes widened at Robert's approach. "Catch you later," he said as he swiftly shoved down the antenna. The plastic console bounced onto the pink concrete beside his barrel chair.

"Sorry I'm late," Shay apologized. He unzipped his yellow windbreaker and tugged it over his head. The fall day was unseasonably warm, in the high seventies with barely a whisper of wind.

Trixie hastily began to clear a place at the table. She squared a pile of *Hollywood Reporters* and dropped them into her straw beach bag. Camp was diligently mopping up his plate with a crusty piece of French bread. A carafe of hazy green olive oil and a bowl of arugula heralded the next course. Behind him, an uncorked bottle of Rodedere Cristal rested in a silver bucket. His stubby fingers choked the neck of the frosty champagne bottle as he poured Robert a glass. "If you won't do the morning shows, I will," he said, screwing the bottle back down into the ice. "This Cole broad's catnip to the media. We've got to counter her story."

Robert half listened as his eyes wandered over the turquoise pool and the pink sand garden dotted with bronzed cactus sculptures. A perfect mix of David Hockney colors.

"Smart people work for you," said Camp. "Libby's sharp, right?"

Robert lifted his fluted champagne glass. "Very."

"Then listen to her. She's nicknamed Krugger 'Mr. Malathion.' "

Robert laughed. Trixie allowed herself an airtight smile. It was difficult to find her face under the horn-rim glasses, thick red lipstick, and spiky auburn hair. Her Partonesque body, however, was impossible to ignore. She was amply stuffed into a puckered white halter and matching slacks.

Camp puffed up like a bullfrog. "The guy's a limp prick. He's a stats-happy accountant, not a cop. I've never seen anything like it. You ask him for directions and he gives you the equation for an ax murderer."

Camp lifted his arms in supplication. One wing sleeve of his silk robe dragged across a bowl of tartar sauce. "Robert, you and I are performers, showmen, communicators. Doni's kidnappers want cash. Whether or not you appear on *The Today Show* makes no difference to them." He dropped his arms with a flourish. "In the meantime your sterling reputation is being destroyed by the likes of this Madison Cole."

Camp tore off a chunk of bread and stuffed it into his mouth. "Perceptions, Robert, perceptions. You've slipped from the prince of Hollywood to the playboy of Hollywood." He swiftly gurgled down a swig of the expensive champagne. His roving eye halted on Robert again. "Who's she anyway?"

"I honestly don't know."

Camp spoke between mouthfuls of salad. "That happens."

Robert grabbed Camp's arm roughly, his pale blue eyes drilling into the publicist's doughy face. "I know exactly who I've been with. This woman wasn't among them."

A nervous twitch upset the corner of Camp's mouth as he quickly backpedaled. "That's all the more reason to appear on *The Today Show*. Or, if you prefer, give a short print interview. *Time* and *Newsweek* are beggin' on hands and knees."

Robert lifted his glass. "Right now, Krugger's clones are interrogating the lady," he said irritably.

"Where does she live?" Trixie asked.

"Malibu." He looked up as Libby rushed over to them from the pool house annex.

"Sarah's in the UCLA hospital," she announced breathlessly. "She overdosed on sleeping pills last night." She gave Camp a stern look. "That's off the record."

Robert felt terrible. He knew that Sarah had been depressed. After repeated polygraph tests, her results were still inconclusive; she had been unable to eat and couldn't stop crying. Over Krugger's objections Libby had sent her home for a few days' visit with her parents.

"Those tests are a crock," said Camp, pouring another round of champagne. "The questions are ludicrous. My needle hopped and wagged . . ." He halted, his pink mouth open, searching for a word.

"Fibrillation," supplied Trixie.

"Yeah, fibrillation," he repeated with gusto. "It was a scene outta *Hellzapoppin'*." He gulped the champagne compulsively.

Trixie's persimmon nails beat a tattoo on his chubby wrist. "Remember your blood sugar, sweetie."

"Sarah got real shaky after those tests," said Libby. She pulled a Filofax from the pocket of her plaid jacket and jotted a phone number on a color-coded page. "The stress put her over the edge."

"Is she gonna make it?" asked Robert softly.

Libby frowned. "She's a basket case psychologically. Krugger's gestapo tactics landed her in the hospital. Sarah's hauling enough guilt without his adding to her misery. To think they once electrocuted people on the basis of those stupid tests."

"It all depends on what you ate for breakfast," Morgan interjected. "I passed with flying colors."

Libby gave him a bum smile. "My point."

Camp looked puzzled.

Libby's eyes bore into Robert's. "From the start I told you that Krugger's grandstanding would get us into trouble. His double-oh-seven routine is infantile. All that techie talk—'We've calculated Doni's whereabouts with heat sensors'—it's patently absurd. Any dullard knows Doni was taken away by either a car or a boat. Brainchild still hasn't managed to figure out which. I've never seen such an inefficient bunch of cretins."

Libby refused to let up. "After I passed my lie-detector test, Krugger handed me a copy of the secret bible on kidnapping. Like I was now one of the club. Later I find out it's his Ph.D. thesis."

Robert had flipped through the massive tome a week before.

"After two thousand pages of graphs, charts, and convoluted research he concludes that kidnappers seize victims from their own socioethnic group."

"What about Patti Hearst?" Camp asked.

"Exactly," said Libby grimly. "The Symbionese Liberation Army was hardly your average Hillsborough family." Fired up, she reached for Shay's glass and helped herself to his champagne. "If you follow Krugger's cockamamy projections the only likely person to have kidnapped Doni is Robert Redford. A Ouija board makes more sense."

Camp raised his glass. "A toast to Mr. Redford."

"Swank, you're drunk," said Libby sarcastically. She examined the label on the champagne bottle. "An expensive binge, I might add."

For the first time in a week Robert listened attentively to their comments about Krugger. He still didn't have the heart to tell them that their phone lines were tapped and their cars and bedrooms bugged. His thoughts returned to Sarah. Krugger would probably maintain that her suicide attempt was a ruse.

"That spook's too anal," Morgan croaked. "Cops don't dress so nice." He slipped on a pair of heavy-framed Gucci sunglasses, then tilted his head back. "That TV show *Wanted Dead or Alive* is catching criminals faster than the FBI." The opaque black lenses were focused on Robert. "Television can work for us if we use it."

"Hold off a bit longer. If we don't get word in three days, I might reconsider."

In Los Angeles that afternoon the westbound traffic on Sunset stood paralyzed. Hundreds of captive drivers stared blankly into the haze of carbon monoxide as motionless rubber tires expanded against the simmering asphalt.

Jack Werts plunged his hand into the box of CDs on the front seat of the Wrangler. He slid Tom Waits into the deck.

Earlier he had made the mistake of visiting the *Newsmakers* office in Century City. The moment he sprawled out on Mara Stykes's sofa Tom Harrington phoned from New York apoplectic over the *Midnight Express* story. With a raspy gasp, the nervous editor upped Jack's salary to one hundred grand, then rudely ordered him to interview Madison Cole for next week's cover. If Cole balked, Jack was authorized to offer cash.

Jack visualized Harrington's lackey editors scrambling about like a herd of Keystone cops when the Cole story broke. Any publication that snagged a follow-up interview with Cole would score a newsstand coup. But Jack also knew that Bill Leggitt's byline meant the story was spun sugar. Strictly clip and paste. Harrington, like the rest, bought the phantom model because he was desperate for a peg to get the kidnapping on the cover again. He was a bottom-line boy.

The traffic began to inch forward. Jack switched to the left lane. It was bumper tag to the Beverly Glen turnoff. A doe-eyed blonde behind the wheel of a white 190SL caught his eye. She smiled at him. With a flip of her hand, she snapped her hair over her tawny bare shoulders. Flirty. Jack grinned back at her. He hugged the fender of the Caddy in front of him to keep up with her. But the Caddy braked abruptly. Meanwhile the sassy Mercedes zipped away.

As he drove up Beverly Glen he thought about the blonde.

Something about her reminded him of Ceci McCann, an ephemeral quality, the fleeting tease. As Tom Waits wailed on about sad barrooms filled with broken hearts, Jack's intense desire for Ceci returned. He sighed aloud, thinking about her lush lips. It had been a long time since a woman's absence had made his groin ache. Unfortunately, the attraction wasn't mutual. He had left three messages for her at NTN, all ignored.

On Mulholland Drive the traffic finally cleared. Jack hit the accelerator. To his right the evening sky darkened over the San Fernando Valley, the panoramic view jarringly interrupted by brown cliffs of thirsty tumbleweed. He braked to a slow roll at the blue-tiled wall that safeguarded Barbra Streisand's house, then cut a sharp right into his rutted driveway. "Damn," he moaned.

The sorry red Studebaker parked in front of the garage meant Sherry Cox was fifty bucks richer. Yesterday, on the phone, he bet against her junk heap climbing the mountain.

The kitchen was empty. A strange, sickly-sweet odor came from the stove. Jack opened the oven door. A blistered chocolate blob ballooned over a rectangular cake pan. He snapped off the gas. Sherry's idea of a birthday cake, no doubt.

An array of wax cardboard containers from Chin-Chin lined the sink. Bait boxes of low-cal chop suey to celebrate his forty-third birthday. Over on the butcher-block cutting board sat a huge bowl of fresh-cut broccoli—Sherry's chow. The thought of her industrious jaw chomping on the raw vegetables drove him to the cupboard for a drink. Cutty and soda. Three swallows, he drained the glass. He poured himself another.

From above came the soft drone of the network news. Jack climbed the creaky back stairs two at a time. The bedroom door was ajar. Sherry was fast asleep under the fluorescent glow of the television set. Her tan arm hugged a pillow, the rumpled sheets twisted about her leg. He slipped into bed next to her.

Then, suddenly, much like being hit by falling debris, Jack realized Ceci McCann was directly in front of him. He sat bolt upright. A head-on close-up of her flawless face dominated the TV screen. Her piercing blue eyes penetrated his. In an announcer-perfect voice she said:

". . . According to our panel of psychiatrists, a child's complete separation from his family creates the most intense fear known in the human species. The child's ability to comprehend reality is severely disturbed by . . ."

McCann was a woman in control, her shoulders back, chin raised, unflinching eyes challenging the viewer. She was magnificent on screen, mature beyond her years, a unique combination of strength and vulnerability. He turned up the volume.

". . . We visited Madeline Veil fifty years after her abduction. Despite a thirty-year marriage and two loving children, Madeline is still haunted by the memory of her captors, John and Betty Doyle. The couple was apprehended in 1940 by Nevada State police two months after little Madeline was found in a Nevada bus station.

"John Doyle died in prison. Betty, now eighty-eight, is bedridden in a Salem, Oregon, nursing home. Every Christmas Madeline receives a card from her. Betty writes 'Dear Daughter' above the greeting. . . ."

Behind Jack, Sherry slid a warm leg around his waist and gently tugged him to her. Absently, he took her slim ankle in his hand and held it, his total attention directed at the screen.

The camera zeroed in on Ceci, who now sat on a floral sofa opposite the grossly obese Madeline Veil. Jack was riveted. He hunched forward. Ceci was Miss Compassionate. Her pleading eyes encouraged Veil to speak.

"I thought you hated trash TV," Sherry drawled as she rubbed the sleep from her eyes with the back of her hand.

"I lied," he said automatically. His eyes remained fixed on the screen.

Sherry jumped him like a playful kitten. Her naked body was glued to his back while she nipped at his ear. "I've a delish surprise for your birthday," she cooed. Her hand slid under his shirt.

"Terrific, babe, that's just terrific." He twisted back and gave her a cursory kiss on the cheek.

She released him. "What's with you?"

"Huh? Let's watch," he mumbled in a detached tone, his attention on the screen.

Sherry peered at him. What was going on? This was very peculiar behavior. No greeting, no deep kisses? Jack never behaved this way. He was an attacker, Jack the Ripper. Especially if she was stark naked. Christ, he hadn't slept with her for over two weeks.

A commercial for McDonald's supplanted the Veil interview.

As if a bell clanged, Jack turned around and grabbed her, clutching her naked body to him, all on fast forward. But the moment the commercial ended, he was once again riveted to the screen. "C'mon. Let's watch," he said to her over his shoulder.

"Boy, is this a switch." She scooted over to be next to him. "And you're the one who accuses me of watchin' junk."

As Madeline Veil resumed the story of her kidnapping, tears washed down her swollen cheeks. It was sad, a bit hokey, Sherry thought. Jack, however, seemed mesmerized by the woman's plight.

Sherry refused to play dead. She scuttled over his lap on all fours. Her agile fingers unzipped his jeans, a surefire way to get his attention.

But Jack continued to stare at Madeline Veil with a drugged, lunatic expression on his face.

Sherry anchored her mouth in his groin. To her complete surprise, he was already rock hard. Who could figure men out? Crouched forward, she applied her lips while she massaged the base of his shaft with her fingertips.

As the camera switched over to a close-up of Ceci, Jack's heart took a leap and, without warning, his cock flexed. Sherry took in a mouthful of milky broth.

Her face intruded between his and the television.

He smiled at her weakly. "Oh, Sherry . . . you, thanks. That was great. Just terrific." He gave her breast a perfunctory squeeze. Toothpaste tubes got more passion, Sherry thought.

"Who'd you think it was?" she asked. She lay back on the bed. Well, she could play it cool too. Ladylike, she folded her hands on her flat tummy.

A commercial for Security Pacific Bank came on, and suddenly Jack's hands were stroking her breasts. He was warm as toast, giddy with happiness.

The man must be ill, Sherry decided. His behavior was too weird.

"You're fantastic," he said. He kissed her lips hard, then asked, almost clinically, "How often do you watch this show?"

"Every day. Tommy's my favorite." She wondered, however, if she would be so enthusiastic about the show in the future.

"How long have these kidnapped victims been running?"

"Two days," she replied. "Yesterday Mitch interviewed a gay Marine."

"Who's Mitch?"

"Look!"

Tommy Train walked onto the high-tech set. Behind him were three retractable screens and an electronic map of the United States. A digital billboard pulsated: " 'Survivors of Kidnapping' produced by Mitch Creed and Ceci McCann." Ceci and a handsome black man appeared live on two screens.

"Eddie Murphy bends like a licorice stick next to Mitch Creed," said Sherry. "The tabs claim he gets more fan mail than any black on TV. Even more than Cosby."

"How can you who work for Morgan Camp trust what you read?" said Jack. But his eyes were on Train. He had only seen newspaper pictures of the talk-show host. He was surprised the man was so damn good-looking. Hip chestnut-brown Armani suit. Tarzan build. Olive complexion. A full head of copper hair that rivaled Donahue's.

But Train was jumpy. Possibly the DTs, Jack thought. There was a continuous change of facial expression, like weather in the tropics. His remarks were glib, crass, unfunny, his choppy monologue that of a local low-rent deejay.

"Who's this Bo-Bo he's yakking about?" Jack asked.

"The show's mascot. A fifty-six-pound kitty that won the fat cat contest." Sherry giggled at her little joke.

On the wall behind Train the electronic map of the United States suddenly beamed red. "Here's the fun part," said Sherry. "Phonathon!"

Train bobbed and weaved before the map like a weather man. Rays of lightning pulsated from the outline of a tiny telephone located somewhere in Iowa. Everywhere were little visual tricks to keep the viewer occupied.

"Hello, Des Moines!" Tommy bellowed.

"My name is John," said a disembodied voice. The phone flashed continuously while the caller was on the air.

"Shoot, John," said Tommy. He spun around dramatically, then tilted his head.

"I am. Right into your face."

There was the sound of a loud disconnect.

Tommy looked somberly into the camera. "Johnny, my boy. Go to the corner and buy yourself a stroke magazine . . ." Before he finished, another phone pulsated in northern California.

"Go ahead, Stockton!" yelled Train with a barker's enthusiasm. His show-biz style was strictly game show.

"Hi, Tommy," a female voice swooned. "I'm Alice. I love you and loooove your show."

"Thanks, Alice," he said graciously. "Now, honey, what can we do for you today?"

"Did the kidnapped lady want to murder Betty Doyle? String up the old lady?"

Tommy liked the question.

"The Doyles were thrown in jail. They served twenty-year sentences. If Madeline Veil ever wanted to kill them she couldn't get to them."

A phone bleeped in Florida. "Tallahassee," said Tommy.

"Fuck you." A burst of childish laughter followed the greeting. Disconnect.

Jack figured there was time enough for two words to be said on air before the caller got axed. "Prime time and this guy doesn't screen calls?"

"That's what makes this show fun," said Sherry. "Teenagers love him. Morgan credits Tommy with the best demographics in America."

"Detroit, Michigan," Tommy barked.

A void of silence. "Are you there, Detroit?"

A gargly cough and then a drunken male voice stuttered: "I got Doni Shay. I got the baby."

Train froze, his eyes leveled at the camera. "What's your name?"

Loud, raspy breathing. "Clem. Yeah, Clem's my name."

"Good, Clem." Train lowered his voice an octave. His tone became chatty, down home. "If you've got the baby, what are you doing with him?"

Another pause. "Smackin' him around a bit."

"Clem, that's real kind of you. Do you expect to get money for the boy?"

A pause. "Yeah." A deep cough. "I want a billion bucks from that actor."

"If you reduced your ransom you'd probably have more of a chance," said Train. Then he abruptly shifted gears. "What are you gonna do with the money, Clem? Take a trip to Mexico?"

"Naw. I'm gonna hire my buddies to blow the—bleep—head off my boss. I hate the SOB."

"Thanks, Clem," said Train. "You've been divine."

130

Jack marveled at Train's detached, emotionless style, given his penchant for high histrionics.

"Mystic, Connecticut."

An elderly female caller said calmly: "Mr. Train, you're a blight on this nation . . ."

Rapid disconnect. Train smiled at the camera, cocky, full of bravado. "Lady, put a postage stamp on your nose and send yourself to a forest fire."

Sherry roared with laughter.

Jack looked stricken. The country was doomed if this was what the younger generation applauded. "Train's crazy, mad."

Sherry nuzzled against him. "Tommy's camp. Don't be such a deadbeat sourpuss. You're just jealous 'cause he's cuter and younger."

"The guy's over fifty."

"Thirty-five max."

The credits for the show rolled. From what Jack had seen, Ceci's interview was the closest the show came to normalcy. Perhaps he was out of touch. Just because he bedded younger women didn't necessarily mean he understood them.

Doni liked to sit alongside Rita in the front seat of the truck. Once again they passed by rows of houses. Whenever the houses changed to tall buildings she would stop and make him climb into the back.

Tonight she drove the truck into a big yard. When they got out she made him get into the back. Then she locked the back door. The glass was dark. Doni couldn't see outside. The hair hat was heavy so he put his head down on the floor.

After a long time, Rita returned. "Get out," she commanded. Doni stayed close beside her. They entered a small house, almost a dollhouse, and went into a room. He had been in many rooms like this one. There was a bed in the middle. But then he saw this room was different. In the corner by the bathroom there was a half-room with a little bed. For him.

Sometimes she would go out and return with a hamburger. Sometimes she talked to him after she removed the hair hat from his head. Other nights, she had tied him to the bed and put a ball of paper in his mouth. She did this before she went away.

He liked it best when she stayed in the room and they watched television together. He liked the sounds and color. As long as she didn't tie him up he was happy. Tonight she didn't leave. Instead, she turned on the television. Then she walked to the mirror and said to herself, "Fucking asshole. Why doesn't the stooge call?"

Her eyes were like the points that his pencil made on paper. She checked her watch and looked at him with a face that was as red as his fire truck.

The phone rang and she said "Hello" right away; then she said, "Where's the money?"

Doni turned back to the television set. He had heard her ask for money before.

With the phone in her hand she reached over and punched the button. The TV died. "Now, I can hear you," she said into the phone. "Yeah, I mailed the tape this morning. Of course, I put enough stamps on it."

Doni looked at a brown spider that crawled over his yellow dress. Many times Rita had told him he was a girl and his name was Tina. But Doni knew he was a boy. He jumped and caught the spider.

"I waited at that damn window for two hours," she shouted into the phone. "The cashier refused to accept the code." She listened for a long time. Then she screamed, "I've done my share of the work. I'm taking the risks while you sit on your fat ass. I've got thirty-seven dollars. If I don't get some support soon, this game's over."

She banged the phone down. She ran into the bathroom then came back to fetch the things she used to fix her hair. She had lots of hair, very black. Like the hair she made him wear every day.

"I can't stand these dinky towns. I'm tired of touring the back roads of America. I'm goin' to go find myself a hunk of flesh and blood. Some dance music and a line or two of coke. Y'know what coke is, kid?"

Doni shook his head.

"I bet you're lying. At those fancy parties there's plenty of coke. Only the highest-quality coke for the stars. My dealer, she sold to Richard Pryor. I bet you didn't know that."

When she finished fixing her hair she flopped on the bed and started to cry. Doni didn't move. From the corner of her eye, she saw him watching her. "What are you lookin' at?"

His eyes dropped to the spider in his hand. It crawled around his finger and started to climb up his arm.

The woman was angry. She banged an ashtray against the table. Before she opened the door, she stopped. "If you cry or try to leave this room, you'll never go home. Stay put, understand?"

The door slammed and the room became very dark. Doni ran back to the small bed near the bathroom. Only once before did he have his own bed.

Finally, he fell asleep.

He woke when two loud voices broke into his dream. It was Rita and a man he did not know. Lights filled the rooms. She rushed to him and lifted the blanket over his head. "Don't move," she whispered. "Leave this bed and I'll kill you."

Doni heard a gurgle of water being poured into a glass. The man had a big laugh like a bear. A roar. Because Doni was hungry, he left the bed and peeked around the corner.

The man was naked. There were tufts of black hair on his back. He had a glass in one hand, a bottle in the other. The woman put her glass in front of the bottle. He tipped the bottle. She sang a song. Doni jumped back because she turned toward the bathroom.

Doni wanted the man to see him. But he was afraid to run out because the woman would hit him. Once when she got really mad, she had slapped him on the head.

The man talked and laughed. The lights went out. There was a yellow glow from the windows. Doni watched a giant black shadow cross the wall as the man climbed over the bed. For a long time, the bed bumped against the wall. The woman squealed and shrieked many times. The man groaned. It was quiet again. Then came the gurgle of the water. More talk until Doni heard the man's steps coming toward him. But the man didn't see him and continued into the bathroom. He shut the door hard.

Doni felt Rita's hand on the blanket. "I'll beat the living daylights outta you if you utter so much as a burp," she warned. "Don't move under there."

Suddenly, the door opened.

"What's that?" asked the man.

She was naked, kneeling down beside the bed. Doni kicked his legs under the blanket. He knew the man could see he was there.

"My daughter," said Rita.

"You said you were alone." The man went back in and flushed the toilet. "She must have heard us goin' at it."

"That doesn't matter," she said. "Come back to bed." Doni listened to their footsteps walk away.

"It sure as hell does matter," said the man. "It's not good for her to hear her mother screwin' a stranger. I coulda got us another cottage, next door."

They continued to talk softly. Funny noises. They sounded happy together.

Then the man's voice grew. "Here's my office number. Call me if you decide to stay over."

"Sure thing," she said.

The door closed.

Doni pushed the blanket away with his hand. She was peeing in the bathroom. A cigarette hung from her lips. She tossed the cigarette into the tub. "You can't appreciate this, kid, but I just scored with an Iowa State Trooper."

13

Robert Shay jerked awake to a piercing blade of sunlight. He immediately rolled over to access the microcomputer embedded in the chrome headboard. The tiny screen was black.

His head collapsed into the satin pillows. He was exhausted. He had spent over half the night lying awake worrying about Doni. If money were the motive the kidnappers would have made contact. Every FBI file indicated that ransom demands were made quickly. Only in political kidnappings did the waiting time extend to months.

He was riddled with fear, convinced now that the motive was political. Why else the delay? He rose up on his elbow and tapped his code number into the keyboard. Chicki had already left a list of messages: Libby was meeting with Starlight's tax accountants in Manhattan; Harry had started shooting at the Federal Court building; Lee Mack had phoned three times. A red light bleeped next to the console. Robert pressed the intercom.

Chicki's voice came from the concealed microphone in the ceiling. "Malathion wants to see you. New info. Very secret." Then she laughed. "For some mysterious reason he brought me a batch of Maria's freshly baked croissants. Probably 'cause I'm the only one who acknowledges his existence."

Robert ran his hand over his hollow stomach. "Tell him I'll be in the basement in ten minutes."

The half-inch spool of tape on the recording machine began to unwind. Shay secured the earphones. Krugger leaned against the cinderblock wall, his leg crossed like a male model's, a gloating, self-satisfied expression on his face.

Robert identified the voices immediately:

—Emmy, it's late. My God, it's three A.M.

—I know, but I had to talk to you. I'm in such pain. I wish you were with me.

—I'm always with you.

—At times I'm so frightened. I feel terribly alone. The ground caves in. . . . I need to escape this prison. I have to fly out and see you . . . for a day, an hour.

—Emmy, you can't. A bearded reporter's been hangin' round the front of the house. It's damn creepy. A female's been callin'. Askin' funny questions.

—We've been so discreet.

—Folks talk. Most of 'em don't mean no harm, they just jabber. An' you're too pretty to be a buddy of mine. In my youth I fathered the offspring of some foxy fillies. That ol' rep sticks like shit to a shoe. We look like what we are.

—Yes. Even Robert knows.

—You best handle that.

—It's difficult. He blows at the slightest provocation. He made a dumb decision when he allowed these yokels to invade our home. Meanwhile he rants at me like a maniac. The only thing he hasn't mentioned is his work. Doni's abduction has replaced his obsession with filmmaking. Isn't that the ultimate irony.

—Is he botherin' you?

—No, no. His guilt has paralyzed him. But I realize what a mistake my marrying him was. We never worked well together. His needs are taken care of by "his team." He doesn't need a wife, he requires an army—and a variety of toy females for sex. What's crazy is that I didn't have to marry him in the first place. I could have given birth to Doni and been done with it.

—Emmy, you've rehashed this a hundred times. Let go. Doni's your fella.

—Reiss suggested electroshock again.

—Stay away from that stuff.

—I know. Your faith in me is better.

—Us ol' alchies are good for spreadin' grace. I been doin' a lot of prayin' lately.

—Are you slipping?

—Naw, I ain't chasin' the bottle. It's Doni, baby. I'm worried about Doni.

—Yes, yes. I wake up at night screaming. I'm scared. I'm sure the FBI's got a glory agenda that involves heroics.

—I can fly out. I got friends in Sag Harbor.

—No, not yet. Reiss says if you're around it will just give Robert an excuse to redirect his guilt into anger at me. He still can't believe I could fall in love with someone else. His ego's that big.

—Emmy, calm down. Remember who loves you. Who's head of your fan club.

—Just hearing your voice helps me so much.

—Remember, baby, I'm here for you.

—We'll talk again.

—Soon.

Robert lifted the headset from his ears and placed it on the table. Seething jealousy boiled up, constricting the back of his throat. "Where does Ventura live?" he asked steadily, willfully controlling his voice.

Krugger sat down in the swivel chair next to him. "Venice Beach."

"The soulful country yarn's a crock," Robert muttered. "The guy hasn't had a decent record since the seventies. His career's over."

Krugger wheeled his chair over to the computer screen and called up a file. "According to *Billboard* magazine his latest album, *Barefoot Alley*, is a modest success."

Robert cursed softly. "Never heard of it."

Krugger turned from the screen and faced Robert. "We did an exhaustive search. He's been surprisingly clean since the Memphis bus accident that killed two members of his band. He's off booze and drugs. Attends AA meetings three times a week. There're no women in his life—except for your wife."

Robert's face reddened. He could barely manage to contain his rage. He slammed his fist into his open palm. "What about money? The guy's gotta have debts."

"Nothing's outstanding. He owns a three-bedroom bungalow on the beachfront. A ten-acre spread in Louisiana. He pays hefty tuition bills for six kids. And, seemingly for charitable reasons, he supports a blind banjo teacher in Nashville."

Krugger switched off the computer. "Emily lied to us, however." His eyes aimed at Robert. "She said Reno never met Doni. This conversation indicates otherwise."

"Investigate those friends of his in Sag Harbor," said Robert curtly.

"We are," said Krugger. He stood up. His voice dropped, his

demeanor cold as ice. "There's another matter. Chicki let it slip that Emily's mother had been committed. You're not leveling with us."

"It's past history," snapped Robert. "The old lady's dead."

The California sun slowly burned its way through the morning coastal fog that hung over Malibu Colony.

"It's astounding how your old girlfriends always come in handy," Sammy said to Jack as they drove past the gated guard booth. Her pink sun visor read: Masters Tournament, Augusta, Georgia, 1984. The tails of an unbuttoned jean shirt hung out over Jack's floral jammers. They looked like they had accidentally bounced off the back of a tourist bus.

A visitor's pass rested against the dashboard of the Wrangler.

Seen from the back, the row of famous beachfront homes was unimpressive, merely a line of cramped garages built too close together, townhouse style. Upon careful inspection, however, it became evident that special care had been taken with every inch of space. Bonsai trees, tended by Japanese gardeners, grew along the courtyard walls. Imported Italian quartz paved the short driveways. The trash buckets, made of top-grade vinyl, had brass clamps for the lids.

Jack parked in front of Crystal Harbison's house. She was an ex-lover who now lived off the spoils of her third divorce. Sammy immediately lifted a blue-and-white Styrofoam cooler from the floor. Two loaded Nikons with four telephoto lenses were inside.

"Hold it, Zippo," Jack cautioned as he surveyed the street for the security patrol.

"Why?" Sammy said impatiently. "Let's stretch our bods next to a spicy Bloody Mary on the deck. Knowing Crystal, she'll have scoped every male in ten miles. She'll have the dirt on her neighbor Mr. Sheffield and his buddy Madison."

Jack hesitated. "I, uh . . . I've got some bad news."

Typical. Sammy braced herself. "Hit me with it."

"Crystal's in Australia."

"Who cleared us?"

"I said I was Sal, her houseboy." Jack slid into the sophomoric Serbo-Croatian accent he reverted to when he was smashed: "Guest passes pleeese for Mr. Werrrrs and his ladeee friend."

"Nifty. So where's Sal? He knows you."

"With Crystal. On a cashmere goat ranch outside Melbourne. The house is sealed tight as a drum."

"Shit, Jack," Sammy groaned. "We need a base to work from."

"Naw, this'll be a quickie."

They drove down the street to Sheffield's house. It was a Pueblo-style box with wood-beamed windows half a block north of Larry Hagman's. A banged-up Dodge Dart was parked in the driveway.

Sammy smiled smugly. "You plan a frontal attack? Ding-dong. Hiya, Madison. Wanna tell *Newsmakers* the lurid details of your affair with Robert Shay?"

Jack squinted at a brown-and-tan patrol car driving toward them. It was every hour on the hour with these guys.

"Get out," he said. A patio door next to Sheffield's house was open.

"Into the jaws of a Doberman," Sammy cracked.

The security patrol slowed down. The officer watched them suspiciously. Jack gave the officer a mock salute.

"Don't overdo it," Sammy hissed under her breath.

They sauntered into the courtyard and closed the gate behind them. The patrol car drove past.

Sammy blinked hard. Around them was a Hansel-and-Gretel fairy-tale world. A stone cottage strangled with ivy sat on a carpet of green moss. Jack leapt onto a pedestaled birdbath and peered into the garden next door. "Two men. Eating bacon and eggs," he reported. "She might be on the front deck."

A major renovation was underway down the block. Piles of lumber were being delivered by flatbed trucks. Sammy hummed a few bars of "Zip A Dee Doo Dah" and with a blasé look on her face headed toward the construction site. Jack followed. In seconds they unfurled their blankets on Malibu Colony's private beachfront.

Jack took a deep breath of the salty air while Sammy stripped down to a fuchsia bikini. She slathered the pale skin of her taut, muscular body with SPF 50. Jack removed his shirt and lay down on the blanket next to her. "How 'bout a civilized expense-account lunch at Ivy by the Shore?" he suggested.

"Suits me fine."

Eyes closed against the hot sun, Jack joyfully began to practice Zen and the art of silent sex with Ceci McCann until his libidinal dream was interrupted by the echo of voices. The approaching men were from Sheffield's yard, one lean and anemic-looking, the other tall. The woman with them had long black hair parted down the middle and hollow cheeks. She was considerably older. His age.

"Are we lucky or what?" Sammy said. The methodical whirrr-click from her fat zoom lens buzzed in his ear.

"Why's she in a one-piece? We get a bonus for buttons."

"Buttons?"

"Belly buttons," she explained. "Harrington runs at least three an issue."

"Don't get sunburned." Jack jumped up and loped down the beach after the threesome. Just as he caught up with them, the trio abruptly pirouetted. The emaciated man kicked a fan of water at Madison Cole. She stooped and slapped two handfuls of the foamy surf across his white shirt. The other man remained serious, unwilling to frolic. Jack could hear patches of conversation. Both men spoke with lower-class British accents, possibly East End.

After they passed by him, Jack swung around slowly. From the blanket, Sammy waved: she was packed, dressed, and ready to leave. Jack knew how she hated the sun.

"Run by me again who this dude Sheffield is," said Jack. They were parked diagonally across from his garage. Sammy polished the lens of her Nikon with a yellow chamois. She kept her equipment in top working order. Her exacting perfectionism drove Jack bats.

"A has-been Brit designer," she said. "Viking furniture, tropical interiors. He ran with the Eurotrash crowd in New York. He's opened up a shop on Doheny, probably to cash in on the Asian market."

Sammy loaded her camera. She studied the trash bins in the driveway. "Recycled garbage, I can relate to that. If worse comes to . . ."

"Last resort only," Jack protested. "Once was enough." They chuckled together at the mutual memory of rooting through John Belushi's trash barrels on Martha's Vineyard looking for evidence of prescription drugs. Coffee grounds, which adhered to every slip of paper, had made the task particularly nauseating.

Before they had time to discuss it further, Madison Cole skipped through the back gate. She climbed into the Dodge and headed for the Pacific Coast highway. Jack tailed her at a respectable distance. A half-mile down the road she turned into the Hughes Market parking lot.

"Bump-cart time," said Jack.

Sammy had strapped a camera to her chest. "I'll be in the bushes, tweetie pie."

139

Inside the supermarket Jack uncoupled a wire shopping cart. He found Cole at the end of a wide aisle in conversation with a pinched-faced butcher. Jack casually shuffled through the lamb chops in the open freezer next to them. Up close, she had leathery, sun-dried skin. Webs of wrinkles circled her eyes. Fleshy thighs had been poured into sharkskin pants. She had a cheap, secondhand look.

The butcher rubbed his hand against her back, then told her to wait as he banged through the swinging doors. He returned with a wrapped package. She thanked him, dropped it in her cart, and rattled on down the aisle.

Jack only used direct assault at zero hour. The thaw-and-charm method was more reliable. The idea was to get as much information as possible before you dropped the A-bomb and revealed your identity. That instant, the store's manager, a suspicious man in a blue dacron shirt with a "Welcome" button, strolled by. Jack quickly grabbed six jumbo boxes of Pampers from the shelf. The manager appeared relieved. A half-dressed man zooming up and down the aisles with an empty cart could mean anything.

By the time Jack turned around, Cole had vanished. He found her at the checkout reading the *Star*. He glanced over her shoulder at the horoscope page. "Amazing how accurate it is," he said cheerfully.

His most effective anonymous pickup technique was to stare ardently at his victim, then tell her she was the spitting image of his dead sister. Most women fell for it. Clearly, the horoscope line didn't have the same effect. Cole hardly stirred. After she placed a carton of orange juice on the conveyor belt, she said, "Once in a great while they're right."

The lady was strictly slow mo.

Jack helped her unload her groceries. She pulled a twenty from her billfold. No visible identification cards.

"Can I buy you a drink?" he asked as she pocketed her change.

"Why sure," she said too eagerly. "The Malibu Inn, down the highway." Jack lifted her shopping bag and followed her out of the store.

"Hey, mister, what about your groceries?" the cashier shouted after him. The pile of Pampers was left unattended in the cart.

"Wrong color," Jack called back.

"Another wacko," remarked the cashier.

"That's exactly why Letterman makes sense," commented a middle-aged surfer on line.

The Malibu Inn was a dank seaside dive. The Beach Boys blared from the jukebox and peanut shells covered the floor. The smell of stale beer and wet bathing suits wafted through a jungle of neon signs and pinball machines.

From the moment Madison Cole sat down, she annoyed the hell out of Jack. She bummed a Marlboro from him, then yelled to the bartender for a White Russian. Models never drank White Russians.

In ten minutes he had her number. She was an over-the-hill hooker loaded with warpaint and bloated with self-importance. If Cole was ever a model, it was decades ago, before the cadaverous hollows under her eyes had developed. Robert Shay could do much better than this.

"You don't strike me as a guy who believes in horoscopes," she said. Jack took in her cloudy eyes, nicotine-stained fingers, the liver spots on the back of her trembling hands. She was coming off something.

"What do I strike you as?"

"A guy who likes football, plays the horses."

Jack exhaled a curl of blue smoke. The clock was ticking. He decided to level. "I'm an investigative reporter for *Newsmakers* magazine." He recited his script. "I need an hour with you, taped. We'd like some photographs."

Cole took a sip of her drink. Her eyes cruised the dark barroom.

He continued his sales pitch. "I can offer you four to six pages. Your words." For sure, her own words. The story had to run in the confession section to preclude challenging witnesses or conflicting accounts.

"That cheap article made me into a loser," she said. "I've got a promising movie career. I didn't like that guy Leggitt. But he paid up front, two grand."

Jack caught a whiff of the rank stench of greed. He studied her chewed-off fingernails as she tapped her cigarette against the tin ashtray. "Robert Shay and I were real close," she confided smugly. "I was part of a party crowd. Those East Coast boys are real nice." Her eyes settled on Jack's lips, then moved up to his eyes in an attempt to be coy. "I've got the details, down to the mole on his ass. I know what he eats for breakfast, what cologne he uses, what shaving lotion, even condoms." Jack felt her knee under the table. Her fingers slipped over his thigh. "The *Penthouse* Pet spread is always the first thing the press brings up about me. Maybe you can change that."

"I can." Jack removed a tape recorder from his pocket. "Let's start."

"Wait."

Now came the hard sell.

"Mr. Bates from the *Tattler* offered two hundred fifty thousand for an exclusive."

Jack didn't blink at the tidy sum. He opted to play in order to test how far things had gone. It was hard to believe this sexual opportunist was the subject of a bidding war. He mashed out his cigarette and beckoned the bartender for another round. "Is there anyone else?" he asked.

"*Exposé* magazine offered one hundred fifty thousand," she said with a practiced smile. "Hart publishers quoted four hundred with a movie tie-in."

Jack saw through her. She wanted to appear a crafty bargainer. She had lifted a few new phrases from each prospective buyer.

"That's more than *Newsmakers* ever pays," he lied. Just last year Harrington had shelled out half a million for the dummied diaries of a rock star. "Why don't you grab the Hart offer?"

Madison was unnerved. She had expected him to fight for the rights to her story. "I, uh . . . they're slow," she said. "Doni Shay might be returned by then."

Jack agreed sympathetically. One of her suitors had explained a story's shelf life to her. If she had any smarts she would liquidate her pack of lies fast. Her media marketability lost value with every passing minute.

"I've got other demands," she said.

Jack listened politely.

"I expect two grand for a dress allowance. Herb Rowen for the photographs. Don Riccidi to do my makeup. José Venda, in Beverly Hills, to style my hair."

Jack chuckled at the absurdity of her requests. Madison sounded like Barbra Streisand negotiating the details of her album cover.

The media was salivating after this woman without examining the validity of her story. It was understandable to offer Donna Rice or Marla Maples a few hundred thousand. Their relationships had been documented. But Madison Cole's story was based on a disreputable tabloid. The sums quoted, if true, were idiotic.

Jack drained his beer. "I've got to talk to my editors in New York," he said. "I'll get back to you."

She scratched her number on the corner of the cocktail napkin. Before he stood up she leaned forward and squeezed his arm. "Remember, you'll get first rights."

Upstairs in the library of his East Hampton mansion, Shay poured himself a drink. Pepper vodka straight. He walked over to the window and stared at the silver-gray horizon and inky black sea. He was furious, ready to explode. He knew exactly when the rift in his marriage began. It started with separate offices. Then separate secretaries and staffs. Then came separate closets and bathrooms. Finally, separate bedrooms. He remembered when Emily had exchanged her wedding band for a Cartier cougar ring. Was that possibly a gift from Reno? Robert had never thought to ask.

It was true that from the start they never attempted to have a conventional marriage. And after Doni's birth there had been a further loosening of the bonds—"creative freedom," they rationalized. Still, in a business where marriage vows were easily broken, they had somehow remained together. Looks, wealth, and power had made both of them sexual targets for ambitious men and women. Several screenwriters had even tried to seduce Emily in order to get their scripts delivered to Robert. In some cases the machinations were laughable.

Early on, they tolerated each other's short love affairs. They even joked about "the perks of the profession." Eventually, however, their schedules—three months at work on films in remote locations with a host of sexually willing partners—took a toll.

Still, in Robert's mind the marriage was never doomed because Doni was a magnet that always brought them back together. The child had a healing effect. He loved them both so much. He was more than the sum of their two parts. He incorporated the very best traits of both of them. For his sake, they had not divorced. For him, they had even tried to conceive another child.

Robert stared vacantly at the rows of screenplays bound in expensive leather covers. The starlets and actresses had meant nothing to him. He had never fallen in love with any of them. Nor had he ever had the time or energy to provide the kind of companionship that they demanded. His marriage had provided the perfect excuse.

In the past he never dwelt on Emily's affairs because he knew instinctively that Doni and her work always came first. Now when he thought about Reno Ventura he exploded with anger. Head of her fan club? How dare he? Robert swigged down the last inch of warm vodka. This wimpy country-western singer had no right to his wife.

He found Emily's maid, Nina, on a pink concrete bench in front of the spa pavilion beside the pool house. The young girl was apathetically tossing handfuls of croutons at a cluster of hungry sparrows.

Inside the dome-shaped building it was hot and humid. Narrow windows in the thick granite walls allowed slivers of daylight to filter through the steamy air. Robert circled the Jacuzzi built like a fountain in the center of the tiled rotunda. A thick cloud of vapor hung over the roiling water. He checked the steam room. Light shone from the rectangular window but the misty chamber was empty. He walked down the Italian-tiled corridor until he came to the massage room.

Emily lay naked on a long narrow table, a terry towel draped over the cheeks of her ass. Robert recognized the masseur. He was the young aerobics instructor from Gurney's Inn who came to the house daily to give Chicki rubdowns. A wispy rat's tail of hair hung down the back of his neck. His strong arms curled over Emily's long, slender back as his oiled fingers pressed into the hollows of her spine.

Shay approached quietly. "I'll take over," he said. The young man disappeared from the room.

At the sound of his voice Emily reared up on her elbows. Wet strands of loosely pinned hair fell down along her neck. The corner of her mouth twitched. She gave him a nasty look, then dropped back down, her forehead resting on her crossed arms. "What's this about?" she asked in a distant, depersonalized tone of voice.

Robert stared down at her supple body. Under the glow of the topaz light a slick puddle of almond oil glistened in the small of her back. Beads of perspiration rolled from the flawless white skin of her shoulder blades. His eyes skimmed over her lithe torso, high hips, and long ballerina legs. Then, without warning, he suddenly gripped her waxed calf muscle. He swiftly slid his hand along the inside of her thigh and slipped it under the towel into the crevice between her buttocks.

Her body snapped like a whip. She twisted onto her side and sat upright facing him, her knees pulled up to her large breasts. Robert studied the fine, tapered fingers of her left hand. "Where's your wedding ring?"

"I rarely wear jewelry." She looked disturbed.

Robert inched his fingers up her shinbone to her knee. With his other hand he lifted her chin to study her face in the dim light. He stood silently, staring at her.

"What is it?" she asked belligerently.

"A wedding band sends the wrong signals?"

Her eyes filled with scornful dismissal. She twisted her face away from his grasp. "I don't begrudge you sex with other women," she said harshly. "Don't accuse me of whoring."

At that moment Robert felt great waves of hatred, jealousy, and love course through his body. He took a deep breath and exhaled deliberately. In a detached voice he said, "You are my wife, after all."

As Robert reached for her, Emily swiftly scooted back to the end of the table. He grabbed her roughly by the ankles and pulled her to him, his strong hands easily pinning her down. She fell back, completely exposed. He took in the whisper of dark hair between her legs, the plum brown nipples.

"To what do I owe this lechery?" She laughed almost hysterically. "Isn't it rather late in the game to be claiming your conjugal rights?"

Robert unbuckled his belt and unzipped his pants. He ripped off his clothes.

Emily took in the size of his erection, the mockery gone from her face. She made an attempt to escape, but Robert tackled her around the waist and threw her lithe body back onto the table. He hunched over and mounted her, straddling her hips with his strong, muscular thighs. His greedy fingers kneaded her big breasts, rotating the nipples between his thumb and forefinger. His tongue filled her mouth while his fingers moved from her breasts and slid under her, digging into the flesh of her ass. Rage boiled up in him. "If Reno Ventura comes near you," he growled in her ear, "I'll kill him."

Emily turned her head away from him.

Robert swiftly locked her wrists together over her head with one hand while the other slid down her small rounded belly. Her body tensed. Every muscle resisted his entry. "Stop this, Robert," she pleaded. "Stop."

For a brief moment their eyes met. Her blazing violet eyes mocked him. "I'm in love with Reno," she blurted. "Can't you understand that?"

A furious rage blasted through Robert. He silenced her with his mouth, biting her lips hard as he entered her. He rode her violently, his cock hammering her body, forcing her to arch and buckle. He wanted to kill her with his force, tear her beautiful body to shreds, possess her completely.

But Emily was strong in her protest. She squeezed his trunk with her thighs and savagely scratched the skin of his back with her nails. "Get off me, you bastard," she screamed. "Let me go."

As she rose up under him, his hand tangled in her hair. He yanked her head back with a sudden motion and kissed her throat, then bit her neck and shoulders. She screamed and spit at him, fire in her eyes. She twisted, trying to wriggle away. Each time, his arms caught her and held her down to the pounding thrusts of his cock.

Then, suddenly, a deep shudder ran the length of her body. As if a bell had sounded, her resistance vanished. With a surprise turnabout she challenged him at full force. Her velvet tongue pressed into the back of his throat. Her legs clamped around him like a vise. When her violent spasms locked together with his, Robert exploded.

Spent, he lay on top of her, his mind empty. Finally, he lifted himself up over her and shook his head like a wet dog. His sweat trickled down in rivulets over her body.

He stared at her: the trembling limbs, hard nipples, and flushed cheeks. She was more beautiful than ever. She shifted, a wry half-smile on her face. "I believe you're jealous."

"What if I am?"

His wet fingers ran over her full lips bruised from his love-making. He stroked her cheek softly. Her eyelids fluttered down. He rose up on his knees and gently traced his fingertips over her body until his hand planted itself in the wetness between her legs.

"Robert, no," she protested. "That's unnecessary."

With a circular motion he began to rub the palm of his hand against her mound. He found her tangy sweetness with his mouth. Again, she protested, but under the touch of his tongue her pliant body responded helplessly, then sparked in a succession of sharp spasms. As she whimpered and moaned Robert slipped inside her. This time he smothered her mouth with kisses and braked often, holding back.

Later, as their bodies settled apart, a dreamy look filled Emily's faraway eyes. "Hooray for Hollywood," she whispered softly. Robert stared at her and braced himself for a barrage of sarcasm. But she remained silent. Finally, she mumbled, "At least we're in sync on some level."

"Wait a minute," Sammy said to Jack as they whizzed south down Pacific Coast Highway. "I gotta get this straight. You want me to offer these snaps of Madison Cole on the open market. Anonymously."

"Exactly," Jack replied as he swerved into the middle lane. A row of yellow blinking arrows warned that the highway narrowed. A pile of debris had slipped from the steep embankment on the left side of the road.

Sammy glanced up at Big Rock. Multimillion-dollar homes now hovered on the scenic rim. Through the window she watched a scrawny female fight against the whipping ocean spray as she jogged along the beach.

"Meanwhile, you're going to tell Mara that Madam X doesn't exist," she said, turning to him. "Abracadabra, she's vanished."

"You got it."

Sammy studied his profile. "Essentially, we'll totally deny this story."

"That's the game plan."

"But why? Why not level? Let Mara know the low-rent bitch is an opportunistic faker. Cole's hardly the first."

"Because the pressure from Harrington is too intense. He'll force Mara to spill the details. If he gets the faintest notion that Cole's ready to play ball, he'll fork over a bundle of cash to her lickety-split."

Jack glanced in the rearview mirror and switched back to the fast lane. "Cole's itchy. If I can stall the deal she'll sell her fairy tale to another magazine. Look at it this way. We've done Harrington a favor. We saved him a million bucks."

"Faulty logic," Sammy replied. "Madison Cole's puss on *Newsmakers* stimulates sales. What's a measly million up against twenty?"

Sammy peered at the parade of cars waiting to park at Gladstone's restaurant, tourists after front-row seats for the sunset. They were bound to be disappointed. It was too damp an evening to slurp Mai Tais on the terrace.

She stared at Jack curiously. "What I don't get is this do-good behavior of yours. You suddenly find God or something?" Before he could respond, she said, "What proof have you that Shay didn't fuck this greedy cash machine?"

"Zero proof. But if he did fuck her, so what? Why should this bimbo jerk us around with ridiculous demands? Why is she allowed to capitalize? Harrington's desperate enough to give her maximum exposure. A *Newsmakers* cover seals her credibility. Even reputable TV shows will book her. I can't stomach it."

They rode in silence down Wilshire Boulevard. At Fourteenth Street Jack turned north and stopped across from Cafe Montana. Sammy's red Toyota Supra was parked at the curb.

"Okay, big boy. If ever I'm quizzed about Madison Cole, I'm deaf 'n' dumb." A look of confusion lingered. "But I still don't get why this story? You've offered big bucks for birdseed before."

Jack removed his sunglasses and checked the scratches on the plastic lenses. "I told you," he said thoughtfully. "I've decided to clean up my act."

"Bonzo!" she declared. "And put us outta business." She hopped out of the jeep and zipped across the street to her car. "Bye, bye, Toots," she called out to him as she U-turned in the intersection.

As he drove home, Jack reflected on the afternoon. He had encountered plenty of phonies over the years, many of them celebrities who fed him polished, practiced stories loaded with hyperbole and outright lies. But even the sleazebags, the ones totally unconcerned about the reputations of the people they maligned, worried over their own public image.

What bothered him about Madison Cole was her lack of self-worth. She saw herself as not having a reputation to care about. And for a buck she was eager to take anyone else down with her.

The line had to be drawn somewhere. If Harrington discovered that he derailed the story it would probably cost him his job, but this time he didn't care. He had made enough sleazoid deals to fill a lifetime. He had polished up an endless number of celebrities so they appeared smart and kindly when in fact they were crass, mean-spirited neanderthals. Most famous people had major ego problems, their desire for fame fueled by deep-seated inadequacies. The closer you got to these media machines, the more you saw their bizarre complexes and self-created loneliness.

Granted, Ceci McCann and her sweet naïveté had something to do with his current state of mind. When he was first out of the gate, the thrill of the chase had challenged him too. Back then, he took great pride in exposing the origins of small-time corruption in Providence, Rhode Island. Unfortunately, the bright lights of Manhattan and a chance to write for a national magazine had seduced him.

He had to admit that he switched to the show-biz beat because of the women. Lunch at the Bel Air Hotel with Morgan Fairchild proved to be more stimulating than a hot dog at Nathan's with some grimy prosecutor from city hall. But Jack was acutely aware that the coverage of Hollywood stories differed from that of hard news. Serious journalism grew out of civic and community concerns; show-biz reporting was purely a commercial enterprise, a way to increase profits and rating points.

And the greed knew no limits. A money-mad culture controlled the news organizations. The concern for in-depth reporting had been replaced by sound bites. Television offered celebrities an open forum for self-promotion. Criticism vanished. Stars shamelessly praised themselves to the hilt. Hollywood celebrities had become America's saints canonized by the media.

Meanwhile the public was being fed scads of dull, often incorrect trivia. Fictitious blather passed as the truth. So what could he do about this, Jack asked himself. Keep Madison Cole off the cover of *Newsmakers* for starters. Bring back sensible values.

As his mind raced he watched a raucous gang of seniors head toward the Sizzler steakhouse for the early-bird special. He felt a great desire to get his life in order before he joined their ranks. Maybe it was time he married a decent woman and raised a few kids—properly. After all, the next generation was going to have to pick up the pieces.

14

From the corner of her eye Ceci saw Shorty enter the fishbowl with Stan Lutz. At the same time the cameraman to her left gave her a twenty-second warning by crossing his arms twice. She held an alert position, prepared to sign off.

Mitch spoke rapidly into camera one, answering a question from a female caller from Boston. "Our research indicates that only 20 percent of children kidnapped by strangers find their way home. Three percent of the children are murdered by their captors. In many cases, however, the bodies are not found."

Ceci's eyes followed camera two as it swiftly rolled back for a wide-angle shot.

"Thanks, Mitch. Thanks, Ceci," said Tommy. He hunched forward, his eyes straight ahead on camera three. "A quick announcement, folks. For the last five nights *The Tommy Train Show* has been the highest-rated prime-time news show on television. It's a landmark for us and we can only thank *you*—our fans." In a booming pep-talk tone he exclaimed: "Stay with us and keep those calls coming! America wants to hear America speaking! Tommy Train loves you!"

A montage of the Golden Gate Bridge, the Statue of Liberty, the Grand Canyon, and Disneyland exploded across the electronic billboard, accompanied by the show's theme, an upbeat bugle roll.

Ceci watched as the red light in camera two flickered and faded. In seconds, the overhead lights came on. A round of scattered applause erupted from a gaggle of well-wishers. Ceci saw Lutz give Tommy a high five. Technicians clambered onto the set. Grinker held out his hand to help her down. "Dracula might have given you two a plug," he whispered.

Ceci flashed him a pained look. She was grateful to have been on air for three successive days.

Tommy bounced from the set and tossed his jacket to his secretary. He loosened his tie as he listened intently to Lutz. The beleaguered network chief rattled off the latest ratings points. After a series of vicious firings at the top of NTN's hierarchy, the task of turning the cattlecar around had fallen on his shoulders. Tommy was his ticket.

For an entertainment executive, Stan Lutz was decidedly unslick. He was a pudgy-faced, middle-aged man with wavy marmalade hair and sallow, greenish skin. His American-made suits never properly fit his portly frame. But his looks didn't stop ambitious women at the network from flirting with him outrageously. Only his wife, Beverly, a 100-pound hellcat intent on pushing her hubby to higher and higher levels of success, was a deterrent.

Shorty Smith joined Lutz and Train, with a thin, beak-nosed man in tow. As Smith introduced Bill Leggitt to the gang, Ceci noted the diamond-and-onyx ring on Leggitt's baby finger. The man dressed like a croupier. Although exceedingly friendly to Grinker, Leggitt dismissed Ceci with an imperious, "you're-pretty-but-irrelevant" smile.

Mitch tapped her on the arm. "Dracula's ordered us to his chambers," he said softly.

"A raise?" she asked as she followed him out the door.

Mitch grunted. "More likely, his preacher routine."

Tommy's office was set up like a classroom. Three rows of empty chairs faced his desk. "Come in," he called out. He was naked except for a purple jockstrap. Ceci averted her eyes from the bulge at his crotch. The gold Cartier dog tags around his neck clanged noisily as he turned away with studied slowness to put on his jeans.

Mitch took a chair. Ceci leaned against the wall and studied a giant tubular tree wrapped in clear plastic, a gift from a fan.

"Ever see one of those monsters before?" Tommy asked salaciously as he yanked a silk T-shirt over his bare chest.

Ceci shook her head. His friendliness made her uncomfortable. She was painfully aware of how dowdy her navy blue jacket and wrinkled madras skirt must appear to him.

"It's a pencil cactus," he said. "Ugly critter but very valuable."

Mitch sighed heavily. He disapproved of Tommy's predictable come-on in the presence of a female.

"Relax, kids," said Train, attempting to cut the tension. "It's a social visit."

He packed while he spoke. Into a Gucci satchel went a shaving kit and leather appointment book. He snapped the buckles. "From now on, you two and the new guy—Leggitt—will handle Shay's personal life." He put a pair of kidskin loafers into a plastic Cerruti bag. He tilted his head in their direction. "If some real news doesn't break soon, we'll have to mimic the tabs, get down and dirty."

Mitch stared at Train as if he had a deadly virus. This approach wasn't going down well with him.

Tommy studied him as he tied his shoelaces. "It's our only choice, Mitch. The FBI won't cooperate. Just sit down with Leggitt and powwow." He spritzed himself with cologne. "I'm still amazed that 'Survivors' captured the public the way it did. These gimmicks work, so use your imaginations. Concoct any harebrained, offbeat angle you can."

Dismissed, Mitch headed for the door. He was incensed. Ceci knew he had expected some time off to spend with his fiancée.

Tommy summoned her before she could leave. His deep brown eyes were warm. "I've got tickets for a smash dinner party tonight at the Hilton. You care to tag along?"

"Er . . . yes, of course," she stuttered.

"My chauffeur will fetch you at six."

There was a formal politeness in his tone. Ceci had never witnessed this side of Tommy. Certainly he had never been very cordial to her.

"And, Sweet Lips," he added, "be a dear and spiff up. Show a little leg. Burn those shrouds you wear on the show."

"Come outta there."

Doni lifted his head from the floor of the truck. He crawled to the door. Rita grabbed his arm and swung him down past the big fender.

He saw grass. Giant trees and mountains. There were no cars, people, or houses anywhere. He was very happy when she closed the door and let him stay outside.

She stared at him. "Your hair's a mess."

With her hand she pulled the hair hat off. He rubbed his hands over his head. He felt fuzzy bumps. They hurt. The air was cool. It felt much better without the hair hat.

"I've got to fix this rag." She held it in her hand and went around to the front of the truck. Doni followed the soft shushing sound her dress made as she walked.

She took a big paper bag from the front seat. Doni didn't get to sit in front anymore. Not even at night. He missed watching the round lights from the other cars. He hated the back of the truck.

She handed him a blanket and then carried the bag over to a tree. "C'mon," she said. She took the blanket from him and opened it. The grass underneath was squishy. It smelled wet. Doni saw a butterfly. He started to run after it but tripped on his dress.

"Hey, klutz. C'mere."

Doni came back to her. She sat in the middle of the blanket. "You've gotta be hungry."

"Yes," he said softly.

"Yes, what?"

"Yes, Rita." She wanted him to say Mommy, but he wouldn't. She gave him a square box anyway.

Every day they ate the same food. But this time there was more. Her hand crashed around in the bag. "You're gettin' too thin," she said. "I brought you a treat. Oreos!"

Doni had never seen black cookies. Maria always baked brown cookies. Rita took a black circle and separated it. She ran her tongue over the soft white center. "I used to love these," she said.

He tried to do the same thing but the cookie crumbled in his hand. Still, it tasted very good. She then gave him part of the hamburger. It was different. He had to chew it like bubble gum. From another bag she pulled a tall bottle. "Chablis for me," she said.

She drank a lot from the bottle and then took a cigarette from the deep pocket in her skirt. Doni watched her light it with a wood stick and drop the box of sticks down on the blanket. He knew those sticks started fires. Big fires. Those fires burned down the houses in the hills around his house. Sarah taught him not to play with those sticks. Rita didn't seem to be worried about them.

She lay down on the blanket and smoked the cigarette like she was eating it. It smelled sweet like cherries. She treated it special. Doni moved away from her. Sarah said cigarettes were bad for you. They made you die.

He crawled away from the blanket, then got up and ran over to some big rocks. It was very cold but he didn't care. He was happy to be outside of the truck. The grass was deep around the rocks. There were blue flowers. Like stars. And small red buttons that popped in his hand. He ate one. It was good. He found a big stick. Tiny white bugs ran back and forth over the end. He started to hit the stick against the rocks.

"Butch, be still," she called from the blanket. But she didn't get up. He looked over at her from the rocks.

"Stop acting dopey," she said.

A white butterfly landed on his stick. His hand opened slowly above it. He caught it by the wings and turned it upside down. Its legs were like short hairs on his arms. They wiggled in the wind. He took it to her.

She pulled away like she was afraid. "What's that?"

He held the butterfly near her and let go. It flew away. Pretty white powder was left on his fingers.

"Stop trying to scare me," she said. She lay down. Her arms stretched over her head. Her feet rubbed against each other. She smiled and then closed her eyes. She was happy.

Doni looked up into the branches of the tree. Light came through in different directions. Birds talked to each other. A fuzzy tail moved. Doni got up to see better. The fuzzy tail rolled into a ball.

A frog croaked. Another. They were in the rocks. Behind the rocks he found a big puddle of water. He picked up a tiny green turtle. It went inside when he tapped its house. He put it in his pocket and climbed the hill.

From the top Doni saw silver trucks zoom back and forth between the trees. Cars, too. He could run there. But the trucks were big and might hit him. He knew not to play in the street. He turned around and ran back. He slipped, fell, and tumbled down the hill. It was great fun. At the bottom he found a wish flower. He filled his cheeks like a balloon and wished for his daddy, mommy, and Snickers. If you didn't blow hard enough it didn't work so he blew as hard as he ever blew. The fuzz filled the air.

When he came back to the blanket Rita lifted her head. "My God, what time is it?" She yawned and rubbed her eyes. "Look at you. You're filthy. What are those green stains on your tights?"

Doni looked at his legs. He didn't see any green.

She looked tired. "This is the shits, kid. I haven't got a penny and I'm supposed to slick you up like a Barbie doll."

She crumpled up the bag. "Never listen to men," she said. "Every one of them is trouble." She shook her head. Her black hair fell down over her eyes.

The old Chevy Impala hissed and bumped its way along Montauk highway. Robert Shay was curled up like a shrimp inside the closed trunk. Through a gash in the floorboards over the rear axle he could see the asphalt road streaming past. The blur of gravel reminded him of being a kid, barreling down hilly curves on his candy-apple red Schwinn, inches away from scraping his knees.

His wrist phone beeped.

"We're free," said Duke. "The racist bastards took me for the janitor."

Robert breathed a sigh of relief. The battered jalopy with its peeling UCLA stickers had done the trick.

As his neck and back muscles knotted in a spasm he cursed himself for passing on the uninhabited island off the Florida Keys that Libby had urged him to buy. For fifty million he could have had his own airstrip. Total privacy and security. In truth, it was Emily who nixed the deal. She objected to Doni growing up in an artificial environment. Now, of course, he realized that children of the rich are different. How stupid of him to think otherwise.

He had always hated the sequestered life that came with being famous. Sure, fame had its glorious moments. Diplomats as well as salespeople provided prompt service and extra comforts. But if you were an artist of any kind the perpetual gang of pushy people clamoring for your autograph inevitably disrupted your work. Moreover, many fans were extremists. Women exposed themselves. Teenagers lay down under the wheels of his car. He thought about Emily. The men were even more aggressive. Dangerous.

The car picked up speed. Robert readjusted his body; the down pillows helped to cushion the bumps. Trying to relax, he sifted through his memory in search of Madison Cole. He had met attractive women everywhere, hundreds of models and actresses, but he rarely spent time alone with them. He vaguely recalled one rambunctious lunch with several young French models last spring. Afterward he brought them by to see the house. But this Madison Cole was an American. There had been no Americans in that group.

The car suddenly backfired, then lurched to a stop. The door slammed and Duke lifted the trunk. Robert looped his left leg over the fender and crawled out quickly. "I don't recommend it."

Duke laughed as he handed him a fishing vest. Shay slipped it over his cowboy shirt and Levis while Duke slapped a beret over Shay's blond hair.

Back in the front seat Robert felt like a man who has just busted out of jail. Everywhere he saw nature's beauty. The sun melted into a sheet of gold that flooded the pencil pines growing alongside the road. Even the fat sea gulls sitting atop a highway sign pointing to the town dump appeared magnificent.

By the time they arrived at the pier in Sag Harbor the sun had disappeared into the horizon. Robert climbed out and waited by the car as Duke lifted his Glock from the glove compartment. He strapped the handsome Swiss-designed gun into the nylon rig under his buckskin jacket. The flyweight model 19 was state of the art. Restricted to paramilitary and government use, it split apart to fit into a shaving can and had enough plastic in it to pass through airport security systems undetected.

A spray of pale stars twinkled in the darkening sky as they

hurried to the boat slips. Rows of sailboat masts clanked in the evening breeze.

Robert's pilot waited on board a ninety-foot cabin cruiser and quickly steered them to the forward deck. Robert settled in a lounge chair as the sleek boat motored through the narrow yacht-choked channel. They headed west toward Manhattan, cruising along the north side of Long Island.

The sea air was damp and cold. Robert huddled under a thick woolen blanket and thought about his own boat, a 180-foot yacht dry-docked in Newport Beach south of L.A. When Doni came home he would take him to Hawaii. They might even sail to Hong Kong.

Duke loped down the deck and settled next to Robert, his restless eyes following the trail of lights that curved away from them on shore. "I phoned a friend on the FBI's hostage recovery team," he said hoarsely. "Krugger's a candy ass like I suspected but he's done his job. European counterintelligence is canvassing the terrorist networks—the Abu Nidal gang, the PLO, Baader Meinhof."

Robert's stomach knotted at the thought of his son held captive in some dank hellhole in North Africa.

"My man says last year the Shi'ites in Iran were seeking an established production company to make a propaganda film."

Robert took a deep breath. "Do you think they'd kidnap Doni to get a film made?"

Duke's pale gray eyes shone like crystals in the damp night air. "I doubt it. If they had taken him for political purposes, we'd know it by now. For some reason, the bastards are hibernating."

Thanks to Charlene's last-minute magic Ceci emerged from the lobby of her building on Wilshire Boulevard looking like a platinum goddess. Her ash-blond hair was a mass of loose, soft curls tied up at the sides of her face with ivory ribbons. Twinkling rhinestones dripped like icicles from her ears.

The black sequined dress that Charlene unearthed was almost a size too small. Ceci's full breasts tapered into the tightly fitted bodice; the skirt flared softly to an abrupt hem that twirled a good four inches above her knees. Her iridescent-stockinged legs ended in spike-heeled sandals tied with silver spaghetti straps.

As the driver opened the velvet-padded door of the Mercedes limo and she sank comfortably into the indigo leather seat, Ceci felt like Cinderella. In her childhood dreams this is what she imagined

Hollywood to be about. She wanted more limos in her life. Diamonds instead of rhinestones.

She promptly flipped open the door of the teak cabinet under the television screen. Six bottles of liquor sloshed softly as the car floated along in traffic. The joys of money. Through the tinted windows she gazed out at Beverly Hills: the spotlessly clean streets, the luxury foreign cars, the high-fashion shops and well-groomed men and women. Life in this tiny triangle of the world was orderly and glamorous. To Ceci it was a dream come true.

The limo turned into the grid of residential streets. These were the Flats, two miles of the priciest real estate in Los Angeles. They pulled into a circular driveway shaded with miniature weeping willows. It was the perfect setting for the pink two-story mansion. As the limo rolled up to the entry Ceci studied the inlaid crests over the huge double doors. A path of butterscotch marble ran from the columned porch to a garden of ornate topiary trees at the side of the house.

Before the driver could ring the bell Tommy emerged. The gold studs on his tuxedo winked at her as he got in. He surveyed her outfit approvingly. "Miraculous. Finally, you look like a woman." He removed his jacket and laid it across her lap. "Take care not to wrinkle it." He plucked a sheaf of papers from a manila folder and began to read.

Ceci shrugged off her immediate sense of rejection. How foolish of her to think there was more to the evening. She was an employee. This was, after all, only a business arrangement.

Tommy tilted forward to adjust his cummerbund. He combed his hair in a hidden mirror that unfolded from the ceiling of the car, then spritzed his tongue with peppermint spray. Reaching for conversation, Ceci commented that the morning's *L.A. Times* had trumpeted the party as attracting Hollywood's A list.

"What else have they got to do," snapped Tommy distractedly. The car pulled up behind a parade of limos in the hotel driveway. "Do you give good speeches?" he asked, scanning his notecards.

"No, not really. I get tongue-tied. I can never remember what I'm supposed to say." She didn't know why she was tearing herself down. It was stupid.

"Then reading from the teleprompter is your gift," he said coolly. His words seemed to hang between them as the limo inched forward. Ceci had noticed that an icy hardness came over him whenever he evaluated a person or an idea.

Impatient with the traffic, people began to emerge from their limos to weave their way through the stalled cars. Ceci saw Angie Dickinson dart from a silver Rolls Royce to the sidewalk. She looked stunning in a slithery red satin gown. Ceci prayed she looked half that good in ten years.

Tommy stayed put. He planned to enter regally. A sea of screaming paparazzi armed with flashing strobes waited for him at the curb.

"Whad'you think of Leggitt?" he asked.

"Nice man." Ceci bit her lip. Another stupid remark, considering she had barely said boo to the man. In truth, she had disliked him on sight.

"He's got dirt on Shay, and you desperately need a producer. With his contacts and your camera presence the marriage might work." He eyed her appraisingly. "This frock you got on is good. It'll turn the kids on. Hon, if you're goin' to make it, you've got to learn to flash it." With that, he reached over and, running his finger under the scoop neck of her dress, swiftly yanked it down. The two sloping mountains of her white breasts popped forward. The sequined fabric barely covered the rim of her nipples.

At exactly that moment the driver opened the door. Three cameras shoved inside and clicked like machine guns. Tommy jumped past them and yanked Ceci out by the hand. As her foot touched the red carpet she heard whistles and jeers from the paparazzi. Their cameras were pointed at her breasts. Some of the lenses actually grazed against her skin. It all happened so fast that Ceci, flustered and confused, was unable to adjust the dress. Tommy chuckled at her attempts to pull up the front as they stood together ringed by photographers.

"Relax," he whispered in her ear. "Loosen up, give the public a peek. Who are you saving those copious cupcakes for anyway?"

Ceci felt his hand slide from her waist down along her hip. "Tommy," she exclaimed angrily as she twisted away.

"I love tight tushes," he said, smiling. He cocked his head this way and that for the cameras. Ceci forced a wan smile. He clutched her to him as they walked across the red-carpeted hallway to the "shooting gallery," where celebrities were herded together like cattle.

"Tommy, over here," shouted a red-faced cameraman. "Tommy, smile," screamed another. "Who's the babe?" yelled another. "Blondie, show some teeth."

Ceci flashed a panicked, uncomfortable smile at the crowd. Tommy let go of her. He was into the star mode—preening, laughing, waving at the press people he knew. She stood dazed and bewildered by his rude behavior. In the car, he had all but ignored her, yet as soon as they were in public he clawed at her like a lion. She was still in a state of shock from his maneuver in the backseat. He had done it purposely so that the photographers would see her breasts. She shuddered at the thought of the photos in tomorrow's columns.

An ill-mannered cameraman stuck his lens practically in her face. She elbowed him. "You bitch," he shot back. Immediately, the ranks behind them swelled. Lights were redirected and the cameras started another chorus of clicks, aimed this time at Burt Reynolds and Loni Anderson, who had just entered the loading zone. Ceci heard the shouts behind her: "Burt, over here." "Hey, Loni." "Loni, you look sssspectacular!" "Give us a big cheeese, sweethearts."

Meanwhile, Tommy stopped to sign autographs and wave to a vocal cluster of his fans. He kissed a baby as three teenage girls scratched at him for souvenirs. With increasing volume, the group chanted "Tommy Train, Tommy Train." A bouncing billboard, held by a chubby red-headed woman, read TRAIN FOR PRESIDENT.

"Tonight's a breakthrough for me," Sherry said to Jack as they drove into the Beverly Hilton's underground garage.

The ski rack on top of the Wrangler barely cleared the low cement underpass. He snatched a stub from the electronic box and followed a Porsche up the graduated incline. Jack knew the parking lot well. Five years ago when he covered the party beat he visited the Beverly Hilton ballroom twice a week.

He marveled at how the Hollywood old guard sustained the public performance again and again. But they were actors, and actors perfected the art of repetition. The real pros even managed to make their twenty-fifth explanation of why-I-became-an-actor for TV talk shows sound fresh and alive. A remarkable tolerance for boredom was one of the requirements of the craft. Out of necessity, the more intelligent often blunted the monotony with drugs or drink.

From the sheet on her lap Sherry read aloud the list of celebrities at the benefit. Liz Taylor was the crown jewel. It had been a year since Jack had attended one of these glitzy photo ops. A few stiff drinks, he figured, and he could enjoy the evening.

Before they entered the ballroom, Sherry slipped a ticket into his tux pocket. "I must check in with Trixie. Three of us are baby-sitting twenty clients," she said with nervous excitement. "I'll meet you at our table."

It was her first night on the job. She had dressed modestly in a dragon-patterned Chinese outfit. Only the thigh-high slits were from the world of Suzy Wong. Jack gave her a peck on the cheek, then savored the muscle of her thigh as she sliced through the crowd. He'd promised to be a good boy, chat up celebs, and push her career along.

He ambled through the lobby. The now dated hotel had been surpassed by the Century Plaza and Four Seasons with their pseudo-European bellmen and complimentary champagne baskets. Tonight Jack found the Americana refreshing. He liked the homey floral carpeting, the coffee shop that served packaged apple pie and white toast, the rooms with their predictable prints and muted colors. He was tired of borrowed European elegance—froufrou for which they charged 250 bucks a night. Their champagne was a $3.99 split from a local liquor store, and the cheese came from Wisconsin.

As Jack entered the barroom Kirk Douglas accidentally brushed against his shoulder. As the older actor turned to Jack to apologize, his eyes lit with recognition. Jack helped him: "Dinner in New York. The Russian Tea Room."

"Of course. Jack Werts." Douglas extended his hand. Three years ago they had spent a rousing evening discussing the Viet Nam war. Douglas proved to be a bright man and formidable opponent. Jack had to admit Douglas was an exception to his "brain-dead celeb" rule.

Sherry zipped over for an introduction and Douglas complimented her on the Flower Drum outfit. A minute later Trixie approached; her wheels clicked when she realized that Jack was Sherry's date. He saw her mentally prepare a list of unknown Camp clients for Sherry to unload on him. The mind of a good publicist never stopped working.

Robert Wagner and Jill St. John paused to say hello to Trixie, who introduced them. Jill reeked of sensuality and all Jack could think of was the photograph of Brezhnev leering at her bottom. Sherry interrupted abruptly with "Duty calls" and scrambled away. Douglas, Wagner, and St. John moved off gracefully and Jack edged over to a small bar dispensing free drinks.

Forward movement was nearly impossible, which made everyone exceedingly friendly. Jackie Collins winked at him, a heavy chain of emeralds about her swanlike neck. A young actress gave him the eye. In the Hollywood crowd he was a nugget: tall, handsome, single, and straight.

After a few bumps, Jack wormed his way up to the bartender, a placid-faced surfer in a white jacket. It was then he saw her. At first he wasn't sure. He looked hard. Had to be. He grabbed a glass of white wine and moved in her direction.

Ceci stood alone in front of a gold-curtained panel. Suddenly Jack's hands were clammy, his heart hammered in his chest. He never expected she would attend this kind of celebrity affair. She waited on the sidelines of the milling, babbling horde. She looked extremely sexy. A tiny black dress barely covered a third of her body. Her hair glistened with pinpoints of light.

Jack felt a pang of jealousy as Stan Lutz approached her with a drink in his hand. He hovered about her protectively. They talked and laughed until Lutz turned his head in response to someone calling him. He kissed Ceci on the cheek and left her for a tiny sour-faced woman. Jack headed over immediately.

The moment she saw him, she attempted to flee into the crowd but Jack cut her off. "Hullo, beautiful." His voice was friendly as if all had been forgiven.

She bit her lip and glared at him. He noticed the faint trace of a blue vein under the pale white skin of her breast and felt an immediate knot of desire. "You're a real sex pistol in that outfit."

A fearful, nervous look came over her face. It was clear she had no desire to talk to him. She looked around for Lutz, but Jack had her cornered, his arm up against the curtain. She smelled delicious. Again he wanted her and was surprisingly aroused by the idea that another man might make love to her before he did.

"When you steal, you clean out the shop," he said softly. "I can't imagine where Tommy Train got the idea for 'Survivors,' can you?"

"Ideas are free," she snapped at him. She tapped her heel impatiently, expecting him to step back from her. The more Jack sought out her eyes, the more she looked away.

"If I remember correctly you were no gentleman that night," she said indignantly.

Jack pinned her body against the wall. "And you're no lady," he chortled.

Lutz approached at an off-balance, loose-limbed gait, the hawk

eyes behind his glasses examining Werts. He waited for an introduction but Ceci was silent. Jack quickly extended his hand. "Jack
Werts."

"I know that byline," said Lutz with a forced smile.

The silence that followed was awkward. The flickering overhead
lights masked their embarrassment.

Jack slipped away and entered the ballroom. It looked like an
inverted wedding cake, the white walls decorated with pseudo-
Grecian columns and gold-tasseled curtains. Two hundred round
tables, bedecked with white bouquets, were arranged by number.
Mayor Tom Bradley cruised the dais until he found his seat behind
a bouquet of lilies. Liz Taylor in a magenta gown with stiff, stand-
up lace collar was seated to his right, Burt Reynolds next to her.

Like everyone at these events, Jack found his head was on
permanent swivel. He spotted Tommy Train at table 8 and when
an obese woman in a puffy chiffon dress shifted, Jack saw that Ceci
was sitting next to Train. She appeared to be his date. Christ, the
old buzzard was twice her age. Before the band struck up an intro-
ductory tune, Tommy headed toward the dais and took his perch
next to the perennially youthful Dick Clark.

Jack almost missed Angie Dickinson slip into the vacant chair
next to him. "Angie," he whispered with a wink when he saw who
it was.

"My God, the devil in our midst." She leaned over to give him
a hug. "From now on, I censor my conversation."

"Just don't censor anything else."

Angie loved to tease. "Never," she said, running her hand
down his back. They chatted about Pamela Mason, a mutual friend
and the doyenne of Hollywood.

Jack was rarely attracted to older women, but Angie broke
another rule. He would oblige her anytime, anywhere, if she would
have him. But after her experiences with the press, she flirted with
reporters outrageously and trusted none of them. A wise dame,
Jack decided.

Jackie Collins, fresh off another best-selling-book tour, joined
them with near-miss kisses and spicy commentary. Once everyone
settled—guests, escorts, husbands, publicists—Jack peered again at
table 8. Ceci's head turned away abruptly. Had she been staring at
him? Jack scanned the guests at her table, a band of pompous NTN
executives and their stolid wives. As he turned back to the table he

spotted Bill Leggitt leaning against a pillar near the exit. "Excuse," said Jack to the group.

He made his way around crowded tables, ducking away from the waiters with their shifting trays the size of sombreros.

"Black Jack," said Leggitt in greeting. He extracted a pack of Dunhills and knocked one forward. Jack took a cigarette. Leggitt snapped a gold lighter and Jack inhaled deeply. Lizard had graduated to expensive weeds.

"That was one hell of an interview you landed with Madison Cole," said Jack. "A smash job. Did you spend much time with her?"

"We made it together."

"Really?"

Leggitt nodded. "She knew the ropes. A fair exchange. It got her name in the news." He looked exceedingly prosperous in his narrow-lapel tux with thin red bow tie.

"I hear you've moved to L.A."

"I joined the wacko world of television."

"For damn good money, I bet."

"You got it."

The orchestra played "Days of Wine and Roses." Sappy music, sappy food. Jack prayed that Dionne Warwick might rise from her chair and put some speed on the evening. "What's the show?" he asked perfunctorily.

Leggitt nodded toward the dais. "Tommy Train."

Suddenly Werts felt ill. The biggest fabricator in the business had wormed his way into a TV slot for a tidy six-figure salary. Journalism was such a racket.

At the podium Tom Hayden railed against big business. Ceci only half-concentrated on Hayden's words. She still smarted over Tommy's rude behavior—that dreadful maneuver of his when they exited the limo. It was a sick, obnoxious public display.

Ceci took a sip of her champagne. Lutz grinned at her from across the table. She smiled at him but her eyes swiftly settled on Tommy sitting up on the dais. He looked like one of the men in the Calvin Klein ads, beautifully posed.

It seemed his every gesture on the show or off was for public consumption. Fame was his lifeblood. Ceci admitted that she too was thrilled the few times people recognized her in the street and

asked for her autograph. The powerful feeling that came from recognition was a natural high, a terrific ego stroke. But she also knew
she could comfortably take a backseat to bigger television stars. She
doubted this was true for Tommy.

Train followed Hayden on the program. He was a superb per-
former with excellent timing, and he took charge of the audience
masterfully. Raw physicality combined with a kinetic energy that
matched his wit. He was exceedingly clever. Most on-air news journalists, like herself, were merely "talent." The strings were pulled
by producers and directors behind the camera. But Tommy was
different. He produced, directed, and acted in his own show. He
was a genius. She had to be patient with his sexual eccentricities,
and she begrudgingly conceded that he was probably right about
her conservative style. Throughout her life, she had been told she
was bullheaded. Adaptability and flexibility were traits she must
learn to develop if she was going to be successful.

Tommy's voice deepened. He praised Elizabeth Taylor and be-
rated the Republican administration for its failure to fund AIDS
research. He finished to booming applause. When Burt Reynolds
approached the podium, Tommy quietly ducked off the stage. He
signaled for Ceci to meet him at the exit.

His limo was parked half a block from the Hilton's gridlocked
entrance, positioned for a fast getaway.

"God, I hate this shit," Tommy said the moment the doors
closed. He stripped away his collar. His heavy cuff links landed in
Ceci's lap. Solid gold *TT*s. "Nice, eh?" he said. "A gift from our
sponsor."

He poured scotch into a cut-crystal tumbler. From an inside
pocket of his jacket he removed an envelope. A neat mound of pills
appeared in the palm of his hand. "Vitamins," he said. "The food
at these events is inedible." He pressed a button on the console.
The smoky glass window unrolled. "My house," he told the
chauffeur.

Ceci wanted to reprimand him for his behavior, but she didn't
know quite what to say. The last thing she wanted—with work
finally going so well—was to provoke his anger.

"Come in for a celebratory drink," he said as they arrived at
the mansion.

Ceci took a tense breath, surprised by the invitation.

"Relax," he said, taking her hand. "This'll be painless." He was
serious, earnest. Ceci stepped onto the flagstone drive and followed

him up the marble stairs. Hugo, his butler, held open the polished oak doors.

"Whip up a banana daquiri for Miss McCann," Train ordered brusquely. "Go in and sit down," he told her before he vanished through a side door.

Ceci walked down a vast Oriental runner, which covered the shining oak floor of the long hallway. Massive beams studded the ceiling, and a series of paintings in antique frames hung on the walls. They were mostly rural scenes, peasant women collecting wheat in sun-drenched fields.

She settled down primly on the edge of a broad leather sofa in the sumptuous living room. A giant picture window afforded a view of the backyard, where a delicately arched footbridge spanned a lake-size swimming pool. It reminded Ceci of the jungle ride at Disneyland.

Hugo reappeared with a festive tropical drink on a black lacquered tray, a glass of canary-yellow liquid, decorated with a tiny tissue parasol. Thirsty from the champagne at dinner, Ceci took a long sip of the frothy drink.

Tommy returned dressed in a form-fitting black jumpsuit. He bounced over to an electronic switchboard on the wall and Frank Sinatra's voice suddenly blasted through the room.

"Sing it, Frankie baby," crooned Tommy as he boogied across the Persian rug on his bare feet. "Isn't that great?" he said, gesturing to her glass. "The perfect bedtime drink. All my sweethearts love it."

A multibuttoned console bleeped from the end table. He lifted the receiver. "Yeah, put her through." An annoyed expression darkened Tommy's features. He covered the mouthpiece with his hand and quietly muttered, "It's Lisa. Claims she's got a Starlight secretary ready to spill . . ." He listened for a moment, then turned the receiver away from his ear. Ceci heard the crisp whine of Lisa's voice. "Of course, you're the best," he said halfheartedly into the phone. "But I got a meeting goin' on." He dropped the receiver abruptly into the cradle.

"Every minute she phones. She's drivin' me bonkers. It's a drain." Again, he was up, pacing. Sinatra softly crooned "One for the Road."

"Miss McCann," he said formally with a swirl of his body, "during this last week you demonstrated to me that you've got the stuff it takes to go the distance. Our little corn-fed filly can become a superstar." He walked over and chucked Ceci under the chin. "That is—ifffff—I provide the platform. I'm thinking about it. But I'm going to give you some advice—once and only once. You've got to bury that holier-than-thou attitude."

He turned to the window and stared at the fluorescent green jungle. "The Saint Theresa save-the-world crap only works on Sunday—in church," he continued. "The kids who watch our show are video Rambos. They expect action. They can't digest the news unless it's presented with humor, sex, and violence. They tune in to get our unique interpretation of what's goin' on in the world."

He pivoted and faced her. His fingers played with the zipper on the front of his jumpsuit. He zoomed it down to his navel, then up. "To hold the kids' attention we've got to dramatize events. Each of us has had to develop a character, a distinct persona. A Batman, Brenda Starr, Lone Ranger."

The zipper swiftly descended down to his belly hair.

"A striptease if you will."

Zip. Back up.

"With great effort you have to market that persona." He sank down, cross-legged, in the leather wing chair opposite her. "Push the familiarity button. Give the viewers a friend they know, an enemy they can hate. A woman they want to fuck." Tommy paused and stared intently at her. "I've worked hard to perfect my own style on the show. I could have been a steel-faced pretty boy like Rather or Brokaw. But because I'm late to the news game I had to put some spin on my performance. There are plenty of stiffs out there in local markets. The blow-dried brain-dead have multiplied like fruit flies. Ceci, you're too sharp to go that route. TV is about the face—and the body. Look how I plan my threads. Hip, the latest from Italy or Japan. I'm a fashion statement. A willfully cool trend-setter. You've got to grab these bastard babies by the balls to keep their fingers off the channel zapper."

He leaned his head back against the chair and sighed audibly. His eyes were on the recessed lights in the pale blue ceiling. "The big surprise to the network—and those mealymouthed TV critics—is that I also hooked into five million lard-assed mommies at home sucklin' their young." He hunched forward. "Y'know why, my pet?"

Ceci shook her head.

"The horny bitches wanna fuck me. That's why. Believe me, that's what life comes down to. To sell anything—trucks or news

—add sex." His face was tomato red. He was incited by his words.

"The women watch because of this." He stood up and bumped his pelvis forward. His organ bulged under the silky black material. "I have a tailor who fits my crotch. Tight, real tight." He then rubbed his hands lovingly over his broad shoulders. "The shoulders in my suits are padded.

"Every night after the show the horny housewives pick up the phone and squeal to each other how outrageous that Tommy Train is. What an exhibitionist he is. My, my, how awful! But I fulfill their secret fantasies. I want those horny bimbos to squeal their little heads off over me."

Ceci giggled. What he said seemed childishly absurd. The room spun slightly. A halo formed around the lampshade.

"When the tabs come to photograph me, I make sure they get me pumping on the Nautilus," he continued. "Ceci, always remember, first and foremost we're actors as well as salesmen. Mitch is the cocky black stud, every white bitch's fantasy. Lisa's our aggressive temptress. She'll stab you in the back before breakfast— the vixen that women love to hate."

He came over to her. He ran his hand into her hair and wound a thick strand around his wrist. "You, my darling, are today's Marilyn Monroe. A bosomy blonde those horny brats can dream about gettin' their . . ." He looked at her with luminous, sentimental eyes. "I bet you're a real blonde, aren't you?" A suggestive smile lingered on his face.

Ceci tensed nervously.

"At ease, hon," he said in a low-powered voice. "If I had wanted you, you'd have been in my bed months ago. I only want to teach to you how to use what you've got."

He sat down and ran his hand along her shoulder. It stopped respectfully at her neck, but his eyes were on her breasts.

"Big knockers are in vogue. Those babes could turn into showy competition for me if you agree to unleash them. C'mon, honey, let yourself stretch and jiggle under some soft sweaters. Good cashmere sweaters, real classy. I've got a British company that'll provide a trunk of their finest stuff if you just mention their name around town. We'll bring back that old sweater-girl look, make it retro chic. It'll give our horny adolescents somethin' to beat off on." Nearly singing, he chanted. "Sweet Lips, you's got the equipment and you's not using it . . ."

Ceci blinked hard. She tried to object, but she couldn't get her mouth to form the words. She felt terribly dizzy, feverish. Her head was loggy. More than anything she wanted to sleep.

"C'mon, baby, relax, put your pretty head down here," he said. His hand pulled her face down on his lap. She closed her eyes while he stroked her hair. How could she be so sleepy? She struggled to stay awake to listen to him.

Tommy ran his fingers back and forth along her shoulder as he talked. "Lisa's a silly cunt, but her confrontational, fuck-you attitude works. Ten college dorms chose her as their poster girl. This means more press, ultimately higher ratings. You, Ceci, are too beautiful to hide it. We've definitely got to display this body on the cover of *Vogue* or *Vanity Fair*. Naked arms and legs on an ermine blanket. If Diane Sawyer can do it, why not you?"

He studied her legs objectively. "There's definitely been an improvement tonight. Where did you get this dress?"

Ceci lifted her head. She half sat up.

"Charlene," she slurred. She felt Tommy's hand rake through her hair. "The hair, too. She did the hair, too?" Her head plopped back down on his lap.

"I noticed that you had Lutz at your beck and call," he said. He pushed her upright. Ceci rested against the leather sofa like a rag doll.

He lifted the glass of yellow liquor. "Drink up, baby." Ceci tried to take a sip but her head flopped over. Tommy shoved the straw between her lips. She felt cold drops of the pearly liquid fall onto her breasts.

Tommy quickly scrunched up a cocktail napkin and shoved it down the front of her dress. He rubbed her chest vigorously as if he were cleaning a fender. His hand burrowed down to her waist. She tried to wriggle away but his arm was firmly anchored.

He chortled heartily. "Squirmy Ceci. Let Tommy clean up your mess. Ceci's been a sloppy girl."

Through her blurred vision Ceci suddenly saw an angry scowl on his face. "This is what I mean," he said loudly. "You're too uptight. Learn to flow with the elements."

He pulled his hand from her dress, then hugged her to him paternally. "We're going shopping at Neiman Marcus, my little Cinderella." His other hand was firmly planted on her thigh. She tried to pull her short skirt down.

"Leave it up," he commanded. "Show those legs to the world." She felt his fingers ripple over her breasts.

"Sweaters will enhance the contours of these melons. Get some sheer blouses with ruffles. Feminine, frilly stuff." He paused. "Somehow I've got to teach you the 'come hither' look, how to make bedroom eyes at the camera. Now you act like a tired workhorse, trying to catch up with everything. Too tense. Maybe you should flirt with me, spark a jealous fire under Lisa. Everybody loves a cat fight."

He leaned back against the sofa. "Tommy's Angels," he said softly. "It's a winner." He repeated, "Tommy and His Angels."

Ceci barely heard him as she collapsed. He stood up and laughed out loud.

Hugo appeared as if by magic.

"Pack her up and get her outta here," said Tommy. "Then tell the driver to pick up Cordero and bring her over. She's been waiting since midnight."

15

The next morning Shay stood on the terrace of his duplex on the top floors of the stately Beresford apartment building in Manhattan. The air was chilly, the sun bright and strong. Below him, Central Park shimmered in the glory of fall. The trees were tinged with brilliant oranges and brandy reds; kites danced their way up to the cotton clouds. On the corner of Eighty-first Street a vendor sold bags of peanuts and salted pretzels the size of frisbees to children getting off school buses on their way to the Museum of Natural History.

Three photographers crouched on the cement sidewalk about one hundred feet from the building's awning. The doormen had chased them away from the burnished brass doors so as not to disturb the residents. The night before Robert had used the service entrance on Eighty-second street to slip by them. Back in the bedroom, a three-thousand-foot master suite, he buzzed for breakfast.

Emily's brushes and combs were left on the marble shelves. She'd been using part of the room to store her theater makeup. A dragon-patterned kimono hung from the back of the door. He pressed the silk to his nose. Her dusty rose scent lingered in the garment. He had debated whether or not to call her this morning and apologize for his behavior but he called Krugger instead. Maybe later.

Emily, he knew, had always been delicately balanced on the edge. There were times when she held on to reality by only a slender thread. Perhaps it was this remarkable ability to slip in and out of reality, to change character so effortlessly and expertly, that had made her a great actress.

As an actor Robert had scored with his rugged good looks and masculinity. He had successfully played the same good-guy hero again and again. But Emily, like Meryl Streep, could conjure up characters at will. She actually seemed to become different people in body and soul. It was a mix of disciplined technique and natural talent, the last a gift from her mother.

Robert thought about Emily's mother, an exquisitely beautiful Latvian immigrant who had the promise of a stupendous stage career until, a year after Emily's birth, she was diagnosed as a violent schizophrenic. Fortunately, Emily's father, a practical, hardworking theater manager, was quite sane. He had instilled a sense of discipline and pragmatism in his daughter. After his wife's fatal heart attack, he never remarried, choosing to lavish his attentions on Emily. At the age of nine, she decided to become a ballerina, and he had provided her with the best lessons available.

Her fierce determination and physical strength earned her a position with the rookie league of the New York City Ballet, but her promising career was shattered in a freak accident when the gate ramp of a jumbo 747 collapsed and Emily and two other passengers free-fell to the tarmac below. Her shinbone splintered apart. Luckily, after two years of therapy she walked without a limp, but she would never be a dancer.

Emily had not had an easy life despite all the present comforts. Robert knew he must be patient with her.

At breakfast, he flipped open *The New York Times* to the metro section, where a brief update on the kidnapping ran down the left column. There were a string of meaningless quotes from Morgan Camp in East Hampton. He glanced at the *Wall Street Journal* and the *Washington Post*. They too ran daily updates, quoting kidnapping experts. More filler. Shay attempted to read some foreign news, but his concentration was shot. He felt like a man about to be sentenced. The best news he could hope for was a stay of execution.

He glanced over at the rows of videotapes that lined the walls, a spillover from the downstairs library. The bulk of his collection—well over 40,000 movies—was in a hermetically sealed vault in the Beverly Hills house. But his precious film collection, like the fine furniture, had lost all value for him. Unlike Doni, it was replaceable.

Unable to eat more than a few bites of cereal, he got up and went to his dressing room. He took a scraggly red-brown beard and a fisherman's hat from the rosewood bureau. Looking in the antique banjo mirror, he secured the beard to his cheeks with two inside strips of adhesive. The floppy hat covered his hair. He slipped into his running shoes and baseball jacket, then galloped down the sweeping circular staircase.

As usual he used the servants' entrance. It was 10:30 A.M. The morning foot traffic on Central Park West had diminished. Uniformed nannies, wheeling hooded prams around wobbly oldsters, now patrolled the sidewalk. The three photographers on the bench across the street barely glanced his way. He hailed a taxi. The cheerful owner of a troop of miniature poodles prancing at the end of their taut leashes wished him good day.

A line of silver trucks with the Starlight Studio logo—a black paw print—were parked in front of the Manhattan federal courthouse. The production crew had cordoned off a twenty-yard square midway up the mountain of steps. Groves of cameras and light stands—small billboards of bulbs that resembled ice-cube trays—were focused on the area. Nearby a gaggle of extras—blue-suited lawyer types and stereotypically trench-coated reporters—danced in a huddle to warm themselves. A biting wind whipped through the shaded canyon created by the solid granite buildings.

A few panhandlers had stopped to gawk, but most New Yorkers, long since jaded by the sight of movie crews, hurried about their business.

From what Robert could see, Harry had already finished pan shots of the crowds erupting from the subway. He was set up for the scene where Lee Mack meets Whitney on the courthouse steps after she has testified against him. The "Et tu, Brutus" scene Libby had called it when their debate raged as to its merit. She had won her case. A lavish allowance for ten takes of face shots had been budgeted to precisely capture the dark moment of betrayal. Whether the scene would work or not was iffy since, in rehearsals, Libby had dubbed Lee Mack "Jaws" because of her inability to bare her Chiclet teeth gracefully.

Robert had slaved over *China White* for two long years. Unlike his trademark adventure sequels and space odysseys, this film was a foray into dramatic art. For that reason he had painstakingly avoided casting the ten-million-dollar men like Cruise and Gibson, choosing capable lesser knowns. The cast was superb. Only Lee Mack had been a last-minute replacement.

Instead of feeling pleased to return to the set Robert felt totally disconnected. It was as if he were visiting some distant part of his past. The minute he stepped from the taxi everything seemed smaller, less impressive than he remembered it. It dawned on him at that moment that moviemaking would never be the same. And for good reason. As famous as he had been for his acting and directing career, he was now even more famous for the tragedy that consumed his life. He had the terrible premonition that in the end this tragedy would be all that history would record of his accomplishments.

Robert paid the cabbie and headed across the street, where Duke Thompson waited beside the studio's Winnebago. Harry Pine tumbled from the trailer. The two men embraced quickly and then Robert followed Pine up the wobbly steps. Inside Lee Mack sprang to life. She was costumed in a faux fifties glen plaid suit, her butter-blond hair swirled in a French roll. Her sorrowful blue eyes welled with tears as her earnest voice rose and fell with words of sympathy. She was an emotional grab bag of pious pity and rueful reassurance.

Whitney weaved down the narrow aisle. His eyes wavered for a second, but he didn't speak.

Their collective gaze was fixed expectantly on Robert. They were waiting for him to take charge of the production—and their lives. After all, he was the general. They were his troops. And *China White* had been his baby. They knew the extent of his passion for the project.

Whitney broke the short silence. "No news?"

"Let's put it this way," Robert said, "no wrap party's in sight."

"Odd, isn't it?" said Harry.

Robert spoke with a deep sadness. "Two weeks ago I woke up in the night dreaming of Doni's death. I saw parts of his body strewn over a highway. Bone-chilling screams came from black tunnels in deep forests." He paused and looked at each of them. "Now, it's different. I still wake with the cold sweats. But I feel this inexplicable inertia. I'm afraid Doni has vanished forever." He glanced down at the script on the table, at the half-eaten bag of M&M's, at the newspapers, theater notices. His eyes dropped to the geometric-patterned rug on the floor of the trailer. "The Stockholm Syndrome can occur, especially with a small child," he said softly.

Mack's round face came close. "What's that?"

"Empathy between the victim and his abductor. Doni will identify the captors as his parents."

"How awful!"

"But it's only been a month," Harry said in a kindly tone.

"Eternity," said Whitney. His rich voice had a stereophonic quality. Robert became aware of the sound of traffic outside the metal walls of the trailer. Harry stepped to the window. He slatted the blinds, then let go a volley of curses. "Shit, two NBC trucks."

Whitney's face went hard. "The lice infested the lobby of my hotel last night."

Robert knew that if he stayed, his presence would disrupt the shoot. "Best I vamoose." He sat down before the makeup mirror and ripped the beard from his face. "Send the last of the dailies to the apartment," he said to Harry as he rolled the disguise into his hat.

Lee Mack scampered up behind him, her blue eyes runny with emotion. "Robbie," she spoke in rushed, embarrassed breaths. "*Playboy* called. They offered a million dollars . . . for our story."

"Our story?"

"Our affair." Up close the heavy makeup made her clownishly ugly. "They asked for pictures of me. Clothed. Proper. They said I can promote the film."

Her painted mouth reminded him of a sea anemone sucking in silt and refuse for its survival. Her long fingers splayed against his shoulder. "Robbie, I told them no. Never would I profit from your distress."

Shay managed a counterfeit smile. Not this week anyway.

Before he pushed open the door, she blew him a kiss from the tips of her fingers. "*Hasta la vista,* my darling."

When the NBC crew saw Robert emerge from the trailer they barreled across the street. Tires screeched. Horns blared. Shay bolted for the private car Duke had waiting. Once he was safely tucked in the backseat they snaked through the heavy traffic on Sixth Avenue in silence.

Robert reflected on Lee Mack. She'd never met Doni nor visited the East Hampton house. She was hardly a suspect. What puzzled him was the abrupt end of his feelings for her. There was a cold emptiness where his sexual fire had been. She had been a first-class blow job and that was it. She had nothing whatever to do with his passions.

The room today was different. It was a separate little house. There were lots of bugs: some flying around Doni's head, others crawling in the cracks. Rita made a phone call right away and then ran out in a rush. She locked the big door. Doni heard the screen slam.

He got up from the floor and walked into the bathroom and lifted the chain in the tub. With his fingers he twisted the shiny loops, removed the chain, and slipped it into his secret bag. He left the rubber circle on the edge of the tub.

Rita got mad if it was missing. She never said anything about the chain. He had four chains in his bag.

He went back to the other room and sat on the floor and waited for the sticky black bugs to come from the hole. They stayed in the wall because it was still light. Doni felt terribly sad again. Very lost and alone. He pulled the blanket off the bed and put the end in his mouth. Then, he began to bounce lightly against the mattress. When he got this way he tried to think about Miss Piggy and the Cookie Monster. The Cookie Monster always made him feel better about himself. But today the Cookie Monster didn't say anything to him so he just kept on banging against the bed. He started to cry. The more he cried the faster he banged. Until he saw the door. Then he stopped. It was shorter than the front door. He got up and ran over to the round knob. He pulled as hard as he could. It opened. The screen had many flies stuck to it. He punched the screen to scare the flies away. It split in half. Red dust covered his hand. It smelled like his model airplane.

Outside it was hot. Pieces of sand were in the air. He felt them in his mouth. The ground looked soft like the yard at his big house in the desert. Not too far away from the door there was a mountain of black tires going in many directions. As Doni stepped through the screen it caught his hair hat. When he turned, the hair hat came away from his head. It hung on the screen like a big black haystack.

Butterflies flew around in his tummy as he ran toward the tires. He stopped at the car seat. It looked funny sitting there without its wheels or windows. He climbed on it and jumped up and down. Puffballs of dust rose around him. He flipped over and then scrambled to the tires. At once, from a tunnel high above, a brown face appeared. A small boy pulled himself through the hole.

Doni smiled at him.

"My hideout," said the boy. He talked in Spanish like Maria. Doni could understand him. "Come, follow me," he said as he ran back up the heap of tires.

Doni was right behind him. It was hard to keep up until he found the ledges and holes. In places the rubber was soft as chocolate. It smelled like the space underneath the cars in Daddy's garage. Doni played like he was a monkey. After a while, the boy slowed down and sat on a bumpy tire. Doni stood next to him, panting.

They were up high now, almost even with the telephone wires. Doni could see a row of houses exactly like the one he and the woman stayed in. On the other side of the houses was a silver trailer. An old dusty horse stood near a bucket. Chickens clucked in the yard. A round brown woman, much fatter than Maria, was hanging up clothes. She picked up a baby from the shade and went inside the trailer.

"My mother," said the boy.

"Your horse?" asked Doni.

"My father's burro."

Doni thought about this. His father had everything, but not a burro. "What's your name?" he asked.

"José."

"You?"

"Doni."

"That's a funny dress," José said, looking at Doni's clothes. Doni's fingers tugged at the material. He hated the dress more than ever right now. He knew José couldn't understand why he was dressed like a girl.

José laughed and jumped up and crawled back into the jungle of rubber. Doni followed closely, afraid he might get lost. In a short time José led him down to the ground where he had made a cave. He showed him a long box. "My treasure."

In the box was a fuzzy yellow ball, a lollipop, popsicle sticks, baseball cards, and a plastic spaceman. Doni knew the spaceman was a Cracker Jack toy. He picked up a tiny white tooth. "Mine," said José proudly.

José showed Doni an airplane on the back of an empty cereal box. Doni quickly punched out the plane. He put the wings into the V-shaped slot and added the tail. Maria and Sarah had bought him hundreds of cereal boxes just so he could make the airplanes.

José tossed the cardboard plane. It hit a tire and crash-landed.

"This way," said Doni. He tilted the nose up and soared the glider into the air. José ran after it, picked it up, and sailed it back to Doni.

The boys laughed and played with the plane until Doni got an idea. "Wait here," he said. He ran back to the house and returned with his secret bag. From it he took four bathtub chains and two dead bugs. "Trade?"

José didn't care about the bugs but he liked the chains. They were heavy.

"The yellow ball and the sucker," said Doni.

"For just one?"

Doni nodded.

"No," said José. "For two."

Doni thought about it. He could always get more bathtub chains.

"Okay."

After they traded, José's mother called him. Before he put his treasures back in the sack, he handed Doni a bunch of popsicle sticks. "A gift, my friend."

Doni offered him a dead bug but José wouldn't take it. "Tomorrow we play again?" he asked.

"Yes, yes."

But just then, Doni saw Rita's truck drive up to the front of the house. He ran back as fast as he could and climbed through the screen. He tried to pull the hair hat from the screen but instead he tore the screen wide open.

"Holy Christ! What the fuck are you doin'?" Rita yelled as she came through the front door. He dropped his bag. The ball and sticks rolled on the floor. Rita yanked him inside and grabbed the hair hat from the screen. She slammed the door so hard the house rattled. She looked at the floor. "Where'd you get this junk from?" The corners of her mouth were way down. She was very mad.

"José."

"Who's that?"

Doni stared at the floor.

Rita went to the back window and moved the curtain over to look outside across the yard to the trailer. "Christ, they're a bunch of illegals. You could catch a disease!"

She rushed over to the bed and started putting things into a big bag. "C'mon, we're blowin' this sand trap. I get paid and you're out rompin' with the beaners."

Because it was almost dark she let him sit up front in the truck. As they drove past the tire mountain Doni climbed to his feet and pressed his nose to the glass.

José stood by a pile of wood. He lifted his arm to wave good-bye. Doni waved back.

Rita slapped his leg so hard he fell down. "Enough!"

An hour later inside the poorly lit trailer, José's mother, Carlotta García, stirred a pot of black beans over a propane stove. His father, Ernesto, hunched over a wobbly table where he sorted the jalapeño peppers he planned to sell at the market the next day.

Carlotta told her husband that José had found a friend at the motel but didn't seem to know if his new friend was a girl or a boy. Ernesto said he better know the difference or he could get into some big trouble later in life.

José, who was playing with the chains on the floor, immediately jumped to his feet. "A boy, a boy," he shouted at them.

His father laughed heartily. He seems to know now, he said to Carlotta. While they laughed, a tape of Doni Shay singing "Happy Birthday" replayed soundlessly on the small Sony television on the shelf over the sink. It was the lead story on Univision's news hour.

José looked intently at the television. "Papa," he said softly.

"Yes?"

"That's my friend."

Ernesto looked at him and then at the screen. "The kidnapped boy is a gringo. Your friend spoke Spanish."

Ernesto ruffled his son's thick black hair and kissed him many times. José curled his small body into his father's strong brown arm, but all the while his eyes were fixed on the tiny screen.

Shortly after noon, Ceci gunned her Saab past the NTN guard booth. So far the day had been sheer hell. When she woke at ten she was still wearing her black dress. Makeup was smeared all over her pillowcase. She felt like a corpse laid out on a slab at the morgue. She had trouble focusing, and her head felt like someone had put a bell jar over it and then clanged the sides with a ten-ton hammer. When she attempted to get out of bed, she crashed in an outright faint on her shag rug. She woke an hour later and, with great effort, crawled into the bathroom where she vomited into the lilac Jacuzzi.

The spin cycle started all over again after she parked her car. It was followed by the now familiar quicksand, the sinking feeling. She pushed open the car door and took four hard short breaths of air.

This wasn't a hangover, it was annihilation. It must have been the champagne. She remembered her insipid comment to Lutz about how pretty the color was. Mistake number one: drinks aren't supposed to be pretty. The beer in Kansas City was ugly and she had never gotten sick from it.

Then she remembered the foamy drink at Train's. She had blanked after consuming it. She felt the familiar rise in her throat and put her head down to vomit on the asphalt. She quickly yanked a tissue from her purse.

She had never felt so lonely. She just wanted someone to love her. A man with strong arms to cuddle her. Jack Werts came to mind. He was suave and debonair but too much of a player. Angie Dickinson and Jackie Collins were plenty friendly to him. She recalled watching them across the room. Then she remembered Tommy's rudeness in the limo. The horrible photographers.

She leaned her head against the steering wheel. A moment's peace. Train's palatial mansion rose up in her mind. He was much wealthier than she had ever imagined. She remembered his black jumpsuit. Strictly Vegas. But after that she remembered nothing. Except the blackness of sleep. And, yes, the chauffeur and her doorman carting her into her apartment. She insisted she was fine and could walk by herself. How embarrassing!

She lifted her head and peered at the gray studio complex. It shifted to the right like an aircraft carrier riding on a black tarmac ocean. She rubbed her eyes. This was scary. She contemplated driving back home. She had never been sick from work a day in her life. She looked down at her slacks. Damn, she was wearing the wrong gabardine pants. Too baggy. And the amber jacket she had planned to deep-six months ago. *Vestis virum facit.* Why was Latin floating on her scrambled brainwaves? She was losing it.

Fortunately, her legs held ground as she navigated slowly down the corridor of the studio. When she arrived at her office she breathed a sigh of relief. Until, that is, she saw the newspaper clippings. Blatantly posted on her door were photographs of a fleshy female with protruding breasts and a tangled mop of blond hair. The *Southland Sentinel*'s caption read: "Tommy Train's new heart-throb." She wasn't identified—not that she wanted her name to be attached to the embarrassing picture. The woman in the photo looked like a young porn star. The other clip, from *Nightbeat*, mentioned Tommy Train at length and noted that he escorted a new producer on his show. Ceci cringed as she studied the picture.

A handwritten note was pinned under the clips: ATTACK OF THE TWIN TORPEDOES.

Grinker's scrawly handwriting.

She angrily tore the clips from the door. Thank God her mom didn't see the L.A. papers.

Inside her office the searing pain shot through her skull again. She stumbled to her desk and found a bottle of aspirin in a drawer.

Mitch's head popped around the corner. "It's about time." Despite his glibness, sympathy and concern shone in his eyes.

Ceci's parched lips mouthed a barely audible greeting. She wanted to disappear under the desk. She felt like she was back in first grade. "What's up?" she asked feebly.

He handed her a mimeographed schedule. Her eyes were unable to focus on the small type.

"Remember Peeping Dicks?" he said.

"How could I forget."

"Your buddy Frankie Fontana is camped in the greenroom."

"Oh my God," Ceci moaned.

"He keeps askin' after you." Mitch smothered a grin. "He has plans to launch your bicoastal fan club."

Ceci massaged her temples. She remembered reading that the Chinese used massage instead of aspirin to get rid of headaches.

Mitch spoke again. "An hour ago Tommy decided to have our three slimeball detectives analyze the Shay kidnapping," Mitch said. The humor had evaporated from his voice. "We've upgraded their status to kidnapping experts."

Ceci felt guilty. She was coproducer of the segment. "I'll come help you . . ."

"Unh-unh," said Mitch. "I've got marching orders for you from Shorty. He's in with Tommy handling some hush-hush crisis. He said to haul ass to Venice. Pronto."

"Venice?"

"Reno Ventura's beach house."

"Reno Ventura?"

Mitch sucked in air. "Wake up, Ceci. We're in the news biz." He tossed the *Tattler* onto her desk. The tabloid flopped open: RENO'S EX RATS: EMILY SHAY'S HIS NEW GIRL.

"When did this happen?" she asked faintly.

"This morning."

"God, I missed it. . . . I've been sick."

"Your reward for dating Dracula. I warned you." He handed her a note. "Here's the address. Leggitt's been there since dawn. He claims to have found a chatty neighbor. Shorty wants you to question her. He needs the tape for tomorrow's show."

Mitch suddenly began to rotate like an eggbeater. She blinked furiously.

"Ceci, you okay?" he asked. "Ceci?"

His body had stopped rocking. He was distinct again.

"I'm fine, fine."

Mitch looked at the aspirin in her hand. "Take it. It'll help."

Alone now, Ceci swallowed the white pellets and stared absently at the file cabinet. She imagined the pills were burning holes in her stomach lining. They weren't working. The pain came again. Stronger, at three-minute intervals.

She didn't even have time to change her clothes. In the drawer she found a cracked compact and some grungy lipstick. She took a yellow scarf from her purse and tied it around her neck, then hobbled over to the mirror on the wall. The scarf sparked up her drab gray blouse. But her hair was flat and snarled. Frightening black shadows circled her eyes. Twenty-four and bags.

* * *

Late that afternoon Robert Shay and Libby Babcock visited the offices of Alexander de Courcy III and Harold Upham, Jr., private bankers to a select clientele. Their lavish rooms overlooking Rockefeller Center were furnished with museum-quality Persian rugs and priceless antiques. Between the pleated silk shades, old masters hung in gilded frames in a setting of calm perfection and old-world gentility. Perched on a Chippendale wing chair, Robert seemed incongruously casual in his faded denims.

Alexander de Courcy III clinked his bone china cup down on its saucer and discreetly coughed into his double chin. "And when exactly do you need this eighty million 'freed up,' Mr. Shay?"

Robert looked at Libby, who sat opposite him in a Windsor chair. "Tomorrow," she said firmly.

A flicker of horror registered in the elderly banker's eyes. He winced and looked at his partner, Harold Upham, Jr., whose countenance also reflected visible distress. Caught off guard, de Courcy instinctively patted the pockets of his dark blue Savile Row suit and corrected his expression with a fastidious smile.

Robert returned his smile. The esteemed monied clan were trained never to show their emotions.

"Eighty million dollars is a significant sum," said de Courcy with judicious restraint.

"Secrecy is of utmost importance," Robert stressed, looking from one man to the other. "No ransom demands have been made. But if the press gets a whiff of this, they'll assume a payment's in progress."

Libby leaned forward and insistently tapped her forefinger on the piecrust tea table. "Get the money together in cash," she said. "Big bills."

Upham's somber face constricted with concern. He shifted around uncomfortably. Robert smothered a grin. Libby had been right. "Tweak" Upham was a nervous Nellie.

De Courcy, however, sized Robert up calmly with hooded eyes. "Mr. Shay," he said gravely, "we're not trying to dissuade you. But we fear that perhaps under this enormous strain you may be acting impetuously."

"Gentlemen, let me assure you I'm in complete control of my senses," Robert said briskly. "Having this sum of cash available to me—without strings—is simply a precautionary measure."

Upham's eyes darted to his. "There's a considerable loss of income involved."

"I expect that."

"It's not a piddling sum."

Robert was perturbed. "Gentlemen, my credit is excellent, yes?" He was one of the bank's wealthiest clients.

"My goodness, sir, yes," Upham countered apologetically. "Starlight's terribly solvent. But the money's part of the international electronic network. As Miss Babcock knows, it's not that simple to extract large sums of cash overnight."

Robert ignored his excuses. "There's a minor addendum, gentlemen. The money must be kept active in some way so its absence goes unrecorded."

De Courcy frowned. "You want us to conceal the withdrawal."

Libby spoke first. "Yes, precisely; until the crisis passes."

"Maybe a loan," suggested Robert. His eyes were intent. "However you do it, the government—the IRS—isn't to know." It was best he made this crystal clear. "The FBI hopes to put up the money in marked currencies. If, at the time, I feel this is a risky maneuver—that it might jeopardize my son's life—I want to have another option available."

De Courcy nodded in agreement. He lowered his voice. "Certain actions must be taken," he said. "Disclosure will be avoided."

"There's another contingency," Robert added.

Again, a twinge of apprehension disturbed Upham's otherwise expressionless calm. He lifted a gold Mont Blanc pen from his desk and clutched it firmly as if it were a string of worry beads.

"I may need to transfer this money into more portable currency." Robert sat upright in his chair. "What is the least traceable, most concentrated form this money can take?"

The glance that ricocheted between the two bankers was a silent dialogue. "Gold bullion," said de Courcy finally. "But that's cumbersome, given the quick transport considerations here."

"Platinum coins. Diamonds. Especially uncut diamonds," Upham suggested.

De Courcy looked at Upham. A swirl of thoughts seemed to condense behind his eyes before he spoke. "Certain nuclear materials are also—"

Libby leaned forward. "You mean nuclear bombs for warheads?"

"Not exactly," he stammered. "However, the seminal materials for these items are easily converted to cash in certain countries of the world."

"God forbid, let's avoid that," said Robert.

Tweak, however, surprised him. "At this juncture we need contacts ready for the quick purchase of uncut gems, gold, and platinum."

"Just how much time do we have to 'grease the wheels' for such a purchase?" de Courcy asked.

"A week," said Libby.

He paled. "Assembling eighty million worth of the highest-quality diamonds will take three weeks."

"So start, gentlemen," said Robert. "And I trust your discretion. No one but the four of us must know about this."

"Naturally, utmost secrecy," de Courcy murmured.

The bankers went with them in the ornate brass elevator to the marble lobby, where two armed guards stood at attention. A liveried doorman pulled open the grilled gates.

The moment Libby hit the backseat of the limo, she moaned. "I can't believe Day Glo. He was flustered by the secrecy clause."

"Tweak was tapdancing," said Robert.

"For sure, extracting eighty mil from 'the international electronic network' takes him about ten minutes."

She had dealt with these boys for twelve years, she should know.

After dropping Libby off at her East Side penthouse, Robert returned to the Beresford. He found his butler, Winston, asleep in the stainless-steel kitchen. The old man sat in a walnut rocker with a black beeper resting on his lap. Shay glanced at the box; the message light was dark. No word from Krugger.

Upstairs in Emily's office he collected Doni's dental records to take back with him to East Hampton. Reflexively, he switched on the television for the evening news. Tommy Train ballooned up on the four-foot screen. Shay had caught the bizarre show once before. He fastidiously adjusted the color. There was a breathless urgency to the talk-show host's speech. He jumped about in an agitated state.

"The videotape you will now see was delivered to our show two hours ago. This is the original uncut version . . ."

Robert riffled through file drawers that contained the family's medical records. Just as he located the folder with Doni's vaccination certificates he glanced at the television. The spattered leader of the upcoming video marked it as a cheap tape. Home-movie quality.

His eyes returned to the balance sheet for Emily's surgery in 1988. When he looked up, a second later, his son's frightened face filled the screen, at point-blank range.

Robert jerked uncontrollably. Papers swirled to the floor as he catapulted to the monitor.

Doni stared straight ahead as if paralyzed by oncoming headlights. Panic flickered behind his glassy blue eyes. Robert's heart fluttered, a spasm gripped his gut. Where did this video come from? It couldn't be one of theirs. The quality was too poor. He began to sweat profusely. His hands turned cold.

Doni strained to listen to something. There was dead silence, no sound. Shay hammered at the volume button.

After a few tense seconds there was a sharp handclap. Doni opened his moist, pink mouth as if to speak. A half-second later he emitted a cracked, high-pitched wail. Robert froze. With unwavering concentration, Doni slowly attempted to sing:

> "Happy Birthday to you,
> Happy Birthday to you,
> Happy Birthday, dear Daddy,
> Happy Birthday to you."

Robert staggered backward, his heart bursting into a thousand fragments. This was a dream, a phantom of his hyperactive imagination. But when Doni bobbed his head slightly in his familiar babyish way, Robert knew this was all too real.

Mechanically, like a robot, Doni lifted his tiny hand. His small fist unlocked, and he wiggled his palm back and forth. He waved at Robert. Confusion and fear shadowed his face. He was about to cry but he didn't. He bravely held back his tears.

The videotape ended abruptly and Tommy Train sprang onto the screen. Shaken, Robert attempted to concentrate on his words: "This home video was delivered by the U.S. Postal Service to our Los Angeles studio at noon today. It was wrapped in brown paper, a Des Moines postmark in the corner. Due to the tremendous volume of our mail we didn't discover the tape until a few minutes before airtime. I made the decision to go with it immediately. I think that the kidnappers wanted you—our fans—to see this tape first."

Winston tottered into the room; his face was flushed with excitement, the beeper in his hand flashing red. Robert grabbed the receiver.

"What the hell's this about?" he shouted to Krugger at the other end of the line. Meanwhile, on the screen, Train introduced a panel of kidnapping experts.

"This nut put the tape on the air before notifying any authorities," Krugger boomed. "It's a dumb and highly irresponsible act. It appears the 'nappers are using this show as a third party—a forum—to relay their demands. The bastards are savvy to our surveillance. It's a ruse to foil us. I'm flyin' to L.A. tonight."

He hung up. Robert grabbed the console on the table. Emily was on one line, Libby on the other. Before talking to them he called his pilot. "Meet you at LaGuardia in half an hour. Get clearance at LAX."

Jack Werts stood mesmerized in front of his television set in his house on Mulholland Drive. His heart ached for the frightened child.

Train bounced back on camera, a mangled grin on his face. Only a thin veneer of concern concealed the bubbling elation over his good fortune. It was supremely lucky for this turkey that the kidnappers had chosen his show to display their valuable hostage.

Jack distrusted him instinctively. For all the public knew, the kidnappers might already have phoned the show with their ransom demands.

Train preened and pranced about the set as he addressed the panel of detectives. "Gentlemen, my first question: Why was this tape sent to me?"

"Because every criminal in America tunes in to your show," quipped Jack out loud.

Without taking his eyes from the screen, he shuffled backward to the overstuffed chair and sat down, kicking a pile of magazines from the cracked ottoman.

"Remember, gentlemen," Train added hastily, "the kidnappers could have sent this video to Robert Shay. That's the traditional approach, isn't it?"

Frankie Fontana, resplendent in a cheap iridescent suit, spoke first. "Da Iowa postmark, it means nothin'. The kid here ain't been anywhere near Iowa." Fontana nervously wet his palm and ran his hand over his pomaded hair. He mugged for the camera, a two-bit imitation Columbo.

"I say da kid's in Iran or Cuba. It's a political snatch. That's why they sent da tape to a news show. The 'nappers are gonna be makin' tough demands. They're goin' to ask da president to free Noriega, somethin' like dat . . ."

Tommy switched to detective number two, Dan Wright. He was a bald man with pitted cheeks. The glint of a loan shark shone in his eyes.

Where in God's name did Train get these so-called experts? A penal colony?

"We're citizens of the electronic age, the global village, if you will," began Wright in a phony professorial tone. "Very few of our good citizens write letters these days. Instead, we rely on the telephone to convey our messages. But telephone calls can be traced."

As he spoke, his jowly face began to tremble. The light in his eye grew stronger. "What we've witnessed here is a crime of the video generation." His fist suddenly slammed down against the fiberglass podium. "Those lazy, shiftless teenagers who stand in the aisles of record stores and dance to blasphemous lyrics. The children of the devil who ignore God's sacred book." His face turned purple as he ranted. "The almighty Bible is the only road to salvation!"

The camera zoomed to Train for a tight shot. "Yes, well, that's a consideration, Mr. Wright." Irritation warped his ready smile. He cut to a commercial.

Jack switched the channel to CBS. Sure enough, the video was being replayed on the local news. As with the attempted assassination of Ronald Reagan, America was being treated to Doni Shay a hundred times.

He clicked back to Train. The camera focused on a hollow-cheeked man with a droopy moustache and dead eyes. SAM BOOT —FRIENDLY SURVEILLANCE, INC.

"The fact that the kidnappers waited this long to strike is important," said Boot.

He appeared the most intelligible of the three.

"They required a good deal of time to secure a hideout for the boy. My guess is they transported him by motor launch to Brazil."

Jack seriously doubted a small power boat could travel from Long Island to Brazil in four weeks.

"I agree with Frankie that the Iowa postmark is meaningless. It merely encourages a wild-goose chase. The drop-off point for the ransom is what's important. I think the abductors will use a foreign country for the exchange."

186

Tommy was pleased with Mr. Boot. "Thank you—and thank you, gentlemen, for your intelligent and enlightening comments."

For the close, Train's voice grew funereal. "I'm both honored and concerned that my show has been chosen to transmit this awful message to the American public and to the Shay family. If the people responsible for this kidnapping are among our viewers, please—I beg you—spare the life of this sweet, gentle child. He's the innocent victim of your ruthless game. I ask that he be returned safe and unharmed."

The phone behind Jack rang. He lifted the receiver as the commercial came on.

"Where have you been?" asked Sammy.

"Right here, glued to this unreal—"

"It's real," she said. "What's horrifyingly unreal is my being saddled with one of Harrington's eager beavers from New York."

Jack ignored her complaint. "Is Harrington goin' to put the videotape on the cover?"

"The likely course. Our whiz kid, along with a thousand other journalists, just requested an interview with Frankenstein."

"Train'll devour him," Jack mumbled. His mind raced ahead. He envisaged a cover shot of Doni Shay from the blurred tape: TOMMY TRAIN IS CHOSEN TO RELAY KIDNAPPERS' MESSAGE. Finally, a solid news-weekly story. What a delicious opportunity to expose Tommy Train for a self-promoting charlatan. And link forces with Ceci McCann. Surely, her survivor series, with its sky-high ratings, had prompted the kidnappers to send the videotape to the show.

"Drop this kid. I'm takin' over this story."

"Clark Kent zips off his Ray Bans," clucked Sammy.

Jack grunted a good-bye and called Mara. Predictably, she was still at the office.

"I'm back from vacation," he crowed.

"Not that easy. I already called Harrington. He's still smarting over the Madison Cole affair. Thinks you deliberately tried to make a fool of him. Apparently the corporate apparatchiks made a stink over the *Exposé* cover story on her." Mara paused. "A salt-rubbed wound, if you get the picture."

"Such a dickhead."

"Dickhead or not, he's the boss."

Jack hung up the phone steaming mad. That schmuck. This was the thanks he got after all the work he'd done for the magazine.

Harrington was a managerial peabrain: power and stock options his twin gods.

Two minutes later the phone rang.

"Train's yours," said Mara. "My ass is on the line. Don't disappoint me."

"Have I ever?"

16

From her vantage point, alone in her Saab at the corner of Pacific and Windward, Ceci McCann didn't buy the hype that Venice Beach was on the move. Exactly what it was the underside of was difficult to ascertain, but it was still the underside.

According to real-estate brochures and local newspapers, the drugs-and-guitar crowd had long been replaced by wealthy yupster professionals. Overnight, the sorry streets of dilapidated shacks had reportedly been transformed into chic split-level condos fortified by impenetrable security systems.

From what Ceci saw this afternoon, it was true. Up to a point. Certainly, the sidewalk artists appeared to have upgraded their enterprise—a host of new art galleries had sprouted along Main Street. And a decent number of tourists roamed through the cleverly renovated shops and restaurants. But, on the other hand, she also observed that scores of hard-core drug addicts still laid claim to the three-mile strip of beachfront.

Through securely locked doors and windows, she contemplated the swirling clouds of the vibrant sunset while she waited impatiently for Bill Leggitt, who had disappeared into the Venice Beach Hotel, a rundown establishment tucked under an arched portico supported by mock Corinthian columns. In the last ten minutes, three unsavory characters had approached her car. One scared the bejesus out of her by jiggling the handle on the back door. The others made obscene gestures as they ostensibly begged for money. Meanwhile, across the street sat two of the saddest bus-bench cowboys that Ceci had ever laid eyes on. Achingly thin, the young boys shivered in their tattered jeans and torn T-shirts. Long, stringy hair flowed down to their shoulders; their sunburned faces hadn't been washed properly in weeks. Back in Kansas City these characters would be labeled white trash. But now that she lived in Los Angeles she came to think of them in media lingo as "marginals," the unfortunates in "the bottom third" who bought generic cat food instead of water-packed tuna.

A faint sickle moon emerged in the darkening sky. Ceci glanced at her watch—Christ, 8 P.M.! She casually slipped the expensive piece of jewelry into her leather purse. The glint of gold was too tempting for the natives. She drummed her fingertips on the steering wheel and flipped the radio to a yesteryear station. Leggitt was annoying the hell out of her. Physically, she found his alligator skin and knowing sneer repulsive. But even more frustrating was the fact that he was a schemer who mumbo jumboed her to death and came up with nothing. He condescendingly called her "Ginger"— and overrode her opinions. The guy had the profile of a loser, the type of creep who hung out in OTB parlors and watched adult videotapes alone in seedy efficiency apartments.

So far, this assignment was a total botch job. She had more or less managed to read the *Tattler* article at stoplights on her drive down to Venice. She had found Reno Ventura's house easily enough. It was a two-story cedar-shake bungalow on a one-way alley that ran parallel to the beach. Built in the 1920s, the house once had breathing space and considerable charm. Today, however, it was choked by a sturdy brown fence and caged with iron grills to keep local druggies away.

Ceci had parked across the street in a four-dollar lot where the attendant promised to protect her car from window-smashing junkies. She walked around Ventura's place. Naturally, Leggitt was nowhere in sight. When a black man with a mohawk hollered at her threateningly, she scurried back to her Saab. On her car phone, she reached Julie Cordero in the office. Leggitt and the crew were twelve blocks from Reno's house. She finally located them at the top of a flight of rickety stairs in a small garage apartment on the Marina Peninsula. Leggitt was getting sauced on cheap red wine with a slutty nymph whose orange hair had one-inch black roots. When he saw Ceci's horrified expression, he pulled himself together and insisted that the crew, who had been nipping at the wine as well, set Ceci up for a quick two shot. Although Leggitt was supposed to have prepped the girl, she was flustered by the simplest questions. She had nothing to say about Emily Shay and had only met Reno once, in the market. In the end the only decent footage they managed to get was Ceci ad-libbing in the alley next to Reno's house. With a queasy smile, Ceci stood there babbling unconvincingly about the improved neighborhood.

Before she could escape, Leggitt managed to hoodwink her into chauffeuring him around to follow up a few sources the orange dye job had given him. At one point, while she waited for him, Ceci opened the glove compartment, fumbled for a bottle of aspirin, and took two. More than anything she wanted to go home to bed. She was tempted to start the engine and leave the jerk.

Why Tommy had hired Leggitt confounded her. She overheard him tell Lutz that "Leggitt helps to broaden our demographic base." What a joke. She was angry at him for saddling her with Leggitt on this sub-basement story. This was her reward for "Survivors"?

Leggitt's knuckles rapped against the closed window. She killed the "easy listening" station on the radio and swiftly unlocked the door. He slid inside, a bag of groceries in his arms. He extracted a carton of Dunhill cigarettes, unwrapped a pack, and dropped the cellophane on the floor. Vile clouds of smoke swirled about Ceci's face. She cracked her window. He made no apology for his extended absence. It was as if she were a hired driver, a nonentity, a cipher.

"Back to your car now?" she asked crossly. The sooner she dumped him the better.

His thin lips curled. "One more stop."

"Please, let me drop you at your car."

"Relax. It won't take long," he replied. The wimp expected her to wait around for him. His mother had done quite a job.

This time, however, she decided to park the car and join him. His destination was the Sand Bar, a seedy dive decorated with huge oil paintings of naked breasts that were being passed off as "art."

"Over there," Leggitt said to her, pointing to a stool at the end of the counter. Predictably, he disappeared into the back room.

Ceci looked around. The joint smelled of fried food, piss, and beer. It was filled with men, sad souls who drifted about in a stupor. She felt terribly uncomfortable. But then what the hell. It was a public place. Anyway, the men didn't look like they were about to jump her.

Exhausted, she put her head down on her crossed arms. From behind the bar a pimply-faced kid tapped her shoulder with his pencil. "Whadda ya want?"

She raised her head and looked at his bloodshot eyes, silver earring, and greasy ponytail. This was not the place to order food.

"Anything diet."

He nodded agreeably and returned with a "lite" beer.

"This is diet?"

"Yeah. A diet beer."

Ceci gave him a spare-me look and took a sip of the white froth. He stared at her. She averted her eyes. A scaly crust covered his deeply tanned skin. He was a sure candidate for basal-cell carcinoma. Ceci was careful to avoid the sun. These California kids amazed her, they lived like there was no tomorrow.

"You look like somebody famous," he said.

"Yeah, who?"

"The fat lady on TV with the accent."

Ceci wobbled her head at him absently. Pathetic, really. The kid was an IQ negative. It was probably good he'd die of melanoma at an early age so the state wouldn't have to foot the bill for his old-age care.

Leggitt charged back into the bar. He was tense with excitement. "We gotta get back to the studio. Fast."

"What gives?"

"A guy in the back says Doni Shay's been on the tube for the last hour."

"He's been found?"

"Not exactly—but he's on our show."

"You're kidding."

Shortly after 2 A.M. that night Robert Shay stood in Stan Lutz's corner office looking down at the NTN studio complex. To the north, the glowing towers of Century City loomed up like platinum blocks. Directly below in the parking lot, a line of squad cars waited beside a giant parabolic dish. Their revolving beacons sent a chalky blue fusion through the thick night air.

Behind Robert the conversation continued to shuttle back and forth like a discordant jam session. This time a piercing high note was hit by Lutz.

"Gentlemen, I'm not for sale! I'm not about to allow the FBI to launch a blitzkrieg through my network and ride roughshod over this operation. You're not going to use Tommy's show as a front for your surveillance."

Robert swung around. The NTN president stood behind his desk, an expanse of smoky glass set on chrome pipes. For the moment Train reclined on a tar-black sectional under a huge bronzed plate engraved with the NTN logo. Across the room Krugger paced back and forth before a pewter wall rigged with television monitors.

Stan Lutz's pudding face was turned in his direction. Once again, he exuded respect and gushing devotion. "Mr. Shay, I'm as curious as you are as to why they chose Tommy's show. Why this network?" He skipped a beat. "And, if we are patient, they may provide us with an answer."

In the last hour Robert had rightly pegged Stan Lutz as a boring TV technocrat. So far, he had not seen an iota of creative juice. Lutz was a protoplasmic hunk who moved about gracelessly, in keeping with his boxy furniture. What didn't fit were the new Gucci loafers. Robert hated stirrup buckles.

Train moved from the couch. From the moment they were introduced, Robert sensed his discomfort. With overblown zeal, the talk-show host had examined Shay's hair and clothes in a painfully obvious sizing up. Such combative vanity wasn't new to Robert, but it usually came from aging male actors or gays acutely conscious of their looks.

It was clear that Train had great difficulty relinquishing his starring role. Lutz's fawning attention toward Robert made the imbalance of power all the more apparent. Shay was enormously grateful he had not started his career in the world of television. The lack of subtlety was overwhelming. Appropriately, he mused, he and Train reflected their mediums.

"Maybe it's a one-shot deal," said Train, loosening his limbs as though he were getting ready for a marathon. "A solo nut case. A loner seeking immortality. Tomorrow he'll deliver another tape to Donahue or Koppel." Train lifted his shoulders, rose up on the balls of his feet, and jerked his head to crack his neck.

Lutz came around the desk, his embalmed smile focused on Krugger. "For the last eight hours your agents have interrogated everyone in this building," he drawled with a Brooklyn twang. "Their presence has threatened to interrupt our telecasts." He abruptly switched to a more genial tone. "We handed over the videotape. The foam carton. The wrapping paper. Our lawyers tell us that's all we're required to do."

"You can't investigate our callers because you think they sound suspicious," said Train, picking up the tempo. "If even a hint of this conversation leaked to the press they would think I was a stooge for the FBI. Unable to control my own show. If callers discovered they were being taped by the cops, I'd lose them. 'Phonathon' makes my ratings."

Train began to gesticulate wildly. "This isn't a police state. For you to interfere with my show restricts freedom of the press. I serve the public, not the FBI!"

It was as if Krugger's shell of restraint had been shattered with a hammer. "Quit dickin' around with us," he snarled. He turned on Lutz with white heat in his eyes. "This isn't a first-amendment issue. It's temporary surveillance. Patch in some lines with electronic tracers uplinked to our satellite. It's totally nonintrusive."

Robert stepped in to plead Krugger's case. "We're not telling you how to run your show or who to put on it—"

"Wait a minute," Train blurted. A calculated gleam lightened his eyes. "What's the quid pro quo here? We lose, you win. Unless"—he studied Shay with a fey smile—"you and your wife agree to be guests on my show."

Krugger surprised everyone with a burst of spontaneous laughter. "Ridiculous. Too dangerous. Too many complications," he said loudly.

His response brought a ceasefire to the conversation.

Robert had no desire to appear on the show. To what end? What purpose would it serve? In any case, Emily would never hear of it.

Though Tommy's self-satisfied expression indicated he loved the idea, he fumbled defensively once he sensed Robert's disdain. He rubbed his chin thoughtfully, then put his hands on his belt, flaring his jacket to display his narrow waist. "There's gotta be a reason for this tape. Maybe the kidnappers expect me to negotiate their ransom demands." He looked at Krugger. "If they got wind the feds were backing me, they might change their plans." Tommy flashed a smile at Shay. "Why not let nature take its course?"

Robert was baffled. Certainly there was no reasonable explanation why a video of his son singing "Happy Birthday" to him had been sent to Tommy Train. Reason and logic had nothing to do with any of this.

"Do you keep back records of callers?" Krugger asked in a hardball tone.

"Oh, fuck off," Tommy whispered as he turned away.

Lutz made an attempt at civility. "Videotapes of past shows are kept in the NTN library," he said graciously. He was nervous. The last thing he needed was a search warrant. "You're more than welcome to view any of them."

"My team'll be over in the morning," said Krugger.

It was as good an exit line as any. Shay gave him a let's-split look. "I want to arrest the sonsofbitches," Krugger said as soon as they cleared the corridor to Lutz's office.

Dog tired, Robert looked at him with weary eyes. "What's the point?"

From the window Train and Lutz watched the phalanx of men emerge from under the concrete lip of the building. Another team of agents circled Shay protectively as he walked to a squad car.

"He's a goddamn Viking prince," muttered Train.

Lutz stared down at the director's blond head. "Wrong," he said. "He's a smart German Jew with an Irish name, no less."

Lutz went to the bar and poured himself a glass of sherry. "A drink?"

Tommy nodded affirmatively. Lutz handed him a scotch.

"Krugger's a prick," Tommy said. He lowered his voice an octave to imitate the flat tone of the agent. "Do we screen calls? Do we save calls?" Smugly upbeat, he started to laugh. "Christ, if only he knew—we cast 'em."

"Don't let me hear that," Lutz warned. "Listen, we're riding high no matter what. If they want to monitor calls, let 'em."

Tommy lifted his glass. "To the Lindbergh Legacy. Like that title?"

"Hmmm, maybe too historical," Lutz analyzed. "Better just keep those retrogrades callin' in. Don't change a thing. The November sweeps are around the corner. For once, somebody out there is on the side of NTN."

After she finished her weekly shopping in the open-air market in Roswell, New Mexico, Carlotta García entered the local police station, carrying two bags of vegetables. The baby was strapped to her hip; her young son, José, tagged along behind her.

Because she was an illegal she was nervous about telling the half-breed officer behind the big desk her full name. Because he spoke good Spanish and did not insist, she finally told him. She also told him that her son had played with a small child from the EZ Motel who looked like the movie star's boy. The police officer asked if she saw the child. When she said no, he seemed disappointed. José stood by his mother's side listening to her conversation as he clutched the hem of her dress.

"He has the sticks and ball," he said softly.

The officer leaned over the desk and looked at José quizzically. In Spanish, he asked him if the little boy he played with had spoken English. José shook his head. Her son didn't speak English, Carlotta informed him.

A disinterested expression drifted across the officer's face. Carlotta García shrugged her shoulders. A few moments passed, then she hitched up the worn strap that held the baby and hoisted the groceries. The officer watched her waddle from the station and cross the dusty street to catch the bus that went to Soma junction.

Since the videotape of Doni Shay had been playing on television, six residents of his district had reported seeing the kidnapped baby. Carlotta García's story was the least convincing he had heard. Nonetheless, he made a few cryptic notes on the standard missing-persons form and dropped the sheet into a mesh basket.

The last sentence of his four-line report read: "José García, 3, claims that Donald Shay spoke with him in Spanish."

"We're going to replay the videotape in the library," Libby called to Robert. She stood in the archway that connected the living room with the overgrown courtyard.

Her statement was meant as an invitation.

"No thanks," he choked out. His anguish was reflected in his eyes. Over the last week he had watched the tape a hundred times.

Libby lifted her hand to shield her eyes from the noon sun and stared at him with concern. From the way she was dressed—a cropped polo jacket, brown skirt, and penny loafers, Robert figured that she'd already visited the offices at Starlight.

"I'll be back," he said, attempting to ease her discomfort. "I need time. To think."

She nodded and reluctantly retired to the house.

Aside from her financial acumen, Robert decided, Libby's greatest attribute was her innate sense of privacy. She was an easy person to be quiet with, but she also unfailingly respected his desire to be alone.

He walked slowly along the oyster shell path past the artificial lake and tennis courts to the steps of the botanical gardens terraced up the side of the north canyon. He hiked through a profusion of violets, tulips, and blue chrysanthemums the size of basketballs. The higher he climbed the more rarefied the vegetation. Flowers gave way to exotic orchids planted among sheltering rock formations. These were interspersed with clumps of wild bamboo, spider ferns, and dense patches of bird of paradise.

Halfway to the top, Robert paused to admire the canyon. The mansion, a salmon stucco quadrangle with a hoof-tiled roof, had been angled to fit snugly into the mouth of the valley. Around the front of the house, towering eucalyptus trees shielded the estate from a private road that connected with Benedict Canyon. Twisted jacaranda trees and blue-needle Canary pines formed a second wall closer in to the house.

Robert truly loved Xanadu. Just four years before he had commissioned Pan Mei to design the structure. European architects ranked the spectacular result with Frank Lloyd Wright's Taliesin. Unlike the East Hampton house, it was no modern UFO job but, rather, a geometric configuration of four lavish courtyards, completely integrating Italian and Moorish styles. With the addition of the video library, screening room, and target range, the estate answered all of his practical needs.

Inside the mansion, louvers of cypress were fitted over the large leaded windows. Robert's team of decorators had purchased every piece of John Stickney's mission furniture they could find. The solid oak straight-backed benches and chairs perfectly complemented the sandstone walls and ruby quartz floors. Although Robert had chosen Stickney purely because it pleased him, the value of the pieces soared with every passing day. When Libby boasted of Starlight's global investments and two-billion-dollar credit line, Robert simply pointed to Xanadu. The mansion, with its precious furnishings, cashed in debt-free at three hundred million. In the end it proved to be his most lucrative investment.

The most interesting aspect of the house was the high-tech security system buried within the thick walls. Unseen cameras and intercoms connected every room. In fact, because of the sophistication of the electronic equipment, Krugger's installation of a telephone-intercept station had taken only minutes.

Every inch of the surrounding ten acres was monitored by cameras watched by a team of rotating guards. At night, a pack of Dobermans roamed along a six-foot corridor that circled the back of the property. The most ingenious feature, however, was the "molehole," the creation of an eccentric inventor who once owned the land. Thirty years before, he had blasted a tunnel halfway through the shale canyon with the idea of creating an underground lab.

When Shay purchased the property he continued the excavation with the intention of making an exit route into the neighboring canyon, but granite formations forced the tunnel to detour into the yard of a humble 1950s dwelling on the valley side of the mountain. When the route was discovered by the geologists Shay immediately bought the shoebox from its owner. From the street the modest ranch house appeared much as it always had except that behind the cedarwood facade was a five-car garage, which housed Shay's Ferrari Testarossa, Emily's 1968 Nile green Corniche, two BMWs, and a Range Rover.

Robert returned to the house via the rear courtyard. On the wide cement ledges the kitchen maids had arranged rows of tomatoes to dry in the sun. His eye caught the glimmer of the mezuzah installed by his mother in the doorjamb. He stopped and stared at it, then lifted his fingers to his mouth and placed a kiss on the narrow piece of silver.

Inexplicably, a memory seized him. He must ask Duke whatever became of Madam X, the crazed fan who sent him swatches of her hair and pieces of her skin in the mail. For years the strange woman had harassed him with phone calls and obscene letters describing in detail the ways in which she wanted him. Many were violent. Then, about six months ago, she broke contact. Vanished. Had she managed to get her life together and organize his son's abduction?

As Robert entered the den, Harry flicked off the set, sparing him the sight of Doni. Libby was seated across the room in a rocker, her legs gracefully curled underneath her body.

"It's too strange," she said.

"Doni's scared to death . . ." Harry began.

Libby gave him a menacing look.

"The quality of the tape's awful," he stammered, changing the subject. "Whoever made it never held a camera before. It's obviously the work of some crackpot amateur."

"Yes," Robert agreed. His blue eyes were keen. "Yes, the nutcase scenario makes sense. Some psychotic testing the water. Keeping it in the public eye, and prolonging the pain." He walked over to the window. "My fear is this screwball's willing to sacrifice himself—and Doni—for that moment in the limelight, that mention in the history books. À la Hinckley, Fromm, Oswald."

There was an anxious stillness as if the right note was suddenly hit.

"Train's uniquely tacky," said Harry, breaking the spell. "A gorilla ego with a high-huckster sales pitch. The set's junk city. It makes *Wheel of Fortune* look like the stage at the Met." He threw his arm over the back of the couch and crossed his legs. "Only teenage deviants can swallow this dysfunctional drama on a daily basis. It's schlock for vidiots."

"Careful—that's our audience too," Libby quipped.

"At a younger age."

Libby hunched forward. She reached for the shriveled Italian olive left on her lunch plate and popped it into her mouth. "Train's an aging Casanova—the TV version of Warren Beatty." She spit the seed into her hand as she looked at Robert. "If the kidnappers do call the show, you sure as hell don't want him negotiating with them. He's about as subtle as an MX missile."

"No shit," said Robert. He sank into the chair opposite them and stared absently at the symmetrically round bull's-eye breasts of the woman in the Gauguin painting over the stone fireplace. He shook his head despondently. "Train's fighting for control tooth and nail. He still expects I'll come on the show."

"Don't," said Libby.

"You can buy the show," said Harry. "What would it cost? A hundred mil?"

"Speaking of which," Libby piped up, "the ready tellers have our cash on the line."

It was then that Robert noticed the film cans on the coffee table. "Last of the dailies," said Harry, touching them with the side of his foot.

"There's a rough cut in the editing room at Starlight," Libby added. "Stuff's sensational. Blockbuster time. I fear we've got a breakout picture on our hands." Her voice was emotionless. She spoke as if she were tallying the budget. These were cold business facts independent of the vortex that presently sucked them into hell. She stood up and exhaled audibly. "I've got a pitch meeting. You wanna come?"

It was a kind attempt to distract him. Before Robert could answer Morgan Camp bounced into the quiet living room, a red silk scarf blossoming from his white linen jacket. "Hi y'all," he brayed. "Here's the media statement." He slapped a sheet of paper into Robert's hand, then pulled a small envelope from his back pocket. "And here's a Xerox of the commemorative stamp."

"Commemorative stamp?" Libby said, an incredulous look on her face.

"I wanna work a deal with the post office. It'll keep Doni's picture circulating."

Libby cringed with disgust. "I can't take any more," she said flatly. "I'm gone."

"Good idea, eh?" Morgan exclaimed.

Libby gave Robert and Harry a weary eye roll, then vanished into the cavernous hallway.

"If Emily's flying out, who's baby-sitting East Hampton?" Harry asked.

"I think maybe Chicki should stay there," Robert replied. "She gets along with the FBI crew."

Camp perked up. "In that case I got a great gal to answer phones. She's worked with Trixie and me for years. Sherry Cox. Smart ticket. Handles the press like a pro."

Robert hesitated, then gave in. "Okay, bring her in for the press calls."

Morgan was enormously pleased. The more people he had on the inside, the more power he wielded. "Now, I talked with Train's producer, Shorty Smith," he said, settling on the couch. "Very down-to-earth guy. He's says Train's willing to make some adjustments for us."

Ceci figured that the reason Stan Lutz had asked her to lunch had something to do with the ongoing uproar over the videotape. Prior to his invitation he had never said more than four words to her.

She downshifted her Saab as she approached Bedford Drive, made a right off Santa Monica Boulevard, and cruised slowly through Beverly Hills until she came to the multistory parking garage on Camden Drive a half-block from The Grill. It was only 11:30. She purposely allowed herself plenty of time to shop for a new suit. After all, how many times in her life would she have lunch with the president of the network? She parked on the top level and took the elevator down to the street.

Rodeo Drive always gave her a charge. Almost everything suited her taste and style, and unlike the pricey shops in Kansas City, the clothes in Rodeo boutiques always exuded an indefinable spark of tailored sexiness.

In Cartier's windows the latest Parisian rings were displayed on wiry branches emerging from folds of buttery velvet. Ceci frowned at her four-year-old emerald ring. The filigree setting made her feel hopelessly old-fashioned. Such elaborate busywork was passé. She prayed Stan Lutz wouldn't notice. Fortunately, from the haphazard way he dressed he didn't seem as keen on clothes as Tommy was.

As she stopped to feast her eyes on the fine leather purses in the Hermès window, two women in black Chanel suits with gold chain buttons entered the store—obviously "Hollywood wives." Ceci had gradually come to recognize this particular breed of female—"the Hermès bag ladies," Grinker had nicknamed them. They drove Jaguars or Mercedes and were magnificently maintained by expensive teams of hairdressers, masseurs, plastic surgeons, trainers, and dietitians. Never a crease or wrinkle marred their perfection. They wore their designer dresses like uniforms that set them apart, as if they attended some exclusive private school. Ceci sighed. At this stage of her life it seemed impossible to keep up with them. Moreover, her lingering midwestern practicality and the fact that she didn't have a rich husband prevented her from buying as indiscriminately as many of these women did.

For all the media hype about Barbara Bush's off-the-rack clothes the truth was that these days designer labels were in. Ceci observed that this fixation with labels didn't just apply to the Hollywood crowd. Designer clothes were being worn by all the top women on TV. Ceci could spot an Armani on Diane Sawyer, a Donna Karen on Connie Chung. A year ago, she had started keeping a notebook, jotting down the jackets, blouses, and jewelry her favorite anchors wore on their respective shows. Later she tried to replicate their outfits.

Ceci made a right through the tall glass doors of Armani. These days, Armani was the badge of a successful career. Even the less serious women—the sexual toys like Donna Rice and Marla Maples—wore Armani. Rock stars wore Armani.

Ceci wandered through the light, airy store as if she were walking through a museum. Appropriately, there were no racks, no feeling of mass production. Instead the delicately printed silk dresses and feather-light cashmere jackets were hung on pedestals much like works of art. They were priced like works of art too. Discreetly, Ceci found a ticket on a rust-patterned silk dress: $2,400. The jacket for two grand was an on-sale item. Then and there she decided to let go of her feelings about money. You had to pay for the best Italian craftsmanship.

Early on in her career she had thought she could wear anything as long as the clothes around her neck and shoulders appeared neat and crisp. But not anymore. The camera picked up the quality of the fabric. Her on-air clothes were critical to her success. They couldn't look cheap or common. The public might accept Barbara Bush in Act III jackets but not their TV anchors.

"Excuse me, aren't you Ceci McCann?" asked an impeccably tailored saleslady. Ceci was momentarily stunned and pleased. Not that many people recognized her.

She took her notebook from her bag and recited three combinations she had recorded. The saleslady ushered her to a private booth and brought her a variety of jackets that matched Ceci's description. Each fit beautifully and each was more exquisite than the last. It was remarkable the way they melted around her body like a second skin. After twenty minutes of admiring herself, she settled on a patterned mocha wool. The accompanying blouse seemed a bargain at $600.

With her old linen suit tucked away in a sleek Armani shopping bag, Ceci dashed across Rodeo Drive into the Bally shoe store. There she found a perfect pair of leather pumps to complement her new suit. Feeling like Diane Sawyer she walked back to the parking lot to dump her past history in the trunk of her car.

The thought that she spent four grand in just two hours caused her some anxiety. A necessary business expense, she repeated to herself in reassurance.

Lutz stood at the bar nursing a drink, listening while a dark-suited man with chrome hair and a deep tan talked excitedly to him. As soon as he saw Ceci enter the restaurant Lutz dismissed his companion and hurried to give her a perfunctory brush kiss.

The maître d' escorted them past tables of businessmen to a back booth. The Grill was a masculine restaurant, a hangout for industry power brokers.

"What have you done to yourself?" said Lutz, beckoning the waiter for the wine list. "You look different. First class."

Ceci pushed her purse along the seat of the booth. It didn't belong with her outfit. It slid onto the floor and she kicked it closer to her, then stretched down as gracefully as possible to reach it.

Lutz seemed unaware of her awkwardness. She smiled at him nervously. Her stomach was doing flip-flops. She turned on some internal dialogue to calm herself. Fortunately, Lutz broke the ice by suggesting a California wine, a Cakebread Chardonnay. The thought of wine curdled Ceci's stomach but she said she'd be delighted to share a bottle.

Lutz surveyed the menu briefly, then stole a peek at her. Their eyes connected and both of them broke into spontaneous smiles. Lutz closed his menu. "Order the New York steak. Primo."

Ceci obeyed. She had planned to bypass salad. She couldn't risk exotic greens sticking to her front teeth and making her look foolish.

"Before we start with the social niceties," Lutz said, "I've got to say I think you're a real pro, an ace news reader and fast becoming one of the best producers on the show. When the Shay situation— our blessing from heaven—resolves itself I've been thinking that you should move to New York and join the network news division."

Ceci's ears burned. Was she hearing right? Was she dreaming this? She clutched a cold fork in her sweaty fingers, unable to respond.

"I'm talking down the line, maybe a year," Lutz added. The waiter brought the wine. Lutz rolled a mouthful around, then told the waiter to pour it. With a trembling hand Ceci clicked her glass against his. She tried to retain her composure but she was so excited she could barely breath.

"We'll bring you in over the assignment desk," said Lutz. "Feminist feathers'll fly but it's about time our gals got the message the eighties are over. Gone. Kaput. Beauty before brains is the operative rule in TV news in the 1990s."

Ceci didn't know if this was a compliment or a put-down. It was, however, a fact. Though NTN's female news correspondents in New York were attractive they were considerably older. Many of them were in their forties. There had been no beauty queens since the days of Phyllis George.

"A knockout will get the anchor slot," said Lutz as if reading her mind.

The food arrived, but Ceci was too nervous to eat.

"Ah, there's another item," he said after taking a bite of bloody steak. "I've got a little project we can start now."

Ceci broke an inch off a skinny breadstick. She put it on her side plate and listened intently.

"At my insistence the news division has finally commissioned a series of commercials. They've collected tapes of ten serious journalists doing their thing." He paused and looked into her eyes. "Gray matter," he said morosely. "What's missing is female glitz.

I sent them a tape of Lisa interviewing teenagers about condoms. They liked it and asked for more. Some body shots of you leaping from a satellite van and rushing videotape into the studio might do the trick."

At that moment two men started to approach the table but changed direction when they saw Lutz was engaged. He looked relieved. "Those guys are Nielsen execs pissed we subscribed to RNX, the new Japanese rating system." He swigged more wine. "What do they expect? Nielsen's rated us number six. According to RNX we're number one." He turned toward her, a ray of light in his hazel eyes. "You know why? Because the Japs are efficient. They aren't afraid to go into the inner-city ghettos and get the numbers. Nielsen hires a bunch of scaredy-cats." Lutz went on. "See the guy at the bar, the one I was talking to?" Ceci looked at the chrome-haired man chatting with two middle-aged women. "A chronic blowhard. Ex-NTN producer who blames Keigel—and me—for the belt tightening." An ugly expression crossed his face. "Why in hell the jarheads don't just read the *Wall Street Journal*. . . . The country's in a major recession."

Lutz readdressed his meal with gusto. He didn't seem to notice that Ceci was barely eating. Between hefty bites of mashed potatoes, he said, "After Kansas City, Los Angeles must be quite a change. La-la land isn't always easy." He whisked the napkin across his pink lips. "Do you have a boyfriend?"

Ceci was taken aback by his question, but naturally, whether or not she had a boyfriend would influence her future move to New York. She explained her situation. Lutz smiled and poured her more wine. She chattered a bit—perhaps more than he wanted to hear —about her life since she came west. Feeling more relaxed, she gave him her rehearsed spiel—nothing profound, just a cute succession of anecdotes: Ceci takes L.A. Easterners always seemed to enjoy it.

Lutz stared at her with rapt attention. His small eyes were fixed on her as if captivated. Ceci found him appealing: he seemed warm and caring. From what she knew about him there was a lot to respect. Harvard educated, he had been a producer for the BBC before he revolutionized a string of cable stations in Florida. The newspapers often described him as a maverick, an imitation Ted Turner. When the Keigel family bought the near-defunct NTN network they hired Lutz to cut losses and turn the dinosaur into a profitable enterprise. He was quoted as saying that NTN was the biggest business challenge of his life. He didn't plan to fail. The once great and grand network would be resurrected.

"You're a very beautiful and intelligent woman," he said, smiling broadly at her. His eyes probed a millimeter deeper than was necessary for normal conversation. He was attracted to her as a woman, Ceci realized.

She blushed, feeling the tug, too. It stunned her. Lutz wasn't an attractive man.

The arrival at their table of a stout dark-haired woman deflected his attention. Lutz rose politely and gave her a bear hug. She introduced the tall man standing behind her as a producer from Paramount Pictures. Stan switched back into his role as network president—joking, friendly, but distant and businesslike.

The two were joined by another man and soon a noisy ring of people surrounded them, paying homage to Stan. As he introduced Ceci, she felt proud being the luncheon guest of such a powerful man.

They parted in front of the restaurant at exactly 3:30. Unlike casual L.A. types, Lutz was an easterner who worked by the clock. Ceci liked that. After he kissed her on the cheek, he said, "I'd rather you didn't mention our lunch to Tommy." He smiled at her. "There's too much happening right now. My plan for your future career is our little secret."

The heavy black door slammed closed and the limo pushed off. The vanity plate read NTN NET. At that moment, to Ceci, it spelled GOD.

She stood savoring the experience. The phrase "your future career" replayed like an aria in her brain. Elation filled her soul. She felt empowered. There was nothing she couldn't do if she put her mind to it. Then with a sharp pivot she turned and strolled up Camden Drive, stealing a glance at herself in the plate-glass windows.

That was it! The rewards of wearing an Armani power suit. She smoothed the clingy, softly tailored jacket and skirt with her hands. Mother had always said, "Dressing your best pays off."

17

Lynn Barnes was in a sour mood as she booted up the main-line terminal of the Atex system in the FBI's Albuquerque office. She called up the master file on Donald Shay and gave it a cursory read-over. The updates were neatly flagged.

For the last two months she had dutifully read the package. A smart woman with a crack memory, she had memorized every detail of the report. She felt she knew Donald Shay better than her own sons. Today's update was more trivia: Doni preferred vanilla ice cream. He called Brussels sprouts "baby balls." His left big toenail might possibly develop an ingrowth. One item caught her attention: he knew how to spell Mickey Mantle and Babe Ruth.

After keying in the proper log-on, an endless list of "sightings" began to scroll down her screen. Since the videotape of the kidnapped boy had been sent to the L.A. television show, calls to local police precincts had increased tenfold. Essentially, Lynn's job was to read each new entry and then assign it a category. She took a sip of her tepid decaf. It was a long and tedious process. Two hundred "sightings" had been added to the system since yesterday.

By noon she was tired and hungry. Her eyes ached and her stomach growled. She had slugged "Coyote" to the grizzled recluse in Taos who sheltered runaways. The police had visited his ranch twice since neighbors reported a Doni Shay look-alike. Lynn figured the community wanted to evict the old codger and hoped to use the Shay 'napping to harass him.

"Southplex" went to the mother who yanked her towheaded child down the aisle of a Miller's Outpost store on a leash. She was a shrew who screamed epithets at bystanders who came forward and told her to stop torturing the baby. Two agents visited her home and found the boy to be her son. The resemblance to Doni Shay was awesome. A carbon copy.

Just as Lynn finished her sixth cup of decaf José García's name flickered across the screen. When she saw that he was only three she was about to deep-six him into the morgue file, but something curious stopped her. José spoke no English. Typical. He talked to the gringo child in Spanish. Also typical. Every gringo child living on the outskirts of Roswell knew some street Mexican. What was odd was José's mother, Carlotta. She did not speak a word of English. A dead giveaway she was an illegal—one of Lynn's pet hates.

She reached past a leather-framed picture of her boys and called Marge Clark, her high school buddy who was now chief assistant for Tom Mendoza, head of New Mexico's Immigration and Naturalization Service. "I was sifting through the missing persons' report on the Shay baby and came across something of interest to your boss."

"What?" asked Clark eagerly.

Lynn knew Marge was especially interested in scoring points with Mendoza because she was up for a raise next month.

"A family of illegals are holed up in a trailer behind the EZ Motel. They're new arrivals. Dirt poor and incredibly arrogant. The wife marched right into the police station and gave the officer her name. Totally fearless."

Marge repeated the sketchy details as she jotted them down. "Sounds good," she said. "I'll run it by Tom this afternoon."

Lynn smiled. She knew Marge would get credit. It might earn her some brownie points too and give her a reason to call him. Mendoza was a hunk. Three weeks ago Marge told her he had left his wife. Lynn pushed the *delete* button on her computer. José García wasn't going to Washington but to the INS office for formal deportation. She switched off the machine and headed down to the company cafeteria.

Meanwhile, in the INS office, Marge Clark processed the information for her boss. Newly appointed to his job, Mendoza was a go-getter who talked of "regaining control of the border." He planned to raise the number of illegals captured to twice that of the previous year and last week he announced a new program of jailing repeat offenders in detention centers in south Texas. In the past, illegals merely declared their wish to go home and were released. Although Mendoza didn't tell the press, Marge knew his goal was to get 600,000 illegals into detention centers by next summer.

Beyond the tinted windows of the Rolls Royce Silver Spur the big mansions of Beverly Hills flowed past like building blocks, one after another. Emily Shay sat next to Maria in the backseat of the car. Snickers snuggled against the thick black cashmere coat that grazed her ankles.

She stared at the pink-and-green awning of the Beverly Hills Hotel as they sped up Benedict Canyon. She hated this part of L.A., the "celebrity grid" Reno called it. To Emily the buildings were oversized and empty. Cold. Her tastes ran to Santa Monica Canyon, Trancas, Ojai, and Montecito. But, like everything of importance in her life with Robert, she had no meaningful say. When they first married he had insisted they establish their home in the most convenient location for his work. Thus, "the Mission," as she called the house disparagingly, was strategically built ten minutes from Starlight in the San Fernando valley and twenty minutes from the animation lab in Westwood.

As they drove by the tract of new mansions with their phony mansard roofs and colonial facades, tears began to slide down Emily's cheeks. Once again, what she loved had been taken from her —first her mother, then dancing, and now her only child. It was too much to bear.

She kept trying to tell herself that it wasn't her fault. But self-forgiveness had never been her strong suit. Her perfectionism was her Achilles' heel. She understood all this; the shrinks had given her the diagram for what made her tick, the intricate pathways like the circuit board of a computer. She saw it all, but despite the brilliant and intellectually tantalizing explanations of her emotions, those emotions refused to be harnessed and jumped off the board. The moment Doni was kidnapped they exploded crazily in all directions. And without the drugs she had no way to control their negative pull—the increasingly intense desire to end her life. She had been without drugs for a week. Robert had called Reiss and forbade him to prescribe even Lithium. She didn't argue because in her heart she knew if Doni died she could never be repaired. She couldn't live in the world or with herself. The only reasonable response to his death would be her suicide. Coldly, she calculated how she would do it. This time, there would be no mistakes. She would use one of Duke's guns. Unlike Robert's, they were loaded.

The Rolls passed through the electronic gates. Although the canyon was bucolic and serene she had no feeling for the beauty of the place. Still, spending December waiting alone in the biting cold of East Hampton seemed pointless. Without the drugs, she was restless. If Doni was alive he was no longer on Long Island. She knew that.

As she stepped from the car, she saw Robert. He stood stock still, framed against the robin's-egg-blue sky. They met on the drive halfway from the veranda. The sexless kiss that passed between them masked their suppressed feelings.

When they entered the house, the butler went ahead, taking Emily's luggage to her suite. The strains of a Brahms symphony echoed hollowly in the stone hallway. Robert stopped her unexpectedly at the arched oak door that led to his bedroom.

"Stay with me," he said.

"Whatever for?"

"It's not sex."

"No?" Her hostility was just under the surface. She realized she wanted to hurt him for all the pain he had caused her.

"I'm frightened," he said.

"So am I," she said with an aseptic smile. "But I'm frightened of us, our lives. We're responsible for this, Robert. We deserve what's happened to us."

"Emily, what are you saying?"

"The way we live. The houses, the parties, the cars, the industry."

Behind Robert's perplexed expression was a growing acceptance of her words. "I can't help it if we live in a media dictatorship." Self-justification filled his voice. "I've tried to stay out of the press. I never flaunted my life-style."

"Have you? Have you really?" A grim smile hardened her face. "The entire world knows you gave thirty million to the USC film school last year. Why does the world know that, Robert?"

"If I've been on a power trip, it's been making movies. Film is a business of exhibitionism. I can't help that."

"Cut the drumroll." Her anger was on full force. "You could have done it differently." Then, as if blasted by Mace, she brought herself up short, her eyes blinking rapidly. "*We* could have done it differently, that's all." She pivoted slightly, then, in a conciliatory tone, added, "I am as much to blame."

He followed her into her bedroom. She opened the shutters over the bed and inhaled the warm, still air of the honeysuckle afternoon. She turned to him. "We have to stop torturing each other."

Robert sat down on the zebra throw that covered the king-size bed. Emily gave him a long, silent look, then took a handful of silk garments from the drawer of an oak bureau and went into the dressing room to change.

He leaned against the Navajo pillows. The smell of burning birch logs wafted in from the drawing room where the butler stoked the fire. The canyon turned fiercely cold with the evening shade.

"What's our boy Malathion up to?" Emily called out to him.

"Still monitoring the tidal wave of calls to the Train show."

She emerged in a white robe. "I see you've got top box office with *Thunderhead.*"

"The numbers have more to do with Doni's kidnapping than with the film."

She emitted a chilly laugh. "I don't think so." She walked energetically to the sliding oak doors and pulled them back. Robert saw the Stairmaster in her training room.

He closed his eyes again. "I think some sicko is intent on making us suffer. He wants to see us twist slowly." Robert lifted his arms up over his head and held a pillow aloft, staring at the woven fabric. "I've racked my brain trying to recall who I destroyed to deserve such vengeance."

"You have relatively few enemies, given the nature of the business," she said.

Emily's violet eyes prowled over his lean body. "Your fly-by-night amours are another matter, however."

Robert sat upright. His eyes met hers. "A jealous woman?" He said it in wonderment.

Emily yanked the pearl barrette from her long, thick hair. "And to think my biggest worry was catching herpes from you."

Robert laughed.

She scanned his face. "This conversation isn't going to get me into your bed."

"There's hope?"

She gave him the sullen smile he knew too well. He watched her buttocks flex under the robe as she walked over to a cedar trunk and removed an Irish fisherman's sweater. He felt the pull toward her, yet there was no right thing to say.

"We're on a roulette wheel," she said as she began digging through her valise. A copy of *Meditations on the Light* landed on the bed next to Robert. "We're in a preordained orbit," she went on as she began to arrange her collection of Swiss skin creams on the mirrored tray of the vanity table.

"Fatalism is death," said Robert.

"Fatalism is realism, my darling. These crazies aren't after money. They're on some lunar cycle." She paused. "What alternatives do we have? Do you think we should go on television and beg them to release Doni?"

"Yes, if I thought it might work."

This time, when Emily swished past the bed, Robert grabbed her arm and pulled her down over him. His hand burrowed under the loose robe. She didn't resist. Unfortunately, his cock was soft, his desire imaginary. He stared out the window over the bed at the forest of tall pines. The bleached sky faded into evening shadows. The room took on a blue glow. He rolled out from under her. "Later."

Disheveled, Emily propped herself up on her elbows. The white robe sliced open to her pelt. "Sure," she said, bouncing back hard against the bed.

Tommy Train's stretch limo rolled east down Hollywood Boulevard. Its destination was the ABC studio where Train was scheduled to be a guest on *Nightline.*

Jack hated conducting interviews in automobiles, no matter how big or well padded, but at this point he wasn't about to argue, since Train had played hard to get for the last three weeks while he warbled to *Time* and *USA Today.*

Werts checked his microcassette recorder resting on the black velvet seat. The sensitive little bugger was picking up sirens, along with Roy Orbison's drone from a CD player somewhere in the front of the car.

"It's obvious," said Tommy as they stopped for a red light at the corner of Hollywood and Ivar. "You've got a twelve-billion dollar industry desperate for raw material and I'm providing it."

Jack glanced out the window at a row of cheap discount outlets and nail salons. Bus benches advertised diet centers and boudoir photography.

"I make no bones about the fact that I'm after numbers. Charles and Di's wedding was watched by seven hundred fifty million people in seventy-four countries. One fucking fifth of the world's population." Tommy reached down and clicked off Jack's recorder. "Off the record: we got global numbers on the videotape and we're gonna publish 'em.''

Oh, why off the record, thought Jack.

Tommy removed his unstructured suede jacket and laid it across the seat opposite them. He wore ultra-creased flannel trousers. His bronze profile jutted forward as he began his Orwellian spiel: "These high-minded critics call my show a Roman circus. Well, I'm sick of their bad-mouthing. I'm a media activist." Restless, he crossed one leg over the other thigh; his manicured hand absently caressed his alligator loafers. Clearly, eco values had passed this guy by.

Jack glanced down at his own black Florsheims. Solid shoes and the price was right. In fact, he felt he was pretty well dressed today. Nice new Arrow shirt. Broadcloth, but what the hell. Couldn't find a tie so it was open at the collar, respectable enough for L.A. He wore what he considered his best suit, a charcoal gabardine bought off the rack, on sale at Macy's in New York. That meant something. Jack instinctively distrusted guys who put time and money into their clothes. It was effete, wimpy behavior. Smarter to put your money into fishing tackle.

Tommy checked to see that Jack's tape recorder was back on. "You'll edit out the profanity," he said. He resumed his for-the-record tone of voice. "What's a newscast without some bias? Who cares if I make it a carnival? Why are they so uptight?" He chortled quietly to himself. " 'Cause I hit the jackpot. They can't stand it. By sheer luck I stepped into the winner's circle. Well, eff-'em."

The phone next to Train's arm blurped. Jack noted his Cartier watch, an expensive trinket, while Tommy began yakking about the next day's show. "I gotta work through some kinks," he said to Jack, excusing himself for a few minutes.

Werts smiled agreeably and turned up the recorder. Long ago he had learned that comments made by the subject when he was unaware of being taped revealed the most about his character.

Jack stretched back in the leather seat of the air-conditioned car. Outside the windows the trash can of Hollywood floated by. "The armpit of L.A." Sammy coined it. Shaggy hipsters, deranged messianics, and bag ladies with bathroom rugs for shawls shuffled across the brass stars of the Celebrity Walk of Fame. A gang of purple-haired teenage mutants cruised next to them in a high rider with an exposed chassis. At midnight, the tribal dance transformed into war and the boulevard went from spray paint to spray bullets.

At the corner of Hollywood and Vine a cluster of baby dolls with painted eyes and juggy chests hawked their bodies in Spandex wrappings—dissolute urchins infested with viruses. There was an eerie placidity to their catcalls. Easy death. Jack thought about Dorothy Stratton and Sharon Tate. If he ever had a daughter he'd raise her in Wyoming.

Train slammed the phone into its socket. "Where was I?" he grumbled.

Jack displayed a good-ol'-boy smile. "Sagely explaining the mentality of TV critics."

"Ah, yes," said Tommy, gathering his thoughts. "While these jealous snipers attack me, the control of the media is being reduced to fewer and fewer corporate hands. We're getting censored information from corporate titans. Even John Chancellor has said the presidential debates are phony." He combed his hands over his thick brown hair. "America needs honesty. I'm the Crocodile Dundee of TV!"

Sure, Mac, and I'm Matthew Arnold, thought Jack. Train tried too hard to come off clever. He missed by a notch. The difference between lightning and the lightning bug.

"Satellite bingo's making a fortune and they don't bellyache 'bout that. I admit I practice shock journalism. You bet I wanna blow some units. Why not? A frictionless fuck is what the networks deliver. Who needs more white noise?"

Jack was getting a crick in his neck. The tape finished. He slipped in a fresh cassette. Although a braggart, Train gave good quote. He was sophisticated in an uncouth way. Essentially he practiced a packaged variety of body-bag journalism not that different from local newscasts. But Train's analysis of TV was hardly fresh. Jack grew bored. He wanted a drink. As they headed through the poor Hispanic neighborhoods of east Hollywood Werts felt the urge to perform.

"Question," he said, mimicking Dan Rather's husky tone. He had long ago discovered that TV people identified with their own.

Tommy cocked a ready eyebrow.

"Why did they send the tape to you? No bullshit."

"Between us, I think it's a fluke," he responded. "Some screwball desperately seeking his fifteen minutes."

Though Train had the integrity of a used-car salesman there was an uneducated charm to the guy. Jack could see why six women had married him.

"A few personal questions," he went on. "The *Tattler* reported that NTN's payin' you ten million a year?"

"I pass," said Tommy. He raised his hands. "The IRS defense."

It was always nice to know that TV journalists were phony hypocrites when it came to revealing their lavish incomes.

"Why so many wives?"

"I've had trouble with women." A gamey smile. "Wives are especially tough, but I'm not alone."

Other than Mickey Rooney, Jack couldn't think of any examples in the six-plus league. But did he have trouble with his producers? Ceci McCann was too pretty for Train not to have made a pass at her.

"There's talk of your using drugs."

Tommy turned ashen. *"Moi?"*

Jack detected a slight tremor in his lower eyelid. Tommy flexed his iron torso under his silk shirt. "I've got the barbell habit. Fifty reps a day. Print that."

He looked too good to be an abuser. A likely ex-user. Clips sent from New York revealed bankruptcy and gambling debts back in his Oklahoma radio days.

"I've sowed my oats," he admitted contritely, a one-real-guy-to-another look in his eyes. "And the tabs are right. I do encourage female fans to submit nude pictures. It's an outrageous gag. But between us—off the record—I hardly spend my day studying photos of overweight women."

"You're notorious for your insult humor."

"Best kind. 'Ziploc yor mouth, ma friend,' " Train croaked. "But not all my viewers are idiots," he protested. "My fans also watched *Sledgehammer*. God, how I loved that show."

Train was truly off center. As the limo cleared the ABC guard booth, Jack asked, "What's your age?"

"Forty-one."

And I'm seventeen, he thought.

In the greenroom, the windowless box reserved for guests and their friends, Jack sipped a cup of black Styrofoam coffee as he watched Tommy on the monitor. Train was making an unsuccessful attempt to charm the pants off Ted Koppel.

Jack was disgusted with his own involvement in this charade. Three species of animals were being lost a day and he sat baby-sitting a megalo. There were so many important issues: AIDS, Iraq,

Noriega, South Africa, the Soviet economy. He got up and bumped the switch. The gray-white luminescence faded to a tiny square.

Because competition from the printed word was prohibited, greenrooms never had magazines, books, or newspapers. But this one did have a phone. Jack checked in with his machine. Four messages from Madison Cole. He dialed her Malibu number. She answered on the first ring. Roy Orbison was silenced in the background. Why was everyone listening to poor ol' Roy?

"I've been trying to reach you for two weeks," she said, sickly sweet. "You were right. *Exposé* did a shitty job. They tried to ruin me."

Jack hadn't read the piece.

"It was awful," she moaned. "They labeled me 'discarded goods' from the Palm Beach-Monaco-Gstaad call-girl circuit. Jack, I've never even been to Gstaad!"

He noticed she didn't say anything about P.B. or Monaco.

"I made a dreadful mistake. I should have spoken to you." She cleared her throat. Took a sip of something. God, he wanted a gin and tonic. He imagined the Malibu waves. The moon.

"I need an article in *Newsmakers*. No cost. Please be a sport. It's important for my career." She paused. "I can reciprocate in other ways."

Madison was hardly Nolan Ryan. Jack doubted her sexual skills had been perfected with age. "Honey, I hate to burst your bubble but the videotape is the story."

"I know. But things change."

"If they change in your direction, I'll give you a call."

215

18

Robert Shay rose from the marble desk in his bedroom office. His work space had been raised like an altar to take in the view of west Los Angeles that stretched to the Pacific. As he ambled outside into the bright sunlight, he noticed a plastic tube of Baby Block 30 wedged between the mossy rocks that surrounded the oval fish pond. Doni. The knife of pain cut into his soul. He picked up the tube and threw it on a chair so the maids would see it and take it away. Despite his gnawing despair, he felt considerably better after yesterday's conference call with George Lucas and Steven Spielberg. Besides being business associates they were his trusted friends. He valued their judgment. Their advice: lie low and wait. Like everyone in Hollywood, they were spooked about the safety of their children.

Robert returned to his study. He had spent the last two weeks plowing through letters from crazed fans who claimed to have knowledge of his son's whereabouts. Not one letter rang true. The videotape had been the only genuine contact, but what was the point of it? What in hell were these people doing with his son? A flood of negative thoughts filled his brain.

On the path below he saw Camp bound up the steps with a young woman in tow. "Ahoy!" Morgan shouted, waving frantically. Robert went down to meet them. The girl wore a hot-pink suit. Nice eyes. She was pretty in a cheap teenage way.

"Sherry Cox, Rob Shay. I know Krugger's goin' to try to terrorize her," Camp said. "I've prepared her." He smiled with all his cheek muscles as if he had just scored a touchdown. "Right, sweetie?"

She nodded at Morgan but her eyes stole over to Shay. He was far handsomer than his pictures.

"*Newsmakers* is doin' a special issue on the video," spouted Morgan, showering them with a faint spray. "Three times in the last hour, Jack Werts, their ace correspondent, requested an interview with you."

Sherry was speechless. Jack hadn't told her anything about this. Of course the bum hadn't returned her three messages either. She moved closer to Camp.

"No interview," said Shay. "No interviews to *Time* or *Newsweek* either."

Snickers nestled against Robert's leg as he gunned the Range Rover into the fast lane, heading east on the 134 freeway toward Burbank. Starlight Studios was located behind Warner Bros. in the heat bowl of the San Fernando Valley.

From the time he was fifteen Robert had wanted his own high-tech studio. Eight years ago, he had bought a forty-acre spread once inhabited by stables and horse sheds. A year later, Libby ruthlessly negotiated with local developers to secure an adjacent thirty acres. When *Blue Lightning* brought in three hundred million in film rentals, Shay realized his lifelong dream.

He drove through gate 1 to the executive offices located in a three-story adobe building nicknamed the Igloo. To the left were the animation labs, to the right five stadium-size sound stages. Each was two hundred feet high to accommodate the mechanical demands of special-effect films. Last year Starlight earned a quarter of a billion renting the valuable stages to outside production companies. Now the stages were taken until June with *Red Planet*. In stage 4 Robert glimpsed the cratered rubber half-moon constructed to resemble the surface of Mars. He pulled the Rover into the yellow neon space, color coded in an offbeat, democratic twist to distinguish Starlight from the other studios with their white stenciled name slots.

Robert was intensely proud of his studio. He viewed it as the workplace of the future with its lush green commons, health-food commissary, Olympic pool, and a state-of-the-art day-care center. At lunch time fathers and mothers could be seen rolling on the lawns with their children. Despite the heavy production schedules, Starlight managed to retain a family atmosphere. It was "the place" for up-and-comers to work: their ticket to heaven. After Roger Corman, Shay had given more film students their first crack at the business than anyone else, and he had a good record when it came to hiring women. By his own admission he was more comfortable working with them.

Perhaps his only professional flaw was a singular focus on techno thrillers rather than dramatic films. After making twenty-seven blockbusters, *China White* was his first film sans special effects. Now its apparent success only added to his misery. Although he didn't subscribe to the historic theme that art requires suffering on the part of its creator, he secretly feared that Doni's abduction was God's way of extracting a pound of flesh. Shay had never accepted or even considered this premise before, but, if this was to be God's price, he'd forsake art.

Robert whistled for Snickers, who had galloped off to deposit his message on his favorite palm tree in the quad. The spaniel loped back and they raced each other up the circular staircase.

Pine's secretary met him at the door to his office. "Chicki just got off the phone," she told him. "She's had it with the Hamptons. She'll be in the office tomorrow."

Robert entered the sandstone arcade, an all-purpose space used for pitch meetings and battle planning. In truth, the big room was a free-for-all adult playpen filled with video games, dart boards, country tables, and an army of life-sized, rubber-faced robots from Starlight's "repertory" company. Robert loved the schmoozy atmosphere. He firmly believed the background chaos loosened up his visitors. The pretentious were annoyed and irritated; the creative kicked off their shoes, shot a few baskets, then settled down and did their best work.

This afternoon the room was empty. He slipped into his office and closed the sliding oak door. Loud, outrageous pieces of modern art covered the walls. Rising up from the floor around the desk, like pilings, were stacks of scripts and magazines. Shay never allowed the maintenance people to throw anything away. From clutter came his best creative material. Not surprisingly, Libby's office was right-angled perfection. Robert liked that too. Yin and Yang.

The intercom bleeped. "How's Bruce Willis's voice for the Martian?" Harry asked.

"Hmmm."

As he stood looking out at the sprinklers soaking the Bermuda grass, Robert realized that the twenty-room log cabin in Telluride, Colorado, was the only residence he owned that had not been publicized by the press. If Doni came home that's where they'd go to live. Then he'd buy a castle in Eastern Europe. A Scottish manor was impossible because of the British press.

Robert watched a cherry picker drive slowly up the asphalt ramp of soundstage 4. A gang of burly stuntmen headed for the wardrobe trailers. Libby was moving full speed on *Planet*.

"Bruce Willis?" repeated Harry patiently.

"I'm thinking."

"Come by the editing room." Harry's voice was sympathetic.

"What's the rush?"

A moment of silence. "*China White*. Cannes in May. Your orders, remember?"

Robert had forgotten. Usually he stood shoulder to shoulder with his film editors to smooth jump cuts and call for reshoots where bridges were needed. But the urge to perfect his movie had vanished. *China White* was far better off in Pine's capable hands.

He signed off as Harry's secretary opened the door. "Oh, I forgot," she announced. "Lee Mack said to tell you she's in villa four."

Robert deposited the golf cart under the red fish-eye at the entrance of the vanilla stucco building. The warning light was off. He pulled open the forty-pound door. The cavernous recording studio was pitch dark save for a cone of light that illuminated a complex digital panel the size of a small swimming pool. Beyond a glass wall was a semicircle of metal chairs, microphones, and sound booms. On the floor were boxes of sand, gravel, and cement used for dubbing footsteps into the score.

Just as he turned to leave he heard a hushed groan. Lee Mack's sleepy head rose from behind the electronic keyboard, her hair wildly messed, her eyes at half-mast. "Robert?" She spoke in a groggy voice. "Robert, is that you?"

She was propped up like an artist's model on the overstuffed purple velour sofa. A thick, sweet smell rose from her body.

"Sorry," she apologized. "I'm exhausted. We got back from Thailand last night. Harry's a goddamn slave driver."

She spoke as if he knew about the trip. Pine hadn't bothered to tell him or if he did, Robert had forgotten.

In the half-light he could see she wore a gauzy summer dress with a deep folded collar that exposed much of her breasts. There was a dazed expression on her wide, angular face.

He ran the back of his hand down her soft cheek and across her lips. Her tongue curled around his finger and sucked it greedily.

His hand dropped lower and freed a breast—the nipple the size of a gas cap. Mack rolled over, offering her rump provocatively. She said, "Back, front or in between?"

Robert's sexual engines fired. The insane intensity of his desire jarred him. In seconds, their hands were tearing madly at their clothes. He pulled the lamp cord. The blackness of the sealed, soundproof room intensified his fevered desperation. He sank into the fat pillows of her warm flesh. Mercilessly, their bodies met to open the shaft between them. With shudders, moans, and avid gasps for air came a rabid, convulsive surge of mindless passion, a vortex sucking him down to its warm, wet core.

Robert's potency came from nowhere like a hostile explosion, a harsh, tragic attempt to destroy the void.

Quenched and trembling, Mack lay splayed under him. Robert got up from her and groped for his pants, the storm in his soul subsiding. With the passing seconds the episode began to erase, like a tape. There had been no intention. Who could ever understand sex?

He dressed in silence.

"It's abnormal to be so quiet." Her voice came from the blackness. "Don't you ever cry?" she asked.

"Over this?"

Impatience touched her voice. "No."

"I've cried."

He walked toward the door, acutely conscious of the squeak his leather soles made.

"Robert! Wait," she said. "I've something I have to tell you."

An irrational panic swept over Robert. For a second he feared that she was going to reveal something awful about his son.

"I'm pregnant," came her whisper from the darkness.

The dry, barren flatlands of the Texas gulf coast went on for miles and miles. With his finger José García wrote his name on the dusty window of the old prison bus as it rattled and bumped down the highway. His father was seated next to him. His mother sat directly in front of them with José's baby sister asleep in her arms.

José took the bathtub chain from his pocket and began to unhook the links with his small fingers. After a while his mother turned around to check on him. When she saw the chain she became upset so he put it away. The chain reminded her of their visit to the police station.

Ernesto's eyes never left the window. He was furious. He had tried to tell the men from the immigration service that he was not an illegal, that he had a passport with a commercial visa, which permitted him and his family to stay in the United States for three months. But the officials didn't bother to listen. Before he could remove the visa from his leather pouch under the bed, they forced all of them into the bus.

He was terribly worried about his trailer. He simmered with frustration when he thought about the burlap sacks of rare spices that were stored underneath. Some of the bags contained his cousin's famous blue peppers. Nearly black in color and bitter-hot in taste, they were prized throughout Mexico. His cousin had paid him a thousand pesos to take the peppers to a man called Pico in Roswell. He and Pico had planned a trip to Sedona and then Santa Fe where cooks at the expensive gringo restaurants had promised to buy the peppers. His cousin had given him money to hire local Mexican grocers to transport the precious spices to the restaurants.

At first, Ernesto assumed the police had confused him with another Mexican, a criminal perhaps. He soon learned from the others on the bus that they were part of a special program. But this was ridiculous, he had no reason to be detained or deported. He was officially scheduled to leave the United States on January 10th.

Priscilla Prager sat behind the intake desk at El Corralon, the newly opened detention camp in Bayview, Texas.

"If you have passports," she said in broken Spanish, "then why are you here?"

Again Ernesto explained their plight. Prager blew a lock of brown hair from her sweaty forehead. She swatted viciously at the horseflies circling her face. Finally, she got up from the shabby wooden desk and took Ernesto and his family into a small room that opened onto the dirt parking lot where the bus had deposited them.

"Wait here," she said. She wrote her name on a slip of paper and handed it to him. "Show this to anyone who tells you to get back in line."

Prager, a Harvard graduate, had signed up for a year of social work with the Naturalization and Immigration Service before going on to law school. Now, after just two months, she was disgusted by the massive bureaucracy of the U.S. government. The García family was the final straw. If Ernesto was telling the truth, and after hearing hundreds of explanations a day she believed he was, then she was blowing the whistle. Tom Mendoza's program of unlimited detention was a right-wing PR campaign. How could Americans preach to the Russians about human rights when this was going on at home? If her dummkopf supervisor gave her any lip she was phoning an ex-classmate who was now a reporter at the *Washington Post*. The abuse of these poor Mexicans had to stop.

Jack Werts drove into the underground garage of the Directors Guild in West Hollywood, a behemoth glass structure modeled after an unspooling film can, that housed three state-of-the-art theaters. The impressive lobby had been especially designed for industry parties and receptions. The Guild was also the place where the show biz press was introduced to new films.

Jack knew that he had no business going to see *Prince of Tides* with his cover story on Tommy Train due tomorrow morning. But deadline pressure was a bummer. A steamroller, really, pushing him to the edge of a cliff. So why not escape it until the last possible second? A little dose of procrastination never hurt. It was part of the marinating process.

He sank down in a plush velvet chair in a side row of the screening room. The usual suspects filed in. The *L.A. Times* critic gave him a friendly nod, ditto the reviewer from *Rolling Stone*. A few flacks came by and said hello. He savored a bevy of attractive females sauntering down the aisle, all with shining eyes and long, tan, sun-kissed limbs—still twenty years away from skin cancer and cataracts.

As the lights dimmed and the credits splashed over the actors' faces, worrisome thoughts about the cover story began to foment in Jack's brain. His reporting was weak. Train had delivered his ego pitch ad nauseam, then nixed his staff's giving interviews. Lutz made NTN into mankind's savior. His puffery was embarrassing to endure. Meanwhile, the FBI spokesperson regurgitated the exact lame-brain quotes he had delivered to *The New York Times* three weeks ago. If anything, the most intriguing stuff he dug up came from a UCLA psychologist who researched the type of people who call TV talk shows. Decent filler but hardly gut-wrenching.

At the end of the film Jack wandered aimlessly through the lobby, then headed down the stairwell to the parking garage. A blanket of leaden air was left in the wake of cars climbing their way up the ramps. As he unlocked the Wrangler a familiar female voice came from behind a cement stanchion. Cupid's arrow stabbed his heart.

"McCann!" he shouted through her chatter.

Much to his surprise, she was warm and friendly. She politely introduced him to her companion, Charlene. "Tommy said really nice things about you," she bubbled. Her misty blue eyes focused on his. She dripped charm. "Have you finished the story yet?"

"Yes," he lied.

"Great," she said enthusiastically. "When's it out?"

"Monday." Better he change the subject fast. "Like the flick?"

"A vanity production," she said, exercising her newly acquired industry jargon. In the last two months she'd learned to read the trades. Before she could continue, Jack quickly invited her to dinner.

"Oh, go, honey," said Charlene, admiring his build. "I've got to fetch my kids in the valley. This way you don't have to tag along."

Ceci was startled by the haste of the arrangement. "I haven't a car," she said, attempting a lame excuse.

"I'll take you home."

Ceci gave him a quizzical look. "Upon leaving the restaurant," Jack said, raising his right hand. "Scout's honor."

A girlish smile lightened her face. "Well, okay."

As they headed west on Sunset, Ceci asked him where they were going.

"San Pietro. Up on Mulholland," he said. "More celebs per square inch than Morton's and Spago combined."

Ceci had never heard of the restaurant though she had eaten at both Morton's and Spago and liked them immensely. She figured Jack's cords and work shirt had something to do with the choice.

As they snaked up Laurel Canyon, he glanced over at her. She sat primly on the edge of the seat, as if she might get dirty. She wore a suede blouse with beige linen slacks. Expensive Rodeo Drive duds. At her temple he noted the delicate gold stirrup of Dior sunglasses. There was a high salmon gloss to her. Decidedly slicker than two months ago. He wasn't sure he liked the change.

"I caught your commercial for NTN," he said with a crimped smile. "That's journalism?"

"Rather and Brokaw do it, why shouldn't I?"

"I haven't seen Rather in a Calvin Klein underwear ad. Yet, anyway."

"What are you implying? I'm fully clothed."

An empty can of motor oil rolled around on the floor, threatening Ceci's pastel pumps. Jack reached down and launched it into the backseat, where it banged against his bait box.

On Mulholland Drive, he snapped down the visor against the orange rays of the setting sun. The light grew dimmer as they wound their way along the mountain road. Through a cleft in the ridge the lights of the San Fernando Valley sparkled through the nickel-plated dusk. A cool breeze came through the open windows. Jack braked as they approached a scenic turnout. Gravel pinged against the metal running boards as the wheels touched the shoulder of the road. A red Corvette was already parked at the rim of the ridge, its lights out.

"Lover's lane," Jack said, his eyes full of amusement. He wasn't about to tell her that San Pietro in the Glen Center was a mere two blocks from his house.

"Every town in America has one," Ceci replied sternly. It was as if she were above that sort of thing. She frowned at him. "Exactly where are we going?" She was obviously dismayed by the circuitous route.

Jack shoved a Harry Connick, Jr., tape into the deck. Strings, brass, and trombones wafted through the car. "This kid's got magic pipes," he said. "Like him?"

"Forties swing stuff." She gave a bored sigh.

Clearly, music wasn't going to be their connection. "So how did your interview go?" she asked. "You got on with Tommy?"

"He specializes in Bullshit 101."

Taken back, Ceci immediately transformed into an action-news anchorette fiercely defending her show. "Oh, that's not true."

"Sure is. He's highly pretentious."

"That's his style," she defended.

"Pretension, my dear." Jack stole a glance at her determined profile. Ceci McCann had an inborn stubborn streak, he knew, but just because she defended her boss didn't mean she was sleeping with him.

"I take it you're fond of him?" he said. There was a double edge to his question.

Disgusted with the insinuation, she made a face. "Not *that* way. He's married."

Jack smiled. "I hear Tanya's on the blink, a serious drug problem."

"Yes, cocaine. But she was cured at the Betty Ford Clinic."

Cured? Ceci had a lot to learn. On all levels. After they passed the fire station he made a left on Beverly Glen. Jack gestured at a cluster of mansions atop a narrow plateau. "Shay's mansion is hidden behind that outcropping," he said. "Nicholson, Beatty, and Brando live there. Eddie Murphy's down in the canyon. The tabs nicknamed the area 'Celebrity Meadows.' Brando's pad's 'Tahitian Terrace,' Beatty's 'Shady Mattress.' "

A minimalist smile came his way. She did, however, lean closer to get a better view of the houses. The dewy smell of her made Jack tingle. He gunned the Wrangler into the parking lot of the Glen Center and tucked it between a Maserati and a Lamborghini.

They settled on the patio amid the ficus trees and heat lamps. At an adjacent table, Michael Douglas ate with Brandon Tartikoff, head of Paramount Pictures. Cher and her mother dined inside beside the open grill. The small café was a neighborhood hangout.

Ceci glowed with excitement. "What's the name of this restaurant?" she asked. Jack's stock had risen. It truly amazed her what a good reporter he was. He truly knew the hot spots before anyone else.

The waiter, a young unemployed actor, handed them menus. Jack could have done without the obvious play he made for Ceci. You'd think the juvenile delinquent would set his sights on Cher. Ceci's busy eyes finished cruising and finally returned to his. "Actually," she confided, "I'm in a jam."

"Can I help?" Sir Galahad was his favorite role.

She looked dismayed. "If I don't come up with a new angle on Shay, I'll be assigned 'Pets Ahoy.' "

Progress was being made. At least this time she was up front about her problems.

"There are worse assignments."

Ceci shook her head. "These 'soft' stories never air."

Jack shifted in his chair. Harrington had been clamoring for a special issue: "Celebrity Children in Jeopardy." If *The Tommy Train Show* beat *Newsmakers* to the punch—cornered the celebs who sell their kids to the media to publicize themselves—Mara might lift her spurs from his flanks. With gusto, he pitched the idea to Ceci. She jumped like a trout for a fly.

"Don't bother with Caroline Kennedy's babies," he advised. "Go for the photo-happy: Cybil Shepherd, Arnold Schwarzenegger,

Ed McMahon. Toss in the TV exhibitionists: Jane Pauley, Paula Zahn."

Two hours later Ceci sat on a rickety cane chair in Jack's living room and stared down at his telephone answering machine. "You've got ten calls waiting," she announced. No response. Her eyes roamed over the messy bookshelves, unused computers, and endless piles of magazines. The living room was a blizzard of books and newspapers. It looked like the PLO headquarters.

"What's this?" she asked, lifting a bottle of wheat-grass juice from the floor.

Jack stood framed in fluorescent light from the kitchen, a mug of scotch and soda in his hand. He came over and peered at the sepia bottle with its homemade scripted label. Sherry's beverage of choice. "Ah, my health-food kick," he said. "I've decided to clean up my act."

Ceci looked at him askance. Then at the torn lampshades and neglected fish tank half-filled with greenish water. A smart-alecky grin flooded her face. "Hiring a maid might be a whole lot easier."

He laughed. "You gotta admit the woodwork's great. Look at those moldings. This baby was built in 1908. A fixer-upper, that's all."

All Ceci saw were map-sized hunks of plaster missing from the ceiling. "A teardown" was more like it.

Jack knocked a pair of mud-splattered fishing boots from the sofa and sank down opposite her. Ceci's slender legs were crossed. Her shimmering blond hair teased him. "I admit I'm not much of a housekeeper. I need a wife."

"What happened to your fiancée?"

"I told you—past history. These days I'm a hermit, monastic."

Even as he said it, Ceci noticed a sliver of black silk wedged in between the cushions of the sofa. She reached over and pulled out a pair of lace panties. "What are these?"

"Good grief," he said. "The last owner must have left them."

"You said you've lived here for six years," Ceci said, mildly amused. She bounced up from the chair. Her own agenda was far more important than Jack's sex life. "It's all so exciting, isn't it?" she said, spinning around the room like a top. "The show, I mean. We're all waiting with bated breath." She came over and settled next to him. "Can you keep a secret?"

Jack nodded.

"For the last month the FBI's been intercepting call-ins via satellite. They pinpoint callers in five seconds. Amazing, eh?"

Jack took a sip of scotch. So Train had lied to the press about keeping the FBI out of the picture. He glanced at the clock over the fireplace: 11 P.M. His cover story was due in New York at 8 A.M. tomorrow. The executioner's bell rang. "It's getting late," he said reluctantly.

But Ceci continued gabbing, Tommy this and Tommy that. After getting the name of his personal trainer, Jack shut down. He had enough on the guy for a book. He lifted himself up from the couch and went into the kitchen. Ceci trailed after him.

There was one surefire way to hasten her exit. "Wanna see my porn tapes?" he said, stopping in the dark wood-paneled hallway.

"Jaaaack," Ceci said, ducking away from his arms. "It's hopeless. You're too much a 'me Tarzan, you Jane' type of guy. Too promiscuous. I find it childish."

Jack chuckled. "A case of mismatched perceptions. I rather think of myself as a bon vivant."

"I like more serious men . . ."

"With money and power, you mean."

"Well, that too," she conceded.

"Take it from Uncle Jack," he warned. "The serious guys are all about machismo. More ruthless machismo." He looked at her affectionately. "To prove to you that I'm not just another aging Don Juan in his orgiastic playpen, I'm taking you home."

"Thank God!"

As his lips nibbled her cheek, she took his arm firmly and pulled him out the back door toward his car.

"What I can't figure," said Steve Klein over his cup of diluted coffee, "is why the García family was put on the roster."

Priscilla Prager wiped her face with a tissue. The Texas heat was a killer. They sat in a greasy roadside café across from the detention center. She was grateful Klein didn't complain. She noticed a change for the better in him since he became a reporter for the *Washington Post*. He was less fussy.

"According to the Roswell police, the Garcías weren't part of their weekly roundup of illegals. The order to arrest them came directly from Mendoza's office. But what makes even less sense is that Mendoza's assistant, Marge Clark, says the tipoff came from the FBI."

"The FBI?" said Priscilla, incredulous. "Why would the FBI be involved with this poor Mexican family?" Possible scenarios began to unravel in her brain.

"Share your thoughts," he prodded.

"Maybe, just maybe, somebody in the FBI is being paid off to shaft poor Mexicans into the detention centers," she speculated. "An under-the-table scheme. If true, that's a front-page scandal."

Klein glowed with excitement. He sensed a story to make his career, get him a permanent spot on the national desk. "It could be somethin' like that," he reasoned. "Has to be. But I need proof."

"Bombard the FBI office in Roswell," advised Priscilla. "Somebody will squeal."

PART
III

19

The L.A. basin was overcast, the stale air thick with a metallic haze. Odd weather for late December, thought Ceci as she drove past the Fox Towers in Century City. She craned her neck to get a look at Ronald Reagan's top-floor office. A stab of pride came from working in the same neighborhood as the ex-prez.

She made a left turn on Olympic Boulevard and finally a right into the NTN complex. The eighty-foot sand palms along the entrance drive had fat ribbons of tinsel wrapped tautly around their trunks. Christmas in L.A. It was Ceci's first.

This afternoon she felt really good about work. Only two more celebrity parents to interview and her segment was ready to air. To get the subjects to talk she had duped them into thinking the focus of her story was Christmas toys. Once they were sufficiently relaxed and singing with the holiday spirit, she zapped them with Doni Shay's abduction. They immediately expressed their horror—and fear for their own children. Naturally, these comments opened the segment.

After the holidays, Stan Lutz had arranged for Ceci to shoot another network commercial. She was terribly excited. This time, she was flying to New York to pose with two of America's finest male journalists. Overnight, the first commercial had given her national status.

The instant publicity had brought ancillary benefits as well. America's top corporations were calling to ask her to sponsor their products. Meanwhile, rich bachelors were sending her party invitations. In the last month Ceci had completely revised her philosophy when it came to men. Never again would she be able to fall in love with a run-of-the-mill guy. To think that she even entertained thoughts of dating Jack Werts sent a shiver down her spine. Hook up with a low-profile journalist and you were destined to a world of obscurity. Given her success, she wanted a husband who had made his mark publicly. She offered the celebrity component that many of these men craved. Moreover, it was a win-win situation. Being the member of a famous twosome insured double exposure. Celebrities were suited to marry their own kind. Look at Diane Sawyer and Mike Nichols, Connie Chung and Maury Povich, Jane Pauley and Gary Trudeau. Why, Ted Turner and Jane Fonda.

After turning off the engine, she fetched the Filofax from her purse and jotted a note to herself. Before she signed any contracts for endorsements, she must hire a crackerjack New York agent.

Train slapped a copy of *Newsmakers* down on his desk. He sprang from his chair like a panther. "Fifty-seven! Shit! Jack Werts makes me sound like a decrepit fossil. A member of the triple-bypass generation."

Ceci sat down swiftly on the folding chair next to Grinker. "The unvarnished truth," Nelson muttered, with a wink her way. She frowned at him. Always the glib smartass.

Pacing back and forth, Tommy continued to rant and rave. "It's as if Werts is on a seek-and-destroy mission," he said, pausing as Stan Lutz came into the room. Tommy's eyes fastened on the network president. "Who gave me the rotten advice to talk to that turkey, anyway?"

In front of Ceci, Shorty shifted his heavy body. Over his shoulder she caught a glimpse of a glossy picture of Tommy on the cover of *Newsmakers*.

"How'd he know about the FBI intercept station?" asked Lisa as she calmly flipped through a copy of the magazine.

Tommy gave Lutz a slit-eyed glance. "I bet Krugger told him," he said. "The fucker."

"At least he didn't report the fifty new telephone lines," said Lutz.

Train riffled through the magazine again, then stopped abruptly. "How in hell did he get this?" he said. He read aloud to them: "Train's snowblinded free-baser fifth wife, Tanya, came home from the Betty Ford Clinic last month . . ."

Ceci felt a tight constriction in her chest. Werts had lied to her. He told her he'd already written the story. The bastard double-crossed her.

Overcome with her own guilt, she blushed uncontrollably. Lutz gave her a curious grin. She tried to look nonchalant.

"The timing's awful," said Tommy. "The ratings are on a steep slide. The negative PR will accelerate our fast fade. We're the flavor of the . . ." He swung his body around and addressed Shorty. "Call that lard-ass Camp and try for Shay one more time."

Shorty grimaced. "After this smear, why should he come on the show?" He rose and walked over to the bulletin board. Some new stories had been tacked on: Burger King Massacre, Montana Celebrities, The Hurried Child. "The news moves," said Shorty.

Tommy snickered. "You think gardening tips will keep our numbers? Get real. Shay sells tickets."

Bill Leggitt, who had appeared to Ceci to be asleep in the back of the room, unhinged his lanky body. His teeth clicked as his lips drew back. "Then quit piddlin' in the tulips and go for the personal juice," he said loudly. "Ginger and I shot great stuff of Reno . . ."

Ceci did a double take. Was he mad or just stupid? Their tape was garbage. Filler.

Lisa came to life. She wore a rhinestone-studded denim jacket and a slinky calf-length skirt that was glued to her buttocks. "I ain't been taping Starlight on spec," she mewed. "It took me a week to smuggle a cameraman into the compound."

"It's shortsighted to run that tape," said Train. "Shay'll hit the roof."

"Bullcrap!" Lisa blurted. "It's Christmas. What are you waiting for? A virgin birth? The kid's dead. Face it."

Train's expression revealed nothing. He glanced at Grinker. Ceci noticed the eco-correct cork briefcase next to Nelson's chair. This week, Mr. Conservation. "What celebs you got wait-listed for the Montana story?" Tommy asked.

Grinker cleared his throat. "Michael Keaton, Dennis Quaid. Possibly McGuane."

"Go for it. Jan three."

"Whoa, I got the Rose Parade dolls."

"Give 'em to Hot Lips."

An audible moan came from Proudfit's mouth.

Shorty interrupted. "McCann's got a celeb pediatrician."

"Did he treat Shay's kid?" Tommy asked.

Ceci sat up. "I'll call and find out."

Stan Lutz rested against his white Jaguar in the parking lot. He opened a pack of sugarless gum and offered Train a stick.

Tommy shook his head. "Slow down with McCann," he warned.

Stan smiled at him. "C'mon. You know icing sells the cake."

"She's too green for those commercials."

"She may be green but she's the image NTN wants to project. Wholesome midwestern looks. Solid intelligence. There isn't an ounce of the dysfunctional druggie in her."

Tommy shrugged reluctantly. "Yeah, Jessica Savitch she isn't."

Krugger stared down at the lunch-hour traffic from the FBI headquarters at the corner of Wilshire and Veteran. According to highway stats more cars passed through the busy intersection in one day than at any other intersection in Los Angeles. It didn't surprise him. Getting home was a bitch. Especially during the holidays.

Behind him, his private line buzzed. "What?" he muttered into the receiver. It was his assistant, on the line about the García family. Apparently a story on that rat's nest had just appeared in *The Washington Post*. The FBI was being targeted by the Mexican consulate and the Binational Center for Human Rights.

"How can we be implicated with the INS?" he said, his voice taut with anger. "What do we care about the García family? Or that the outhouses at El Corralon are flooded? I want to know what peabrain crossed the wires this time."

He could hear the young FBI officer hem and haw. "This may sound crazy but I've done a full investigation, sir, and I think that our missing persons' bureau ordered the Garcías' detention."

"What A-hole did that?" Krugger shouted.

Incompetence always unsettled his stomach. He reached into his desk drawer for his bottle of Tagamet pills. The last thing he needed was the *Washington Post* ridiculing the bureau again.

"We don't know who or why," was the reply.

"The orders came from somewhere," Krugger snapped. "It must have been drug related. Call the DEA. They must be in on this."

Doni had been in the back of the truck for many hours. Long ago he had finished the water in the small milk carton that Rita had left for him. She had never left him alone for so long.

He crawled over to the empty bag of potato chips. He put the crinkly paper in his mouth and licked the last tiny pieces of salt from the crevices. Then he chewed on the crackling paper. It tasted awful but he was very hungry.

After a while he went over to the door. The long metal handle was cold now. He felt the sides of the truck; they were very cold too. He took his hand away. Even the floor was cold. He made potty in the corner. He stayed away from the puddle because it smelled bad. Where he kept his ball and sticks was a better place to make a fort. He wondered if José was playing cops and robbers in the tire fort. He loved the soft round circles of rubber. You could fall all the way down—like off the Empire State Building or from his daddy's airplane—and not hurt yourself.

For now, he played with the ice-cream sticks José had traded him. The sticks made a family: a daddy, a mommy, and a dog. Not Snickers, but a big white dog with a furry tail and floppy paws. His paws were like white roses.

Doni thought hard about roses. They had been put all around his mommy when she was sick. When he closed his eyes the smell of his mommy flooded his brain. The ugly smells went away. Mommy's white smell made the floor soft and his blanket warm. He became groggy and fell asleep. When he woke, his mommy was gone. His face was very hot even though the floor was cold.

The next morning the sun made the walls of the truck light brown. It became very hot and hard for him to breathe. He stayed asleep more now. Often, he didn't finish playing with his stick soldiers before he became tired.

All at once the door banged. The noise frightened him so much that his chest thumped. Rita stood outlined in the sunlight. He ran toward her. He was so happy to see her that he cried.

"I'm sorry, kid," she said. "I got into a jam. I got carried away. I shoulda stuck to the slots." She lifted him gently from the truck and put him on the ground. She touched his face with her hands. "You've got a fever."

Rita looked very nervous and upset. Doni knew a fever meant he was sick. She rubbed his head. "Tonight I'll get us a decent motel. With a color TV. You can have a bed of your own. Just don't pass out on me, okay?"

Doni nodded. He closed his eyes and fell asleep in her arms.

When he woke up he was under a soft blanket in a white room. Rita's back was to him. She was smoking and talking on the telephone. On the dresser he saw the buzz machine she had used to cut his hair.

"I did," she said. Her voice grew angry. "Don't tell me what I did or didn't do."

She hung up and turned around to him. "How do you feel?" She came over to the bed with a bag of red candies. He took one. It tasted good. She put the bag next to him. The phone rang again.

"Drop dead, you motherfucker!" she yelled into the receiver. "I don't care what you say, I'm driving to L.A. I got friends there." She slammed down the phone.

Her hands were shaking. She took a funny-looking glass bottle from a drawer. "My magic lantern," she said to him.

Doni ate another candy. He watched her light the lantern. Smoke moved around in the neck like a piece of cotton. Her face grew red as she sucked the cotton into her mouth. Finally, she blew out a long puff of smoke. "Hell, Butch, we'll have fun in L.A.," she said. "Serious fun. None of this gambling shit."

Doni felt better. He ate another candy. He knew L.A. meant Los Angeles.

Because the García family had become the target of a *Washington Post* investigation, the INS had separated them from the other Mexicans in the detention center. Representatives from the ACLU and the Hispanic Legal Foundation had taken up their case. Their independent counsel, paid for by the Hispanic Fund, insisted they be freed since they had committed no crime. But the Minority Freedom League, who also represented them, encouraged them to remain in the detention camp to publicize the injustice of the program. Meanwhile, in an attempt to save face, the INS still maintained there was a valid reason for their detention.

Pleased with the progress of the case, Priscilla Prager watched José playing in the sandy yard outside his family's cement barracks. It was just a matter of time until they were released. She was proud of the story Steve Klein had written. Teams of energetic reporters from *The New York Times*, *Sacramento Bee*, and the *L.A. Times* had descended on the center. They wrote powerful, gripping stories about the subhuman conditions, the lack of decent food and medical care.

She took her lunch bag from the noisy half-fridge near the window and went down to the yard, heading for the tree under which José was playing. She offered him half of her cheese sandwich and they chatted together in Spanish. Finally she asked if he was eager to go home and he told her he was because then he might find his friend Doni.

"Who is this Doni?" she asked. He explained about his gringo friend who wore a dress. Priscilla laughed, thinking it was a fantasy. She didn't know many folktales but she knew the Mexicans had some wonderfully clever parables for children.

José looked up at her. "I'm sorry I caused my mother and father problems."

She stared at him. How dreadful, the little boy thought their detention was his fault. "But you didn't cause these problems for your family," she explained.

"*Sí, sí*," he said. "I did. My mother went to the police because of my friend Doni."

Priscilla slowly lowered her sandwich onto the waxed paper. The afternoon heat was overpowering. She pressed her fingers to her temples. Suddenly, she felt the heavens above crash down on her. MISSING PERSONS, FBI, BOY IN DRESS, GRINGO, DONI SHAY.

"My God," she said. Chills ran up and down her arms. She knocked over her carton of iced tea as she dropped on her knees in front of José. "What does your friend Doni look like?" she asked, barely able to control herself.

José cocked his head. He described Doni's funny hair. He told her about the airplane. The tennis balls and the sticks.

A three-year-old child couldn't possibly make this up.

Priscilla picked him up in her arms and ran to find Carlotta.

20

It was dark when Robert drove over to Lee Mack's house in the Encino hills. Duke sat next to him. He turned in the driveway and parked in front of the bright red enameled door. A string of Christmas lights had been draped across the portal. A plastic wreath of shiny green holly circled the brass knocker.

For a moment the two men sat in silence while the cold night air seeped into the Rover. Thompson slouched down in the seat. "You handle this," he said. "I ain't comin' to rescue you."

As Robert stepped from the Rover the door of the house opened. Lee Mack stood framed in the doorway, encased in skintight acid-washed jeans and a tricolored satin jacket; a lacy tank top restrained her prodigious chest.

She planted a moist, sloppy kiss on his cheek. "Don't be cross with me," she said. "*Your* savage libido got us into this."

Despite their four-month affair, Robert had never been in her house. The living room was chaotic. Gaudy yellow walls were set off by snow white wall-to-wall carpeting and hung with a series of posters from the low-budget Italian films she had starred in. An artificial Christmas tree decorated with blue bulbs dominated the wraparound window overlooking the valley. A cheap oil portrait of Lee hung in the maple-paneled den. She had told him she lived alone. For the last six months, anyway.

"Look at it this way," she said, handing him the medical report. "He's my Christmas gift to you."

Robert read the results of her amniocentesis test. The three-month-old fetus she carried was a healthy male.

"You know it's yours," she said, stepping behind the counter of the open kitchen. "Work the arithmetic. How much more proof do you want?" She poured herself a cup of cider from a saucepan simmering on the stove. "I've even given up booze because of our baby."

Robert stared at her. Mack's blue eyes skittered away, not ready to meet his gaze. The spoon clicked against the cup as she stirred the cider nervously. "If you're still unsure, we'll have a blood test done right after the baby's born," she said. "They're 97 percent accurate."

He turned away and walked over to the living-room window. The twinkling city lights of the valley floor brought a fleeting moment of serenity. He noticed the ultrasuede sofas, the fur rug under the driftwood coffee table. The modest house was a love nest of sorts. Odd that they had never fucked there. He wondered how many men had.

"I've also got eggnog and cranberry mimosas," Lee said, opening the door to the fridge. Robert returned to her side. A box from Domino's Pizza was on the counter, two dirty plates in the sink. He lifted the lid. The pizza was half-eaten.

"Have a piece?" she said.

"Cider's fine."

She carried two mugs of steaming liquid to the coffee table. Her shapely rear brushed lightly against him as she sat down. Her snug jeans showed no bulge. It was difficult to imagine that Doni had a potential half-brother in her belly.

"Why did you have amnio?" he asked.

She gave him a fey smile between sips of cider. "Because I'm older than you think."

Shay had never believed she was twenty-eight. Her liposucked ass was a giveaway.

"I wanted to make sure the baby was healthy," she said. "Because, well, I've been thinking . . ."

Robert felt like he'd fallen down a rabbit hole. He wasn't ready for this. Not now. "Last week, you said you scheduled an abortion."

The statement floated between them. He didn't want to push her.

"Well, yes, I did say that. But then I started seeing his cute squishy red face. He'd be a wonderful child. A handsome genius like you. A great kid. I felt maternal urges. Breast-feeding. Carrying to term." Her eyes watered. "My mother says I'm lucky to be carrying your child."

Robert looked at the Naugahyde-cushioned bench at one end of the large window. It was heaped high with needlepoint pillows scripted with corny slogans, a bushel of crepe-paper flowers, glass ashtrays filled with ribbon candy. The phone rang; one short, sharp ring. The answering machine had been set to pick up. Lee Mack slid across the sofa and linked her arm companionably through his. "If anything awful should happen to Doni, you'll have another son."

Robert said nothing. He tried to remember what Libby had said about Mack. "A pair of powerful lachrymal glands," that was it.

He lowered his head and rubbed his neck. Did he need another child? Did he want this woman, a valley girl from the land of stretch pants and foam curlers, to be the mother of his son? His second son?

Mack rose from the couch and went over to the fireplace. She tossed a Duraflame log onto the dying embers. The fresh flare turned her long hair a pale golden rum color. She took another log, then another, and threw them onto the crackling blaze. In seconds, the fire roared. Blue-tongued flames lapped over the flagstone. She'd overdone it. The way she overdid everything. It had worked with sex, however. He recalled their total immersion on the straw mattress in Thailand. Binge fucking. Humid primal soup with no tomorrows. Then Robert heard Sarah Silverman's panicked, desperate voice. A haunting image of Doni returned.

Mack came back to the sofa and curled her body against his. "Wanna get laid?" she said in a bantering tone. He had heard the line too many times, from too many women. It peeled off like cheap varnish. Mack reminded him of a plastic Kewpie doll, a cheap car ornament hanging from the rearview mirror. He studied her objectively. She wasn't sophisticated but she was big, beautiful, and healthy. From the way she fucked, he knew she was promiscuous.

"You don't show," Robert observed.

"I usually don't."

"You've been pregnant before?"

She moved away from him and lifted her feet onto the beveled edge of the glass coffee table. Her spike heels nudged the dish of peanuts. She had a garish vulgarity he'd never noticed before.

"Four abortions," she said. Her eye caught his. "Oh, Robert, can't you see why—now that I'm older—having this baby—your baby—means so much to me."

There was something terribly unsettling about the beatific smile lighting her omnivorous mouth.

He stood up and roamed over to the bookshelf where he lifted a pewter plate. A tourist memento from the Leonard-Spinks fight in Atlantic City. Next to it was a picture of Mack with Donald Trump. There were other pictures of her. Mostly with men. No pictures of her parents in front of the proverbial white-picket fence. He knew nothing of her background.

"Have you finished with *China White?*" he asked.

An agitated expression disturbed her seeming serenity. "Some poster art and I'm free. But," she paused and the corners of her mouth drooped, "I've been axed from *Red Planet.*"

"I hadn't heard."

"Libby held auditions last week. Scuttlebutt has it that Michelle Pfeiffer and Martin Sheen got the parts."

It made sense. They had been considered from day one.

"You see, Robert, it's the perfect time for me to have a baby. My agent says that producers won't be beating on my door until *China White*'s in the theaters. But that's nearly a year away."

She pursed her lips. "Naturally, if I had landed the lead in *Planet,* well, this decision whether or not to have an abortion would have been less difficult to make."

"You couldn't play Zodine pregnant."

Mack chuckled. "I sure couldn't. In those neoprene body skins. It would be hysterical." She looked down at her nonexistent belly. "This big fat stomach lapping over those tight crotch numbers. Can you imagine my boobs in three months? Watermelons!" She emitted a harsh laugh. "A Martian mommy!"

While she babbled on about the film, Robert considered the ramifications. An illegitimate son would destroy Emily, who was slowly making her way back to him emotionally. He had always taken great pains to ensure that he didn't father a herd of illegitimate children. Christ, he had no intention of getting stuck like poor Marlon Brando, forever financing his unruly offspring. Once before, he paid an actress a hundred thousand to have an abortion. The second time it was a film student who settled for two hundred grand. She'd gone on to be a fine documentary producer. He looked at Lee Mack. This was quite a different situation.

"Lee, it's the worst possible time for me to have another child," he said softly, trying to be tactful. "It's too crazy. Maybe later, after Doni . . ."

A look of total dejection came over her face.

He took her hand. "I'll compensate you for the abortion." Their eyes met. Mack's face twitched violently. "I don't want your money! How dare you! God, I thought you were a better man than that."

In that instant Shay knew exactly what she was after. "Money can't replace this precious feeling I have in my belly," she cried as she rubbed her hand over her stomach. Abruptly, her voice softened. "It's *your* baby. That's special to me."

She raked her hands through her hair as she paced about the room. "What might have changed my mind was my career," she announced coolly. "And even then I would have made you promise to get me pregnant again." She stopped and searched his face. "If that had happened, well, then I might have considered aborting your son!"

Robert shuddered. How quickly sex went from ripe to rotten.

Jack Werts stood on the back porch with a Guinness in his hand. A coyote howled in the canyon. The night was damn cold, the coldest Christmas Eve he could remember in Los Angeles.

In the moonlight he surveyed his bathtub Porsche, wheelless, choked with ivy. A thicket of greasewood and sumac had overtaken the yard. He took a swallow of the dark, bitter beer. He'd never be accused of wasting water. No sprinkled-lawn syndrome here. His yard was gardened by nature before xeriscaping had become the rage. He sat down on the broken swing. The wind from the canyons whistled around his head and cleared his mind.

The truth was he had lost Ceci McCann. Like most of the pretty young girls who arrived in town, she had swiftly been transformed into a gold digger. Another enameled blonde cruising Beverly Hills in a Rolls with her initials stenciled on the door. These days he had discovered to his sorrow that the younger variety of these platinum barracudas even passed on sport fucking. They demanded a portfolio, not a prick. He had six grand in his savings account. Max. On the upside, he still had a full head of hair. He drank to that.

"Jaaaaack," came Sherry's voice from the upstairs window. Barbara Mandrell's Country Christmas blared from the television. "A female's on the phone for you."

He took the call in the kitchen.

"I'm invitin' you to a blowout New Year's Eve party," said Madison Cole.

"I'll be on a boat."

"Where to?"

"London."

"My fave town." She sounded smashed. "Well, we must have dinner then, after you get back."

"Fine, leave the details on my machine," Jack told her, hanging up.

"Yet another woman?" Sherry said, sauntering down the stairs in a frilly red negligee, Jack's Christmas gift.

"The Malibu druggie," he explained half-heartedly.

"She still expects a story?"

"They never let up."

Back upstairs, Jack switched on PBS. He felt testy. Alistair Sim as Scrooge in *A Christmas Carol* was dependable.

"Oh, gumdrop, how borrring," said Sherry, pouting. She teased him with the Vitality vibrator, a power mower with rubber pads—her Christmas present to him. When he objected, she whispered, "If you're nice tonight, I'll give you a tip."

Later, he acquiesced. Before they dozed off, she whispered, "The Shays are goin' to the forestation fund-raiser at DC-3."

"Huh?"

"I can't talk about it. Just go if you want to see them in the flesh."

Two canyons away, Ceci McCann waited in the bar of the Bel Air Hotel, sipping a glass of Dom Perignon and marveling at the twenty-foot Douglas fir in the corner. It was the most exquisitely decorated Christmas tree she had ever seen. Small bouquets of lacquered fruits hung in clusters from the heavy boughs. Cherry-red pomegranates and sun-yellow grapefruits were artfully bunched together near the trunk; translucent grapes and burnished walnuts were invisibly threaded amidst the outer limbs. The riot of natural colors was illuminated by flickering imitation candles.

It was 11:30 P.M. The hotel lounge was filled with a mellow crowd of out-of-towners. A black nightclub singer crooned "White Christmas" at a Steinway grand piano. The brandy snifter before him blossomed with ten-dollar bills. Ceci felt a sharp pang of loneliness as two old friends kissed good-bye at the door. This was the first Christmas she'd ever spent away from Kansas City.

Her melancholy vanished the moment Stan Lutz returned to their table. He glanced anxiously at the birch logs crackling in the fireplace. His mood seemed to have darkened after phoning his wife.

Ceci raised her glass to him. "Merry Christmas."

"If only Beverly could be more like you," he said softly. "Beautiful, buoyant, carefree. A woman in love with her work and not obsessed with my making it to the top." His hazel eyes reflected pain and hurt. "Beverly won't be satisfied until I knock Ted Turner and Rupert Murdoch off their pedestals. That's a heavy order. Impossible, really. The truth is I'm tired of corporate infighting. I'd like to root in L.A. for a few years and build the entertainment side of NTN. Escape the New York shark tank." His gaze lingered on her. "You're young. It's hard for you to understand."

"You're hardly old," Ceci replied diplomatically. "I have friends. I hear from them that all high-powered marriages are difficult."

Stan smiled appreciatively. He was in the mood to unload his frustration. "Yeah, you'd think her designer business was enough." He swilled down his glass of champagne.

Ceci felt terribly sorry for Stan. He was a sweet, loving man. Not handsome but kind and keenly intelligent. He had married the wrong woman and now he was paying the price.

He beckoned the waiter to bring him more champagne. "We're scheduling 'Celeb Kids' late January," he said. "Your segment's masterful. Perfect for the Feb sweeps." He looked straight into her eyes. "You've become a real star, Miss McCann."

Ceci blushed. "I've got a lot to learn."

"What's on camera is all that counts. That you've got in spades, which reminds me . . ." Stan dreamily directed his eyes to her. In the firelight his face appeared thinner. A teddy-bearish warmth about him made her feel comfortable and safe. The piano player broke into "Jingle Bells," and chimes rang from behind the bar.

"Have you heard of the Meiko Toy Company?" he asked, slipping his arm around her shoulders.

Ceci shook her head.

"They're the most prosperous toy outfit in Japan. Half the toys sold in America come from their factories." He hesitated while the waiter removed a plate of salmon canapés from his tray. "Yesterday Mr. Hosai, the president of the company, called. He's the brother of a prominent Jap who has offered to finance our drive to take NTN global." Lutz tilted his head forward and lowered his voice. "With his billions behind us, NTN will be the first American network to beam into Europe and the Soviet Union. In months, we'll dominate the international advertising market. Murdoch won't know what hit him."

Excited by his words, Lutz stuffed a canapé into his pink mouth. For a moment, his face looked fat and lumpy—like "mashed potatoes." Ceci immediately banished Grinker's nickname for him.

"Anyway," he continued, "Mr. Hosai has a business proposition for us—for you."

Ceci's eyes gleamed with intrigue. What did a toy conglomerate want from her?

"You're aware that we syndicated Tommy's show in Japan?"

She nodded.

"The Shay kidnapping brought you to their attention." He paused. He wrestled with how to proceed, then opted for speed. "They hope to persuade you to be the real-life model for an anchor doll they plan to manufacture next year."

Ceci choked on her laughter, then caught herself, seeing his troubled expression.

"I admit, I was skeptical too," he said. "But Mr. Hosai is persuasive. The project is bigger than Barbie. The accoutrements—toy news vans, TV monitors, and cameras—come with the package. They include a full wardrobe of reporter's clothes from bush jackets to evening wear. Miniature NTN logos on every piece of merchandise."

Ceci smiled at his enthusiasm. "But why me? Why not a generic character? Like Annie Anchorette," she asked in bewilderment.

"They want a credible hook. You're image-tested as most appealing to girls four to ten."

"I'm overwhelmed," she said mockingly.

But Stan was dead serious. "They've proposed a thirty-million-dollar ad campaign to launch the doll. Overnight your name becomes a household word."

Ceci smothered a smile. "I'm not sure that's the kind of notoriety I . . ."

His look silenced her. "There's big money in this for you."

With that, she listened more attentively. After all, Lutz had always had her interests in mind.

"A two-million-dollar contract to start," he said flatly. "And, my dear, if the doll takes off, an option to renew on your terms."

Under a multitude of stars, Stan took Ceci's hand in his. A graceful swan floated silently across the glimmering pond in the white moonlight. Barely aware of the cold, they walked along a garden path to his bungalow, where a fire roared in the fireplace. In the bedroom silk pajamas with gold piping were neatly laid out on the emperor-size bed. French doors opened into a private garden where wispy palm fronds cast plumelike shadows on the crenellated sandstone wall.

Their lovemaking began quickly and easily. Although Ceci had qualms she didn't resist. She was lonely and if she was going to sleep with someone, why not a network president who cared about her career. Wisely, she'd come to realize that her notions about the sanctity of marriage were hopelessly dated, like much of her wardrobe.

In the glint of moonlight she felt Stan's body encompass hers. To her surprise he was more barrel-chested than fat, and his skin was smooth as silk, practically hairless. And though he wasn't particularly well endowed he was totally loving, almost adoring. Again and again his hands caressed her breasts, kneading, running his fingertips around and around her nipples. He called her "my precious," "my kitten." He seemed to adore and savor every inch of her. The idolatry was a turn-on Ceci hadn't known before. Younger men, she realized, lacked the connoisseur's appreciation. Tonight she felt valued in a totally different way.

"Bear down, press against me," he whispered as he began to lose control. His tempo accelerated until he peaked in a wondrous moment of passion. Ceci held him to her. She was grateful to be spared the usual raves about her tits and tight pussy. Younger men's rantings seemed gross and sophomoric now that she was in Stan's arms.

In time, he rose and returned to the bed with a Baccarat crystal goblet of lemon gelato. "I've got to tell the Japs about the endorsement," he said, spooning the white ice into her mouth. He brushed the hair from her forehead with a paternal gesture. "Two million can't hurt," he said. "It's good for you—and for NTN."

A thrill ran through Ceci's body. Now she could buy her condo on Wilshire. She bubbled with quiet happiness.

21

Three days after Christmas, Jack drove west on Ocean Park Boulevard toward the Santa Monica airport. He marveled at how swiftly the restaurant scene had moved to the west side of town. Overnight, hordes of chic industry types had exchanged the Polo Lounge for DC-3.

As he turned in to the parking lot he immediately spotted a welcoming line of bucketed seedlings. He checked his invitation. Recycled paper. Jack couldn't figure why Robert Shay chose an environmental fund-raiser for his debut. The crowd would be strictly avant, conservation their latest kick. Well, Shay probably considered himself new Hollywood. Frankly, Jack thought the distinction was a crock. The only difference was that the new Hollywoods had their teeth bonded whereas the old dolls had black gums from caps.

But when it came to watering holes, DC-3 was something special. The impressive space was the size of an airplane hangar and decorated with explosive offerings from the Santa Monica art scene. Over the giant glassed-in kitchen, a banner screamed SAVE THE RAIN FOREST.

Jack quickly strode past an abstract sculpture made of tortured debris and gazed down at the airstrip below. The row of vintage planes made the trip worth it. World War II props painted bright tangerine were parked next to wide-winged gliders and Royal Air Force bombers with ancient decals. Arms folded, he swung back around to the crowd. It consisted of legions of tanned, ponytailed jocks in wrinkled suits. Sierra Club groupies, no doubt, plus a few Earth First terrorists spiffed up for photo ops. For this gang, sewage treatment had been raised to high art.

Directly in front of him, a Birkenstock-sandaled hippie chatted with a poodle-haired girl in hundred-dollar jeans. As usual, the party was low on ethnics. Two hedge-hair blacks from the music biz filled the minority quotient. And, of course, the ubiquitous foot-ball team of Hispanic waiters.

Plenty of high profiles though. Tom Hayden, the self-appointed environmental king, presided. The Malibu gang was well repre-sented: Cher, Larry Hagman, and Ali MacGraw. Meanwhile, Ste-phen Bishop, Kim Carnes, Bobbie Shriver, and Ted Dansen milled about posing for photographers. Poor Sydney Pollack was being accosted in a corner by a CBS camera crew. "Yeah," he guiltily told the interviewer, "I feel terrible driving a big car . . ."

Certainly Jack had nothing against conservation, but the hy-pocrisy of the event annoyed him. The vast majority of Hollywood stars rode around in gas-guzzling limos and had eight-jet showers in their stadium-size bathrooms. Now, suddenly, they were preach-ing the wages of excess. How could they dare tell the masses to conserve water or cut wattage when the security systems that pro-tected their lavish homes used enough electricity to light up a third-world city?

He spotted one honest soul: Ed Begley, Jr. Slathered in sun-screen, the actor had arrived on his bicycle.

A karate chop hit Jack between the shoulder blades. "Hey, Romeo," said Sammy Voight with a soft whistle.

He swung around. "Whaddidja do to your hair?" he blurted.

Her fingers ran over a half-inch of red stubble. "A boot-camp cut. Doncha love it?"

Jack digested the sight. "It fits the skull-and-bone earrings."

Sammy ignored his teasing. "Too many symbiots," she com-plained. "Press/celeb ratio's eight to one." Symbiots was Sammy's shorthand for the show-biz gravy train.

"Ace celebs," Jack commented.

"Naw, it's the same gang from the animal-rights rally. Their pictures are already sitting on Harrington's layout table in New York."

Behind them, Tom Hayden began his pitch: "The lead levels in our blood have dramatically dropped thanks to . . ."

Sammy flashed a sarcastic smile. "He makes me want to club a baby seal." She unlooped one of her cameras and put it in its case. Adjusting the strap, she added, "The guy's political ambitions are so transparent. Such a fool. Jane's pockets were a lot deeper than greenhouse gases."

A waitress in clunky shoes and kiddie socks came by with a tray of Thai beef sticks and buffalo carpaccio.

"Bye, bye, Bowser," said Sammy, grabbing a hunk of raw meat. "I don't want to sound like a spoilsport." She paused to chomp down. "This is a nifty-poo party and all that . . . but, sweetheart, I don't see Mr. Shay. I don't even see his shadow, Morgan Camp." She smiled smugly. "Are you sure Sherry had her antennae screwed on tight?"

At that instant, Jack spotted Joe Krugger making his way to the bar. "My word, it's Mr. Emotional," said Sammy.

"Theirs not to reason why," he quipped. He headed over and introduced himself. His name registered and to Jack's astonishment, Krugger offered his hand. "Sterling piece you did on Train."

This was remarkably good fortune. Clearly, there was bad blood between Train and Krugger. Better he move fast. "Any new leads?" he asked.

A paralyzing "no" hit his ears.

Ten thousand times in his career Werts had confronted the immutable brick wall. Too old and tired to play Humpty Dumpty, he handed Krugger his card. "If you ever get the urge, I'd appreciate a call."

Behind them, a crowd of people rushed to the terrace. Beyond the glass windows, a police helicopter dropped from the sky.

Sherry Cox had just earned herself two dozen red roses.

The digital panel read 5:15 P.M. as the pads of the chopper touched the tarmac. By now, Robert figured, Harry had informed Libby that Lee Mack had the lead in *Red Planet*. He was grateful he wasn't there. Babcock was a bitch on wheels when she blew.

Behind him, Emily was combing her hair. Exactly why she had insisted they come to this fund-raiser puzzled him. With the exception of movie premieres, she rarely appeared in public. And with closetfuls of fur coats in Paris and New York, she was hardly an active environmentalist.

Krugger and his agents came running through the gate and whisked them across the airstrip to a side elevator in the terminal. Tom Hayden was waiting for them upstairs. He promptly introduced them to the head of the Environmental Defense Fund.

Flash bulbs popped around them. Robert marveled at Emily's upbeat and accommodating behavior. She actually squeezed his arm before the cameras. Reflexively, he returned her affectionate gesture.

When the hoopla cooled down, Krugger guided them to a booth

that afforded a full view of the airstrip, chasing away a teenage girl with a Leica who approached them for a picture.

"See that guy in the blue blazer at the bar?" he asked.

Shay studied the black-haired man who sat quietly by himself nursing a beer.

"He wrote the *Newsmakers* story on Train."

"Don't encourage him," said Robert curtly, "or he'll be over here buggin' me for an interview."

Krugger kept his eyes on Werts. "Somehow, I don't think so. He's a different breed."

They had been driving for a very long time. But it was better in the back of the truck because Rita had given him many new blankets. Doni made two big caves. The one near the back door was for his soldiers.

Yesterday, Rita put a tree of yellow bananas in the back with him. Even though he was tired of eating them he loved the itsy-bitsy spiders that lived inside by the center. He had captured five of them. It was hard to keep them though. When it was dark in the truck they crawled away.

Rita slowed down. They made many stops and starts. Car headlights flashed against the back window. Doni began to get excited. Finally, they stopped. The humming of the engine turned off. Rita got out and slammed the door. He ran to the back door but it was a very long time before she came to open it. When she did, she climbed in. Outside he saw buildings. Dogs began to bark. Mean yaps and nasty howls. They sounded big and scary.

She separated the blankets. "I gotta wrap you up and carry you." Doni grabbed his treasure bag as she pushed him into the center of the blankets. "Act dead," she said.

Doni lay down obediently while she pushed his body along the bottom of the truck. He pretended he was a log rolling down a hill except it was flat and the ride was short.

He felt her coughing as she hoisted him into her arms and carried him up a few steps. His ear was pressed to her chest. Through the blanket he heard her heart beating. After a few more steps she kicked a door with her foot. She tried to put him down but instead dropped him like a package. "Shit. Man, it's dark as a fuckin' tomb in here."

Doni cartwheeled out of the scratchy blanket as fast as he could. He got to his feet and dashed down the short hall. Everywhere boxes were piled high with big dust balls on the floor. This place was different from the other places. Bigger. He sprinted back to her.

"You're never to leave this apartment," she said meanly. But Doni wasn't in the least frightened. He was too happy to be out of the truck.

"What a dump," she said as she took his hand. They went into a small room with a mattress on the floor. She threw the blankets on it. "This is your room. I'm sleepin' on the sofa up front."

Doni hid his treasure bag under the blankets while she dragged a stool over to the lamp hanging from the ceiling. "Cattle musta lived here," she said as she climbed on the stool. She removed the shade from the light. Dust filled the air. Rita looked at him. Her face turned ugly. "This hellhole is the best those sons of bitches can do? Let me tell ya, kid, when you got no use, your rich friends desert you. They got me hangin' by my ass."

She stepped over to the window. It was closed and covered with dirt. To Doni, it looked like the wall. "You sleep," she said, rubbing her arms to keep warm. Then, all of a sudden, a loud pop-bang sounded in the driveway.

Rita froze, terrified. A metal chain clanged against the iron bars outside the window. She reached for Doni. Voices screamed in the alley. There was a bright flash of light. Shadows on the windows. The roar of a helicopter overhead. Through a loudspeaker, a voice shouted, "Police!" Another set of footsteps ran down the driveway. In the distance they heard another pop-bang, much louder this time.

"Twelve-gauge," whispered Rita, her body rigid.

The dogs barked wildly. Then, almost as quickly as it started, it was quiet and dark. After a few seconds, a baby cried. A blast of music came from upstairs.

Rita let go of him. "Beanersville," she hissed. "Dealers peddlin' cheap shit. Man, this joint's a crackerbox. We're apt to get busted by narcs. What a joke thadda be." She stood up. "A goddamn pile of shit we're in."

After pushing the stool over to the wall she switched off the light. "I'm goin' out for a pint. Pray to the tooth fairy I make it back alive." Before she closed the door, she hesitated. "Calm down and quit fidgeting. And don't upchuck on me 'cause I ain't cleanin' it."

The lock clicked.

Doni skipped and skidded around the mattress. He crash-dived into the blankets. He liked them messed up and inside out. They made good caves. He started to jump up and down. Something sharp stuck him. A curly wire. He yanked it from the mattress and put it in his treasure bag. He could get a baseball card from José for it.

That night, through the louvered blinds of Reno's bedroom window, Emily gazed at Venice Beach. The boardwalk was deserted except for the presence of two cops. They straddled bicycles tilted against their legs as they talked together under the blue glare of a phosphorescent street light. Down the way, a vagrant approached.

A torn T-shirt with EAT SHIT AND DIE was emblazoned across his scrawny chest. When he saw the cops he stopped and began to forage through a trash can.

For a brief second the scene reminded Emily of the undulating black-and-white boardwalk in Rio de Janeiro. There was the same scent of urban violence, the promise of a vast ocean in the impenetrable blackness. Four years ago she had vacationed in Copacabana with Robert. Their passionate lovemaking on the floor of their balcony suite in the Grand Hotel had produced their son.

She gave a withered sigh as she turned around to Reno. He rocked soundlessly in the antique chair behind her, his hand against his chin. A sly, sweet smile lightened the rawboned handsomeness of his face. He rose and encircled her with his long arms. His fingers unbraided her hair; his hands cupped her head. He touched his lips to her neck.

Emily's eyes rested on the row of laminated Harley jackets on the wall. Sixties nonsense he swore he was going to toss every time she looked at them.

The house was seventy years old. It contained layers upon layers of history: the man, his family, his music. There were no marks of renovation; no retro-chic bullshit. Reno abhorred pretension.

Staring at his grandpa's brass bed, Emily remembered the night when Reno bound her hands to the tall posts. She recalled the smile on his face the lusty afternoon he nicknamed her "Zinger." With a spasm in her heart, she thought about the hard-soft elements he so beautifully combined, his playful nature during their most raunchy lovemaking.

She studied the guitar that leaned against the walnut bureau. It was a fancy lacquered job, black as the Stealth bomber and laced over with eye-splitting chrome. "That monster would do Elvis proud," she whispered in his ear.

He let go of her body and lifted the guitar fondly as if cradling a baby. His agile fingers plucked three soulful cords. He looked at her thoughtfully. "I give up the boozin' and brawlin' and you got me checkin' into heartbreak hotel."

He always spoke in this slow, laconic manner. The canny smile on his craggy face signaled a worldly mind that had gathered its education from the scholarship of the road.

"The wild blues and strawberry reds never hurt you like the chocolate browns," he crooned softly. Then, with the pick, he slashed violently across the strings. "He come back to you? Is that it?"

She said nothing as he put the guitar back down. He came to her and buried his damp face in her neck. She felt his yearning, his loving hunger. Her resolve began to fragment as he held her in his arms. Like a spooked colt she abruptly twirled away. Detached— that was the attitude she wanted to convey despite the fact it was not what she felt. She fussed with her Chanel suit. Ironically, it was the same suit she had worn when she consulted with Marvin Mitchelson about a divorce seven months before.

Finally, she responded to his question. "Yes," she said, "he's come back." She stared at the row of pencils on the rolltop desk, the cubbyhole filled with sheet music. She glanced at him. "The pain and horror have brought us together. I realize how intensely he loves Doni." Her voice broke with emotion. "I don't know that either one of us will be able to survive his . . ." Tracks of tears glistened on her high cheekbones. Reno gently blotted her eyes with his handkerchief, then hugged her with great warmth.

"We survive," he said in a distant voice. "We survive."

How well she understood. He too had known great agony. Two years before, his eldest son had been killed in a motorcycle accident in Georgia. Somehow Reno had made it back.

They shared pain on many levels: the anguish of the artist, and now, the loss of a child. He had supported her through the doubts she had felt as an actress. It was difficult to allow powerful emotions to course through her night after night on stage. He had mastered his own pain by putting it into the lyrics and melodies of his music. She had tried to master it with technique. Before she lost Doni, the intensity of her stage emotions had a profundity and depth that her real life lacked. If anything, real life was merely an exercise class to hone her acting skills.

Now this had changed. Reality had crushed her. The abject fear that coexisted with naive hope could never be duplicated on stage. This reality was a madness. Technique dissolved in the face of true madness. The center unraveled.

"Easy, amigo," Reno said, attempting to comfort her. God, how she loved him. He understood the ongoing pain of her life. Her brilliant husband only understood showmanship. With regret, she released herself from Reno's arms.

He followed her down the carpeted steps to the parlor. A smell of saddle soap rose from the cracked leather divans, the scent of furniture polish from the old walnut tables. The worn state of the house was as comfortable as an old flannel robe.

Before she opened the door, she turned back to him. Unable to raise her eyes, she tentatively touched his bolo tie. Her nails traced the stitched pattern of his western shirt. He leaned over and brushed his lips against hers. His kiss tasted of apricot tea. "A hundred and thirty-two days without a drink," he said. "Thanks to you."

"Oh, Reno," she cried. "I love you. I'll love you forever."

The guileless look in his eyes filled her with remorse. The spark of pain grew in him slowly like a flame.

"What if Doni is returned? Then what?" he asked.

"God, yes, I hope . . ." She bit her lip. "The pressure is too great for me to say anything . . . for now I have to stand by Robert. Divided they will kill us."

"They?"

"The kidnappers, the press. You. Myself."

He grabbed her to him. "I want you more than any woman I've ever known." She whimpered softly, a plaintive cry.

Reno buzzed the electronic gate to the alley and Emily's driver backed up the Rolls. The windows of the neighboring houses were dark. The ocean fog lent a cold dampness to the night. Reno pressed his hand into the small of her back. Just as he leaned over to kiss her an explosion of white light torched their eyes. Another round of flashbulbs burst in their faces. Reno dashed forward and almost caught the shadowy figure, which, escaping, fled into the row of carports. Reno tore after it.

Shivering in the alley, Emily heard the distant screech of wheels. Her driver opened the door of the car. "Sorry, Mrs. Shay. I didn't even see the bastard," he stuttered apologetically.

Reno returned, his breath jagged. "Blazin' assholes," he cursed. "I was afraid of this. I told you we should have met—"

Emily lifted her fingers to his lips to silence him. She kissed his cheek and quickly slipped into the car. It was too risky to spend any more time outside.

Still as a statue, Reno watched the rear lights become pinpoints in the fog. He kicked the painted boulder beside the fence. The pain sealed his frustration. "One day at a time," he told himself. "One day at a time."

In his music studio he sat down with his guitar and strummed into the darkness. "What was it with this town," he crooned. "This town, this town. Why did the John Derek haircuts always win in the end?"

Malcolm Bates strolled into the King's Head at half past midnight. The English pub on Santa Monica Boulevard was relatively quiet. On weekday nights the limeys were home trading green cards. Malcolm spotted Sam Sloane at a back table with a well-built girl. He stuck his hairy face between them.

"Bates!" exclaimed Sam. He tipped back in his chair. "Meet the *Daily Sun*'s centerfold."

"Pleasure," said Malcolm.

"The film's in the lab," said Sloane. His brown eyes flickered toward the girl. "Give us a second, luv. I got some private business." He pulled a ten from his pocket. "Get yourself a plate of chips."

"Whaddabout my picture?" she cooed.

"Later. Now, scoot."

They watched her wiggle past the dartboards to the bar. "Brass knockers," commented Sloane. He gulped a mouthful of draft before he got down to business. "It went swimmingly. I got a perfect shot. You can see the moles on their necks." He smiled faintly. "The maniac flew after me like a bat outta hell. Almost gave me a concussion."

Bates was pleased. His fat lips beamed a smile through his shaggy red beard. If he pulled off this coup he scored the "celeb watch" on St. Bart's for a month. Full expenses.

22

The chilly morning air from the dormer window cooled Jack's sweaty face. The rancid taste of stale cigarettes and sour booze filled his mouth. In the oak trees next to the house the chickadees squawked dementedly. The tiny suckers had to have a Yamaha synthesizer. It was impossible for six birds to maintain such volume. He closed his eyes and mashed the pillow under his head as he tried to reconstruct the fleeting fragments of his dream.

The face of Doni Shay fluttered back and forth like a hologram. Jack remembered that he was with the boy. They crawled under a bridge, faster and faster, before the entire structure collapsed like a house of cards. That was it. Cards. He had been jarred awake by the distinct feel of a card in his hand. He remembered it vividly. The Joker.

The unsettling dream goaded him from his stupor. He got up, stumbled to the closet, and dug out his crumpled jogging shorts. A diet of scotch and cigarettes was no way to control his weight. In step with the New Year, the transformation from mush to muscle had to come.

He drove down to Santa Monica and parked in a deserted beach lot. Above him, the plaintive honking of the seagulls blended with the glum, overcast sky. He began jogging along the shore at a slow gait, then accelerated to a moderate pace. When his intake of air was comfortably in synch with his muscle expenditure, he ratcheted his speed up a notch. He held each plateau until the hollow pain in his chest from strained breathing subsided.

During the last mile, his flaccid muscles protested the punishing pace. His mind was the only weapon to fight gravity, inertia, and the descending speedometer of his body. Jack willfully envisioned Ceci McCann's torso twitch under his weight. His body shot forward. The muscles in his legs contracted faster, his lungs pumped harder. He flew down the third mile.

Later, bent and panting like a dog, he laughed at himself. Always a woman. For some men the catalyst was money, for others, it was power. For him, it was the approval of Ceci McCann.

From the beach he drove over to Santa Monica Place. Once a ghost town of 1950s ready-to-wear shops and musty dime stores, the renovated pedestrian mall now boomed with sidewalk cafés and novelty shops. Jack strolled past a freshly painted kiosk selling ADOPT A BEACH T-shirts and then ducked into the Broadway Deli.

The restaurant had been designed to capture the feel of a 1930s Deco cafeteria. Of course, the dangling halogen lights, backlit signs, and faux Eames chairs brought it up to the minute. In fact, it was *the* hangout for quintessential thirtysomethings. Every guy in the place sported a ponytail and wore a black shirt buttoned to the neck, the accepted uniform of wannabe movie execs.

Jack hated the joint but Sammy was amused by the crowd. Grudgingly, he had to admit the food was decent, although the word "deli" had been stretched to include thirty varieties of olive oil and chocolate waffles the size of small cushions.

"Mr. Werts," said the hostess. She stood beside a cashier's cage that resembled a passport gate. The lady was vintage California vacant. She came from that species of straight-haired blondes that populated the beach communities of Newport, Malibu, and Santa Barbara. "This way," she said absently. She slapped at her purple tights with a handsome black-and-white menu.

As they approached the table, Sammy lifted her head from a pile of newspapers. A plastic visor shaded her pale face, bicycle shorts hugged her thighs. "Creampuff," she exclaimed.

"Salamander," he muttered.

Jack immediately observed that the thirtysomethings didn't bother reading newspapers. God, how he preferred the boisterous gang at Factor's Deli on Pico. At least he could count on old Jews still reading newspapers. Unlike the young ones who had sold out to the visual arts.

He reached for the sports section of the *Washington Post*.

Sammy slapped his hand. "Forget that."

"Forget the Redskins?"

She fished the *Tattler* from the heap. Jack feasted his eyes on a half-page picture of Emily Shay and Reno Ventura in an open-mouthed kiss. He pointed at the byline. "Malcolm rises from the dead."

"Save your praise. It's gobbledygook."

Sammy was right. The story was pure retread except for the line about Emily consulting a divorce lawyer.

An overly upbeat waiter came over. Jack ordered ricotta blintzes, coffee, and a Corona.

"Ten to one Harrington's gonna demand Ventura for the cover," Sammy warned.

"Banish the thought."

His coffee arrived in a pint-size French breakfast cup. He found the sports section just as a gaggle of anorexic blondes with magenta lips filed into the booth behind them.

"DGs," said Sammy, giving them the once-over.

"DGs?"

"Development girls. Mills College graduates desperate to be studio execs." She folded back the op-ed page of *The New York Times.* "Instead, they become fetch-and-fuck machines for baby-boy executives."

Jack wondered how much this tirade had to do with her girl-friends not getting their scripts produced. He contemplated the blondes. Too emaciated for his tastes.

"Do me a favor," said Sammy. "Give your ol' pal Bates a call. Find out how Sam Sloane got this picture."

"Why? Who cares about the soap opera?" He noticed that the Raiders were in second place.

Sammy removed her visor. "Maybe they're related."

Jack looked at her. "You mean Ventura kidnapped Doni Shay?"

"No, hardly Reno." She pondered the situation. "Shay's ex-girlfriend possibly."

Jack frowned. "You've seen *Fatal Attraction* too many times."

Robert found Emily in her studio, a cluttered attic that overlooked the back courtyard of the mansion. He hesitated at the door, attempting to calm himself.

She stood with her back to him, brushing graceful spirals across a large canvas, her loose shirt and Docker's pants splattered with flecks of paint. Suddenly aware of his presence, she twisted around, softly questioning the interruption.

With violence in his heart, he marched into the room and threw the newspaper at her. It slapped open, knocking over a canister of brushes. She barely glanced at the photograph. "Please, don't be cross," she said with a pained expression. She spoke with an air of surrender. "It's not what it appears. I can explain."

"You bitch!" he shouted, the fury in his soul unleashed. His brain seethed, a cauldron of conflicting emotions. "Omnivorous cunt," he muttered contemptuously. "I hoped—naively, I see now—that we had something going between us. A spark, at least. At a time we needed to pull together."

Emily coldly turned away and faced the canvas. She took a fat brush in hand and made a jagged black slash through the muted colors.

"I'm no fool," he said, moving toward her. "I know we have a long way to go to find love again. And given the damage we've done to each other, it may be impossible. But for Doni . . ." His voice faltered. "Until he's released, I hoped we could put on a show for the press. For the FBI, at the very least."

Robert was overcome by myriad feelings. "I hoped our renewed commitment might somehow help us get him back." He blinked back tears. "If only they had demanded money . . . if only . . ." He stared at the profusion of violets in the windowbox while he regained control. "And what's this about Mitchelson?" he asked calmly.

Emily gave him a sharp look. "Christ, Robert. That was last spring when you were unable to extricate yourself from the pixie-faced winner of the scriptwriting contest. Remember? In her love letter, which I so luckily stumbled on, she insisted you had promised to divorce me."

He turned away. Overhead, the intercom buzzed. Chicki had them on the remote camera. "Libby's downstairs," she announced.

Robert left the room fuming. He still couldn't believe he'd lost Emily to Reno Ventura. A cowpoke loser. Jeez, Kristofferson was leagues above this guy.

Libby glared at him like a bull ready to charge. "Your romp in the hay may cost us seventy million bucks," she snapped. "For a supposed genius, you're sure a slow learner."

Robert lifted his eyes, indicating she must lower her voice.

"Oh, puh-lease. The gossip's all over the lot. Everyone at Starlight knows about this. Mack's got a megaphone for a mouth."

She stepped over to the mantel to cool down. But her eyes met his in the gilt mirror. Acid seeped into her voice. "The abortion's done, paid for by Starlight's insurance program. That's the good news. The bad news is that Pfeiffer's lawyers are suing us for contract default. I hear she passed on films with Coppola and Scorsese."

Libby turned and faced him. "It gets even worse. Martin Sheen now wants off the picture. And Duval refuses to play Captain Mylar."

Robert was acutely uncomfortable. "What's the solution?"

"Fire Lee Mack."

"I can't," he protested. "She had the abortion for me."

"You don't even know if the baby was yours," Libby shrieked. "Mack's slept with half the directors in town. Only they're smarter. They didn't give her parts in their films—let alone a seventy-million-dollar film."

Libby closed her eyes for a moment, attempting to regain her composure. This time, her words came more evenly. "Robert, the meter's running, you've got to act fast. Give her cash, a Mercedes, promise her a part in a future film—at another company. Anything she'll accept."

She spotted the *Tattler* on the rosewood coffee table and studied the photo of Emily and Reno. "That Chanel suit is five years old. They pasted their pictures together. More tabloid garbage," she sneered, dismissing the story. Her eyes pierced his. "But Pfeiffer's lawsuit, which is being filed by Gibson Dunn, will be blasted around the globe by all the media heavies." She snorted with disgust. "You can kiss your Prince Charming days good-bye."

Disturbed by the commotion, Emily appeared in the arched doorway. "What's wrong?" she asked.

Libby looked directly at Robert. "You explain it." She turned and headed for the foyer.

Krugger spoke to Robert in a compressed tone of voice. "A three-year-old boy in New Mexico claims to have played with Donald." He hardly sounded convinced. "Other witnesses told police the child was a girl, but José, the Mexican kid, and a cleaning woman, disagree. We pieced together a profile of a young, dark-haired woman traveling with the child."

Robert grew impatient. "That's all you got."

"At fourteen bucks a night, the EZ motel hardly keeps decent records. The woman gave the name Rita Sanchez."

Robert was skeptical. "Doesn't make any sense. Doesn't seem likely that . . ."

"Except for the possible connection with Maria's relatives," Krugger said.

His words hit Shay like a fastball to the brain. "I thought you sealed that can of worms?" he said.

"The relatives, yes. But the friends of relatives, no."

Stan Lutz's office looked like the VIP lounge at LAX. Shorty, Leggitt, and Grinker were stationed on the sofas. Tommy trotted back and forth, shouting orders into the phone, straining at the spiral cord like a dog on a leash. His voice was filled with restrained hysteria.

The atmosphere in the room was charged, but it was a queer tension, as if a plane had crashed and the details were as yet unclear.

As Lisa trailed in after Ceci and Mitch, Lutz grabbed another line and spoke fast. His surveillant eyes gave Ceci a covert, intimate glance.

Her cheeks flamed self-consciously. It had been over two weeks since she'd seen him. On Christmas Day, he had sent her a bonsai tree accompanied by a tender note, but he didn't call.

"What gives?" Lisa demanded.

"Tape two arrived," said Grinker. "Delivered by Domino's Pizza."

Ceci looked at Mitch, astonished.

Shorty broke into their conversation. "The FBI has the kid in studio four. They're grillin' the life outta him."

"Domino's Pizza?" said Lisa.

"The carton was theirs," explained Grinker. "One of those insulated vinyl deals they use to keep food hot."

Leggitt supplied the details. "The kid's thirteen, black. Riding a ten-speed. He said a white woman handed him the package. She gave him twenty bucks and told him to bring it to the studio. The kid thought it was a pizza."

"Where'd this happen?" asked Mitch.

"Fairfax and Melrose."

"Where's the tape?" Ceci asked.

"Yeah, when can we see it?" said Lisa.

Mitch looked troubled. "What's wrong? Is the baby disfigured?"

Grinker nodded in Lutz's direction. The network president's voice grew louder.

"If Shay comes on the show, we'll hold off. Otherwise, the video airs in ten minutes." His small eyes ricocheted around the room. "I don't care what Krugger says," he brayed into the receiver.

Ceci realized he was talking to Morgan Camp. Lutz shook his head. "That's our timetable," he said firmly, hanging up.

Everyone began to talk at once. "Play it for them," Tommy said, silencing the confusion.

The video countdown began on monitor 4. Doni's face appeared, bravely resolute. His small voice called, "Where's Mommy?" Blank fear filled his big blue eyes. His small arms reached to them as if he expected to be lifted. "When will I see you, Mommy?" he asked distinctly.

As glassy tears rolled down the boy's smooth cheeks Ceci struggled to remain calm. Then, miraculously, Doni stopped crying and stared straight ahead, remarkably self-possessed. "Please come and take me home. I'll never get into trouble. I'll be a good boy. Forever 'n' ever."

The tape went to gray.

"Psychological warfare," said Lisa.

"No shit, Sherlock," intoned Grinker.

Ceci couldn't believe what brutal savages these monsters were. The tape was designed to destroy the sanity of . . . of who? Emily Shay?

Train turned to Lutz. "What's with Camp?"

"The FBI won't allow Shay to come on."

Tommy swore under his breath. Briefly, he glanced out the window at the towers of Century City. "How was it that Krugger's agents missed the delivery boy?" he asked.

"Camp says Krugger's on a wild-goose chase," said Lutz. "The FBI's got an all-points alert out for a blue seventy-nine Datsun truck—whatever that's worth."

"The kidnap vehicle?" Lisa asked.

"Presumably."

Train looked at Shorty. "We'll throw that tidbit in after the tape runs." Swiftly, he began to discharge orders. "Lisa, call Camp back. Tell him we're bringing a dupe of the tape to the mansion. Drive over with a crew. We need Emily's response. An on-the-spot, after-the-fact interview."

Lisa groaned at the impossibility of it.

"Okay, okay, if you can't get the Shays, try for the butler, the maids, even Camp. We've finally got a foot in the door, don't blow it." He glanced at his watch. "Leave now. Go."

Tommy focused on Ceci. "You and Mitch get down to studio four. Interview the kid. Extract every fuckin' detail. Get a full description of the woman, the color of his bike, what he ate for breakfast."

Train whipped around to Shorty. "We might think about callin' in some actors to dramatize the transfer." He turned to Leggitt. "Get details on the Datsun truck. McCann can tape a thirty-second news spot—'FBI's now investigating dot, dot, dot.' "

Train laid a heavy hand on Grinker's shoulder. "Take a crew over to West Hollywood. Interview anybody who saw anything. Shoot the corner, the shops, street signs." He paused. "After that, get your ass to the federal building. By then the video will be airing continuously. Get some flustered quotes from the FBI flunkies." He looked at Lutz. "That'll fill a full hour. The other networks won't know what hit 'em. They'll be a half-hour behind us."

Without delay, everyone filed from the room. Lutz grabbed Train's arm. "The 'nappers are gonna call in. I can feel it."

"Yeah, fine," said Tommy. His nimble mind was already blocking segments of the show. "We're fuckin' hot. Hotter than hell."

23

For the past three weeks Jack Werts had stayed holed up in his house on Mulholland and followed events in the Shay kidnapping on TV. The second videotape generated even more hysteria than the first. Committees of outraged mothers proposed new laws against kidnapping. NTN went to an all-talk format with endless panels on the subject. It didn't take long for the other networks to catch on.

Against Jack's advice Harrington put the delivery boy on the cover of *Newsmakers*. Much to his surprise the New York reporter did a halfway decent job on the story. Predictably, the electronic media kicked into high gear and made the thirteen-year-old kid a major celebrity. After a guest spot on *The Oprah Winfrey Show* with his five brothers and sisters he signed with Creative Artists Agency. Two days later, Liz Smith reported that he had landed a substantial role in Eddie Murphy's new film.

Following the delivery boy, *Newsmakers* had put Emily Shay on the cover with a sympathetic story written by Mara Stykes. It was a highly polished piece with the bulk of the quotes coming from Emily's theater friends. Reno Ventura denied any involvement and insisted their relationship was purely professional. Ventura was a likable guy who pulled in audience sympathy. After the controversy, his album *Barefoot Alley* soared to number two on the charts.

Jack was left to cover developments on the Train show, which had expanded to an hour format. Two top anchors were sent out from New York while Tommy radically transformed his freewheeling style. Almost Koppel-like in his restraint, he became the voice of logic trying to make some sense of the situation. The ploy worked. The print media christened NTN the "network of record" on the kidnapping. Instantly, the Train show signed quality advertisers, which translated into lucrative ad dollars for the starved network.

Ironically, at the same time, the tone of the viewers changed dramatically. A natural censorship set in. Loonies quit bothering to air their insults. Jack suspected that many of the crazies had been deleted by the FBI. The result was boring fluff. Syrupy calls had transformed the show into the Hallmark-card hour.

Meanwhile, the Shays made a statement to the press. Again, they implored the kidnappers to spare the life of their son. It was routine pablum. The FBI officially announced they had uncovered one of the kidnap vehicles in a junkyard in Mexico City. The truck had been registered to a Connecticut veterinarian who had reported it stolen nine months before.

The only rumble that even mildly whetted Jack's appetite came from Lee Mack. The fledgling actress had offered Harrington an elaborate tale of abortion and abandonment involving Robert Shay. Harrington passed on the package because the medical records she presented as proof were under an alias. From Bates, Jack heard that a London tabloid had purchased her spiel for three hundred grand.

Jack switched off the tube, tired of listening to Phil Donahue interview experts about international child-slavery rings. He went into the kitchen, poured himself a Perrier, and added a half-inch of Angostura bitters, his New Year's resolution to cut down on the sauce.

He took a slab of fresh sturgeon from the fridge, cut off half a cube of rich yellow butter, and knifed it into a cast-iron skillet. The artery-hardening hunk of saturated fat reminded him of Sherry, the health queen. Last week, she had sent him a convoluted "I need my space" note all knotted up with sappy phrases about her love for him. Spinoza she wasn't, but he got the message. "Total commitment to her work" meant she was fucking Morgan Camp. He did actually feel a pang of sadness, which astonished him. But he could survive nicely without the endless bills from Victoria's Secret charged to his credit card.

As the fish spit and sizzled in the pan Jack noticed the invitation to the NTN affiliates' party on the windowsill. He had planned to pass on the event until Mara called and informed him that Train was scheduled to make an appearance. According to the invitation, the party was for *Marked for Murder*, a corny sit-crime that was the only top-ten show NTN had on its roster. The gaudy fetes were staged seasonally for the fat-cat owners of local TV stations.

He gulped down the Perrier. If Train did show there was the

unpleasant possibility of a confrontation. Too many times he had encountered subjects who were less than pleased with the stories he had written about them. It was a thorny situation at best and, in some cases, violent. Norman Mailer nearly took a swing at him.

The fact that Ceci McCann might make an appearance was a plus. The ubiquitous commercials had made her famous. It was remarkable, really. What Ronald Reagan was to Westinghouse and Bob Hope to Chevrolet, Ceci was to NTN. Her appearance had changed as well. Her golden hair was fuller and lighter, her clothes more stylish. She fit the medium perfectly.

Despite the impossibility of the situation, the itch in his groin grew. His cock had a will of its own that transcended the details of reality. He snapped Jimmy Buffet into the CD player and attempted to redirect his lewd thoughts to the succulent fish. After a few bites, he put down his fork and knife, strode over to the bar, and poured himself a shot of Wild Turkey. Shit, he'd go. What better did he have to do this Friday night?

Shortly after two o'clock in the morning, Robert Shay awoke, tortured by nightmares. He listened to the wind howl through the canyon, the rain beat against the tile roof while morbid thoughts massed like thick black clouds in his brain. To disperse them, he tried desperately to hinge some hope on Krugger's phone call. The agent had flown yesterday to Albuquerque to investigate new evidence involving the García boy.

Robert tried to sleep but it was hopeless. By seven, he would be exhausted. When he got up and went into the marble bathroom to get a sleeping pill, he heard the faint drone of Doni's voice.

He followed the sound to the den, where Emily sat immobilized before the screen, her face drained. The second tape with its message had plunged her into a clinical depression. Now only powerful tranquilizers kept her from taking her life.

Robert slammed his hand against the button. Emily said nothing, her dark violet eyes unreadable. He sat down next to her, wondering how she had escaped the nurse who slept in her room. Perhaps it was good, a sign that the life force still stirred within her.

"I think"—she seemed to be struggling to speak—"Krugger's wrong. The kidnappers expect us to appear on television." She looked directly at him. "And if they aren't interested in our money, perhaps their accomplices and relatives will be." Robert felt the force of her determination. "How much reward money should we offer?" she asked.

His words came slowly. "If I pay two million for a script, twenty million for our son is reasonable."

A loud voice woke Doni. The seal man was shouting at Rita in the front room. Doni crawled from under his blanket and went over to the door.

"You're chippin'," he said. "What a fuck-up. You're strung out. Look at yourself."

"Sure, sure. I scored a couple," Rita cried. "But I ain't speedin'. No, man. I'm well enough to know I ain't takin' the rap."

"Relax. It's a minor delay."

"Minor delay," she yelled.

Big music started upstairs and Doni couldn't hear them anymore. He went back to his blanket and listened to the dogs bark. He had named them Fur and Alarm. Fur sounded terribly mean but he was nice too. During the day he talked to Alarm in happy yaps. More than anything Doni wanted to go outside and play with them.

A door slammed. The seal man had left.

Later, Rita came back into the room. "Why the face?" she said. In her hand she had a plate of food. "I brought you steak. But I ain't cuttin' it for you."

Doni took the meat in his fingers and began to tear it with his teeth. He was hungry. It had been a long time since he'd eaten.

"You can't breathe in here," she said. She opened the window a tiny bit, then sat down. She looked very sad. "I'm dead without wheels," she said. She began to sob into her hands. When Doni finished eating he put his hand on her arm. She dried her eyes with her dress. "Hell of a deal, kid. We're locked in and I ain't feelin' good. All I can get is cheap shit."

After awhile she left and then returned with a plastic jug of water and a doughnut. It had red and white sprinkles. This time when she left she forgot to turn off the light.

Quickly, Doni took the paper box from under his blanket. He opened the top carefully. They were all there. Teensie, tiny dots, smaller than the little round seeds Maria put on the bread before she put it in the oven. Yesterday, he squished the biggest one and found many white specks inside its belly. He figured that was a mama seed bug.

After a few seconds Doni closed the lid. If he kept it open too long they would jump out and bite his arms and legs. He wasn't scratching now that he had them in jail.

Between two papers he kept his collection of arrowheads. He made the points from pieces of the wall. They were big and looked good but when he tried to throw them they came apart. José was too smart to trade his soldiers for these arrowheads.

As Doni arranged his stick soldiers in a row on the floor he thought about the seal man. The doughnut had something to do with his visit. But Rita didn't sound happy. In fact, she was angry all the time. More and more she forgot to bring him food. He wanted to help her but he didn't know how.

24

On Friday evening Jack Werts drove his Wrangler up to the valet station under Chasen's green-and-white-striped awning. Directly ahead of him, the red-jacketed parking attendant opened the door of a gleaming black Mercedes with a chrome belly guard. Bill Leggitt stepped from the car. His hair was brilliantined back, gangster style. The white silk scarf around his neck was draped casually over his tuxedo. A lissome blonde, wearing a skimpy chiffon dress, emerged from the passenger side. Leggitt took her arm and guided her through the paparazzi gathered at the entrance.

Another attendant opened the door of the Wrangler. The snotty kid grunted disparagingly at the sight of the dilapidated interior. Jack climbed out. "Twerp," he muttered, confidently adjusting the bow tie of his tux. He inhaled the warm night air redolent of magnolia and hibiscus, squared his shoulders, and strode past the meager troop of photogs.

Despite the crush of people, Jack liked the feel of the dark, clubby restaurant. Established in 1936, the decor was that of a gentleman's hunting lodge: tufted leather settees, duck prints, shaded wall lamps, thick oxblood carpeting. The only Hollywood touch was the endless row of autographed pictures of ancient stars interspersed with humorous cartoons and caricatures. Glancing at a drawing of George Jessel, Jack thought it appropriate that NTN chose the legendary show-biz haunt for its affiliates' bash. The paunchy small-town tycoons with their bejeweled and beribboned wives thrilled over the chance to chow down at Ron and Nancy's favorite eaterie. This was Friars Club territory, home to Frank Sinatra, Merv Griffin, and Zsa Zsa.

Like a churning windmill the maître d' steered the boisterous crowd through the paneled corridor to the California Room. Unlike the rest of the restaurant, the spacious, high-domed space was light and airy. A forest of ficus trees, festooned with pin lights, were stationed before the tall windows. White helium balloons danced on tinsel strings. From above, a revolving mirrored ball shed rays of confettied light on enormous buffet tables decorated with ice sculptures and miniature fountains.

In the center of the room rose a monumental twelve-tier cake. A glittering NTN logo twirled at the top.

Jack ambled past a trellis of crab and shrimp conveniently propped up alongside the bar. Tattinger's champagne flowed from frosty bottles poured by white-gloved waiters. He stared at the platters of clams casino, oysters Rockefeller, rib-eye steaks, and the silver tureens of Chasen's famous chili. He liked the old place. It was an honest establishment that served copious quantities of high-grade cowboy chow. Like everywhere else in L.A., the prices emptied your wallet, but at least the food filled your belly. For one night he was delighted to be spared the spa cuisine. As far as he was concerned the Supreme Court should forget abortion and outlaw peanut tortillas and pint-size pizzas.

He quickly sized up the crowd. The NTN affiliates were overfed honchos accompanied by plump, dimpled wives they had married for keeps. These solid citizens contrasted starkly with the glitzy Hollywood stars who, Jack noted, were strictly third-rate has-beens and hopefuls, many hardly recognizable except by die-hard couch potatoes.

Still, they were physically impossible to ignore.

The tall, muscular males had the lean, conditioned bodies of sexual gymnasts. They wore neon cummerbunds and rhinestone studs. The tips of lizard cowboy boots poked from under their tuxedos. The females of the species were hard-faced synthetic beauties with bodies sculpted by the scalpel and Stairmaster. They were wrapped in spangled rubber-band dresses designed to display their hardball breasts and iron thigh muscles. Jack smiled. A truly either/or crowd.

As he waded through the merriment, he sensed a crescendo of excitement. An increasing buzz, almost a nervous anticipation. Amidst the commotion, Tommy Train appeared. The talk-show host walked through the throng like Charlton Heston parting the Red Sea. He raised his arms as if blessing the audience. Victory signs were in his eyes.

Almost immediately a reporter from *Entertainment Tonight* sidelined him. Delirious with the attention, Train spoke to the camera as if addressing a religious congregation. The white light of fame spurred him to higher and higher levels of intoxication. For an instant, Tommy looked directly at Jack, but he was too self-absorbed and flushed with self-importance to recognize him.

Unable to stomach the hurrahs, Werts headed for the bar. It was then he saw Ceci. She stood in a shrine of magically bright light from a row of candles on the banquet table. She looked like a young Grace Kelly in a room full of aging Lolitas. The perfect princess of NTN.

Her intense blue eyes were focused on Train with the adoration of the Magi. Suddenly, she saw Jack and blanched. "Gawd! Werts! You've got your nerve."

Maintaining her guard, she looked at him with an ingenuous expression. "Brave to show your face," she said with a sneer that distorted her pretty mouth.

"I'm here for round two."

"With me?"

"Who else?"

"Select another opponent," she said. "Just being seen talking with you sullies my reputation—and casts suspicion on my integrity."

She about-faced with an aloof toss of her blond mane. Stan Lutz joined her and guided her to the ET cameras. With a clumsy gesture, he patted the shoulder of his star pupil. "Push the February sweeps," he whispered. He stood back like a father to watch her perform.

Jack observed the glee in the network chieftain's eyes. Lutz was a brilliant tactician who had started playing water boy to higher-ups from day one. His keen sense of the line between flattery and obsequiousness had worked wonders on Arthur Keigel.

Tired of the circus, Jack backed away. As usual his common sense had been damaged by his lustful desires. A wave of self-pity began to seep into his soul as a local photographer tapped his elbow. "Malcolm Bates is in the bar, askin' after you."

Sure enough, in the front corner of the lounge the tabloid king and his gang of cannibals had commandeered a horseshoe booth under a forty-year-old picture of George Burns. "Black Jack. Join the riffraff," Bates shouted to him.

"What are you doin' at a low-level TV gig?" Jack asked.

"Enjoying ourselves." Malcolm's bushy brows bounced with delight. "Best freebie in town." He offered Jack a Gauloise cigarette. Werts made an unpleasant face.

"We hoped Shay might put in a cameo," said the limey sitting next to Bates. He took a lion-size bite of an unwieldy sandwich he had assembled from the buffet tables. At that moment the stud on Malcolm's tux apron popped. The gold clip flew into a neighboring champagne glass to hoots and roars.

Malcolm ignored the jeering. He touched Jack's arm. "We hear Shay's gonna offer a big reward. On Train's show."

"When?"

"Next week."

Jack cursed softly. That explained the delirium. "Lutz is so happy I thought he'd split his pants," he said dryly.

Bates wiggled his nose. "I hear the blond anchor, McCann, is suckin' his dick."

Jack blinked hard. The evening was getting really grisly.

Bates reached his arm around Jack's neck and pulled his face close to his. "After the toasts, Lutz is gonna announce the birth of ITN."

"ITN?"

"The International Television Network. First American network to go global. Financed by the Japs."

While Jack was estimating the millions of dollars Keigel and Lutz might make off such a deal, Bill Leggitt sauntered past their booth. The flimsy blonde had been traded for a redhead. A pair of round white breasts rested against her chest like two scoops of vanilla ice cream.

Bates gave Leggitt a dirty look. "That braggart says he's clearing two hundred grand a year, plus expenses."

"A piss-poor reporter," chirped the *National Enquirer* columnist from across the table. "Fagan fired him from the *Midnight Express*."

"For fabricating stories," added the limey, standing up. "Like the rest of us don't?" He took off for a buffet run.

The men watched Leggitt enviously. "The cadaver doesn't deserve a kitten like that," Bates said.

Jack gulped down his scotch. "Money talks."

"Especially in this town."

"In any town," Jack replied. He'd learned his lesson. Glumly, he contemplated the model of the space shuttle that hung from the center of the bar. Leggitt's newfound prosperity severely depressed him. S. J. Perelman's description of Hollywood came to mind: "A dreary industrial town controlled by hoodlums of enormous wealth." Man went to the moon but show biz never changed. Jack ordered another scotch.

The limey returned with two plates filled with oysters and clams. He gave one to the table, the other he unloaded in a plastic bag. "For the missus," he explained as he slipped the squishy packet into his pocket. "Twenty-four bucks at the Santa Monica fish market."

The jocular ribbing and updated gossip of the tabloid tribe distracted Jack for a while, until a drunken reporter called out, "Behold! The publicity chieftain with his squaw."

In the doorway stood Morgan Camp with Sherry Cox on his arm. That wasn't the worst of it. When Sherry turned to greet a Camp client, Morgan's meaty paw slid down her sequined rump. As Jack had suspected, there was more to Sherry's burning the midnight oil than press releases.

Two strikeouts and it was only ten o'clock.

He sank down in the booth as the lovebirds joined a gaggle of TV stars that included David Doyle and Cheryl Ladd. Sherry fluttered about Morgan, adjusting his tie, patting down his few remaining strands of hair.

"Nice piece, his new lady," said Bates with an appreciative glance.

Jack picked up his drink, excused himself, and slipped from the booth. The evening had become unbearable.

Too wired to go home, Jack made a left on Bundy off Santa Monica Boulevard. He headed for Eureka, Wolfgang Puck's latest salt lick for celebs. On Friday nights, the restaurant had the best bar scene in town.

A valet with dreadlocks opened the door of the Wrangler. Before getting out, Jack ripped away his tie and cummerbund and tossed them in the back. Stepping onto the sidewalk, he felt better already. He glanced at the seventy-foot sand palms that lined the entrance. Their shaved beards were obscene. They reminded him of a girl who once shaved her pubis for him. Christ, he needed a drink—or a woman. He wasn't quite sure which or in what order.

From the outside the huge sandstone building resembled an Egyptian temple. Inside, it was an industrial-baroque brewery that housed two stainless-steel tanks of beer alongside a cavernous room filled with tables. When it came to the decor, no expense had been spared: steel chairs, black stone floors, oversized brass-and-copper bolts that carried out the distillery theme. The errant tangle of halogen lamps dangling from the ceiling perfectly replicated a Paul Klee painting. The place was either tantalizing or revolting, depending on how drunk you were.

Werts edged through the rambunctious bar crowd. It was the full L.A. spectrum: fighter jocks, chantilly-lace maidens, yupster lawyers, and gold-chained body builders. To Jack, it looked like an updated version of Elizabethan England.

He quickly ordered a silver bullet and as he sipped the icy gin surveyed the predictable lineup of Holly Golightlys. Fey blondes and brunettes sleek as Dobermans stood ready to snare the owners of the Masaratis parked out front.

"The rough footage sucked," complained the man in Gucci loafers standing next to him. A moustached fellow in a herringbone jacket slapped the man's back. "Burn the negatives. That's how you survive it," he said loudly. "You have to bend the rules to get what you want."

Jack took another swallow of gin, his attention caught by a host of golden daffodils in the corner—a trio of ripe-lipped blondes with pouty expressions who waved to and fro for each new guy that passed. The short, peppy one with HUGS NOT DRUGS scripted across her T-shirt made eye contact with him. Jack pushed his gin away and called to the waiter for a beer. If he did get lucky and score, these baby dolls were performance artists who expected back flips in bed. He needed all his faculties.

Directly across from him, an intriguing Medusa toyed with her drink. With incredible sophistication, she plucked the lemon wedge from her empty glass and began grating it across her teeth. Slowly. Very slowly. A perverse, knowing smile curled her lips. She wore a black bustier and sheer paisley skirt. Ready for action.

Before Jack could move in, a young guy in a blue blazer approached her, a nice-looking kid, topsider type. His "Howdy" elicited a treacherous snarl from Medusa, who let him know she was shopping for somethin' else. Jack turned away. It wasn't gonna be him either.

For a few minutes, he addressed his beer and calmly studied the kinetic art on the walls. In keeping with the factory theme, it blinked and whirred like a series of conveyor belts. Appropriate, mused Jack. Since America had lost its manufacturing base, the only use for factories was in restaurant design.

Gucci Loafers accidentally bumped him with his arm. "John Wayne's dead, pal," he roared to his friend. "There aren't any heroes, not in the movie business."

Not in any business, thought Werts glumly. Except ol' Winston Churchill who said, "Success consists of nothing more than going from failure to failure without a loss of enthusiasm." All at once, Jack realized that what had been gnawing at him for the last few months was his loss of enthusiasm.

A shrill female voice cut through his bittersweet reverie.

"Jaaaaack Werts."

Madison Cole's sharp crimson nails dug into the shoulder of his tuxedo jacket. A wet kiss hit his lips. She pushed Gucci Loafers aside to make room for her friends. The guy was a string bean in a white Panama hat. He had cloying spaniel eyes and floated in a vapor of heavy cologne. The girl trailing him was a slovenly feline in mesh stockings with a bumper sticker for a skirt. Certifiable. All three.

Madison draped her hand over Jack's thigh. "We've come to sweep you away," she said, semiloaded on stimulants. To his shock, Jack felt a momentary flare of desire. "Our ride deserted us. Give us a lift up the coast and we'll take you to the best party of your life."

"How far up the coast?" he asked. After all, she could mean San Francisco.

"Malibu." She reached over and finished his beer. "C'mon, don't be a killjoy. Let's boogie!"

Overcome by an increasing sense of inertia, he agreed. "Okay," he grunted.

Medusa gave him the finger as he walked past her.

When they hit Pacific Coast Highway, Spaniel Eyes settled with Mesh Stockings in the back seat and lit a joint. Madison took a hit and passed it over to Jack. He took a long, hard drag. Good shit, but it did nothing for his mood.

The four-lane highway was a smooth ribbon in the bright moonlight. Fortunately, traffic was light. At 1 A.M. the coastal road warriors were tucked in for the weekend. On the radio, Peggy Lee's "Fever" played forever. Jack began to feel somewhat better.

As they zoomed past the Malibu Pier he tried to dissociate himself from Madison's constant chatter. It was hard to say what her problem was. The two in the back were a puzzle too. Jack detected the trace of an Australian accent in Spaniel Eyes; Mesh Stockings was strictly local flora.

Eric Clapton's "I Shot the Sheriff" blared from the radio.

"Turn it up, turn it up," Stockings wailed in his ear.

"Shut up, marblehead," hissed Madison. "Your taste in music is shit."

"She's a May Company model," protested Spaniel Eyes.

While Jack tried to find the key to their non sequitur conversation Madison switched off K-ROCK. After rummaging through his box of CDs, she settled on Bonnie Raitt.

"You can't believe what I've had to put up with," she moaned.

Yes, I can, thought Jack.

In time, Madison got restless and started searching around the dashboard. "Where's your car phone?"

"I don't approve of 'em."

"How neanderthal," she crowed. "Everybody in the drug business has one." She pulled a brown vial of pills from her purse and downed a handful.

Mesh Stockings suddenly popped her head between them. "Why are you dressed in that tux?" she asked.

"I came from a funeral."

"That's sad," she said, then vanished into the darkness. Jack figured she'd been giving Spaniel Eyes a blow job. It was that kinda night.

Two miles past Pepperdine University they made a right on Coral Canyon road. They climbed a steep embankment, snaking around thickets of dry scrub and boulder outcroppings. Except for a few horse ranches, the area was largely unsettled.

"Edgar's got the estate on the market," said Madison, instructing him to turn onto a narrow dirt road. "Four million, would'ya believe?"

On first appearances, the house wasn't much. A neglected two-story Spanish villa with a parade of cars, mostly foreign, parked haphazardly in the gravel driveway. Jack parked the Wrangler in what felt from the bump under the wheels to be the remains of a rock garden.

"I don't wanna walk," whined Stockings as she climbed from the back seat.

"Shut up," Madison snapped. She clutched Jack's hand possessively. Spaniel Eyes was relieving himself in the bushes on the other side of the car. Jack heard his stream hit the dry leaves. Like a band of gypsies, they headed for the dimly lit house, the raw sea breeze biting viciously at their backs.

On the porch, stone urns had been upended and the ceramic tiles underfoot were chipped and missing. From a row of pleated wood doors came the sound of heavy metal along with the sweet scent of hashish. They stepped into a cathedral-ceiling living room where a spaced-out crowd, mostly in their early twenties, drifted about like zombies.

It was one of those Malibu drug parties where introductions were passé—the Blue Velvet generation.

"Get 'em to put on 'The Cure'," wailed Stockings, disappearing down the dark hallway. Spaniel Eyes padded after her.

Jack took a hard look at the place. Except for a few pieces of Mediterranean furniture, everything portable had been removed. There were no carpets, drapes, or paintings. At that moment, a skinhead with steel-toed boots slid down along a wooden bench to make space for them. Madison smiled graciously at the tattooed monster. "Let's get a drink," she suggested, preferring to prowl.

They walked into another room lit with black candles big as dock stumps. The house was sizable; twenty rooms downstairs at least. They entered the kitchen. Empty bottles of beer and wine filled the dirty porcelain sink; a black trash bag brimmed with garbage. Jack poured some cheap red wine into a used paper cup. Madison opened the fridge to retrieve a can of Budweiser from a thicket of brown bags. A hulking biker came in behind them. The rattler on his bicep uncoiled as he banged a six-pack of Coors into the fridge. Before he left, he swiped an open bag of chips from the counter.

Madison sauntered onto the patio, where she introduced herself to a group of quasi-normals sitting around a white iron table. Back in the kitchen, two maize-haired sylphs joined Jack. Painted for war, they wore tiny jeans skirts and no stockings. It took a minute or two for him to realize they were hookers. He had a hunch they were a package deal: two for the price of one. The runt held back, plucking her nails, while the other searched the cupboards.

"The assholes drank my whiskey," whined the aggressor. Jack savored the flesh of her loins as she stretched over the counter to reach the top shelves. He was tempted. He took a swallow of his rancid wine and gleefully imagined himself lewdly tangled up with them. Suddenly, the runt got jumpy. "There ain't a liquor store for miles," she complained.

"I know, I know," said the temptress.

She was on Jack's wavelength. Before he could move he felt her hand slide between his legs. Her fingers fondled his crotch through his tuxedo pants. Her eyes, however, were miles away. The lady was on Planet 19. He noticed a row of tiny red welts on her bare white arm. Tracks. With a sigh, he pushed her away. "Another time," he said softly. Horny as he suddenly was, these biodegradables weren't taking him to the grave with them.

"Let's scram," said the runt. "The guy's a priest."

Jack chortled good-naturedly. She mistook his tux for liturgical gear.

Madison reappeared, smoking a joint. "Edgar's upstairs," she said, tossing the roach in a plastic sack of melting ice.

Together they climbed the spiral staircase. A shaft of yellow light came from a door at the end of the long hallway. On a king-size bed, a man's naked ass pumped two white legs that opened and closed like an accordion. "I'll introduce you later," Madison said with a laugh.

The drafty hall opened onto a huge balcony overgrown with ivy. Wide cement stairs flowed down to the lower yard. Sand crunched under Jack's shoes as they walked to the railing. Beyond the sloping hills, the Pacific gleamed, an infinite pond of polished pewter in the moonlight.

Jack lit a cigarette and stared at the carpet of green scum floating on the swimming pool below. Madison took the cigarette from his mouth and flicked it into the ivy. "Nasty habit," she said as her arm circled his waist. Before he could protest, she said, "I never slept with Robert Shay." Her eyes narrowed. "Leggitt paid me with ten grams of coke." She sighed audibly. "At the time I was hurtin' bad."

That was pretty much what he had figured.

Back in the upstairs hallway, a nervous young girl crashed into Madison head-on. They exchanged a hasty greeting. The kid was emaciated, too wasted on drugs to be a hooker.

Halfway down the stairs, Madison turned to him. "She's Leggitt's squeeze. Or was, in the Hamptons. I don't know who she's with now."

Jack was dumbfounded. The waif was a heavy-duty druggie. "What's her scene?" he asked.

"A nowhere lady."

Later, sitting on a patio bench behind the house, Madison casually unzipped his pants. She knelt down and began to stroke his cock with her lips and tongue. He felt the soft back pocket of her throat. Though aroused, he was fixated on Leggitt's ex-girlfriend. He pulled away, concocting a meek excuse about virility problems and the need to find a bathroom.

Instead, he wandered back upstairs. He found the girl wrapped in a ratty wool poncho sitting cross-legged in the darkest corner of the balcony. A hard-core addict, she sucked at the stem of her glass pipe with the urgency of a baby at the bottle. Her glazed eyes remained blank at his approach. Then, unexpectedly, she offered the pipe to him. Jack sucked on the straw-sized stem as hard as Madison had sucked his cock. He took down a lungful of the hot cloudy smoke. Within seconds, a jolt of white lightning hit his cranium. The ceiling of his skull blasted to smithereens.

He knew then his sense in not trying crack before.

With great effort, he managed to register the pleased look in her eyes. Vague sexual nuances passed between them. Though still reeling, he noticed she had a lean butt, an even leaner smile. Her mink brown hair was unkempt. He tried to focus on her arms, covered by the long sleeves of her black leotard.

She dragged again on the pipe. Not a flutter of emotion rippled in her dead eyes. Jack marveled at her stamina. She'd been at this awhile. She promptly offered him another go-round. He declined, still recovering from the initial punch.

Gradually he collected his thoughts. He moved closer to her and put his arm around her skeletal shoulders. "How do you know my friend Leggitt?" he asked.

The girl's face turned ash gray. Terror filled her eyes. She recoiled at his touch and swiftly gathered her gear. "I gotta find my friends," she said, retreating toward the house.

Jack hardly had the energy to stop her. Instead, he contemplated Leggitt's relationships with women. He knew Legs had a long-standing reputation for using and, Bates once said, abusing them. What had he done to this girl? Jack went after her.

Down in the living room an obnoxious man was arguing with Madison. He was a slick dude in a silk shirt, gold wristwatch, and flannel trousers. It was impossible for Jack to determine what the argument was about but after a few minutes the guy's stocky Latino pal came over and quieted him down. As the Latin turned away Jack glimpsed an 8-mm. Beretta tucked in his ankle boot. He took Madison by the arm.

"Leggo," she said. "That's Edgar. I'm stayin with him."

Despite the fact that he was loaded, Jack's gut instinct immediately told him their host was a Colombian drug lord. He released her arm and flopped down on a grungy couch beside an unwashed guy with a matted beard and rubber-tire sandals. Jack closed his tired eyes on the scene and eased his head back against the pillows. He slept for a while. When he woke, his powers of perception had returned. He looked at his watch—5 A.M.—then got up and walked down the road to the Wrangler.

As he drove down the hill in the pale light of dawn, broad streaks of fleecy white clouds came alive above the tranquil ocean. He made a left on Pacific Coast Highway. Cruising for breakfast, a squadron of seagulls flew over the churning white waves like fighter bombers.

A few miles past Malibu he pulled into a roadside deli and ordered a jumbo container of hot black coffee. He sipped the brew as he drove south toward Sunset Boulevard.

Scenes from the crowded night began to flicker through his mind: a slow-mo replay of Chasen's—Ceci's dismissive sneer, Tommy's bizarre bragadoccio. Jack could almost smell the sour breath of Malcolm Bates as he drooled over the redheaded trophy who clung to Bill Leggitt's arm. Suddenly, he remembered the chilling eyes of the emaciated druggie. Where had he seen that look of paralyzing fear before? Of course, Doni Shay. Both victims—both taken advantage of.

Other memories from the miserable night rose up, one by one. Jack recalled the reporter from the *National Enquirer* saying that Leggitt had been fired from the *Midnight Express*. It was odd that Legs never mentioned this. Suddenly, Jack remembered an echo of Leggitt's voice—where was it, in Bobby Van's, saying—"I'm on assignment for the *Express*." Why had Leggitt lied? Perhaps to cover his failure. But that was ridiculous. Among tabloid rogues to be fired was a badge of honor.

Somewhere in the depths of Jack's mind something shifted. Like fragments of glass in a kaleidoscope, the events of the night shattered apart, then adhered in a new and peculiar pattern.

Wasn't there a Newtonian law that said for every rise there came a fall? NTN's profit margin was enormous, Robert Shay's loss devastating. Was there possibly a connection?

Jack's brain clicked as if the dial on a combination lock had twirled to zero. "My God," he said aloud.

25

Under the blazing New Mexico sun, a turbulent twister whirled around the government helicopter in the sandy field across from the EZ Motel. Robert Shay left the cracked window and rejoined Krugger beside the evidence neatly laid out on the chenille bedspread. "The forensic department did a superior job," said the agent.

Robert leaned over to reexamine the short, stubby hairs mounted on the black cardboard. Doni must have a butch, he figured. Possibly a punk dye job.

Krugger lifted a manila folder from the knotty-pine nightstand. It contained the blowups of Doni's fingerprints found on the floorboards and paneling. "You must appreciate the difficulty involved in identifying these," Krugger boasted. "Six families inhabited this dump after your son."

Robert felt a spark of hope as he contemplated the pitiful one-room shack. He sat down on the edge of the lumpy bed and removed the Gideon Bible from the drawer. Pages had been torn away. From the mirror he took down a yellowed postcard of a flamenco dancer. The back was blank.

He went over to a shabby brocade chair and pounded a cloud of desert dust from the seat with his fist. Next to it was a steel-framed cot covered with a flimsy mattress. Had this been Doni's bed?

In the cramped bathroom the sink was stained with rust, the brown porcelain in the claw-foot tub streaked with cracks. Speckled linoleum curled around his sneakers like wood shavings. "Are they poor or is this their idea of a hideout?" he said over his shoulder.

"Hard to know," replied Krugger. "It appears they concealed him by traveling in Hispanic areas of the country."

Back in the bedroom Krugger crouched over a chalk-marked triangle in front of a rotting plywood door. Robert squatted next to him.

"A high concentration of the prints were found here," said the agent, waving his hand over the pitted planks. His hand sliced through the spider webs around the rusty hinges of the door. He straightened up and kicked it open. Robert followed him into the yard.

The hot sun baked the back of Shay's neck as his eyes roamed from the deep ravine heaped with deflated tires to the weatherbeaten silver-bullet trailer. Two squad cars were parked under a nearby clothesline. "When do I meet José?" he asked impatiently.

Krugger squinted at him. "Early next week."

"Why not this afternoon?"

"The media's all over the detention camp. Human-rights activists have destroyed the town. Your presence would create a holy war." He raised his hands to his forehead, shading his eyes. "The naturalization service officially releases the family on Monday morning. He'll be in my office by noon."

When they returned to the motel, he said, "If it's any consolation, I spent two hours with the boy and a translator. He and Doni played together. That's it. Remember, the kid's only three. What does a three-year-old know?"

Robert wasn't about to argue.

"The problem is Rita Sanchez," said Krugger. "She used a fake driver's license. We can't trace her." He took an exasperated breath. "The truck was torched in Mexico. Bad luck. Or somebody paid off the scrap dealer."

As they headed back to the chopper, Robert planned his own strategy. Tomorrow he'd fly down to Mexico City, meet the repo guy, and take a look himself. On Monday, he'd wine and dine the García family. Joe Krugger couldn't be trusted.

Later that same afternoon Jack Werts woke with a start. For a few minutes he stared blankly at the clock on the dresser. Then, on an impulse, he lifted the phone and called Brian Fagan. It was 6 P.M. in Florida. Fagan, a family man, would undoubtedly be sitting down to dinner.

A lilting Irish voice answered. Fagan's wife. Pleasant and friendly, she put Jack through to her husband in the yard. "Fagan here," boomed the editor of the *Midnight Express*, the second-biggest tabloid in America.

"What's up, Jack?" Fagan inquired. "Tired of *Newsmakers*?"

"Always, but that's not the reason I called."

Jack invented a cock-and-bull story about the possibility of collaborating on a book deal with Bill Leggitt.

"Don't get involved," warned Fagan. "Legs is a lazy SOB."

Jack cut to the quick. "Did you fire him?"

"You bet! Three times."

"When, exactly, was the last time?"

Fagan was silent for a moment. "August, I believe."

"Before the Shay fiasco?"

"Right," said Fagan. "At least a month before."

Jack paused. "Can you tell me why?"

Fagan had no qualms about dumping on his ex-employee. "I assigned a story on Christie Brinkley and Billy Joel. He diddled 'round for two months, squandering twenty grand. When the *Enquirer* reported that Joel and Brinkley were in Europe, I canned him."

"Where did Madison Cole come from?"

"Oh, that," said Fagan.

A child whined in the background. Jack held the wire while Brian attended to his needs.

"Madison Cole," reminded Werts.

"Last year, Leggitt pushed for a story on Robert Shay. He spent five grand on the project. Then in May, he sent us a batch of anemic reporting. Shreds, nothin' of interest." Fagan cleared his throat and lowered his voice. "Personally, I think he was nailin' a society tramp out there. Anyway, a local photographer managed to snap a picture of Shay strollin' in the woods."

"The Cole picture?"

Fagan clammed up. "I'm not about to reveal our secrets."

Jack heard the sizzle of the grill. "Cookin' swordfish?" he asked.

"Shark."

"Well, enjoy. And thanks." He paused. "Oh, yes, one final thing."

"Yeah?"

"How did Leggitt get a job on the Train show?"

"Beats me," said Fagan. "They never bothered to call me. I woulda set 'em straight."

At 10 P.M. that night Ceci McCann, clad in pink flannel pajamas, hunched over her marble bathroom sink, massaging her gums with her electric toothbrush. As the nylon bristles swirled away, she mentally cataloged her chores for the next morning. It was going to be a hectic day. After twenty laps around the UCLA track, she had to deposit her new Missoni dress at the Italian tailor on San Vincente. The skirt had to be hemmed by Wednesday in time for her flight to New York.

Stan Lutz's secretary had reserved a room for her at the Pierre. It was discreetly understood that after her videotaping, she would spend the night with Stan. The prospect sent chills through her. Her wardrobe must be perfect. No glitches. With three Armani suits and two Missoni dresses in her new leather suitcase, she'd blow these sophisticated New Yorkers away.

Her critical eye caught a frayed fingernail on her left hand. Fortunately, she had a hair trim and manicure scheduled at 10 A.M. Afterward, she had to stop by the beauty-supply outlet and sample their natural makeup line. She shuddered, remembering last Friday's catastrophe. The skin base Charlene had always used on her face had inexplicably created a rash of knobby red pustules. The problem must be solved before Wednesday.

Her calculations were interrupted by the piercing buzz of the intercom. She went to the metal box and touched the black button with her forefinger.

"A gentleman is downstairs with a bouquet of roses," said the concierge.

Ceci sighed. Probably another loco fan. "Who is he?" she asked. After an exchange of muffled voices, the concierge said, "Mr. Lutz."

Ceci's heart skipped a beat. Stan, my God! He had escaped Beverly. "Ah . . . send him up," she stammered.

Heart pounding, she raced to her closet. She snatched a cashmere sweater from its box and tugged the elastic band from her hair. A pair of white jeans came down from the peg on the wall. Off came her pj's. With one leg halfway into the jeans, she halted. No, no, no, she told herself. Too preppy, you dumbbell. Sexy. Look sexy. From a lacquered pink drawer she grabbed a white-lace negligee. Brand-new, for their second night together. She frowned as she pulled the gown over her head. It was his fault he was jumping the gun.

In the mirror over the vanity table, she adjusted the straps. It was odd that Stan hadn't given her some warning. A quick call from his car phone at least. Before she could finish the thought or lift a powder brush to her face, the front bell chimed insistently.

Well, she thought, he'll just have to take me as I am. She closed her eyes and with a sweeping gesture pulled the gold ram's-head handle of the double doors.

Like a waterfall, a huge bouquet of pink roses cascaded into the apartment. Half-hidden behind the flowers was not Stan Lutz, but Jack Werts. Ceci shrieked with anger when she saw him.

"My, my, my, my . . ." said Jack, a wry, amused grin on his face. His eyes were fixed on the strategic slits of sheer lace over her breasts. "Business attire?" he said mockingly.

The roses landed on the antique armchair in the foyer. He marched into the living room as if he owned the place.

"You asshole," Ceci raged as she stormed after him.

He spun around. "Sorry to disappoint you." His eyes traveled down her body.

Momentarily silent with embarrassment, Ceci hugged her arms over her breasts.

"Don't worry," Jack said with a chuckle, "for once I'm not the least bit interested in fucking you." He walked over to the window and looked down on the twinkling lights of Bel Air.

Ceci collected herself. "Why in God's name are you barging in here at this hour?"

He settled down on the white sectional. "I've got some questions to ask you." His eyes were disturbed. He was dead serious about something.

"Ask," she demanded. She snatched a hand-crocheted afghan from the sofa, slung it around her body, and gingerly perched on the chair opposite him.

"Where was Leggitt today?" he asked.

"Leggitt?" Her voice cracked with annoyance. "Working. We were at the Westwood Marquis interviewing Mia Farrow. He's the producer on 'Celeb Kids.' "

"What's he doing tonight?"

"I'm not his mother. Call him and find out."

Jack glared at her.

She gave him a curt, hostile nod. "We're due in the studio at noon tomorrow. Shorty had problems with our tape—"

Jack interrupted. "He's free tonight?"

"I guess."

"Y'know where he lives?"

"Yes, he has a rented house in Mandeville Canyon. I gave him a lift—"

Werts stepped over and rudely lifted Ceci by her arm. "Get

dressed," he demanded. "We're gonna play real journalists for once."

"I will not. You can't tell me what to do. I've got a busy—"

He shoved her roughly toward the bedroom. "Move it." When she resisted, he stepped around her and walked down the hall. He lifted the discarded jeans and sweater from the bed. "Put these on," he ordered.

She refused.

"You put them on or I'm putting them on you," he threatened.

"All right, all right."

She changed behind the closet door. Clearly, he wasn't about to rape her if he told her to get dressed as fast as she could. She grabbed a handful of pins from the dresser and stuck them in her hair. Better humor him. How long could it take, anyway?

Bored and angry, Ceci sat beside Werts in the Wrangler parked diagonally across from Leggitt's house. Two coach lamps in the brick driveway beamed a yellow arc on the English country cottage.

"That rabbit hatch must cost him five grand a month," said Jack absently, handing her the Sunday calendar section of the *Los Angeles Times*.

"I can't read in the dark," she snapped as she let the newspaper slide from her lap. Jack leaned across the seat and took a penlight from the glove compartment.

"Oh, stop it. I don't want to read. I want to go home. I have an appointment at 10 A.M.," she whined. "This is stupid. Why are we spying on Leggitt?" She raised her knees and put her moccasined feet on the dash. "Why don't we just go knock on the door? He'd be more than happy to see us." She tossed her head. "Y'know, you're nuts. You've lost your mind!"

"Shut up and inhale the carbon monoxide." He took a sip of cold coffee from a paper cup and once again attempted to read the sports section in the reflection from the streetlight.

But Ceci refused to quit. "We've been here for over an hour. I can think of a thousand better things to do at 11 P.M.—like sleep."

Before she could go on, Leggitt emerged from the front door, his black hair slick as motor oil. He wore white ducks and a loose, bold-patterned shirt. He gave a guarded look about the yard before he opened the door of his car. It was a two-toned vintage T-bird with porthole windows.

"Snazzy mobile," observed Jack.

"He rents 'em. A different car each week," said Ceci.

Jack started the engine and followed Leggitt down the dark canyon road, staying at least six car-lengths behind.

Ceci switched on the radio. "Surfin' Safari" bellowed through the car. "This is dumb, dumb, dumb," she moaned.

They trailed the T-bird east on Beverly Boulevard toward downtown. As they drove into the pit of the L.A. basin the smoggy night air began to thicken into a metallic neon soup. Finally, Leggitt made a left on Wilton and headed north into Hollywood.

Jack drove slowly along the rundown streets. Geographically, Hollywood was a ghost town of long-gone movie idols. The brass stars in the sidewalk were tombstones. Now, jalopies and low riders were parked along the curbs; graffiti branded every building. On the side streets, anorexic druggies prowled for five-dollar bags of crack. It was as if they had arrived in a slum of Mexico City without ever having boarded an airplane.

Ceci sat bolt upright. She pushed down the button on her door. "Cripes, what a nasty neighborhood."

"Germane observation."

Leggitt made a right into the driveway of an old stucco four-flat lit up bright as a football stadium to deter drug dealers. Jack parked across the street behind a broken-down station wagon.

They watched Leggitt emerge from the T-bird and climb the stairs to a sheet-metal door. He banged hard. The door opened a crack and Leggitt disappeared inside.

"I hate to say this about anyone on my show, but he's probably buying cocaine," said Ceci. "Grinker insists Tommy hired Leggitt for his drug connections." She shook her head. "Bill's a creep."

A white 1960 Chevy with spinners and tuck-and-roll squealed to a stop next to them and two Latinos got out. A black kid emerged from the darkness. After some words, the kid gave them a plastic baggie. They gestured toward the T-bird in the driveway. The black kid shrugged. The Latinos returned to their car and peeled rubber.

For a moment Jack contemplated going in but decided he might blow it. Somebody in there knew Leggitt. He studied the front windows. Iron bars were bolted to the wood frames for protection. He unrolled his window and peered down the street. A group of Hispanics were huddled in the parking lot of the Sinclair paint store on Santa Monica. Day laborers waiting for work? At midnight? Junkies, more likely.

Ceci took an emery board from her purse and anxiously began filing her nails. "Not only is this stupid," she said accusingly. "It's dangerous." She stopped filing. Her voice cracked with fear. "Rock houses. Stray bullets. You've heard of them?"

Jack didn't respond. He picked up the newspaper and flicked on the penlight. He started to read about the resurgence of real-estate prices when a red Ferrari convertible pulled up beside the Wrangler. The headlights snapped off. A dead ringer for Sonia Braga stepped from the sports car. Her hips beat with the rhythm of a rumba as she sauntered toward the glass door of a stucco cell block. Somewhere a baby screamed. The woman paused and spun around to smile at the bald man in the car. The twinkle of gold sparkled from her front teeth.

Ceci slouched down low in the seat. "This is a combat zone," she hissed. "We're gonna die in the crossfire." Jack ignored her. He lit a cigarette. Annoyed by the smell of the tobacco, Ceci cracked the window, then rolled it back up again.

Five cigarettes later, Leggitt emerged from the apartment. He jumped in the T-bird and started the engine. He drove north toward the big Sears store that loomed over the wasted neighborhood.

"Okay?" said Ceci. "This proves your point. I work with a dopehead. Now, let's get back to civilization."

"Not yet."

"Are you mad? We're smack in the middle of a drug ghetto. If you want to play hero, report the place to the cops."

While they argued a girl wrapped in a black shawl left the building and skittered up the walk toward Santa Monica Boulevard.

"Sit tight," he said. "I'm makin' a house call. Keep the doors and windows locked."

Ceci glared at him as if he had gone over the edge. "Yeah, fine, great, thanks for your concern. I'll call 911 when I hear gunshots."

Jack walked up to the door and knocked. A rustle of curtains came from the neighboring window. A fat man, at least two hundred fifty pounds' worth, stood there shirtless. "Whadda ya need?"

"Your neighbor, the lady, is she home?"

"How should I know." The man slammed the window shut. Jack felt the tremor through the porch. He checked behind him, then jumped down and followed the narrow alley around to the back. A chicken coop had been wedged between a cinder-block wall and the adjacent apartment complex. Fumes of garbage filled his nostrils.

The back entrance was fortified with iron bars. Jack knocked for a while, then waited. Next door, a pair of husky Rottweilers began to bark and bang their bodies against a chain-link fence. Strains of Hollywood gospel poured from the windows upstairs.

Ready to call it quits, Jack returned to the alley. As he passed the back window, he noticed it was open. Barely a half-inch. He rapped his knuckle against the sill. "Hello, hello," he hollered. "Anybody home?"

A shadow moved in the window across the alley. A face appeared. The man retreated when Jack looked at him. He had a gun in his hand.

Jack knocked on the sill again. "Hello. Donald Shay. Are you there?" He put his ear against the bars.

Silence.

Doni was preparing his platoon of stick soldiers for their climb over the mountain of blankets when he heard the strange voice. He didn't move. It sounded like a man was in the room with him.

When he heard the voice again, he realized it came from the window. He still didn't move. It might be Rita. Once she tested him to see if he answered. When he didn't she gave him a big sucker.

He gathered his soldiers together and put them in his treasure bag. Then he put the bag underneath his bed. He went inside his blanket cave. It was very dark but safe. In the distance he heard Alarm yap and yelp.

The strange voice didn't come back.

Doni kicked away his cave and scratched the bumps on his legs. He thought about the cats. Sometimes they screeched by the window. Where did they go? There were no pops tonight, either. Rita told him they were gunshots. He wasn't sure. In the movies, gunshots sounded much bigger.

Earlier, seal man had come to visit. He shouted at Rita like a general. She cried and cried. She came back into the room and dragged him out to see seal man. But seal man hid in the closet. From behind the door he said he didn't want to see Doni. Seal man was very mad. He yelled at Rita. She yelled back. She stopped yelling when seal man said he would get her a car. She took Doni back to his room and locked the door.

Later, when she came to clean his potty her hands were shaking. She coughed up tiny pieces of white water. "I'm falling to pieces," she said. Sarah used to say that too but she wasn't really. Doni felt bad for Rita because she was.

He crawled off the bed. He was hungry. He drank the last of the water in the plastic bottle.

The strange voice called "Hello" again.

Doni didn't move. He listened as hard as he could. He was sure it was a man. He went to the window. The edge was high above his head. The "Hello" came again, even louder.

"Anybody there? Donald Shay, are you there?"

Doni pressed his little hands to the wall. The man called Donald Shay over and over. That was his name, Donald. Not Tina. All of a sudden he felt frightened and cold. He began to tremble. He was confused. He felt terribly lost. Then he remembered he was a lost baby.

He began to cry. He was afraid it was the seal man, back again, playing a trick on him in the dark.

Jack stepped away from the window. He looked at the apartment across the alley. The man with the gun stood in the shadows. Somewhere in the darkness, another window slammed shut. He felt foolish. Clearly, the downstairs flat was empty. Ceci had been right. Leggitt had a drug habit. That explained the coked-up ex-girlfriend, the obsession with money, the missed deadlines. Jack wanted to kick himself. Wishful thinking had gotten the better of him. He had invented villains where there were none.

As he walked back up the alley he began to formulate a face-saving explanation for Ceci. Several feet past the building he heard a child sobbing. He stopped and listened with concentration to pinpoint the source, then raced back to the window.

"Donald! Donald!" Jack yelled fiercely at the top of his lungs. He pressed his ear to the iron bars. A child was crying in the apartment. Again he shouted, "Donald Shay!"

This time, from behind the torn, rusty screen a tiny, muffled voice whimpered, "Daddy."

Jack gulped air as he ran for the street. Ceci peered at him with amazement as he leaped into the Jeep and started the engine. He floored it, screeching around the corner on two wheels. All the while he swore at himself for not installing a car phone. Behind the Sears store he skidded to a halt at a glass-enclosed phone booth. He jumped out and punched up Sherry's number. Mercifully, she answered on the first ring.

"Mega emergency," he said. "I've got to talk to Krugger immediately."

"It's two A.M.," she groaned.

"A favor."

She paused. "You saw me at Chasen's."

"It's okay, honey. We do what we have to do."

She seemed relieved. "Hold on, I'll try to get him on my beeper."

After a series of electronic clicks, the FBI chief came on the line. Jack swiftly filled him in.

"Werts, if this is a ploy to get an interview, I'll have you locked up for life," Krugger threatened. It took another round of assurances before the agent promised to send some men.

Breathing hard, Jack hung up. He wanted the FBI to bash in the apartment. If the child turned out to be the girl's baby and nothing more, he didn't plan to get saddled with breaking and entering. With a brisk step, he hopped into the driver's seat.

Ceci scowled at him. "Would you kindly tell me what's going on?"

"I don't know yet but we're gonna find out real soon."

As they arrived back at the four-flat a battered Buick drove up and idled outside. Jack double-parked across the street. A moment later, a vanilla Olds arrived and Krugger jumped out. The bodybuilder with him had a piece bulging under his nylon jacket.

Jack left the jeep and ran across the street. Two unsavory-looking men got out of the Buick. Krugger introduced them to Jack. Scooter, the wiry one, hopped around like a junkie. A 9-mm. semiautomatic was stuffed down the front of his stringy denim cutoffs. Lucas, the giant, spoke in monosyllabic grunts.

The agents went to the sheet-metal door and pounded with fists of iron. Neighbors scurried away from their windows like cockroaches. After a few minutes the men abandoned the porch and went around to the back. When no one answered, Krugger nodded to Lucas, who pulled a .38 from his jacket and clipped a silencer to the muzzle. With neat efficiency, he blew off the rusty hinges of the iron bars.

Jack followed them inside.

The place was a dank flophouse with exposed pipes and pockmarked walls. The kitchen hadn't been used in years. A yellowed Security Pacific bank calendar flipped to June 1976 hung on the wall. Cupboard doors had been torn off; a piece of plywood rested over the sink. The windows were opaque with soot. The hum of a small refrigerator was the only sign of life.

"Over here," Krugger mumbled. A naked bulb hung from the sagging ceiling in the living room. A torn bedspread had been thrown over a battered green couch. "Better Homes and Gardens gone south," Jack grunted.

A brand-new Panasonic answering machine sat on a Formica table and beside it, a syringe, a packet of rolling papers, a wad of cotton balls, and a plastic bag filled with pills. Scooter fingered the packet. "Poppers," he said. "Minor-league stuff."

Jack noticed a moth-eaten sweater tossed over a canvas chair, a western belt on the floor. A copy of *The Racing Form* was jammed under the couch. Cosmetics littered a cracked glass table with rust-spotted chrome legs.

The men gathered in the dark hallway, where Jack joined them. "This better be good," said Krugger. He pulled a Koch pistol from under his trench coat and stealthily sidled along the wall to the closed door.

Guns drawn, Lucas and Scooter flanked him protectively.

Krugger twisted the dead bolt. The door opened slowly.

Lucas jumped in first, Krugger right behind him. In the dim yellow light, Krugger's face went slack. "Sonofa . . ."

Jack managed to sneak back into the front room. He swiftly put in a call to Sammy and gave her the address. He cupped his hand over the mouthpiece of the phone. "Shoot first, ask questions later."

26

At two A.M. Robert and Emily were roused from sleep and hustled into an unmarked patrol car by a rookie agent who had been assigned the graveyard shift at the mansion. As they sped down the dark, zigzagging curves of Benedict Canyon, Robert, half-awake, scooted forward and asked where they were going.

"I honestly don't know," the agent replied. The headlights of an oncoming car illuminated his grim expression. "It's a top-secret code." The patrol car jackknifed onto Sunset Boulevard. "From the neighborhood, I can tell you we're not goin' dancin'."

"Oh, why not?" Emily said sarcastically. She burrowed into her oversize wool coat to escape the cold. Her long hair was haphazardly bunched under a felt fedora.

"What's the address?" Robert asked.

The agent pressed a button on the dashboard and a police siren wailed from the roof of the car. "Santa Monica and Western. The armpit of Hollywood."

Robert exchanged glances with Emily. Her face lengthened. "If this turns out to be another of Krugger's bum leads, I'll kill him," she said soberly.

They blew down the Sunset Strip at sixty miles an hour, wildly crisscrossing the double line, weaving through a blinding row of frozen headlights. By now Robert had little faith in Joe Krugger. Yesterday Duke had told him that the naturalization service, not the FBI, had uncovered José García.

He slumped down and watched the neon bars and boarded pawnshops of Hollywood whiz by. On every other corner pathetic groups of ravaged losers sold themselves to the passing traffic. As the patrol car crossed Hollywood Boulevard Robert vividly recalled the night he planted his palms in the soft cement block outside the old Grauman's Chinese theater.

He glanced over at Emily. She was curiously quiet. Only when they passed the garish mini-mall that had destroyed the lawn of the Hollywood Cemetery did she speak. "Sad, isn't it? I wonder if poor ol' Valentino knows what they've done to his grave site."

Hollywood *was* sad, Robert thought. Tragic. He felt a chill of apprehension shoot down his spine. Given the looks of the neighborhood, he prayed this hasty excursion was a wild-goose chase.

The agent killed the siren a block before they made a right off Santa Monica Boulevard. In seconds they screeched to a halt next to a cannibalized 280Z. Three Mexicans with beer cans in their hands were sprawled on the car's roof trying to get a bird's-eye view of the activities across the street.

Robert and Emily followed the agent up the walk of the graffiti-covered building. Emily's hand gripped Robert's arm, her nails digging into the sleeve of his jacket. "This place is ghastly," she mumbled.

A skinny junkie hovered outside the fortified door like a mosquito. The agent turned to the Shays. "He's one of ours, I think."

"Let's hope so," said Emily.

The man abruptly twisted his head in their direction. His eyes never left the street. "Go on inside," he told them.

They entered a claustrophobic tomb that stank of rot and decay. The bleached white light from the porch streamed in through barred windows, creating a jail effect. Robert felt a shudder of panic bolt through Emily's body. "Please, God, let him be alive," she prayed. He took her hand quickly. It was icy cold. His own knees began to shake and sweat drenched his body. In that moment, he had the horrible premonition that his nightmares had finally exploded into reality.

Crouched down in the front seat of the Wrangler, McCann bolted upright when she saw Robert and Emily Shay step from the patrol car. "Oh, my God," she whispered to herself. "Enough of this." She slid her arms into the sleeves of Jack's parka and bumped her rear over the gear shift to the driver's side of the car. It was safer to exit in the street since a mob of seedy derelicts had congregated on the sidewalk. "Please, Heavenly Father, protect me," she prayed as she locked the car door behind her.

"Hey, white woman, you're goin' the wrong way," a voice called out. A psycho in a torn T-shirt came around the other side of the car. Ceci tore across the street. The clatter of the chopper blades overhead gave her a fleeting sense of security. Before she could lift her arm to knock on the door a jittery druggie leaped from the shadows. He lunged at her, then stopped short when he got a closer look. "Who in hell are you?" he said incredulously, flashing his badge.

"I'm with Jack Werts."

He stepped aside and let her through.

Krugger stood at the end of the narrow, darkened corridor, a tense smile on his face. Before Robert or Emily had a chance to speak, he gestured toward the partially opened door.

Robert entered the room first.

It took a millisecond for the scene to register: the dull topaz light from the naked bulb, the foul stench, the bundled rags and trash heap of fast-food wrappers. On the gutted, mildewed mattress, the *Newsmakers* reporter was hunched over a bald, emaciated child who held a bunch of ice-cream sticks in his tiny hand. The mangy, wasted-looking head turned and two alert eyes glowed through the gloom.

"Doni!" Robert cried.

"My baby!" Emily screamed, shoving past him.

Doni's arms, hands and fingers outstretched, paddled the air, reaching for them helplessly. "Mommy, Daddy," he rasped as Emily snatched him from the ratty pile of blankets. His little arms circled her neck. Robert scooped both of them to his chest and began kissing his son with desperation.

Tears poured down Emily's cheeks as she clutched her child, stroking and caressing him with trembling hands. With frenzied fingers she touched the tufts of hair on his scalp.

"What have they done to you? What have they done?" she said hysterically. She ran her hands over his protruding ribs and distended stomach, over the scrawny legs that extended from his filthy shorts. "Skinny, so skinny!" she cried. "My God, you've been starved!"

Her fingers stroked the swollen red sores on his dirty back. "What's this?" she said in horror.

"Flea bites, ma'am," Lucas said. "My kid gets 'em all the time," he added reassuringly.

Robert was horrified. His son's gray pallor and luminous eyes gave him the appearance of an AIDS baby. He had aged prematurely. Self-conscious from the attention, Doni shyly bowed his head and pushed against Robert's chest for protection.

"Let's get out of here," said Emily, as if taking in the squalor of the room for the first time. But Doni lifted his head and tugged insistently at both his father's and mother's hands. "Wait," he said clearly.

Robert smiled broadly. Tears of affection flowed from his eyes. "Unload your cupcakes," he said softly to his son. It was a silly phrase Doni had always loved.

Doni giggled with delight. His beaming smile lighted the dingy room. He wriggled for Robert to put him down. They watched as he slid across the mattress and pulled a dirty burlap bag from under the far edge. "My treasure," he jabbered proudly. "I got good stuff. For José."

"José," Robert said. He glanced at Krugger. "José García?"

The FBI chief shrugged. "Apparently."

Emily crouched down next to Doni on the mattress and gazed at him lovingly as she patiently watched his smudged hands jerk open the coarse material. A pile of rubbish spilled onto the rotten floorboards. He picked up several sticks. "My soldiers," he said. He looked over at Jack.

Werts came forward and gave Doni the remaining sticks. They had played war together while waiting for Robert and Emily. "Take good care of these fellows," he said with a wink. "You never know when you'll need them."

Emily smiled at Jack. "We can sort them when we get home," she said to her son. She quickly removed her coat and with Robert's help wrapped Doni's near-naked body in the soft cashmere. Only his head and his treasure bag, held tightly in his fist, protruded. As Shay carried him past Werts and the agents, Doni twisted in his father's arms. He looked directly at the men, his blue eyes enlarged with concern. "Where's Rita?" he asked.

Emily immediately covered the back of her son's head with a flap of the heavy coat. "These gentlemen will take care of her," she said evenly.

Ceci was dumbfounded, a stricken look on her face. Her eyes met Jack's. "Leggitt, that bastard," she blurted.

Jack put his arm around her as they followed Krugger down the hallway. Suddenly they heard shouts from the porch and a series of light bulbs flashed in the darkness. Jack ran ahead, pushing his way around Lucas to get a look at the photographer. When he saw it was Sammy, he breathed a sigh of relief. She stood her ground, arguing furiously with Scooter. Before the agent could nail her, she slithered away and disappeared behind the cinder-block wall.

Krugger whirled around to Jack. "You told her?"

"Hey, look," said Jack, somewhat apologetically. "Who can pass on an exclusive family shot?" He beamed at the agent with a demented smile. "I'm an inveterate journalist. A story's a story. What can I do?"

"Keep your mouth shut till we catch these thugs," Krugger snapped.

True to form, the moment the Shays drove away in the patrol car Lucas and Scooter tried to hustle Jack and Ceci into the street. "Vamoose," Krugger called from the porch.

Jack charged right back up the stairs. No yuppie cop was going to prevent him from being in on this. "I'm staying for the finale," he said coolly. "You owe me one. A mighty big one."

Krugger stared into Jack's determined face. He capitulated reluctantly. "Okay, get your asses back inside." As they went past him, a look of sheer disgust darkened his face. "Bloodsuckers," he muttered.

Jack and Ceci leaned against the far wall of the kitchen. Krugger, alert as a marine, stood in the deep shadows of the archway. A match scratched in the corner of the room as Lucas lit a cigarette. The glow of the orange tip moved back and forth, to and from his lips. Scooter's short, shallow breaths came from behind the door.

Outside, on the street, the noisy night life of the drug ghetto had resumed. From the dark apartment they could hear brazen dealers catcall to cruising cars. In the alley, the chained dogs barked ferociously at the continuous patter of footsteps. Jack glanced at the neon numerals on his watch: 3:10 A.M. Retail sales might be off but the drug business was going great guns.

It wasn't long before they heard footsteps on the front porch. Jack stiffened. Ceci drew an audible breath as a key was inserted into the lock. The tarnished brass knob turned to the left. Several seconds passed before another key slipped into the lower lock.

The metal door grated against the linoleum floor as it opened. The girl, outlined by blue light from the porch, entered with a bag of groceries in her arm. She closed and bolted the door. Her breathing was labored.

As she touched the light switch, Scooter jumped her. She let out a bloodcurdling scream. Jack recognized her as the girl from the Malibu party just as Scooter's raised arm tried desperately to contain her swirling mop of matted brown hair. The black cape fell away from her thin body. A leather halter covered her breasts. Faded black jeans were stuffed into cheap leather boots. Her arms flailed at the wiry cop, hysterical fear in her wild black eyes.

Lucas closed in from behind. Like a hunted animal, the girl whirled to greet him with a knee to his groin. Scooter countered with a swift knuckle to her chin. Stunned by the blow, she lashed at him in a frenzy, fists helplessly beating the air.

Lucas pinned her with an effortless clamp.

Kicking wildly, she spit at him. "Lay off, you ape," she cried, edgy fear in her high-pitched voice.

Steady as a tanker, Lucas steered her to a chair Krugger had pulled out from the broken table and forced her down. Krugger moved in, his eyes zeroed on the girl's face. "What's your name, Squeaky?"

Coked to the eyeballs, she twisted haughtily from Lucas's grasp. "Lemme go," she said. The burly agent dropped his arms.

She looked at Krugger. "Hey, man, why you buggin' me?" Then she looked back at Lucas. "I don't live here. I never been here before." She stood up to leave. Her eyes met Krugger's. "I gotta go . . . go find a laundry."

"Yeah, and I'm on my way to a prom," he said. He roughly shoved her back into the chair. Jack saw a ripple of fear as she sized the men up. Her skin was deathly pale, her lips thin and papery. Her red-rimmed eyes darted anxiously about the room, stopping a moment to peer at Jack intently. A toilet flushed upstairs, a tidal wave that shook the shabby room.

Her eyes shifted to Krugger. "What the fuck is this about?"

"You tell us, honey," he replied. "Your ass is fried." He flipped his wallet open in front of her face. "You're under arrest for the kidnapping of Donald Shay." He recited her rights.

It hit the girl hard that the men were cops, not druggies. She hunched her shoulders and crossed her arms fiercely. "I told you I don't know nothin'," she said. "A guy gave me his key . . . to pick up some stuff."

"What stuff?" needled Scooter.

Krugger decided to take a gamble and interrogate her before legions of lawyers and shrinks could correct her hopped-up, panicky state. "Where's your stash?" he said.

Scooter pulled her pencil-thin arms away from her body to inspect for tracks. There was a gruesome scar across her forearm. He bunched up a syringe and some Baggies in his hand and shoved them under her nose. "C'mon, baby, the rig isn't for waterin' the plants."

With his fist, Krugger pushed the girl's chin his way. Her belligerent eyes met his. "We'll start over," he said irritably. "Once again, what's your name?"

"Fuck off, you motherfuckers!" she screamed. "I don't know you're a cop. I don't trust you. I want a lawyer."

Krugger gave her a contemptuous sneer. "You trust your buddies? They left you, baby. All alone in this rancid hellhole holding the merchandise. That's a human being you had back there." He grabbed her by the neck. "A human being!" He pressed his face up next to hers. "You think they care about you? Wise up. C'mon, who's in on this? You didn't mastermind this production."

"I dunno what you're talkin' 'bout," she said. Her eyes dropped to the floor. She wasn't about to play ball. Then abruptly, as if she were in a slow-motion trance, her face turned ghostly white. Her hands began to shake violently. Foamy spittle formed at the corners of her mouth. She collapsed in a deep wheeze.

"Cool the heat," said Lucas. "She's freakin' on us."

"Where's your stash?" Krugger hammered away.

"I ain't got none." She attempted to raise herself. Her skinny, blue-veined hands gripped the corner of the table with such force that the knuckles turned white. "I need a shot . . . anything," she begged. She gestured to the bag on the floor.

The girl's face contorted in pain while Lucas dug through the brown paper. Her cheeks were wet with sweat and tears.

"Hey, relax," said Scooter. "Take it easy." He took a dirty shirt from the floor and gently mopped the moisture from her forehead.

Lucas unscrewed a pint of Cuervo and handed it to her. She grabbed the neck of the bottle and frantically gulped down the pale yellow tequila. She finished off half the bottle.

A placid, detached expression came over her face. "I ain't freakin'," she said calmly.

In a surprise move, Krugger ripped the pint away and stuck his face close to hers. He came at her again, like a barracuda. "Okay, then. What's your name?"

"Rita," she said softly. "Rita Sanchez."

"Rita, baby, they don't give a rat's ass about you," he shot back. "You're gonna hang for this. There's no fairy godmother waiting in the wings. For them, maybe. But not for you."

At his words, the girl flinched. "Fuckin' cowards," she mumbled. "I ain't takin' the rap for those motherfuckers." Seized by panic, she began to tremble. She reached for the bottle. Krugger held it behind his back. "Talk first, drink later," he said coldly.

"The cheatin' bastards, they put me up to this," she sputtered. "I did the best I could to treat the kid good. Good as I could with no cash. From the beginning I've been the goddamn guinea pig. I been set up. Sure, I dealt some toot . . . but I never stole nothin' in my life. Never. You gotta believe that!"

Krugger handed her the bottle. She gulped down the liquor hungrily.

"Who's pullin' the strings? Who's in this with you?"

Ceci moved closer to Jack and clutched his arm. "Should we tell him about Leggitt?" she whispered.

Jack raised his hand. "Wait."

The girl put the empty bottle on the table. Then, as if a fissure had opened in her soul, she began to cry. Krugger stepped back and waited until the raging tears softened into wrenching sobs. She reached for the tequila and desperately sucked at the glass lip. Dazed, she dropped the bottle on the floor. It made a hollow sound as it rolled under the table.

No one moved.

She glanced back at Jack with a demented half-smile. Then she tilted forward and looked at Krugger. "You wanna know who's callin' the shots?" she said, a weird look of triumph in her bloodshot eyes. Her voice dropped an octave. "Bill Leggitt, that's who." Then, from deep within her throat: "And behind Leggitt . . . Mr. America. Tommy Train!"

Ceci gasped in horror. Jack felt the weight of her body slump against him.

27

The last day of April was fifty-two degrees, chilly by L.A. standards. A blustery wind had whipped the smog from the basin, leaving the air clear as glass. The Santa Monica mountains had the freshness of the High Sierras. Behind Jack's house, a family of blue jays squawked plaintively in the row of eucalyptus trees.

From the back porch he watched beams of afternoon sunlight dance over the swirling piles of unraked leaves. It was unfortunate he had chosen such a beautiful day to move, but he had made his decision and it was final. He was chucking the glitz of show business for the wilds of the great Northwest. So far, he had a tentative hopscotch plan. He'd spend the winter on the San Juan Islands off Seattle where an old fishing buddy had generously loaned him his house. The rest of the year he'd rustle up free-lance work around Cody, Wyoming. He had a hunch the "range" states were making a comeback. Riding high on his heroic investigation of the Shay kidnapping, he could earn substantial money from fancy New York magazines for ecology pieces: The Last Mustang, The Endangered Bison, that sort of fare. He'd make enough to get by and be a happier man. He truly believed people arrived at their professional destiny around the time they hit forty-five. Hollywood wasn't his destiny. It had been a long detour on the highway.

He went into the house. The living room looked like a garage sale: books were down from the shelves, artifacts strewn about the floor, storage cartons everywhere. He groaned at the mess. Moving was such a pain it called for a drink. On the way to the kitchen he flicked on the stereo, then remembered it was disconnected. He unearthed a ghetto blaster from a pile of debris near the door and plugged it in. *La Bohème* sent strains of serenity through the chaos.

He poured himself a beer and contemplated his collection of books. There were too many to haul in the trailer. He decided to store them and then eventually ship the entire caboodle to his new abode. Maybe, by that time, he'd have found a wife to sort them for him. He shut his eyes and envisioned a raven-haired beauty with incandescent blue eyes, wearing Ralph Lauren chaps and nothing else. He opened his eyes to a wilted fern on the windowsill. A bad omen.

Jack took a sandwich from the fridge. As he bit into the soggy bread and hardened prosciutto he spied a copy of *Newsmakers* atop a pile of newspapers destined for the dumpster. He retrieved the magazine and briefly studied the picture of the Shays on the cover. He smiled proudly. Last week, he heard his story was being nominated for a Pulitzer, bringing a status to the magazine it didn't deserve.

Predictably, Harrington had offered to raise Jack's salary fifty grand. He even flew to Los Angeles, something he hated to do, fearful he might be seduced from his corporate mission by the sun-and-fun mentality, and begged him to stay on. But Jack had resolved that this was his last story. It was the appropriate time to quit.

No sooner had he returned to the living room than he heard a car in the drive. Through the bay window, he watched Ceci Mc-Cann's Saab coast into the dirt turnout. Long blond hair in motion, she scampered toward the house, an eyeful in a honey angora sweater and silky tan slacks. As sweet and yummy as a caramel, except that he had never liked caramels. They ruined your teeth. In the end they were never worth the trouble.

She waved at him from the porch.

He opened the door and she galloped past him with a *TV Guide*–cover smile on her face. At the sight of the room her eyebrows shot up. "You moving?"

"Yep."

Her eyes stalled on the trophy marlin that rested against the grandfather clock in the corner. Its raging glass eye and razor-sharp black sword were impressive. For a moment her pretty face soured, then her curious eyes began to roam about the room. "What happened to your girlfriend?"

"She shacked up with Morgan Camp."

Ceci looked shocked.

"It's a business arrangement," he said dryly. "Camp changes 'associates' once a year."

The notion that Werts was truly single made Ceci uneasy. She rapidly switched the subject. "Keigel's worried the whole network may collapse. Yesterday Leggitt squealed like a rat to the prosecutors. He told them about a half-million payoff deposited in an offshore bank by Tommy."

Jack smiled, delighted they had concrete evidence nailing Train. Already they had an ironclad case against Leggitt and Rita Sanchez supported by a trail of fingerprints and telephone calls from motel rooms throughout the country.

"The bums'll be locked up for life," he said confidently. "They don't have a prayer in hell of ever being released."

Ceci nodded solemnly, then turned and sailed over to the sofa. She brushed against a large, handwoven basket from Kenya. The prickly palm tips snagged her sweater and, with mild annoyance, she delicately unhooked the material. "I assume you've heard the news about Rita?" she said offhandedly.

Jack shook his head.

"She has AIDS. Mitch says she'll die within the year."

Jack felt suddenly sorry for the girl. Ravaged by crack and heroin, she was just another pathetic victim of the drug culture, too easily exploited by everyone.

He gazed at Ceci. "Only Lutz is the wild card." He yearned to lambast the schmuck for the benign simpleton routine he had attempted to sell the press but decided to be judicious, given Ceci's involvement with him. "It's hard for me to believe he was entirely blameless."

"Oh, Jack. He didn't have anything whatsoever to do with the kidnapping," she said vehemently. "And now he's lost his job."

"Cashing out with ten million in stock is hardly—"

"Stan's been terribly humiliated," she protested. "He's a broken man, his reputation ruined." Head bent, she whispered, "Even his wife left him."

"That's convenient; you can move in."

"Me? What would I want with an exiled network president?"

Jack had no idea whether Lutz was guilty or not, but at that moment he did know he didn't love Ceci McCann. The disease of fame had done irreversible damage to her immune system.

She rose and flitted over to his big oak desk. On top were a pile of his published stories. The blockbusters. Hundreds of them. She casually riffled through the stack, then whirled back to him. If anything impressed her about him, it wasn't showing on her face.

"I came by to apologize," she said with a resigned sigh. "For being such a jerk."

Hope didn't spring eternal but there was a kind of divine justice in her admission. "Apology accepted," he said graciously.

"And," she announced, "I wanted you to be the first to know I'm leaving the business."

An opportune time, thought Jack, since Train's crime had destroyed the careers of everyone on the show.

"I've signed with William Morris for six commercials. Shampoo and toothpaste to start." Her perfectly aligned, gleaming white chompers beamed at him. "I've enrolled in acting classes too. My agent expects I'll get a TV spot within the month."

She began to flirt with him like an actress angling for publicity. He noticed she had developed the affected "hair toss," a mannerism perfected by L.A. starlets.

"I still can't believe it," she said with a toss. "I should have known Tommy was a bastard. But at the time he seemed a hero to me." She tossed again. "What's that called," she asked, sweetly perplexed, "when your hero turns into a felon?"

He laughed. "Disillusionment."

"I've learned from this," she said. "I see how different we are. Basically, I'm not a journalist. I don't care a fig for uncovering things. That insatiable curiosity you have to get to the bottom of a situation no matter how grimy it gets, well, I haven't got it." Spry and buoyant, she bounded forward and hoisted the strap of her purse over her shoulder. Gucci was discreetly embossed in the thick leather.

When she kissed him on the cheek Jack decided he still liked her, but in a different way. Ceci wasn't a bad kid, just initially miscast. Hollywood had a way of doing that to people.

He watched her Saab lurch over the rutted driveway. In six months he knew she'd be driving a Jag with racing stripes—and he'd be driving a pickup truck.

And why not? He smiled broadly. As Sammy said, in L.A., wheels are the windows of the soul.

Before he had time to get the second load of cartons into the front yard, a stretch limo fit for the Rajneesh made its way toward the house. At every pothole, the mammoth car dipped and tilted like an aircraft carrier. It parked thirty yards away, afraid to come closer.

Two men emerged, both dressed in dark blue three-piece suits. They looked like morticians from McCallahan Mortuary.

Jack tucked his Superman T-shirt into his Levi's and strolled out to meet them, trying to recall if he had broken any laws lately.

"Mr. Werts?" gushed the portly, florid-faced man. The skinny fellow stuck close behind him.

"What can I do for you?" asked Jack. The big man offered his hand. He had a steel grip. "I'm Alexander de Courcy III. This is Harold Upham, Jr."

The small guy was an odd bird with a flimsy handshake. He squinted disagreeably at the pot of dead geraniums on the steps of the porch. A look of condescension seemed permanently etched on his face.

"We're Mr. Shay's New York bankers," said de Courcy.

Whatever was going on, it sounded good. Jack swiftly ushered them inside.

"It took a stream of phone calls to locate you," said de Courcy, as he sat down. He cleared his throat. "It came as a surprise to find you were listed."

"That's what phone directories are for," said Jack.

"Nice trophy," Upham remarked, admiring the stuffed marlin.

"One of my better catches."

"Hardly your best," said de Courcy. He flipped open an attaché case and removed a white envelope, which he handed to Jack. "From Mr. Shay. A little gratuity, shall we say, for your help."

Jack's eyes never left the men as he slipped his finger under the flap and removed the check. He studied the figure calmly. Twenty million dollars. Made out to him. He counted the zeros again. To make sure.

"There's a stipulation," said de Courcy. "Your benefactor asks that no public mention be made of this transaction . . . lest it encourage rash acts in the future."

"I get your drift," said Werts. A series of cymbals began clashing in his ears. He was barely able to conceal his glee.

"You can draw the money any way you desire," said Upham. "But we suggest tomorrow you come by our branch office in Beverly Hills. We'll be more than delighted to advise you on taxes and investments."

"Don't worry, I'll be by." He wanted to shout. Instead he creased the check with force and tucked it into his jeans pocket.

De Courcy smiled and briskly clapped his hands. "Enough of this, yo, ho, ho. We're off."

Before their land yacht disappeared from sight, Jack rang Sammy.

"Punk face, we're flyin' to SF for dinner tonight."

"On what? Breadcrumbs. You quit your job, remember?"

Jack sang into the receiver. "Put on your high-heeled sneakers, let's twirl, baby . . ."

"Christ, don't tell me you're in love again?"

"Let's say we're gonna celebrate my buyin' a new truck."

That evening, Robert and Emily Shay stood on the granite terrace of a modest house they had rented in the high desert north of Palm Springs. From the jutting butte they were witness to a magically colorful sunset. In the west, fleecy pastel clouds were gently draped over the purple sawtooth mountains that circled Lake Arrowhead. Twenty miles to the south, the sky was darkened over a strip of Interstate 10 dotted with cars speeding home to Los Angeles.

On a patch of grass in the yard below, Doni played catch with José. Emily's eyes caressed her son as she watched his small arm wind up like a propeller. He released the rubber ball with all his might, then abruptly fell on his can. Emily laughed. Her hand dropped from the railing and she looked at Robert. "He'll end up an army brat, y'know."

Better an army brat than dead, Shay thought, although he didn't say it. For now, he felt comfortable living in rented houses. Adopting a gypsy lifestyle put them one step ahead of the media. He slipped his arm around Emily's slender shoulders. She reached over and tugged gently at the blond hair on the nape of his neck. "You need a haircut," she said.

"How about a ponytail?"

She wrinkled her nose.

As Robert began to massage her shoulders the phone in his shirt pocket beeped. Emily pouted dramatically at the intrusion. He rapidly unfolded the wallet-sized device and held it to his ear.

"You comin' by tomorrow?" Libby asked. She and Harry were shooting *Planet* in the Mojave Desert a hundred miles northeast of the house.

"Can't."

Robert had promised to fly Doni and José to Santa Barbara to watch a Little League game.

"Did you decide on Cannes?" Libby persisted.

"I'll pass."

Without wasting a second, she said, "This'll warm your heart. When Lee Mack called for travel dates she told Harry how insanely happy she was for you."

"Spare me."

"Exactly."

Robert clicked off and slipped the phone back into his pocket. Emily glanced away.

Except for an occasional B-52 bomber homing in on Edwards Air Force Base, it was hauntingly quiet. As he listened to the wind blow sand against the granite cliffs he thought how appropriate it was that Lee Mack had hooked up with the new baby-faced director of bloody thrillers, this month's box-office golden boy.

He gazed at Emily. Quietly introspective, she smiled at him. He felt a sublime peacefulness. Released from the horror of the last seven months, the burden of despairing guilt had finally lifted. Already he was jotting down notes for a new script: a breed of fearless animals conquer the earth, sapient creatures who render humankind extinct.

Emily reached over and took his hand. Her eyes sparkled in the fraying light. "We are lucky, very lucky," she whispered softly.

He leaned down and touched his lips to hers.

Doni knew Sarah waited near the house. She had told him, three times already, to come inside and wash up for dinner. But José didn't have to go home yet so why should he. He turned his head and looked up. Mommy and Daddy were kissing. Yuck. No chance they would help him.

Before he had time to untie José's kite—the Red Hornet had knotted up terribly with Black Bat—Ernesto appeared from the other side of the hill. His eyes big as golf balls, José jumped to attention at the sight of his father. Ernesto took his son's hand and led him away. Doni followed them to the edge of the grass and waved good-bye.

It was okay 'cause it was a short good-bye, only until tomorrow. He was so happy José and his family lived next door. His mother now helped Maria in the kitchen. Even their food tasted better. Mommy had said that, and she was fussy.

He turned back to the house, then started to spin around like a twirly top. Dizzy, he fell down on the grass and played dead. The moment Snickers saw him lying down, he trotted out from under the house and began to chew at Doni's shoelace. Doni grabbed him and kissed his ear to make him stop but he wouldn't. Finally Doni bumped his head against Snick's furry nose. That did it. Snick shook like a rug then kerplopped.

Doni stretched out flat next to him. Way above, a speck of silver dragged across the sky like a zipper. A jet. But he didn't care about airplanes because Daddy had promised that they could sleep under the stars. Duke bought special tents for camping in the desert. Already Daddy had showed him pictures of rattlesnakes. Spike said they must take salt tablets to keep the water in their body. Doni had begged Mommy to let him take one of the big white pills for practice, but she wouldn't let him.

Still, she said she would camp too. That was good because she was the best at seeing the Big Dipper. And the guy with the belt.

He kicked his legs up and walked in the sky. He was so happy. Mommy and Daddy and Snickers were there with him. It was such fun. Only once in a while did he think about Rita and seal man. When he did, he remembered the good parts. The black cookies with the white centers. The mountain of tires. The littlest soldier.

From the start, Doni knew the littlest soldier would win the war. He was small but he was strong.